"There's no escapin' it, if you ask me," said Niall Murray. "It's on everybody's mind, there's no escapin' it. He was at our meeting last week. He was on the field with us not more than two short days ago. And now he's gone. And 'twasn't as though he'd got some terrible sickness and passed away quietlike in a nice clean hospital bed. He was murdered, he was. Somebody plotted it, just like them Pharisees in the Gospel. And what's more, the police think that one of us might be the culprit!"

He'd said it! He'd said what was on everyone's mind.

Several long moments of silence followed as those around the table reevaluated each other. They'd worked together. They'd played together. Relied on one another. Was it possible one of them could be a murderer? Was it likely that one of them had killed Hank Hunsinger?

"May well b… e

The…

P…

Also by William X. Kienzle
Published by Ballantine Books:

ASSAULT WITH INTENT

KILL AND TELL

SHADOW OF DEATH

SUDDEN DEATH

WILLIAM X. KIENZLE

BALLANTINE BOOKS • NEW YORK

 Published in the United States of America by Ballantine Books, a division of Random House, Inc., New York, and simultaneously in Canada by Random House of Canada Limited, Toronto.

Library of Congress Catalog Card Number: 84-28268

ISBN 0-345-32851-5

This edition published by arrangement with Andrews, McMeel & Parker

Manufactured in the United States of America

First Ballantine Books Edition: April 1986

For Javan

ACKNOWLEDGMENTS

Gratitude for technical advice to:

SGT. ROY AWE, *Homicide, Detroit Police Department*
RAMON BETANZOS, *Professor of Humanities, Wayne State University*
BRIAN CRAGG, CHRIS AND MARY MURRAY,
MRS. VINCENT (MARGARET) MURRAY,
Gaelic League/Irish-American Club of Detroit
KENNETH J. FAWCETT, M.D. *Assistant Director of Laboratories, Mt. Carmel Mercy Hospital*
THOMAS H. GALANTOWICZ, M.D., P.C.
JIM GRACE, *Detective, Kalamazoo Police Department*
DONALD GRIMES, *Pharmacy Services, Samaritan Health Center*
SISTER BERNADELLE GRIMM, R.S.M. *Pastoral Care Department, Samaritan Health Center*
GAIL JOHNSON, *Southfield Public Library*
TIMOTHY KENNY, *Principal Trial Attorney, Wayne County Prosecuting Attorney's Office*
RUDY REINHARD, *World Wide Travel Bureau*
KATE DORSEY RICHARDSON, *Campbell-Mithun, Minneapolis*
WILLIAM G. SHINE, *Security Manager*, Detroit Free Press
ANDREA SOLAK, *Assistant Prosecutor, Wayne County Prosecuting Attorney's Office*
WERNER SPITZ, U.M.D., *Wayne County Medical Examiner*

With special thanks to Chris Godfrey, Mike Keller, Dave Tipton, Jay Shoop, and the 1983 USFL champion Michigan Panthers, and to Judge Peter B. Spivak, without whom Father Koesler could never have dared enter the world of professional football.

1

"THIS REMINDS ME OF A CARTOON."

"What?"

"I said, *this reminds me of*..." The band ceased playing, making shouting almost unnecessary. "...a cartoon."

"Which cartoon would that be?" Father Robert Koesler leaned toward his friend and onetime classmate, Father Patrick McNiff.

"I can't remember where I saw it," said McNiff. "It was years ago. But it showed a couple of women sitting in the very top row of a stadium. Down on the floor of the stadium were a bunch of dots that represented football players. And one woman was saying to the other, 'Their shoulders are really falsies.'"

Koesler grinned. He and McNiff were part of a sellout crowd watching a football game between the Pontiac Cougars and the Chicago Towers in Pontiac's Metropolitan Stadium, sometimes called PonMet, more frequently the Silverdome. By those attempting to enter or exit the parking lot, it was frequently called names never found in a family newspaper.

In any case, it was billed as the World's Largest Domed Stadium. Koesler and McNiff were seated in the next to the last row on the upper level.

"Couldn't you get anything higher than this?" McNiff's sarcasm was evident.

"Pat, what you don't understand is that these are among the best seats in the house."

McNiff snorted.

"No, really," Koesler insisted. "Wait till play starts again. From this vantage, you can see the pass patterns and the defensive alignments. It's like watching all the *X*s and *O*s on a coach's blackboard, only they're alive. It's really an exciting place to watch a game from."

"You're telling me that we've got the 'overall picture'?" The PA was blaring; McNiff was forced to raise his voice. "Is that in any way like the 'overall picture' of the Archdiocese of Detroit that Cardinal Boyle keeps telling us he is the sole possessor of?"

"A kissing cousin. Good grief, that PA is deafening! It's a wonder the players can hear themselves think!"

Hank Hunsinger, the Cougars' tight end, stood toweling the back of his neck during the commercial time-out. He could hear clearly the taunts, threats, and imprecations being directed at him by several of Chicago's defensive team. Through some acoustic anomaly, the public-address system did not affect the noise level at the playing surface nearly as much as did the racket made by the crowd as the teams approached the scrimmage line and throughout each play.

The Towers' defensive team roundly hated Hank ("the Hun") Hunsinger. In that, they were joined by every other defensive team in the league. In one of the most violent games ever devised by civilized mankind, Hunsinger was notorious for his dirty play. If there was an unfair advantage to be taken, he took it. Always. If there was an opportunity to hurt an opponent, he hurt him. He was notorious in the league as a cheap-shot artist.

Hunsinger didn't care. He had not entered a popularity contest. Getting his job done, by whatever means, was his aim.

That he did get his job done was duly noted by his

teammates. The Cougars, even if they did not much favor his methods, respected his skill and experience.

Again, Hunsinger did not care.

The referee blew his whistle and pumped his right arm, signaling the thirty-second period during which the offensive team must begin play.

The team's center stationed himself some ten yards behind the line of scrimmage, raised his arm, and cried, "Huddah!" Which was as close as he would come to "Huddle."

The players formed an uneven oval, with the team's center as its focal point. The last to enter the oval, and the only one lowering himself to one knee, was the quarterback. Bobby Cobb was black. Notable only because, although blacks outnumber whites on most pro football teams, it is rare for one to be quarterback.

As he knelt within the oval, Cobb was singing softly, "We shall overcome." Such was his style.

In addition to being an extremely violent game, professional football had become one of the most stressful of competitions. Split-second decisions were now the order of the day. Decisions whose outcome would involve, eventually, millions of dollars—in advertising revenue, gate receipts, concession income, television revenue, bets, and, finally, the value of the franchise.

Of all the decisions made on the playing field, none was of greater significance than the quarterback's. Bobby Cobb's reaction to all of this was a studied nonchalance. He was good at what he did. He knew it. He intended that his attitude of relaxed confidence be contagious. Usually it was.

"'. . . Deep in my heart, I do believe, we shall overcome someday.' Well, gentlemen, let's eat 'em up. Or, as the experts in the booth like to say, We're going to continue to establish our running game." His tone became businesslike. "Blue! Right! Thirty-six! Let's see some daylight! On two! Break!"

With a communal clap of hands, the team ambled deliberately to its offensive position. The play called for the fullback to run through a hole cleared by the right tackle and the tight end, who, on this play, would align himself as the final lineman on the right side.

As Hunsinger lowered himself to a three-point stance, he gave neither thought nor care to anyone's assignment but his. He was to block the strong-side linebacker. Then, as the running back passed that spot, Hunsinger was to proceed downfield to take out the strong safety. For the moment, his attention was riveted on the linebacker, his first target.

The crowd noise swelled. The spectators in the coliseum were eager to see the gladiators do battle. Bobby Cobb would shout the play again—or change it—first calling to the right, then to the left, to make sure all heard it correctly.

"Set! Two—thirty-six! Two—thirty-six!

"Hut! Hut!"

The ball was snapped. Plastic shoulder guards popped; players grunted, yelled, and cursed; padded arms were flung out as weapons; huge bodies launched into each other. One side would win this isolated moment of combat, the other would not; that's the way it always went. For even if there was no advance, that was a victory for the defensive team.

It was a rookie-type blunder. Hunsinger knew it the instant he made contact. He had charged off the line of scrimmage and cut sharply to his right, eyes fixed on the numerals on the linebacker's jersey. The initial contact was solid. For good measure, Hunsinger thrust his helmet at the linebacker's chin. Butting an opponent was legal but extremely dangerous. The possible injury to his opponent did not trouble Hunsinger.

But a split second after contact, he realized his feet were not properly placed. They were too close together to provide a solid base. Simultaneously, the linebacker, sensing Hunsinger's mistake, stepped aside and, grasping the Hun's jersey, threw him to the turf like an oversize ragdoll.

Having disposed of the blocker, the linebacker tackled the ball carrier.

A one-yard gain. Second down, nine to go. No one in the stands doubted whose blunder it was.

In the TV booth, the announcer was informing those at home with the aid of instant replay that "old number 89 really blew that one. And cost his team some valuable yardage."

"Nice block, Hun," the linebacker gloated over his shoulder. "Best goddam shot I've ever seen you throw."

Hunsinger picked himself off the Astroturf, one part of him registering the boos that were cascading upon him from the fans, and returned to where the center's "Huddah!" again summoned. In the huddle, the fullback, who, unprotected, had been hit hard, glanced balefully at Hunsinger, who continued to stare at the ground. Inwardly, the Hun was seething.

Cobb slid into the huddle on one knee. He had received the next play from the coach through a substitute. "Gentlemen, neither I nor the bench is satisfied that we are establishing our running game. So we'll try again. Slot! Right! Forty-six! Think you can take the 'backer this time, Hun?" Rhetorical sarcasm. "On three! Break!"

Hunsinger assumed the three-point stance, his mind once again centered on the strong-side linebacker, the same player who had just humiliated him. It would be different this time: His opponent would pay for his small victory.

But first, Hunsinger had to be certain that there would be no unexpected defensive formation that would force Cobb to call an audible—changing the play at the line of scrimmage.

"Set!" Cobb shouted to the right. "Three—forty-six!"

It was the agreed snap count. The play would be the one called in the huddle. Now that bastard would pay.

Hunsinger was not sure in just what manner payment would be exacted. He would rely on his vast experience in foul tactics to improvise something appropriate.

"Three—forty-six!" Cobb shouted to the left. "Hut! Hut! Hut!"

The ball was slammed into Cobb's hands. He pivoted and pitched it out to his halfback. Twenty-two very large men again moved from a tableau into violent action, one team endeavoring to tackle the ball carrier, the other trying to block that effort and advance the carrier. In the end, that was what this game was all about, blocking and tackling.

Again, Hunsinger sprang from his stationary position and headed for the strong-side linebacker, not head-on this time, but slightly to one side. As he had hoped, the linebacker attempted to "swim" by the block. Swinging his right arm in a wide, over-the-head arc, he tried to brush past Hunsinger, pushing the tight end's right shoulder back, much as a swimmer cuts through the water.

Perfect. Hunsinger had maneuvered himself and his opponent so that no game official would have an unobstructed view of his actions.

The linebacker's upraised right arm left his entire right side exposed and unprotected. Even with all the padding players wear, ordinarily there is no protection for the chest area.

Hunsinger planted his right foot and drove his fist into the linebacker's upper diaphragm. The punch didn't travel far. It didn't need to. Indeed, it could not have, else the officials likely would have spotted the foul. But Hunsinger was a powerful man; as his punch buried itself in the linebacker, the Hun thought he felt the man's rib snap. He clearly heard the sharp expulsion of air as the linebacker collapsed and rolled over in agony.

Whistles sounded. The play was over.

Hunsinger looked around. There was a pileup some fifteen yards upfield. The play had worked. He checked for penalty markers. Apparently no foul had been detected. The field markers were being moved upfield. The men carrying the sticks wouldn't be moving them if the head linesman hadn't beckoned them. And he wouldn't have signaled them if there'd been a foul called.

Perfect. Hunsinger moved to join his teammates.

By now players, coaches, and fans were aware that only twenty-one players were up and about. The injured linebacker had curled into a fetal position. Several teammates hurried to his side, peered at him, but didn't touch him. The trainer and an assistant ran across the field. They managed to move him onto his back. He could be seen now by the fans and TV viewers only from the waist down. He was not moving his legs to and fro in pain. He was not moving at all.

The fans were hushed. Many relished the violence of this game, but most shrank from the sight of serious injury.

Even the TV commentators had missed Hunsinger's blow. Nor had any isolated camera recorded the action. The TV people spent this official time-out running and rerunning the play as it was recorded on instant replay. Each time the halfback carrying the ball passed the point of the collision in question, one of them would call out excitedly, "There . . . there, see? You can see the linebacker go down, but the camera got there too late to catch the block that flattened him." Then the film would be played backward and the linebacker would miraculously rise from the turf.

No one on either team had seen what happened. The Cougars simply assumed that it had been one of those unfortunate accidents that happen when two strong people run into each other. Not that some of Hunsinger's teammates did not harbor some suspicions, given his well-deserved reputation.

The Chicago team, on the other hand, took it for granted

that there had been a deliberate foul. Most of the Towers loudly cursed Hunsinger.

Few fans could hear the curses. By now, the linebacker had been taken from the field on a stretcher, to the fans' sympathetic and commendatory cheers. And the band was blasting over the superloud public-address system.

For his part, Hunsinger noticed that one of his shoelaces was twisted. He bent down to straighten it. He was oblivious to the threats and curses being hurled at him from across the scrimmage line.

"Hun, you bastard, you're gonna pay for that!" The Towers' middle linebacker was a formidable specimen.

Hunsinger did not hear him. Nor did he notice that several of the linebacker's teammates were physically restraining him from instant delivery on that threat.

The referee's whistle sounded. The Cougars had thirty seconds in which to get a play under way.

"Huddah!"

Bobby Cobb slid into the huddle. "It seems that everyone is convinced that our ground game is at least good enough so's we can risk a pass. Red! Left! Seventy-three! Hun, give me a sharp post pattern. On three! Break!"

Hunsinger lined up on the left side of the five interior linemen. The plan was for him to delay a few moments at the scrimmage line, blocking as Cobb retreated to set up for the pass. Then, after the two wide receivers, X and Z, had begun their patterns, designed to clear the middle zone, the tight end, Y, would cut sharply across the middle into the clear.

"Set! Three—seventy-three! Three—seventy-three! Hut! Hut! Hut!"

Hunsinger retreated the prescribed couple of yards, both legs pumping to give him balance as he helped his neighbor, the left tackle, block. Suddenly, he slid off the block and charged several yards upfield. Then, he broke sharply and diagonally across the center.

Cobb, under considerable pressure from charging Chicago linemen, at the last possible second caught sight of Hunsinger's maneuver and fired the ball at a spot where he hoped Hunsinger would be in another second. Cobb was then slammed to the turf by one of the Towers who finally broke through the block.

Under his breath, Hunsinger cursed. The ball would be high and away from him. Instinctively, he tried for it. A pass receiver was paid for catching the ball, not for missing it, and certainly not for refusing to try. Hunsinger liked being paid. A lot.

He leaped as far and as high as he could. He was able just to tip the tightly spiraled pass and somehow bring it under control with the fingers of his left hand. Quickly, he gathered the ball into both hands, and tucked it tightly to his chest.

He knew there was no way he could land on his feet. Nor was he surprised when he was bent like a bow by a brutal tackle from the rear. He was, though, surprised and not a little shocked to suffer sharp, repeated blows to the small of his back after landing on the turf.

"You goddamn Hun!" The Towers' middle linebacker repeated the imprecation over and over as he made a punching bag of Hunsinger.

Whistles came from every corner of the field. Yellow penalty flags fluttered to earth. The deafening cheers that had greeted Hunsinger's remarkable reception were transformed into choruses of boos directed at the Chicago player.

Officials pulled the linebacker away. The referee escorted him to the sidelines, where his coach was informed of his official ejection from the game.

With assistance from the trainer and a couple of teammates, Hunsinger slowly got to his feet. As he was assisted from the field, the volume of cheers exceeded that which had greeted his catch.

"Look at that! Did you see that? That bastard oughta be thrown out of football. The commissioner is going to hear from me tomorrow!" Jay Galloway, the Cougars' owner, was furious.

He was in the owner's box, his face almost pressed against the pane of the permanently sealed window that gave a panoramic view of the stadium. In the booth with him were his wife, Marjorie; the team's general manager, Dave Whitman; his wife, Kate; and several of Michigan's movers and shakers.

A subtle smile played at Marjorie Galloway's lips. The smile had been there from the moment of Hunsinger's injury. She hid it by cupping a hand over her mouth, as if in horror or concern.

"Somebody do that to a dog anywhere in town and the cops'd have the guy in jail before he knew what hit him. That's a million-dollar property that bastard was pounding on!" Galloway lit another Camel. His previous cigarette was only half smoked. He noticed it when he placed the newly lit cigarette in the ashtray. He snuffed the smaller butt.

Dave Whitman noticed the double-cigarette incident. From long association with Galloway, Whitman recognized the signs. Ordinarily a decent fellow, Galloway could and frequently did present a Mr. Hyde side when it came to his team.

A big part of the problem was that Galloway's team was also his bread and butter. Unlike owners of other pro football franchises, Galloway was not enormously wealthy from independent enterprises. Every nickel he paid in rentals, advertising, salaries came out of his pocket. That alone made him one of the testiest owners with whom to do business.

It had been a near miracle that he'd been able to secure this franchise. He had put together a consortium of wealthy local merchants and businessmen, convincing them that they would find both himself and the franchise profitable investments. Both of which had proved true. Then, one by one, he had bought them out until now he was sole owner.

But the crown rested uneasily on his head. Now there was no one to fall back upon. From time to time, frankly, it frightened him. But he held on to his expensive trinket. Among the goals Galloway set for himself, his ultimate goal was to be Somebody. The Cougars were his vehicle toward that goal.

Basically, Galloway was an insecure man. And insecure people can be trouble.

It was typical of him to think of one of his players as a property. To Galloway, the players, trainers, and coaches represented investments and expenditures. And Hunsinger was one of his most expensive investments. Hunsinger's salary was second only to Bobby Cobb's.

It was not all that common that a tight end be paid so much. But Hank Hunsinger was as vicious at the bargaining table as he was at virtually everything else in his life. He had come to the Cougars from the University of Michigan, where he had been Big Man on Campus, accumulated an abundance of press clippings, made a national name for himself, and become extremely popular locally; hordes of Michigan fans showed up at the Silverdome just to catch the Hun's act.

However, instead of being on the field performing for the customers, he was now on the bench and injured. And no one knew just how injured he was.

Jay Galloway trained his binoculars on the activity surrounding Hunsinger on the sidelines. As he pressed the glasses to his face with his left hand, his right hand was shaking so badly that cigarette ashes fell to the floor.

Dave Whitman noted the trembling right hand and shook his head. Impossible, Whitman decided, for the man to slow down enough to smell the flowers.

"Hurt?" Jack Brown, the Cougars trainer, pressed a few likely spots on Hunsinger's back where fresh discoloration promised more hematomas. Not all that many bruise-free areas remained on the Hun's body.

Hunsinger winced. "Congratulations, Brownie; you found 'em. Now go play with your tape and leave me the hell alone!"

Brown knew well that he was not alone as a target of Hunsinger's verbal abuse. Undaunted, the trainer raised Hunsinger's jersey and sprayed ethyl chloride lightly over the newly injured areas.

He should have expected it, but the freezing mist against his back startled Hunsinger. "Goddamn it all to hell, Brownie, I told you to leave me the hell alone!"

Brown shrugged and sat down next to Hunsinger. Acrimonious as he was, Hunsinger had been injured. And it was the trainer's responsibility, short of involving the team doctor, to make a judgment on whether the player could return to the game or whether he was done for the day. He would watch Hunsinger closely for any sign of further distress.

Meanwhile, on the field, the Cougars were not faring well.

Cobb's pass to Hunsinger had advanced the ball to the Towers' 35-yard line. But the next two running plays had netted only a yard. At third down with a long nine yards to go, it was an obvious passing situation. If that failed, it was field-goal time.

Niall Murray, the soccer-style kicker imported from Ireland, sat down on the other side of Hunsinger. Murray, like many of the rookies and younger players, looked up to Hunsinger as the old pro who had paid his dues and had amassed experience in this game.

"Well, then, man . . . " Since the Hun continued watching the action on the field, Murray found himself talking to Hunsinger's profile. "It looks as if they'll be callin' on me soon, don't you t'ink?"

Hunsinger, without turning his head, nodded.

"I've been tryin' to figure it, Hun. Near as I can tell,

the way it lines up right now, I'll be goin' to be kickin' from about the 42-yard line." He paused to see if there was any objection to his calculus thus far. "That means a field goal of over fifty yards."

Hunsinger nodded again.

"Well, then, that's stretchin' my limits a bit, don't ya know." He paused again. "Hun, I'm a bit nervous about that." He paused once more. "Hun, d'ya have any words for me at all?" As some indication of the straits in which he found himself, Murray extended a hand before Hunsinger. The hand trembled slightly.

Hunsinger took note of the tremor. "Think," he prescribed, "of something tranquil. A rural scene in Ireland."

Murray's brow furrowed. He returned in memory to cherished vistas in counties Sligo, Mayo, Galway. Searching for something tranquil, he could think of nothing to surpass a waterfall he had once spent several hours contemplating. That would be Slaughan Glen in County Tyrone. In the North.

The very thought of the North and its troubles was disquieting.

"Hun, it's not workin'."

Hunsinger kept his eyes on the field of play. Clearly, this was an annoyance. "Try thinking of how relaxed you are just before going to sleep."

That would not work; Murray knew before trying. From childhood on, he'd always had trouble falling asleep. If he now dwelt on this painful process, he knew he would become even more unsettled.

"No, Hun. That'll not do it at all."

"Okay," Hunsinger would turn to the ultimate weapon. "Think about the best lay you ever had."

First, Murray had to translate. He knew English well enough, of course. After all, hadn't it been said for centuries that the best English in the world was spoken in Dublin? But sometimes he had problems with American colloquialisms. Now he had to ponder the sexual connotation of the verb *to lay*.

Well, now, this would not be difficult; he'd never had intercourse with anyone but his wife. But which of their many couplings had been best?

Certainly not their wedding night. That had been a disaster. But shortly thereafter, they'd got the hang of it. And it just kept getting better as time passed. So, it was reasonable to consider the most recent bit of lovemaking just the other night.

Murray became almost lost in the most pleasant memory. As his mind became more and more absorbed in the lingering, unhurried love play leading to simultaneous fulfillment, a warm serenity glowed in his loins and suffused his entire body, indeed his entire personality.

Trainer Jack Brown, who had taken a more than casual interest in this process, noticed the tremor leave Murray's hands, and noted the bemused smile on his face, indicating the kicker was physically many miles removed from the game.

Damn! thought Brown, if that isn't about the best demonstration of Transcendental Meditation I've seen.

"Incomplete pass," the play-by-play man shouted needlessly into his microphone. His viewers had seen for themselves. "Eddie, the Cougars needed that one. That brings up fourth and long. Now we'll have to see what Coach Bradford will do. Will he punt and try for the corner? Or will he try for a field goal? The next few seconds will tell."

"That's right, Lou." The color man watching his monitor began analyzing the previous play, being shown to the TV audience in all the glory of instant replay and stop-action. "That was a simple 'flag' pattern with a three-step fake inside. See, now we're isolating on Kit Hoffer, the tight end who replaced the injured Hunsinger.

"See, he leaves the scrimmage line—and right there he gets bumped by the linebacker. That's okay; that's within the first five yards. Now he's heading downfield. See, now the strong safety picks up the coverage. Now watch Hoffer plant that right foot and break to his left. The safety buys the fake and heads inside. One, two, three steps. Then Hoffer cuts toward the flag. And see, the pass is thrown behind him.

"Lou, I think it's just that Cobb hasn't had enough work with Hoffer. Bobby knows Hunsinger's every move, when he's likely to cut, and most important, how fast he can run. It's tough on Hoffer having to play behind an old pro like the Hun, who's out there on almost every offensive play. But this young man has got the goods. On that last play, he just outran the ball. Cobb didn't allow for Hoffer's speed. For a big guy, he sure can move. But you just wait. Once the Hun hangs 'em up for good, this young Kit Hoffer is going to be one of the great ones. He's got all the tools and he comes to play."

"Okay, Eddie. Now back to the live action. Coach Bradford has decided to go for a field goal. But I don't know: That's gotta be a try of about fifty-two yards. Cobb is kneeling just at the 42-yard line. The Towers are jumping around, trying to distract Niall Murray, the Sligo Sidewinder. But Murray looks pretty cool and collected. I don't think I've ever seen a kicker look that calm. He's just standing perfectly still, not flexing his arms or anything.

"There's the snap! Murray moves into the ball. It's up. It looks true. Has it got the distance? Yes! Yes, it's just over the crossbar. It's good! A 52-yarder! How about that!"

"That's right, Lou. A 52-yarder. Not a record, but certainly something to write home about. You can see in this isolated replay. The kicker is waiting for the snap of the ball. That's not a still picture, folks; it's just as Lou described: Murray standing just like a statue. There, now: Cobb places the ball; Murray moves into it. Cobb and Murray are following the flight of the ball. Now they know it's good. See Cobb. He's jumping up and down. But look at Murray. He's just standing there with a smile on his face. Very strange."

"Right, Eddie. Strange. Maybe that's the way they do things in Ireland.

"Well, that makes the score Cougars 34, Towers 32. The Cougars went from a one-point deficit to a two-point advantage. But you can see why Coach Bradford would have preferred a touchdown. Now the Cougars can be beaten by a Chicago field goal. So, that's it: 34-32, Cougars up with 3:28 to go in the game. And we'll be right back after these commercial messages."

On the floor of the Silverdome, Niall Murray was teeing up for a kickoff, after the TV and radio commercials, of course. He had come out of his quasi-trancelike state and began to realize what he had accomplished. Wasn't that fine, then: a 52-yard field goal! He'd have to explain the significance of that to his wife, Moira, tonight. From time to time, she would say, "What you do is fine and all... but just what is it exactly that you do then?"

Moira was a fine lass, but she had an amazingly difficult time comprehending some of the basics of football.

Now that Moira had come to mind, it was only natural that Murray should return to the pleasurable recollections that had so relaxed him before the field goal.

He was startled, then, by the referee's whistle. It took him an extra moment to remember that he was expected to do something. Kick the ball.

With a pleasant smile playing about his lips, Murray kicked off. The ball soared high and deep to the other end of the field.

Ordinarily, play immediately after a kickoff actively involves twenty-one of the twenty-two players on the field. Usually, the kicker is exempt from any further contact. And mercifully so; most modern kickers are veterans of the game of soccer, not football. Generally, they are much smaller than the standard-size football player. And more fragile. They are expected to pursue and attempt to tackle a ball carrier only under conditions that would anticipate suicide.

It was odd, then, that Niall Murray, still wearing a silly grin, continued down the field after having kicked off. He wandered into the path of a burly lineman, who, having nothing better to do, flattened him.

Murray was the recipient of a swinging elbow that caught him across his face mask. He went down like a felled tree. The back of his helmet bounced once off the hard artificial turf before coming to rest. Then, the entire body of Niall Murray came to rest.

The Cougars' trainer and his assistant rushed to the side of the fallen warrior.

Murray appeared to be unconscious. Still the smile remained.

Before calling for the gurney, Brown tried smelling salts. Murray moved his head, at first tentatively. He opened his eyes. The smile disappeared.

"What's your name?" Brown asked.

"Uh . . . Murray . . . Niall Murray."

"What should happen in Ireland?"

"The Brits should get out."

"He's okay. Let's see if we can get him on his feet. It's a lucky thing he was wearing that cage or his face really would look like the map of Ireland." Brown assisted Murray to his feet.

The crowd applauded appropriately. Obviously, they appreciated anyone's unexpected recovery.

"Shit! Look at that! There goes my kicker!" Jay Galloway had just resumed his seat for the kickoff. Now he was back on his feet. "Maybe they ought to outlaw the whole goddamned Chicago team."

"That's the bad news, Jay," said Dave Whitman. "The good news just came up from the bench: Hunsinger seems to be okay now."

But Galloway was inconsolable. "What happens if we

need another field goal? There isn't another player outside of the Mick who's that accurate."

"There's another bit of good news, Jay: They just announced today's attendance—80,902, SRO."

In spite of himself, a smile appeared briefly. "Yeah, but where they gonna be next week if we can't field our best men?"

Whitman eased back onto his upholstered stool and sipped his Scotch-and-soda. It had crossed his mind many times that joining Jay Galloway in this enterprise might not have been an entirely smart idea. But it had become a venture to which he had grown increasingly more committed.

Galloway and Whitman had grown up together in Minneapolis, attended the same public schools, primary and secondary, followed by the University of Minnesota. But when they began their business careers, their paths diverged. Galloway tried various entrepreneurial roles with varying degrees of moderate success. Whitman started with International Multifoods and attained a responsible position in public relations before Galloway had lured him away.

Galloway had a burning ambition to be Somebody. Whitman was very much more the hard-headed businessman. Secretly, he planned to take over ownership of the Cougars some day and make the team into the franchise he knew it could be.

On the field, the Towers had used up little more than a minute's playing time in moving the ball from their 25-yard line to their 42, where their drive stalled. They were forced to punt to the Cougars, whose punt-return specialist caught the ball at his 10-yard line and advanced it to his 35. At that point, two minutes remained in the game. The automatic time-out was called as the two-minute notice was given to both teams.

The Cougars' offensive team began to gather on the field. Kit Hoffer, on the assumption that Hunsinger was still disabled, trotted onto the field, pulling on his headgear.

Near the Cougars' bench, Hunsinger approached Coach Bradford. "I can play," Hunsinger informed him.

Bradford wordlessly looked over his shoulder at the trainer. Brown, who had expected the query, nodded. Bradford looked back at Hunsinger and nodded.

Hunsinger trotted out to where his teammates had loosely gathered. The crowd, noting his reentry to the game, cheered loudly.

"Get outta here, kid," Hunsinger said to Hoffer, "the Man's arrived."

Disappointed at not being allowed to continue, and angry at the cavalier manner in which he'd been dismissed, Hoffer left the field red-faced.

Orders from the Cougars' coaching staff to Bobby Cobb were to play conservatively, chancing as little as possible. If the Cougars could grind out a couple of first downs, using up the remaining two minutes, they would be two-point victors.

The strategy reflected neither Cobb's style nor his liking. He had experienced too many stupid mistakes happening with this type of thinking. The Towers would guess that the Cougars would be playing close-to-the-vest football. So they would bunch up, "dogging" and shooting the gap, trying to stop the run, and trying to strip the ball from the carrier. But orders were orders.

Two consecutive running plays gained four yards. It was third down and six yards to go for a first down—the classic third and long.

A guard brought the next play in.

Cobb slid into the huddle. "Okay, gentlemen, we'd better make this one work or we may be in a lot of trouble. I-formation! Left! Twenty-five! On two! Break!"

The play called for the halfback to run off left tackle. Hunsinger was to block the linebacker.

They settled at the line of scrimmage. Cobb crouched

low, hands tucked under the center's crotch. He viewed the defensive formation and decided this play had two chances to work: very little and none.

"Three!"

It was a different snap count than he'd given in the huddle. He was changing the play. This would be an audible. He had each teammate's undivided attention. In a split second, a number would give each of them an entirely different task to perform and in yet another split second they would have to adjust to this new play.

"Ninety-two!"

It had changed from a running play to a play-action pass. The offensive linemen would appear to be blocking for a running play by pulling, and giving the appearance of leading a sweep around end. Cobb would fake a handoff to the fullback, who would continue, emptyhanded, through the line. If the linebackers bought it, they would be pulled into the line of scrimmage, thus opening up some of the short zones.

"Three! Ninety-two! Hut! Hut!"

The ball was centered; everyone was galvanized.

In the "pit," bodies crashed in a heated push-pull contest. The fake sweep began to the left. As Cobb retreated, he pretended to tuck the ball into the fullback's gut. The linebackers fell for it and crashed into the line. Hunsinger found the vacated zone.

Cobb retreated only four steps, then quickly released the ball. It was a perfect pass. Hunsinger gathered it in and broke straight for the goal line. However, before he could get completely clear, the fleet free safety nailed him with a desperation shoestring tackle.

And then the fun began.

"Boy!" exclaimed the TV play-by-play man, "that just goes to show you what experience will do for you, Eddie. Hunsinger gathered that pass in and immediately headed upfield. Like a horse heading for the stable, he knew where that first-down yardage was, and went for it."

"He certainly did, Lou. We'll see it on the instant replay—wait a minute. Something's happening on the field. Hunsinger did something after the whistle blew. I think he kicked the defensive player who tackled him. Now, a big lineman from Chicago—I can't get his number yet—but that Chicago lineman jumped on Hunsinger and began punching him. Now they're rolling around on the turf—they're really laying into each other."

"They sure are, Eddie. The officials are trying to separate them and, at the same time, keep the other players out of this scrap. You hate to see a game end like this . . ."

"Oh, dear. Oh, dear." Grace Hunsinger shook her head as she peered at her large-screen color console. "If it isn't one thing, it's another. Now, that's the second bit of trouble Henry's been involved in this afternoon. I don't know what gets into that boy."

"What's that?" Mary Frances Quinn, Mrs. Hunsinger's companion, woke with a start from her nap.

"It's Henry again, Mary Frances."

"What's he done?"

"Gotten into another fight."

"Oh." Mrs. Quinn sighed. "Well, I suppose boys will be boys."

"You know, Mary Frances, I used to worry a lot about Henry when he was growing up. He had a habit of going about with undesirable companions. God knows, my dear husband—God rest him—was not wealthy, though he left us as well as he could."

"I know."

"And we tried to send Henry to good schools. I just don't know what gets into that young man."

"Now, Grace . . ." Mrs. Quinn adjusted her recliner chair into the upright position. "You're just not feeling well this afternoon. You know Henry is a good boy. He's certainly been good to you. And he's in an honest profession. At least there's nothing criminal about it. And all of the papers say that he's one of the best players in the league. He's earning all that money, and he will surely be able to secure a good position for himself after his playing days are over . . . what with the name he's made for himself.

"Come on, now. All will be well. We know that everything is in the hands of God. And that God is good."

Mrs. Hunsinger looked at her companion sharply. "Yes. I suppose that's true. Oh, but look." She gestured at the TV screen. "What's going on now?"

"Why, it looks like that man with the striped shirt is escorting Henry over to—what do you call it?—the sidelines. You don't suppose Henry is hurt, do you?"

Mrs. Hunsinger leaned forward and stared intently at the screen.

"He's outta there! Done for the day!" the referee declared to Coach Bradford.

"Now, wait a minute, Red. My boy could have been provoked, you know."

The referee couldn't suppress a grin. "Coach, believe me, the Hun started it. And the other guy finished it. They're both out of the game. That's it; they're outta there." The referee trotted back to the field of play.

"Brilliant, Hun." Bradford looked disgustedly at his player. "A fine lot of good you're doing the team on the bench."

"Screw the team!"

Blood gorged Bradford's face and neck, "I'll see you in my office tomorrow morning." He had never been closer to striking one of his players.

"Well, Eddie, with the Hun out of the game and the two unnecessary-roughness penalties offsetting each other, the ball remains on Chicago's 49-yard line, where it will be a first down for the Cougars. And there's just a minute, twenty-five seconds to go."

"That's right, Lou. Coach Bradford has established his

pattern now in these closing seconds. He'll keep it on the ground, hoping to grind out the yards, maintain possession of the ball, and hang on to win this one."

"Right you are, Eddie. Now, back to live action. The Cougars break their huddle and come out in an I-formation. The Towers have a five-man defensive line with everybody bunched up close. Boy, a pass just now would sure surprise them! But, it's not. Cobb takes the ball and hands off to his fullback, who goes over right tackle and—hold it: There's a fumble, there's a fumble! The Towers are claiming they've recovered it. And the referee agrees with them. The Towers have the ball on their own 46-yard line!"

"Well, this is just the break they've been looking for, Lou. Remember, all they need is a field goal to win."

"That's right, Eddie. And Chicago quickly breaks out of their huddle. They line up in a spread formation. The Cougars have added a fifth defensive back, so they are in the nickel defense with three men rushing. Morand takes the ball and fades to pass. He sets up in the pocket. Now he moves up. He spots his wide receiver, Finnegan, in right flat. Finnegan's got it and he steps out of bounds, killing the clock. The head linesman places the ball at the Cougar 47. A pickup of eight yards. It'll be a second and two for a first down and just fifty-five seconds in the game.

"Now Chicago breaks from its huddle again and lines up in the shotgun formation, with Finnegan split to the right, Thomas to the left. The ball is centered back to Morand, who scans the field as the pass patterns begin to develop. Robinson, the big tight end, is wide open over the middle. Morand sees him and hits him. Robinson avoids one, two, tacklers and wisely steps out of bounds, again killing the clock."

"The Towers are playing heads-up ball. They've got a first down now at the Cougars 30, with just forty seconds to go. They're already within Tom McAnoy's field-goal range, but they'd like to get a bit closer. They've got time for two, maybe three more plays, and that'll be it. My guess is that they'll keep it in the air. Though they could run it with all of their time-outs left. Now, back to Lou and the next play."

"Right you are, Eddie. Okay. Chicago comes out of the huddle. They're in a spread formation again. They might just try one in the end zone. There's the snap. Morand fades back and—oh!—it's a draw to the fullback, Markham. The Cougars are really caught looking. Markham gets by the line of scrimmage and stiffarms a linebacker. Now the cornerback and strong safety have him hemmed in. Markham reverses his field and picks up a couple of blockers on the way. Now he breaks downfield again. Two good blocks and he's got only one man to beat. He's at the 25, the 20—and Conor Bannan, the free safety, nails him with a sure, solid tackle at the knees. Markham immediately signals for a time-out, with just three seconds left and the ball at the Cougar 17. Wow, what a run!"

"What a run, indeed, Lou. While Markham almost ran the Towers right out of time, he accomplished what he set out to do. He's got the ball in easy field-goal range. Of course, it's a bit much to say that any field goal is easy when the outcome of the game depends on it. And now we are down to the last play of the game. Talk about your cliffhanger, this is it. And here comes Tom McAnoy trotting onto the field. Lou, in his long career, this guy has put many a foot into many a football."

"That's certainly right, Eddie. But none of them—not all his field goals or extra points—was ever more vital than the one coming up. The game hinges on his next kick, and even with all his experience, he must be feeling the pressure.

"Well, here it comes. The two teams line up. The Cougars' defensive backs are charging around, jumping up and down, trying to distract the kicker. The fans are screaming their heads off. It's bedlam. I don't know if the players on the field will be able to hear the signals. But, okay, here we go. Morand is kneeling on the 24. McAnoy is standing perfectly still, his arm swinging gently back and forth, establishing his rhythm. Hold on, this is it! There's the snap! Morand spots the ball. McAnoy moves into it. It's up—and right through the middle of the uprights! The back judge and the field judge have their arms raised. It's good. No flags are down. And time has run out . . . time has run out for the Cougars this day."

"Lou, the Towers are delirious over their 35-34 victory. But the Cougars are a discouraged bunch of athletes. Both teams are headed down the tunnel to their respective locker rooms. And the fans—I think the fans are in a state of shock. A moment or two ago they were raucous and confident, but now they can't believe their eyes. I wouldn't say you could hear a pin drop in this gigantic stadium, but they're sure a lot quieter than they were."

"Right, Eddie. And we'll be back to wrap things up right after these commercial messages."

The door to the Cougars' locker room was closed to everyone save players, coaches, trainers, administrative staff, and, of course, the owner.

In the breezy tunnel separating the home and visiting teams' locker rooms, and leading into the stadium in one direction and out to the parking lot in the other, stood the ladies and gentlemen of the media.

The members of the Chicago-based media, along with some wire-service personnel and a few Detroit newspaper people, were in the Towers' locker room. Chicago had no reason to embargo the media. The Towers were winners, at least on this Sunday afternoon, and they were in an ebullient and communicative mood.

The Detroit television people were clustered outside the Cougars' door. They were becoming more restive by the moment. Along with film clips of the game, which would be easy enough to come by, the TV reporters were expected to bring in hard-hitting, insightful, exclusive, controversial, and perhaps damning interviews. But between the reporters and those interviews was a locked door.

"What do you suppose is going on in there?" asked one TV cameraman of another.

"Whatever it is, if we put it on the eleven o'clock news, we'll have to precede it with one of those warnings, 'Parental discretion advised.'"

"Yeah, 'Parental discretion advised'—but not expected."

"Let's just say that in this case, the boys were not in a jocular mood in the locker room after the game."

The two chuckled quietly. Cameramen could be jovial and laidback. They were not the ones who, at approximately eleven-fifteen tonight on all three network-affiliated stations, would be seen, on tape, asking questions of tired, angry, and very large athletes.

At long last, the door was opened and, like the Israelites spilling through the dry bed of the parted waters of the Red Sea, the reporters entered the Cougars' dressing room.

Having been ejected from the game, Hank Hunsinger was a trifle ahead of his colleagues in the transformation to civilian life. He had showered and, now clad only in boxer shorts, was seated before his locker. He was a man of compulsive ritual. Many a reporter had become nearly mesmerized during an interview with the Hun, simply from watching his meticulous, unchanging rituals—clothes or uniform always donned in the same order, pads in a preordained sequence, each shoelace lying flat against the shoe, tape removed in exactly the same way, always.

Most of the initial attention was focused on Hunsinger, the only Cougar ejected from a game so far this season. Reporters crowded around his open wire locker and the stool on which he sat. The TV sungun cast its unreal illumination in the area; questions came seemingly from everywhere.

Hunsinger—like those of his fellow players experienced in being interviewed—was cautious in his statements. Television, with its relentless closeups, could reveal not only answers and comments, but also the interviewee's attitudes, whether he was serious about a statement, or lying. The print media had three options: They could quote correctly, and in context. Or they could misquote. Or they could quote correctly, but out of context.

It was akin to Woody Hayes' opinion of the possibilities of the forward pass: It could be either complete, incomplete, or intercepted. In both the interview situation and the forward pass, two of the three outcomes were bad. But there were times when there seemed no alternative to talking.

"How about it, Hun, did you get hurt out there today?"

"Football's a rough game." Hunsinger mopped a perspiring brow.

"Come on, Hun, you were mixed up in two fights this afternoon. That's extracurricular rough. You hurt?"

"You wanna see the bruises?"

"It wouldn't help; I couldn't tell the new ones from the old ones."

"What we wanna know, Hun," interjected another reporter, "is, are you gonna be ready for next week's game?"

"Of course. You know what they say: You can't make the club from the tub."

"You took a real beating out there today, Hun. Make you think about hangin' 'em up? Think this might be your last season?"

"Nah." Hunsinger very carefully adjusted the cuffs of his shirt. "I'll know when the end's in sight. I got some good years left. Besides, the club is depending on me."

Several reporters choked back guffaws. It was common knowledge that Hunsinger, probably more than any other player in the league, ranked the welfare of his team rather low on his list of priorities, a list that had himself at the pinnacle.

In another part of the room.

"Was that the longest field goal you ever kicked, Niall?"

"It was." Arra, he thought, they could've looked it up.

"And your biggest thrill?"

"Well, now, I don't know about that. I suppose it would be pretty close." Murray paused in toweling off his back. "Actually, there was that time I scored the winning goal, as well."

"Winning goal?"

"Winning goal in a match with Cork a few years back."

"Cork? You talkin' about soccer?"

"Indeed."

"No, football. Your biggest thrill in football?"

"Oh, yes. Indeed. By far."

"Niall, you seemed especially calm out there today. How'd you manage to stay so calm?"

Murray's blush almost seeped into his neck and shoulders. "Ah, now, that would be my little secret. We've all got to have some secrets, don'tcha know."

And in another part of the room.

"You don't have many closed-door meetings, Coach. What did you tell the guys after the game?"

"Well, we pointed out a few of the mistakes we made today." Bradford had closed the emotional door to his anger when he had ordered the opening of the locker-room door. Now he was putting on his drawling good-ol'-boy Texas charm. "Don't want the boys to ferget. Strike while the iron's hot, and all that."

"Was there any one play or player that turned the game around, Coach?" The obvious target of the question was the fullback and his fumble that had given Chicago the ball for its final, victorious drive.

"No. Now I know whatcher drivin' at. But we're a team. We're a family. We win together. And we lost together. No one player's more responsible than anyone else for either outcome."

The reporters all knew that there was one glaring exception to the coach's claim of togetherness philosophy.

"Coach, if you had it to do over, would you play that last series as conservatively as you did?"

"Fellas, if I 'llowed myself to second-guess myself, I'da strung myself up by the neck until dead long ago.

"No, that was the way to play it. Put the ball up and you're just beggin' for an intercept. You keep it on the ground. You don't look for the fumble. I reckon we'll be doin' some work on ball-handlin' this week."

And in still another part of the room.

"What's this loss do to the Cougars' season, Mr. Galloway?"

"It's not the end of the line. Don't bury us too soon, fellas."

The owner prized all media coverage. But he had a special place in his heart for television. Not all that many people read newspapers, and radio had a comparatively small sports audience. But everybody watched television. Every time he was on, friends went out of their way to mention they had caught him on the tube. It was an important way of his becoming Somebody.

"But it evens your season at five and five—and now Chicago is one up on you."

"Let's just not call the season over when we've got eight big games to go. And one more with Chicago. I'm confident at this point that we'll make the playoffs."

"Thank you, Mr. Galloway." The TV lights were extinguished; the crew headed in another direction to interview someone else.

Galloway felt an impulse to call them back. They hadn't talked to him nearly long enough. He had lots more to say. He would wait right where he was in hopes another crew would set up here and ask him some questions—interesting ones for a change.

And in another part of the room.

"How did you feel in that last series, Bobby, keeping the ball on the ground? That's not the Bobby Cobb style."

"Look, they pay me pretty good to toss the ball around. For the same amount of money, I'd be glad to throw in a little thinking. But, as it stands, all they want is a strong right arm and a loud voice. You guys want to talk strategy, go see the coaches."

"You missed on that big third-down pass to Hoffer, Bobby. What went wrong?"

"Just a matter of timing."

"That's all?"

"That's all, my man. He's a rookie, and he's faster than the average tight end. We haven't had a chance to work much together yet. But give us a chance. He's got all the tools. He could be our next pheenom."

"Playing behind Hunsinger?"

"The Hun can't play forever."

"The Hun's got a no-cut contract."

"Not with Father Time he doesn't."

"Seriously, Bobby; how's Hoffer going to break into the lineup and get regular work, let alone a starting position, as long as the Hun is around?"

"You know, it's like that old song: Old tight ends never die; they just fade away."

"That's soldiers."

"Whatever."

"Now, you know that Hunsinger is, in a manner of speaking, the franchise, Bobby. As long as he's on the team, Coach Bradford's got to play him. I mean, everybody knows the coach is under orders from Galloway to play the Hun. If the Hun doesn't play, the Silverdome isn't filled. And that hits Galloway in his most sensitive area, the wallet."

"Now you're talkin' about the Man and the Man. And both of 'em are right in this room right now. I suggest you gentlemen go right over and ask them your questions."

Most of the reporters did just that, leaving Cobb to peel off a perspiration-soaked jersey. Generally, he was among the last to leave the locker room.

Elsewhere in the room.

Kit Hoffer sat alone.

His locker was only one removed from Hank Hunsinger's. It might as well have been a mile. No sungun had illuminated Hoffer's space. No strobe lights had flashed to blind him briefly. No reporters had asked him a single question. No coaches had said anything to him. He sometimes thought Jay Galloway knew him only because his paycheck helped to drain the owner's finite resources.

Hoffer's uniform, clean and dry aside from some nervous perspiration, hung from its hook. He shrugged out of his athletic supporter. It fell to his ankles. He removed his left foot and, in a well-practiced move, propelled the strap into his locker. Naked, he stepped into the shower area.

There was little banter from the players already in various stages of showering. Even if some, like Hoffer, had been only brief participants in the game and felt like engaging in some horseplay, they would display only somberness. The coaches, especially Bradford, would appreciate the funereal atmosphere a loss should engender.

Hoffer stepped into the steamy, powerful stream of water. It pounded through his hair and into his face, and flowed down his body. It felt good, as hot showers do, but there was nothing special about it. From the days when he was a little kid playing football in the Catholic Youth Organization, through high school and college, he'd taken his lumps in games. And always in the shower he had assessed the damage the foregoing game had caused. Athletes generally experience an automatic sort of self-hypnosis during competition—unless the injury is very serious. Then, of course, they know immediately they're in trouble. But the usual bruises and nicks would present themselves to be recognized only as the soothing hot water found them.

It had been a very long time since Hoffer had gone through such an accounting. Too long. He had not been noteworthily hurt since training camp. Which spoke volumes about his playing time during the succeeding games.

As far as his pro career was concerned, if Hoffer had not had bad luck he would not have had any luck at all. Twice he had been cut from teams before the season began. That both cuts had occurred in the final days of training camp was little consolation. But the Turk had visited him twice. And both times he was cut not because he was less talented than his competition for the position. No, the first time, his mother's death had cost him a week of training-camp time. This, coupled with the fact that his competition had no-cut contracts and the head coach had no alternative but to retain the players whose contracts bound them to the team. The second time it was because he had been injured.

This year had been different only to the extent that while Hunsinger had the precious no-cut contract, no other lineman had one. So Coach Bradford, knowing the Hun was nearing the end of his career, and aware of Hoffer's great natural talent, had kept him on the team.

But Hoffer, though technically still a rookie, had already lost two years in a profession that was notoriously brief. And he was rapidly losing a third year. Nothing stood between him and fame—and with it, big money—but Hunsinger.

Hoffer stepped out of the shower's steady stream. He felt physically fine—unfortunately. Well, he asked himself, how many bruises do you expect to pick up running just a couple of plays and carrying a record of no passes caught?

But he had plans. It would be different. And soon.

* * *

"Do you know how many nudes there are in here?"

Father Koesler smiled. He and Father McNiff had just been seated in the lounge area of the Machus Sly Fox, not far from the Silverdome. Koesler would have preferred the main restaurant area. But he knew they were lucky to be seated anywhere. The restaurant was packed, mostly with fans fresh from the game.

Of course Koesler had noticed the large painting of a voluptuous nude hanging in the lounge. It dominated the room. Being oblivious to the painting would require an ability to overlook the Grand Canyon.

But he had to smile at his friend, Pat McNiff, a typical Irish-American priest obsessed with all the evils that could be laid at the door of sex—read Women. As long as Koesler had known McNiff—and that had been forty-two of their fifty-five years of life—Pat had always been at least slightly more conservative than any of their confreres. McNiff usually caught up with the rest of the world, eventually; but he always arrived late, kicking and screaming.

"I give up." Koesler had not tried counting. "How many nudes are there in this room?"

"Twenty!"

"Twenty?"

"Twenty!"

Until now, Koesler had been unaware of the exact nature of any of the other paintings hanging in the lounge. Alerted by McNiff's curiosity, Koesler began gazing more intently at the other paintings.

"Don't look," McNiff cautioned in a stage whisper. "People will notice you're looking at naked women." He always pronounced it "nekkid."

"What do you mean, don't look? *You* looked."

"That's different. I counted. You're looking. There's a difference."

A waitress came to take their drink orders. She smiled at Koesler. She had seen him looking at the paintings. Koesler blushed.

McNiff ordered a martini; Koesler a bourbon manhattan. Neither priest smoked. Koesler had quit several years before. McNiff had surrendered the habit more recently, in deference to triple-bypass heart surgery.

"Don't you recall the sage advice of our old speech professor, Father Sklarski?" Koesler reminded. "'Look, but don't touch.'"

"Sure. I just prefer the advice of our old rector, Henry Donnelly, 'The look is father to the touch.'"

"You would." Koesler began studying the menu. McNiff did the same.

"God, what a game!" McNiff commented from behind his menu.

"Huh? Oh, yeah . . . a real barnburner."

They returned to their menus for several minutes until, simultaneously, they decided what they would order.

"If only the Cougars could have held onto the ball," McNiff said, shaking his head. "We had that game in the bag."

"It happens. Frankly, I thought we were playing too conservatively."

"Well, for Pete's sake, what did you want them to do—pass?"

"Even though I know in advance that you are not going to like this very much . . . yes."

McNiff flung his napkin the short distance from the table to his lap. "Isn't that just like you! Taking chances, not going with the percentages."

"Sometimes the dramatic pays off. Don't you remember how bunched up the Chicago team was the last time we had the ball, everybody crowding around the scrimmage line? They not only wanted to hit the ball carrier, they were up there to strip the ball away."

"We're pros. We're paid to hold onto the ball."

"But," Koesler continued, "just think what might have happened if Cobb had faked a running play, then dropped back and passed."

"It probably would have been intercepted."

"Maybe, maybe not. It could have been a touchdown. Then the game would have been iced."

"Or it would have been intercepted," McNiff repeated.

"We lost the ball anyway."

"That's hindsight."

"The Monday morning quarterback is always right."

The waitress brought their drinks and took their dinner orders. Koesler ordered ground round, medium. The Machus Sly Fox would join the considerable list of restaurants about whose hamburgers Koesler could testify. McNiff would have scrod. Having so said, he glanced at Koesler. Silently, they shared the old joke that *scrod* was the pluperfect of *screw*. One of the consequences of their long and close friendship was the ability to communicate wordlessly.

Koesler cupped his manhattan in both hands, trying to help the ice melt. With his index finger, McNiff began stirring the ice in his martini. Just as he always did. Just as he always had, beginning with his very first taste of hard liquor. That epic event had taken place in Koesler's suite at Sacred Heart. At the time, each had been a priest for ten years. And thereby hung the tale.

When Koesler and McNiff were ordained as priests, they and their entire class had taken—been forced to take—a pledge that for a period of ten years each would drink no alcoholic beverage more powerful than beer or wine. Such a pledge had been required of everyone ordained by Cardinal Edward Mooney.

Long before the ten years had passed, most of their classmates had rationalized their way around that pledge.

After eight years as a priest, Koesler had been appointed editor-in-chief of the archdiocesan newspaper, the *Detroit Catholic*. In his new role, Koesler found it necessary—or thought he did—to join his new colleagues in newsgathering, reporting, commenting, and drinking. If that was the bad news, the good news was that Koesler soon learned, through the school of honest mistakes, the necessity for moderation.

In any case, after the allotted ten-year period, McNiff presented himself to Koesler for his baptism in hard liquor. As was the case in all McNiff's more important endeavors, he imbued the occasion of his first serious drink with a melodramatic ambiance. One could, in one's imagination, hear the roll of kettledrums.

McNiff, solemnly announcing that he was placing his immediate alcoholic future in Koesler's trusted hands, warned, "You ain't gonna play fool-around with me!"

Koesler assured him that no horseplay would mar this sacred moment. He repaired to his inner sanctum, where he prepared McNiff's first drink. He dropped several ice cubes in the glass, poured in a few drops of Scotch, and filled the considerable remaining space with water. Technically, it was an alcoholic drink—the lightest McNiff would ever taste.

The presentation was suitably solemn. McNiff sat pondering his initiation into the realm of serious drinkers. He once again extracted Koesler's assurance that there had been no hanky-panky in the drink's preparation.

McNiff stirred the ice with his index finger; for years, he'd been watching confirmed drinkers do that. Finally, he took a sip, rolled it around his palate, swallowed it, looked up brightly, and commented, "That wasn't so bad."

Now, as Koesler watched McNiff stir his martini, a drink considerably stronger than his first, the long-ago scene flooded his memory.

"Besides," McNiff picked up the thread of their conversation, "any offensive chance we had in that game was shot when Hunsinger got thrown out."

"Oh, c'mon, Pat; the Cougars' entire offense isn't tied up in one player."

McNiff nodded gravely. "Who does Bobby Cobb go to when we need the big play? Nine out of ten times," he answered his own question, "it's the Hun. If he'd been in the game at the end, I'd almost go along with your crazy pass play."

Koesler smiled. "For you, that's a real act of faith."

"The Hun can get the job done. He's been doing it for years. I don't know what we're going to do when the Hun hangs it up, as, inevitably, he must."

"There'll be someone else, Pat. There always is."

"Who's the Hun's backup now?"

"Hoffer. Kit Hoffer."

"Yeah, that's the guy. What'd he do today? One incompleted pass!"

"The ball was thrown behind him! Good grief, what do you expect!"

"The Hun would have caught it."

"Oh, sure, and then made it disappear."

"You mark my words, Bobby: Kit Hoffer is never going to fill the Hun's shoes. And remember, you heard it here."

"Please, Pat," Koesler said lightheartedly, "don't be so hard on Hoffer. He's one of my parishioners."

There was that moment of genuine surprise that, from long association, Koesler recognized.

"I didn't know that."

"He moved in earlier this year, when he won a spot on the team."

"No kidding! You got a pro football player in your parish!" McNiff's childlike awe was manifest.

"Not only is he a parishioner; he got me involved in a Bible discussion group."

"A Bible discussion group! What happened? Did you find a spare moment that wasn't filled in with meetings, Masses, or paperwork?"

The waitress brought their salad. Koesler noticed for the first time her clinging black dress with its fetching décolletage.

He ordered a bottle of Blue Nun. He had never taken enough interest in wines to become an oenologist. Someone had once mentioned that Blue Nun could accompany meat, fish—anything. Since he was having meat and McNiff fish, he quickly decided on the easiest solution. Besides, for two men in clerical suit and roman collar, Blue Nun had a nice ring.

He could not help reflecting on McNiff's questions. Koesler had always considered the priesthood a hard-working, busy profession. But how priestly occupation, as well as the world, had changed since they had been ordained in the mid-fifties! Then, Catholicism had found itself in the middle of a rhythm-only baby boom, campaigns against steady dating and a nefarious new publication called *Playboy*; the beginning of what might become either the newest or the ultimate technological explosion; and the last throes of a climate in which "Father" knew best.

How things had changed in thirty years!

Now, few could remember why steady dating had been a problem. Teenagers of the fifties had passed along that victory, as well as the triumph of their music, to their children. If steady dating was no longer a problem, undesired pregnancies, as well as abortions, the occasional consequences of steady dating, now were.

Catholics, by and large, had settled the issue of family planning to the satisfaction of their own "informed" consciences. Almost the only Catholics who still found a problem with most means of birth control were a few priests, many bishops, and, of course, the Pope. With almost all these gentlemen, the problem remained no more than theoretical.

Playboy, despite all Catholic efforts to have it removed from store shelves, was alive and well. The magazine had spawned so many imitators that had, in turn, so strained the limits of decency that the mother of them all was now quite bland by comparison.

Word processors were ubiquitous. Long ago, they had put the final nail into the coffin of that noble instrument, the Linotype machine. And now so many children had computers that these electronic wonders had replaced books, comic books, Big-Little Books, television, and, of course, outdoor exercise. The nuclear club had grown by the year. So much so that most first-world countries as well as some second-world countries had the capability to at least initiate the final holocaust. And in all this technological race there was no semblance of a contemplative balance. Reflecting on the present state of affairs, Koesler concluded that the seven last words of Western Civilization might well be, We Have the Technology to Do It.

Finally, as far as Koesler was concerned, the day of "Father"—in the sense of the good old parish priest—knowing best was irretrievably gone. There had been a time, spanning centuries, when the local priest had been the best-, sometimes the only, educated person in an area. The serfs worked while the monks studied. Ethnic immigrants to the USA clustered in their ghettos around their priests. Even in the 1950s, the parish priest had been the general practitioner who instructed, counseled, mediated, arbitrated, processed, and at times acted as an employment agent. Now, in this age of specialization, Catholics, like nearly everyone else, took their problems to specialists. The priest as amateur marriage counselor and seat-of-the-pants psychologist gave way to the professional.

Koesler stabbed a piece of lettuce and dabbed it in the house dressing. "As far as our time being overscheduled with meetings and Masses, I'll give you that one. God knows, between parochial and diocesan meetings, there's not an awful lot of time left over. And with the priest shortage, each of us has more Masses to say than ever before. We used to be able to at least take turns with all the weddings and funerals. Now, there's hardly anyone around to take a turn.

"But the other thing you mentioned, Pat, the paperwork, the administration; I think we can get rid of a hell of a lot of that."

Finished with his salad, McNiff cracked a bread stick. "Oh, you do, do you? Well, it's not going to go away. So who's going to do it? Who's going to be around running the plant? Who's on duty at the door? Who's available in case of emergency? Who's there when the parishioners need somebody?"

"The ultimate answer to most of those questions is, our business manager."

"Business manager! You got a business manager? When did you get a business manager? Where did you get a business manager?"

"About, let's see, maybe six months ago." Koesler sensed McNiff's pique over not having been told. "It just never came up in any of our discussions."

Koesler waited while this new information was assimilated. McNiff did not adjust easily to surprises. "It's one of the men from the parish," Koesler explained. "Ed Dorsey. I don't think you've met him. A little while back, he retired from Ford. He was an executive there. It was his idea; he didn't know what to do with all that time. He suggested he take over the office. So now, between him and our secretary, Mary O'Connor, the parish is doing better than ever. We give him a little stipend. It isn't much . . . but then, he doesn't need much. We just wanted to show him our gratitude."

McNiff was not at all sure he liked the idea. But then, he seldom liked any new idea at first blush. "But who takes care of the parishioners, their spiritual needs? Neither what's-his-name—Mr. Dorsey—nor Mary can confer sacraments. Neither of them is trained to give spiritual advice."

Koesler chuckled. "I didn't abdicate, Pat; I just hired a business manager. I'm around much of the time, catching up on odds and ends, preparing homilies . . . like that. And if I'm not at the rectory, I call in periodically to get any messages. And if someone wants to see me, he or she makes an appointment. Just as they do with their doctors, dentists, and lawyers.

"You ought to try it, Pat. In a parish like yours, you've got to have a number of retirees who could step in and help. They'd probably be grateful to be asked. It would free you up. All those Masses and meetings make demands on us that we can't escape. But there's no reason we have to add to the burnout the rest of the time."

The waitress cleared away the salad dishes—my, that was a décolletage!—and served the pièces de résistance. McNiff was still digesting the business manager concept. "Okay, so the business manager relieves you from hours of answering phones, taking care of the books, managing the janitor, ordering supplies, making sure equipment is kept in good repair"—McNiff was unaware that he was enumerating tasks he would be relieved of if he had a business manager—"but what do you do with the time you've saved? What do you do, Father, all day . . . I mean, after you've said Mass?"

Koesler smiled. "There's lots of things, Pat. I go back to the seminary, audit some classes. Bone up on some of the new theological trends. Spend a bit more time visiting ill parishioners. There's a nursing home in our parish. I go there every once in a while. Those folks really need company. We've started a few prayer groups in the parish. And," he paused and chuckled, "then there's the Bible discussion group . . . how's the fish?"

In response, McNiff freed a segment of scrod, dabbed his fork in tartar sauce, speared the morsel, introduced it to his mouth, and chewed, a smile indicating approval. "How's the hamburger?"

"Fine."

"How does it stack up against the hamburger in every other eatery in town?"

Koesler grinned. Of course, being together as much as they were, McNiff would be well aware of Koesler's penchant for ordering ground beef.

"I would say"—hamburger was one of the very few secular subjects about which Koesler felt qualified to expertly pontificate—"this is only slightly lower in quality than that of the London Chop House. And considerably lower in quantity than that of Carl's Chop House, but then, Carl's is especially appropriate just before or after famine."

McNiff sipped his wine. "Nice." He knew as little about wine as did Koesler. "So," McNiff returned to the previous topic, "you joined a Bible discussion group. As the leader, I suppose."

"Nope; just a member. Not even first among equals."

"Not the leader! Then why in God's green world would a priest join a Bible discussion group? The other members can't all be priests!"

Koesler smiled as he swallowed a morsel of potato. "No, they are by no means priests. As a matter of fact, they all belong, in one way or another, to that team we saw get beat this afternoon. As for the reason I joined, it probably has a great deal to do with my inability to say no."

"All Cougars!" Three surprises in one mealtime were not good for McNiff's digestion. "Come on! Come on!" he gestured, fingers curling into his palm, "let it all out. You'll feel better for it."

Koesler touched a napkin to his lips. "As I said, my parishioner, Kit Hoffer, asked me to join this discussion group. I'm not sure why. But I've got a hunch he feels a little insecure in that group for one reason or another. So he wants his friendly parish priest along."

"Well, one incredibility after another. Who'da thought that a pro football team would have a Bible group?"

"Not that surprising when you get into it. It's kind of an offshoot of the Fellowship of Christian Athletes... you've heard of them?"

McNiff nodded.

"They sponsor prayer meetings, especially on the

mornings of game days. It's a very active, nondenominational organization. Actually, there are three discussion groups among the Cougar personnel. But ours—we call ourselves the God Squad—is the only one of the three that has allowed in an outsider." He paused. "I guess that's not so odd when you look at the disparity of our members."

McNiff's expression invited amplification.

"There's Kit—and me, of course—Jay Galloway, Dave Whitman, Jack Brown, Bobby Cobb, Niall Murray, and Hank Hunsinger."

McNiff whistled softly. "What a conglomeration! The owner, the general manager, the trainer, a priest, and four players. How did—"

"I'm not sure. I think it was organized by Brown, the trainer. As for his motive, I can only guess at it. For one thing, I think he wanted to bring management and player personnel together. Management is certainly represented by Galloway and Whitman. But why he singled out the players he did is beyond me. Come to think of it, he may have invited other players to join. In any event, I assume he picked Cobb because he's the hub of the team. And Hunsinger is the most notorious—or should I say he seems to be most in demand as far as publicity is concerned. Murray, as an immigrant and rookie, and Hoffer, as a rookie and backup to Hunsinger, would have to be about the least secure members of the team." He stopped, then added, "I'm not claiming that these were Brownie's reasons. But it's the best scenario I can come up with."

McNiff finished his entrée and was sipping coffee while being very thoughtful. "The one who seems most to stick out like a sore thumb in that group is Hunsinger. If you can believe what you read in the papers, the guy's an out-and-out hedonist. And, on top of it all, I think I read that he's a Catholic!"

"Right on both counts. He is a Catholic, though certainly not a practicing one. He alone of the group always seems rather cynical. I'm only guessing, but I think the reason he's in this bunch is that he wants as few things as possible going on behind his back. I think he knows he's nearing the end of his career. So any meeting that Kit Hoffer attends, Hunsinger is probably sure to be found there.

"As for the rumors about his private life, I guess there must be some truth to them. Our meeting last Tuesday evening was at his apartment. Talk about a swinging bachelor's pad! Until I saw the Hun's place, I'd only read about things like that. Mirrors everywhere, especially in the bedroom—even a mirror on the ceiling above a bed that's set up on a platform."

"What for—the mirrors, I mean?"

"It enhances the sexual experience for some people. Or so I've been told."

McNiff pondered that for a moment. "You met on Tuesday. Do you always meet on Tuesdays? Weekly? Monthly?"

"Weekly. And, yes, always on Tuesday evenings. Tuesday is sort of the football players' day off. Next Tuesday we meet at Galloway's home."

"Any chance they would allow another member?" McNiff would be so proud to tell his parishioners that he was rubbing elbows with and dispensing theological opinions to real professional football players. "After all, if I get myself a business manager, I'll have a little extra time on my hands."

Inwardly, Koesler winced. He wished McNiff had not asked that favor. The group was already of a size where it was difficult for each one to fully express himself. And then, too, it was just not the sort of group wherein McNiff would be comfortable. With a lay bunch such as the God Squad, McNiff would inevitably attempt to enforce his interpretation of Scripture. Except that it wouldn't work with these men.

"Tell you what, Pat. The first time there's a chance to

bring this up with the group, I'll do it. But I wouldn't hold my breath if I were you. I don't get the impression they would let anybody else into the group. As it is, it's a bit unwieldy. But I will give it a try."

Koesler meant what he said. McNiff seemed satisfied with the promise.

Meal completed, they settled the bill, going Dutch.

McNiff had met Koesler in the restaurant parking lot before the game. Koesler had driven them to the stadium and back. They now parted, each taking his own car.

En route back to St. Anselm's, Koesler thought about this odd Bible group. It certainly was composed of provocative but strikingly different personalities. He had gleaned a few new insights about the Bible from the group's discussions. But, being a student of human behavior, he had learned a great deal more about the men who participated. Each was interesting in his own way. Especially interesting was their interrelationship.

It was Koesler's understanding that Galloway and Whitman had grown up together in Minnesota. He would have expected theirs to be a more fraternal relationship. It didn't appear to be. Neither seemed to hold the other in much respect.

Kit Hoffer was, of course, Koesler's parishioner. But he was surprised at Hoffer's attitude during the meetings. He seemed to resent Hunsinger, which, given Hoffer's position on the bench behind the Hun, was natural enough. But Hoffer's resentment appeared to spread to both Galloway and Whitman, as if it were their fault he spent so much time on the bench.

Niall Murray, fresh from Ireland, was obviously not entirely at ease in a strange land and in a mostly foreign game. Outside of kicking a ball, he knew little of the refinements of pro football. And he seemed somehow oddly dependent upon Hunsinger.

Just from his interpretations of Scripture, it was clear that Bobby Cobb needed to control any situation in which he found himself. A practical attitude for a quarterback. The fly in Cobb's ointment was Hunsinger, who was not one to be heavily influenced, let alone controlled.

The trainer, Brownie, seemed the catalyst. Frequently, he bridged the gap between management and employees as well as between the players. This did not surprise Koesler, since it was Brownie who had initiated the group.

Finally, there was Hunsinger. One of the more interesting and flamboyant characters Koesler had ever met. It seemed likely that the Hun was doing his best to negate his Catholic upbringing. Koesler had known a few people like that, but none to compare with Hunsinger. He seemed the least likely of any of the members to be part of a Bible study group. Why had he accepted Brownie's invitation to join?

As he had explained to McNiff, Koesler believed that the Hun realized he was nearing the end of his physical ability to compete and couldn't afford to have anything going on behind his back. Especially anything that he might even remotely construe as potentially threatening to his position. Particularly with a group that included his employers, his quarterback, and his probable replacement. In this, the Hun resembled the slow-witted person whose eyes are in constant motion because he cannot afford to miss anything.

If there was a common denominator to this group, it was that the feelings of everyone, with perhaps the exception of Brownie, toward the Hun ranged from dislike to contempt. This negative atmosphere bothered Koesler greatly. He had the premonition that something evil would come of it.

The black Continental glided almost silently through the dark, narrow maze of streets. It was almost as if whoever had laid out the city of Grosse Pointe Farms had wanted to make it difficult for a stranger to find anything. Perhaps that had been the intent.

Bobby Cobb, however, knew where he was going. He'd been there many times. Usually, as was the case now, for a postgame party. It didn't much matter whether the Cougars won or lost; there were postgame parties virtually all over the Detroit area. The prestige of these parties could be measured by the quantity and quality of real-life football players in attendance. Obviously, it was the fate of most parties, given the relative paucity of players, to remain plebeian.

The Continental began encountering a solid series of parked, mostly luxury cars. He was nearing his destination.

Several attendants blocked the semicircular driveway at the Lake Shore address. They were there to block entry to anyone but the arriving Cougars and to park their cars. Nonplayer guests might have to park quite a distance away. But the players had run as far as they would be required to for this day.

Cobb slid gracefully from his car, leaving the motor purring. A young attendant, newly hired for this job, held the door for him. Admiration was evident in the attendant's eyes. Quickly, he studied Cobb as thoroughly as possible. It would be his responsibility to describe the famous quarterback to his fellow students at the University of Detroit Dental School tomorrow. They would want to know all about Cobb. And the attendant would tell them. About Cobb's sharply chiseled features; his chocolate-colored face and hands; his closely cropped, kinky black hair with the trace of gray at the temples; the blue turtleneck, maroon blazer, and gray slacks, none of which could hide the rippling muscles beneath; and those huge hands, which, when wrapped around a football, made it appear to be no larger than a grapefruit.

Cobb was aware in general of what the attendant was thinking. It was not an uncommon reaction to his presence. In a few moments, the same sort of phenomenon would occur at the party inside this mansion.

Cobb understood the phenomenon. He not only understood it, he utilized it. As he did with almost everything else that suited his purpose.

Professional football players, particularly the stars, or, as they were more commonly called in the game, pheenoms, were celebrities. Their photos appeared in the newspapers. They were interviewed on television. Stories were written about them in magazines. Most important, on Sundays, occasionally on the other days of the week they performed.

Detractors tried to disparage their work by claiming they were paid extremely well simply to play a child's game. Further, that their IQs qualified them for little more than children's games.

There was no denying that some, the pheenoms, were paid exceedingly well. But their profession had developed into a science of precision and perfection, with physical and mental rigors that few with smug intellects could have met.

In any case, they were certified celebrities. Their fame was equaled by few aficionados of their sport. And those few fans who could match the players press clipping for press clipping nearly always lacked the players' physical presence. The players, almost all of them, lived up to the description "bigger than life."

All of this subliminal self-awareness accompanied Bobby Cobb as he entered the mansion.

"Hey! Hi, Bobby! What's happenin'?"

Damn! He couldn't see who had greeted him. He couldn't see a thing. Long ago someone had decreed that to be intimate, luxurious and stylishly pretentious rooms had to be kept so dark that it required half an evening for one's eyes to grow accustomed to the dimness.

"Yeah," Cobb responded blindly, "how's it goin' with you?" He hoped there was no hand raised for a high five. If there was, he certainly could not make it out.

Cobb remained near the door, waiting for his vision to

adjust, and noncommittally returning salutations to blurry figures, all of whom seemed friendly. Gradually, he was able to see sufficiently to chance leaving his island of security.

An arm fell heavily across his shoulders. Cobb tensed instinctively but briefly, then smiled. People shouldn't do that to an athlete, especially during the playing season. If Cobb had been a lineman or a linebacker, the gentleman standing next to him might be flat on his back nursing some broken part of his body. All a matter of conditioned reflexes.

"Bobby, how're you doing?"

"A little sore, sir. But I guess that's to be expected."

Cobb recognized the voice instantly. Senior partner in one of Detroit's most outstanding law firms. And important to Bobby Cobb, who was only a few scholastic hours and a bar exam away from becoming a lawyer.

"Waiter," the attorney beckoned, "get Mr. Cobb here a drink, will you? What're you drinking, Bobby?"

"Dewar's on the rocks."

"Sure thing, Mr. Cobb." The waiter hurried off.

"That last series of plays this afternoon, Bobby, that wasn't like you, keepin' the ball on the ground." The lawyer, arm entwined in Cobb's, tried to steer him off into a corner.

"I'm not the coach, sir."

"So it wasn't your idea." The lawyer seemed gratified.

"No, sir." Cobb tried to communicate the impression that he could take orders, which was the truth.

"What would you have done if you were the coach? What would you have done if the coach had given you your head?"

"Crossed them up. The Towers were bunched up tight. The last thing they were giving us was the run."

"So?"

"We needed a play-action pass. Fake a run up the middle, flare out, and hit the S receiver along the sidelines.

He could easily have gone all the way. Even if he hadn't, the Towers would have been so deep in their own territory they could never have come back and scored."

"You'd take a chance on an interception?"

"No, sir, I wouldn't. Not as long as I was throwin' the ball."

The lawyer smiled again. Cobb had demonstrated that he was a take-charge guy with plenty of self-confidence. Just the kind of personality one might want in one's law firm.

In Cobb's plans for himself was a partnership in this prestigious law firm; building and enhancing his reputation. Then a jump to the political arena. Mayor of Detroit, if that were possible without a term on the city council. Then, bypassing Lansing, on to the House, and eventually the U. S. Senate.

It was all well within the realm of possibility. He had the talent. All that was needed was promotion. He needed every headline, every moment on camera that he could get.

His only competition for the limelight was that damned Hunsinger. The Hun with his strong local popularity. U of M to the Cougars. A playboy lifestyle that kept him in the forefront of everything from the sports pages to the nightly news to the gossip columns. Hunsinger could catch a football. Outside of that singular accomplishment, the Hun wasn't worth a pile of crap.

The waiter slipped Cobb's drink into his hand, measuring the enormousness of that hand against his own. All this was so that tomorrow he could describe to his friends, with a little embellishment, the legend of a quarterback's mitt.

"You're coming up for the bar pretty soon, aren't you, Bobby?" The lawyer turned to face Cobb.

"Yes, sir."

"Listen, why don't you come see me after the season? Just give my girl a ring. Maybe we can do business together.

Would you like that?" He knew the question was rhetorical.

"Yes, sir, I would. Very much."

"Hey, Bobby, c'mon over here!" One of the other Cougars was calling from across the room.

"Would you excuse me, sir?"

"Of course." The lawyer patted Cobb's arm and directed at him a benevolent paternal look that carried the unspoken bromide, Be good, but if you can't be good, be careful. "Go on, now. Have a good time. God knows you paid your dues this afternoon."

Cobb inched his way across the room. With the wall-to-wall crowd, each person was a new obstacle. Almost everyone wanted to talk to him. Several asked about the conservative play of that last series. Each time, he passed the question off with a brief, flip explanation. The only person in the room entitled to a detailed explanation was Cobb's future employer. And he had already received the full commentary.

As he crossed the room, women, oblivious of their escorts, rubbed seductively against Cobb. He raised his eyes to heaven. So many women in the world and so little time. But he needed neither the complication nor any trouble with any of their companions. Like as not, some hotshot with too many drinks under his belt would seize the occasion to prove he could take the great athlete. And there he would stand with no pads, unprotected against some drunk who had nothing to lose but his teeth. With his luck, Cobb figured the best that might happen would be that he'd break a hand and be out for the rest of the season. So he graciously apologized to each woman who airily threw herself at him.

At long last, Cobb reached the man who had called to him. "Hey, Bobby, I thought you needed some action." It was the Cougars' center, an amiable gentleman built like the proverbial brick house. Mercifully, he had reinserted the bridgework he went without during games.

"This where it's at, Spud?"

"Shit, yeah, Bobby." The behemoth grinned. "It's about time don'tcha think? I got this little fox for me and I got this one for you."

Cobb inspected the foxes. Spud held one under his arm. Her feet were not touching the floor. Cobb thought Spud neither knew nor cared about that fact. The other young woman Spud held around the neck. He thrust her toward Cobb. Both women had fixed smiles as if they had been cast from plaster of Paris.

"Not tonight, Spud. Have you seen Niall?"

"The little guy? Yeah; he's upstairs in one of the bedrooms. But I don't think he's asleep yet." Spud roared at his venture into humor. He then scrutinized both women, the one in his hand and the one under his wing. Deciding to take them both, he moved them off toward the rear of the mansion.

Cobb hurried up the stairs, nodding at and brushing by those he encountered on the staircase. He tried two rooms before he found Murray in the third.

The young Irishman was seated on the side of a bed, which was covered with a red satin quilt. Stretched out on the quilt was a young woman in a white slip.

Actually, Murray was more slumped than seated. He seemed transfixed by several lines of white powder spread out on a piece of wax paper on the nightstand. He looked up momentarily when Cobb entered. "Hi, there, Bobby, then. What're you doin' here now?"

As Cobb approached, the girl moved apprehensively to the far side of the bed. Murray's concentration returned to the neatly arranged powder.

Cobb quickly and expertly appraised the woman. Neither a con artist nor a whore. One more groupie wanting to know firsthand, as it were, if all those muscles were genuine. This one obviously was abashed at Cobb's expression.

"Has he had any yet?" Cobb nodded toward the powder.

The woman shook her head. She did not blink. Nor did she remove her gaze from Cobb's face.

"Hey, Niall, babe, what's happenin'?"

"Hi, there, Bobby, then. What're you doin' here?"

"Had a little bit to drink, have you, babe?" Cobb could smell the sweet odor of bourbon.

"Some."

Cobb shoved lightly; Murray fell back on the bed. "The trouble with you Irish is your image. You're supposed to be great drinkers, but you can't hold your liquor." Cobb slid Murray's loosened tie up to his neck, closing his shirt at the collar.

"The trouble with you coloureds," Murray's speech was slurred, "is your image. You're supposed to be sex maniacs. And you are as well."

Cobb pulled Murray to his feet and got him into his jacket. "You don't want to get that white stuff up your nose, Mick. With or without booze. With booze, it could kill you. Any which way, it's gonna scramble your head. Next thing you know you won't be able to find the goal-post and you'll be kickin' my balls instead of Wilson's. Then you and me, but most importantly me, will be the laughingstock of this city. And I don't intend for that to happen. I intend to own this city for starters."

It was obvious that Murray was understanding none of this. Cobb was handling him as if he were a ragdoll.

"Who got you started on coke, anyway?"

"Huh?"

"I said, who got you started on coke?"

"Oh, the Hun."

"It figures."

"Huh?"

"That bastard! He's got a knack of corrupting everything he touches. He'd pull the rug out from under me if he got the chance. Only he ain't gonna get it."

Cobb supported Murray and began walking with him. Actually, Cobb virtually carried the Irishman. They would leave the mansion as close as buddies ever get, eliciting from other guests hopeful observations on racial harmony. Cobb would deliver Murray, untouched by alien hand, to the forgiving arms of his wife.

"Hun a bas'ard," Murray slurred as he was inserted into Cobb's car.

"That's right, little Mick. You just learned a lesson that could save your life. But it won't do much for the bastard."

Everywhere he looked, there was Hank Hunsinger. That was because his three walls were mirrored, top to bottom. The fourth wall was a picture window.

He removed his jacket, wincing as he did so. He was growingly aware of this afternoon's slings, arrows, and pummeling fists. Football commentators are fond of stating that when receivers leave the ground to catch a pass, they are "vulnerable." And when they're tackled midair, they "pay the price." Unless the commentators have undergone the experience firsthand, they would have no notion of just how high that price is.

Hunsinger entered the large walk-in closet. Neatly displayed was an extensive wardrobe of expensive jackets, coats, and foul-weather gear. He arranged his jacket on the appropriate hanger in the section reserved for green and green coordinates. A place for everything and everything in its place. He made certain the jacket he had just hung and the ones on either side of it were hanging free of each other so that no wrinkles would be inflicted.

He crossed the living room to the kitchen. Both rooms were outstandingly large. But then his entire apartment was several times more spacious than the average apartment. He had money and, being of sound mind, had decided to spend it.

He opened the liquor cabinet. Everything. Well, perhaps not everything. The best of everything. He selected a Scotch and poured it generously over several ice cubes.

He returned to the living room and stood by the window, swirling the Scotch gently.

The Detroit River, vital artery of the Great Lakes. And Belle Isle, jewel-caressed on either of its shores by the river that separated Canada from the United States. Hunsinger never tired of the sight. Few did.

He sipped the Scotch. Cold to the taste, it spread warmth through his body. His memory broke free and returned to the antithesis of all this—his youth.

Growing up in Detroit's southwest side. Poor. Although he hadn't known they were poor. They always had food. Not top grade, but enough.

He remembered 1954. He had been just seven years old when his father died. From then on, it was just Hank and his mother. She had gotten a job as housekeeper in the extensive convent that housed the nuns who taught at Holy Redeemer parochial school. Tagging around after his mother, he had become somewhat of a pet to the childless nuns—which largely accounted for the sufficiency of average food at his disposal. The nuns could not afford top-grade food, but with what they had, they pampered this growing boy.

Oddly, he had attended public, not parochial, school. His mother told the nuns this was in accord with the wishes of his late Protestant father. She then confessed her lie to the priest, but could not bring herself to tell the nuns the truth: that with the little they paid her, she could not afford even the modest tuition at Holy Redeemer. What did the nuns know about it, in any case? Shielded by their vows of poverty, the trifle they were paid went to their religious order, not to them individually.

All in all, it was a pleasant enough life. The first time Hunsinger realized they had been poor was when as a young man he saw pictures in the newspaper of poor homes, and recognized them as being identical to that of his old neighborhood. The houses of the poor were easily relatable to the home in which he'd grown up.

He had liked the nuns. Through and because of them, he had stayed at least nominally close to his Catholic faith. And his mother's place of employment gave her the opportunity to become a fanatical Catholic, attending several daily Masses, novena devotions, taking communion daily, and going to confession weekly.

As for Hunsinger, outside of his close and uncluttered relationship with a lot of doting nuns, he became a creature of the streets. He grew quickly into a very big boy, and kept growing. His personal maxim—Do unto others, then split—was a drastic paraphrasing of the gospel admonition. He was conscious of that. Very early, long before it became a popular credo, he had become primarily, indeed exclusively, concerned about Number One.

He perceived early on that excellence in athletics could lead to a life in the fast lane not only for poor black kids, but for big white kids too. So he applied himself. He won all-state honors in basketball, baseball, and football at Western High. He was awarded a full scholarship at the University of Michigan. Drafted in the first round by the Cougars in 1969, this was his sixteenth season with the club. He was well past his playing prime. Each year it became increasingly tempting to hang 'em up. But each year the contracts got sweeter and more irresistible.

However, the end could not be far off. Another season or two at the most. Even now, he had lasted longer than any other tight end in the history of professional football. He survived now mostly through a host of illegal, dirty tactics that he had mastered over the years.

He was hated. He didn't care. He would not now compete, nor had he ever competed, for Mr. Congeniality. Even members of his own organization hated him. Well, that was a concomitant when one was exclusively concerned with taking care of Number One. It didn't matter.

After all these years, he was quite good at taking care of himself and protecting his rear.

Thinking of the care and feeding of Number One, he glanced at his watch and returned with a start to the present. It was nearly time for Jan to get here. She was becoming an expert in the care of Hank Hunsinger. He must prepare himself for her arrival.

He set his glass, empty save for the remains of the ice cubes, on a nearby table. He had not been aware of having finished the Scotch. He noted that he was a bit lightheaded. It had been a long time since he had eaten. No matter; it might even add a dimension to the upcoming wrestling match with Jan. Booze had helped him in the past.

He turned on the television and, after making a few adjustments, slammed a cassette into the Betamax. It was a movie featuring two, then many more evidently consenting adults, engaged in explicit sexual activity. It had no redeeming social value whatever. The Hun had been delighted to discover that Jan seemed to find voyeurism stimulating. Hunsinger certainly did. He turned down the volume; they could provide their own moans and groans live.

He moved to the bedroom. Again mirrors—wall to wall, floor to ceiling, and ceiling as well. Lest there be some lingering doubt as to what was intended as the focal point of the room, the large circular bed was mounted on a platform.

Hunsinger removed his clothing, placing each item precisely in its appointed place, making certain that when trousers and shirt were hung, adjacent garments would not be wrinkled.

He stood naked in the center of his bedroom examining the multiple images of himself. The muscles were not as sharply defined as they once had been. But they were still evident. His six-foot-four, 232-pound body still resembled an ancient sculpture of an Olympian. He ran his hand through his salt-and-pepper brush cut. Almost no one wore his hair in a brush cut any longer. Hunsinger did it for the sole purpose of extending the image of a Hun that he carefully and profitably nurtured.

Life was good. And in a little while it would get better.

He removed his contact lenses and placed them in the Bausch & Lomb disinfecting unit, switching it on. He could still see, but fuzzily. A combination of nearsightedness and astigmatism blurred his vision.

He entered the bathroom. There were neither shower doors nor curtains. Not even a stall. The shower was an adjunct of the enormous sunken tub. He turned the powerful jet of water on and waited until it became very hot, then slipped into it. It beat against his head, back, trunk, buttocks and legs. He moved slowly back, forth and around in the spray. So much better than the shower at the stadium. There it was crowded, hurried, and invariably followed by further perspiration as one dressed while others were showering. The steam kept pouring into the locker room. Then there were those damn television lights that further heated the area.

This was nice. He could feel tight muscles loosen and relax under the relentless beat of the waterjet. He was in no hurry. Jan could join him in the shower when she arrived. It had been too long since they had started an evening by showering together.

He reached for the shampoo, second container from the left on the shelf beneath the shower head. He could not read the label, but it didn't matter. It was the correct shape, and besides, he always kept the shampoo second from the left on the shelf.

He unscrewed the cap of the plastic bottle, poured a generous measure of shampoo into his left hand, and replaced the open bottle on the shelf—second from the left.

He let some of the shampoo flow from his left to his right hand, and then began to rub it vigorously into his hair and scalp. With his brush cut, he was able to get the liquid to his scalp quickly.

Something was wrong.

He pulled both hands from his head and pressed them tightly to his chest. There was a terrible constriction there. It felt as if someone had placed a steel band around him and was tightening it rapidly. A heart attack? The very thought induced a further sense of panic. He was alone. No one would come to his aid.

Suddenly, his entire body began to shudder. The shuddering intensified. He shook as if he were a ragdoll being battered about by a malevolent child.

He tried, but could not control the violent shuddering. It became a spasm. Now his body was completely out of control. His hands shot to his neck, which had stiffened so he could not draw a breath.

It was not so much that he fell as that he was thrown to the floor of the tub. His legs shot out stiffly, straight and rigid. He tried to breathe, but could not. He could feel his respiratory muscles tighten. His skin was turning from bluish to a purple discoloration.

Suddenly his body arched, then balanced on his head and heels. It stayed in that taut position for long seconds.

Then, as unexpectedly as it began, it ended. His body relaxed, and gave one more massive shudder. He was dead.

The shower played unimpeded against the far wall. It ran down and formed a small pool where the body of Hank Hunsinger partially blocked the drain.

Not much later Jan Taylor let herself into the apartment.

"Hun?"

No answer.

She noticed the television was on. She also noted the images on the screen. She shrugged. So it was going to be one of those nights. Plenty of kinky sex. She loathed it, but would never let on to Hunsinger. He might be an animal in bed, but he did keep her well.

She removed her coat and carefully hung it on the hook inside the closet door. The Hun had appointed that specific hook for her hanger and apprised her of the importance of always, without exception, using that hook for her coat. Left to her own devices, she would have thrown it over a chair.

She could hear the shower running. She toyed with the option of waiting till he finished before announcing her presence as if she had just entered. It would spare her the unnecessary repetition of getting wet again. She had showered before leaving her apartment. And it would save her the indignities of Hunsinger's shower routines. A far greater consideration.

On the other hand, it was entirely possible he was waiting for her to join him. In which case, her absence would infuriate him. And the last thing she needed was a furious Hun.

She shrugged and entered the bedroom. The sound of the shower was much clearer now. The lack of any sound but that of the water beating against a wall seemed somehow ominous, although she did not focus on any specific reason for her apprehension.

While she removed her clothing, hanging each item on the designated hangers, she noticed the small red light indicating that his "cooker" was working and that his contact lenses were being cleaned. All the better to see you with, my dear.

Naked, she entered the bathroom. Although she had been girding herself for the worst, she certainly had no way of anticipating this.

She screamed. Over and over. Then she ran from the bathroom.

Lieutenant Ned Harris was in Hank Hunsinger's bathroom. It was the scene of the crime and he was being careful not to miss a single detail. Very soon, investigative specialists would be swarming over the apartment, each performing his or her task. Before that happened, Harris had the rare opportunity to commune with the place where death had occurred, where, probably, murder had been committed. He would never again in this case have this perfect opportunity to be in this specific location where vital clues and silent testimony told no lies. As he studied the apartment, he allowed the everyday inanimate objects to talk to him wordlessly.

Harris was an inch and a half to two inches more than six feet tall. His build was slender but powerful. Aquiline features and a receding hairline set off his deep black skin. He had been a part of the homicide division for most of his professional career. He loved it.

His partner on this case, Sergeant Ray Ewing, was interviewing the witness, Jan Taylor, in the living room.

Ewing, at five-feet-eleven, with a stocky physique, somewhat resembled singer Steve Lawrence. He also had Lawrence's pleasant voice and engaging smile.

Harris and Ewing had been the sole occupants of their squad's office at police headquarters on that otherwise slow Sunday evening when they got the call from the uniformed officers who had responded to Jan Taylor's 911 call.

"Would you mind going over that one more time, Miss Taylor?" Ewing continued to scribble notes on his pad. "Why would Mr. Hunsinger take another shower when he got back here after the game? He would have taken one before leaving the stadium, wouldn't he?"

Jan dabbed at her eyes with a corner of her handkerchief. She was obviously distraught. Ewing chose to reserve judgment on the reason for her anxiety. It might have been the sudden loss of whatever Hunsinger had been to her. It might have been the shock at what she had found in the bathroom.

"He was never satisfied with the shower at the stadium." This was her second time through the second-shower phenomenon. She wondered why she had been asked to repeat the explanation. "What with the heat in the locker room, the steam from the showers, and the lights from the TV cameras, he said he always felt as sweaty after that shower as he had before."

"So?"

"So he always took another shower when he got home."

Ewing noted the slight show of color in Jan's face when she reached this part of her testimony the second time through. He surmised that the second shower probably was for her benefit. Taking stock of her, he did not blame Hunsinger.

"Always?"

"The Hun," Jan replied, a touch caustically, "did everything he did *always*."

"And what time was it when you entered the apartment?" The third time for this question.

"About six-thirty, or a quarter to seven."

"And was that tape in the videocassette deck playing?" First time for this question.

"I . . . I don't recall."

"It was playing when we entered the apartment. If it was on when you came, did you turn it on?"

"I . . . I guess it must have been playing when I came in."

You bet it was, Ewing thought. And that tells us much about the relationship between the two of you and why you're going to be on the shy side of telling us much about it.

"Then you went into the bedroom. Why was that?"

"I heard the shower. I knew Hank couldn't hear me with the water running and I wanted him to know I was here."

"And then you said you noticed that Mr. Hunsinger's disinfecting unit was operating. It was cleaning his contact lenses?"

"Yes. I just happened to glance over and saw the red light lit."

"Anything significant in that?"

"Well, it told me he hadn't been in the shower very long."

"How's that?"

"The unit turns itself off after about twenty minutes."

"So he would have been in the shower something less than twenty minutes. Then he wouldn't have begun his shower much before you got here."

"That's right, I guess."

"Are you married, Ms. Taylor?"

"No."

"Ever been?"

She hesitated a split second. "No."

"Ms. Taylor?" Lieutenant Harris had been standing in the doorway between the living room and bedroom for some time. Jan hadn't noticed him. His words startled her.

"Yes?" She looked up at him.

"Could you tell us why there was a bottle of DMSO in Mr. Hunsinger's bathroom?" Harris had heard enough to learn that Jan Taylor would have been in a position to know just about everything about Hunsinger.

"He kept some here and some at the stadium. It was for pain. Mostly in his shoulder. Sometimes his knees. He's had a lot of operations. He never knew when the pain was going to flare up. I guess it's supposed to be a controlled substance, but..." Her voice trailed. She couldn't understand why with a man dead the police were concerned about DMSO. Even though it was not approved for use as a painkiller, anyone could buy it as a solvent in any number of stores. It was like worrying about bank robbers being illegally parked.

"I'm not so concerned about its being a controlled substance as I am about why it would be on a shelf in the shower area with other toiletries. And why the DMSO container should be open as if it were being used during his shower."

Jan appeared perplexed.

"If you'll accompany me to the bathroom, I'll show you . . ." Harris stepped in the direction of the bathroom as if inviting her to follow him.

"Is . . . is he . . . uh . . . still there?"

"Outside of turning off the shower, nothing's been touched, Ms. Taylor."

"There must be some other way . . . without having to see him again." She thought for a moment. "Wait; that's all wrong. Hun kept the DMSO in the medicine cabinet. It was never on the shower shelf. Where did you find it? Where was it on the shelf?"

Harris consulted his notes. "The second container from the left."

She need only a moment to consider this. "Second from the left? That's where he kept the shampoo."

"Are you certain?"

"Absolutely."

"Always?"

Ewing, smiling, broke into the conversation. "Apparently when Mr. Hunsinger did anything, he always did it the same way. A bit of a compulsive, I take it."

Jan nodded.

Ewing sensed that Harris had no more questions for Jan. Nor had he. "I have your address and phone number, Ms. Taylor. We'll undoubtedly have more questions as this investigation continues. So we'll probably be in touch with you."

"May I leave now?"

Ewing glanced at Harris before dismissing Jan Taylor.

"Come on," Harris said, "I want you to see a few things."

"She lied to me twice," said Ewing as Harris led the way back to the bathroom.

"Oh?"

"Yeah. She knew the skin flick was on when she came in, but wouldn't admit it until I confronted her with it."

"And?"

"Claimed she's never been married."

"What makes you think she has?"

"Ring indentation on her third finger, left hand."

"Could have been an engagement ring."

"Could have been—but I doubt it. Very heavy hunch." Ewing smiled. "It may come in handy if I have to question her again. I can tell her, 'You lied to me before; why should I believe you now?'"

"Detectives do not live on hunches alone."

They entered the bathroom and crouched near the body.

"Can you figure the grin?" Ewing asked.

"No. It's grotesque. His eyes are wide open, like he was terror-stricken. And then he has this fixed grin. It doesn't fit together at all. And look here . . . " Harris pointed to areas on Hunsinger's nude body. "See here, on his hands? Looks like some kind of rash, doesn't it? And up here, on his scalp . . . and you can see it all over his head through that short brush cut: the same kind of rash. Whataya think?"

"I dunno. Suppose it could be contagious? Some kind of contagious disease?"

"I don't know either. That's why I called Doc Moellmann."

"Willie Moellmann? On Sunday night? You got a death wish?"

"Willie knows that I don't call him at home unless it's serious. He's on his way here."

"You and I ought to team up more often. With my brains and your clout, no killer would be safe."

Harris grinned and stood up. Ewing did the same.

"There's the DMSO." Ewing nodded at the uncapped second bottle from the left. "What the hell is it, anyway?"

"I'm not positive. I read something about it somewhere. It was supposed to have been a miracle drug of the 1960s. Supposed to alleviate almost any kind of pain, from arthritis to toothache. Somehow, it never got on the market."

"Hmmm. Looks like Hunsinger was using it. It's the only open container on the shelf. But why would he use DMSO in the shower?"

"Wait . . . what did that woman say? The slot second from the left was for the shampoo. And he kept the DMSO in the medicine cabinet."

They looked at each other and together headed for the medicine cabinet.

"Sure enough," said Harris, "here's the shampoo. If Hunsinger was as compulsive and meticulous as we've been given to believe, do you suppose somebody switched bottles?" He frowned in thought. "But . . . if so, why?"

Ewing began to hum tunelessly as he made several quick trips between the shower area and the medicine cabinet, taking notes as he did so.

"Look at the two bottles, Ned: They're identical in size and shape. Both tall, cylindrical containers. Both with ribbed caps. Both caps can be unscrewed or opened by their fliptops. Both bottles hold six fluid ounces. As far as size, shape, and heft go, they're identical. But one has a boxed label stating clearly that it is DMSO, 99.9 percent pure dimethylsulfoxide. And the other one has a lion monogram and the trade name, Royal Copenhagen, on it."

"Okay," Harris reasoned, "we know that Hunsinger needed help with his eyes. His contacts are still out there in the cooker. Maybe his eyes were bad enough so he couldn't read the labels."

"Okay," Ewing returned, "but look at the color, Ned. The DMSO container is white opaque. The shampoo bottle is translucent and you can see its pink color plainly through the bottle."

Harris shrugged. "He had soap in his eyes?"

"A killer could count on that?"

The doorbell rang. It was the Wayne County medical examiner, Dr. Wilhelm Moellmann. Ewing ushered him into the bathroom. All three stood still and silent as Moellmann made a cursory preliminary study of the body.

"Remarkable specimen," said Moellmann finally. "Who was he?"

"Hank Hunsinger," Ewing said.

"Hmmm. Who?"

"Hank ('the Hun') Hunsinger," Ewing tried.

"Hmmm. I seem to have read the name somewhere. But where?"

"He was a professional football player," Harris explained. "With the Cougars."

"Ah, yes, of course. That would explain the mammoth size. And all those contusions. And all those scars. His surgeon would have been well advised to put zippers instead of stitches in his knees." Moellmann looked about for some show of appreciation of his humor. Finding none, he squatted to study the corpse more closely.

While Harris filled Moellmann in on what the two officers had found, Ewing proceeded with his investigation of the premises.

"This is what concerns me," said Harris, finally arriving at his reason for calling the medical examiner. "This rash here on his hands and here again on his scalp."

Moellmann studied the rash. He did not touch it. "It is peculiar. And, you see, there are similar marks here on his neck and there on his chest."

"Any ideas?"

"Ideas? Ideas! You mean guesses! Guesses, like Quincy makes on TV! No, no guesses! This is science, not television!"

A brief but spirited performance. Harris had been subjected to many similar ones by Moellmann. On reflection, Harris decided he should not have asked the question. He decided to stay on surer ground.

"How about the DMSO, Doc? Can you fill us in on that?"

Moellmann rose as did Harris.

"Ah, yes, DMSO," said Moellmann, staring at the opened container on the shelf. "A most intriguing compound. It never got FDA approval, but that hasn't stopped people from buying it. At one time it was thought to be the ultimate and harmless answer to pain. This much can be said of it: when applied to the skin, it penetrates the skin and immediately enters the bloodstream. Many have testified that upon application, it relieves their pain immediately."

"Then why didn't it get FDA approval?"

"Now, then, my memory grows a bit vague. I believe the problem lies in testing it. In any such test, there must be a control group."

Harris immediately called to mind all those kids with the cavities because they were in the control group that wasn't using the sponsor's toothpaste.

"The control group," Moellmann continued, "should receive some sort of placebo, some admittedly ineffective substitute for the substance being tested. Something like a sugar pill instead of aspirin. But they've never been able to come up with an appropriate placebo for use instead of DMSO, because the application of DMSO usually causes a reddened skin and a very bad breath. People in the control group would know they were not being given DMSO because no other substance causes both an inflammation of the skin and the strong breath."

"Red skin?" Harris mused.

"Yes, red skin," Moellmann repeated.

Harris and Moellmann as one looked down at the corpse. Their gaze was fixed on the rash on Hunsinger's hands and scalp.

"I wonder . . . " said Moellmann.

Ewing entered the bathroom, carrying a gallon plastic container. "Found it in the kitchen! Strychnine, if you can believe the label. But from what we've seen here, if I had a last dollar I wouldn't bet it on the truth-in-packaging in this place."

"Where would anyone get strychnine these days?" Harris asked. "It's off the market, isn't it?"

"I thought so," Ewing agreed.

"Oh, yes, definitely," Moellmann affirmed. "You can't get it anywhere these days. Commercially, that is. Nixon signed an order taking it off the market back in 1973, I believe."

"Well, either this is or it isn't," said Ewing, hefting the half-filled container. "But at least the label says it's strychnine."

"Intriguing," Moellmann murmured.

"Doc," said Harris, "there's going to be more than the usual pressure to get this one locked up . . . and soon. Hunsinger was a celebrity, especially in this area. This is going to be in the papers, prominently, and on all the newscasts, not just locally, but nationally." Harris hated to get where he was going with this plea. He well knew how Moellmann resisted any pressure to expedite a case. But, in this instance, it needed saying. "So can you hurry this one along a bit?"

Moellmann gave no indication of having heard Harris's plea. He kept looking from the rashes on Hunsinger's corpse to the DMSO to the container Ewing was holding. "Intriguing," he murmured. "A very simple plan. So simple one might even call it ingenious. That is, if it all works out." Then, to the officers, "We'll want to get at this first thing in the morning. Have it all shipped down as soon as the technicians finish." He ambled distractedly toward the door, rubbing his hands together. "How clever," he muttered. "What a clever plan. But how did he make it work?" He resembled a crossword addict confronted with the world's toughest puzzle, to which he might hold the ultimate clue.

As Moellmann exited, the police technicians arrived.

Harris and Ewing briefed them on the situation and the probable evidence that should be gathered. Shortly, officers were everywhere, taking pictures, dusting for fingerprints, packaging evidence—taking particular care with the twin containers of DMSO and shampoo—and interviewing neighbors of the Hunsinger apartment.

Ewing and Harris disengaged themselves from the hubbub.

"Whatever we got here?" Harris was gearing up for an up-to-the-moment summary.

"One dead football player," Ewing responded. "A probable homicide by means as yet undetermined. If a homicide, then the perpetrator had to be in this apartment before Hunsinger arrived this evening, or while he was here."

"That's right. Hunsinger was alive this afternoon. Some eighty thousand people saw him at the Silverdome. And additional hundreds of thousands saw him on TV. He left the stadium, as far as we know, under his own power. He gets home—something, something, something—he steps into the shower, and bingo, he's dead."

"He gets home," Ewing supplied, "he puts a skin-flick cassette on TV—something, something, something—he showers, he dies, his girlfriend arrives. What about her?"

"Too early to tell. Not likely she'd off him and then report it to the police. Though it's happened."

"We'll have to find out where she's been today."

"It'd be good to know when's the last time Hunsinger showered at home before tonight. If something in that shower killed him—something in the DMSO bottle maybe—and if Hunsinger is the creature of habit he seems to be, then whatever killed him was put in there sometime between his previous shower and the one tonight."

"And"—Ewing glanced around the room, but he was so familiar with investigative routine he was not distracted—"if not the Taylor woman, someone else got in here and set it up."

"There's a security guard on duty downstairs. Let's go down and check on just how secure this building is—oh, and let me do most of the talking."

Ewing grinned. "What's the matter? I get along pretty good with black people."

Harris winked. "You do okay for a honky. But there was something familiar about that guy when we came in. I think I might know him from a previous bust."

The two took the elevator down twenty-one floors to the lobby. In the foyer, they spotted the guard. Clearly he had been flustered, first by Harris and Ewing, then by the arrival of the investigating crew. He had phoned his supervisor, who was with him now.

Introductions were exchanged. The officers explained that they wanted to question the guard. The supervisor took over door duties while the three men moved to a nearby empty office.

"We want to know all about the security here, Mr. Malone," Ewing began. "We know you only work here. It's not your security system, so you can be very frank."

"In fact, Mr. Malone," Harris was gazing at the guard so intently that Malone was becoming visibly upset, "this is a homicide investigation, so it is not to be taken lightly. Answer carefully and be sure you tell the whole truth."

"Homicide!" Malone licked his dry lips. "Mr. Hunsinger!" He knew which apartment they had come from. "Mr. Hunsinger dead? Oh, God almighty!"

"He's dead, Mr. Malone. And we've got to know everything you know about him," said Harris. "Start with when he got home after today's game."

"I don't know."

"What do you mean you don't know?" Harris's tone suggested a short fuse that was burning.

"I don't know. He's a resident. He probably parked his car in the basement garage, then took the elevator from there directly up to his floor. He wouldn't have passed through the lobby."

"That's all the security you got? People walk into the basement and go anywhere in the building they want?"

"Wait; it ain't that bad. At least not now. It's better than it was."

"Why don't you just tell us about the security system, Mr. Malone?" Ewing was more conciliatory.

"Sure." It was comfortable in the apartment's all-season climate control, but Malone had begun to perspire. "See, the way it used to be, we'd be in this cubicle, all glassed in, just next to the front door in the lobby. Visitors come, we'd let 'em in, check with whoever they come to see. If everything checked out, we'd let 'em take the elevator up.

"Wasn't too good a system. For one thing, we never had no record of who the visitor was. Sometimes they'd slip by. You know, come in with a resident or something like that. Then, we was right up front, you know. If someone wanted to take out the guard, they could just do it. You know, Mr. Hunsinger ain't the first one to get killed here. This can get to be a pretty lively place from time to time."

Ewing nodded. He easily recalled that within the past year a couple had been victims of a drug-related homicide here. Neither he nor Harris had been in on that case. But he remembered how the investigating officers had complained of the odor. The couple had been dead four days before their bodies were discovered. The place could indeed be pretty lively, or, more properly, deadly.

"Not good. Not good." Malone shook his head. "But just last Monday they installed a new system. See, Mr. Hunsinger could enter either in the basement—the garage—or through the lobby 'cause he got a key. But them who don't have keys gotta come through the lobby. See, they can enter the lobby, but when they do, we got this camera that's mounted on one wall and swings back and forth. Then, whoever's on guard monitors the camera. We can see everybody who comes through the lobby.

"Then, 'cause the visitor don't have a key, they gotta ring the bell. When we buzz 'em through, we already got a look at 'em. Then, when we let 'em in they gotta register in the guestbook. Then we still check with the resident before we let 'em go up. That is, unless the resident lets us know ahead of time that he's expecting this particular person." Malone seemed pleased with his performance. "See, it works pretty good now."

After a moment's silence, Harris said, "Yeah, we saw your system when we came in." He turned to Ewing. "Think you could break it, Sergeant?"

Ewing smiled. "I'll give it a crack."

Harris and Malone joined the supervisor in the guard's station, while Ewing went into the lobby. He knew what to do.

First, he stood outside, peering into the lobby. He watched the TV camera as it panned the lobby. Carefully, he timed its swing. Eight seconds from left to right; eight seconds, right to left.

Ewing timed his entry for the moment the camera's focus left the front door. He flattened himself against the wall on which the camera was mounted. Stiffly, he walked the length of the wall to the inner door. At a short distance, he studied the lock. It appeared to be no different from other locks on doors that could be buzzed open.

Once more, he waited for the moment the camera's focus moved away from the door. Quickly, he moved to the door, inserted the thin blade of his pocketknife, and lifted the lock from its catch. He entered, opening the door just enough to let himself in, then letting it close behind him. He crouched beneath the window of the guard's station, moved beyond the station, stood erect, then nonchalantly strolled back to the room from within the inner lobby.

Both Malone and his supervisor stared at Ewing open-mouthed.

"How'd you do that?" asked the supervisor. "We didn't see you once on the screen!"

"All I can tell you," Ewing responded, "is that it wasn't all that difficult. All you'd have to know is that the system was there and have a chance to study it for a while.

"Now, you said that the new system was installed last Monday . . . that right, Mr. Malone?"

Both men nodded.

"And you also said that with the new system, visitors had to sign in. So anyone who visited with Mr. Hunsinger since, say, Tuesday of this past week would be aware of the system, would have had the opportunity to study it, at least briefly, and would also have signed in. Now, the question: Where is your log of the people who have signed in to visit any resident since last Monday?"

"Right here," said Malone, turning the opened guest-book toward Ewing. "We got a brand new book when we started registering visitors. It's hardly been used at all."

Harris took the book eagerly and began to run his finger down the list of names looking for anyone visiting Hunsinger. He found what he was looking for recorded on Tuesday evening. He turned to Ewing. "Get a load of these names." Harris pointed to a succession of seven signatures, all signed in as visitors of Hunsinger, then said to Malone, "Were you on duty Tuesday evening last?"

Malone nodded.

"Did you call Hunsinger and check on these people?"

"No, sir. Mr. Hunsinger left word that he expected them."

Ewing read each name as he recorded them on his notepad. "Jack Brown, Dave Whitman, Bobby Cobb, Jay Galloway, Kit Hoffer, Niall Murray, and Father Robert Koesler." Ewing, smiling, looked up at Harris. "Guess which one of the above doesn't fit with the others?"

"You mean you know who all of them are?" asked Harris.

"With one exception, I think they're all members of the Cougars organization."

"Koesler."

"That's it."

"How does he do it?" Harris shook his head. "There must be hundreds of priests in Detroit, but every other year or so, Koesler gets involved in a homicide investigation. You've worked with him before, haven't you?"

"Yeah. But I didn't get the impression he was all that happy about being involved with a murder case."

"Just lucky, eh?"

"I guess."

Harris went back to sliding his finger down the pages, in search of more Hunsinger visitors. Coming to the end of the listed names, he looked at Malone with some irritation. "I thought you said all visitors were registered. What about Jan Taylor? We know she was here to visit Hunsinger today."

"Oh, no; she don't sign in." Malone ran a finger between his starched white shirt and his neck. "She's got a key."

"A key!" What had begun as a rather narrow list of suspects was beginning to expand. "Okay, how many people have keys to Hunsinger's apartment—which key, I assume, also works on the building entrances?"

"That's right, sir. Just Miss Taylor and Mr. Hunsinger's mother."

Harris shrugged. "Okay," he said to Ewing, "add mama to the list."

"Is nothing sacred?" Ewing grinned as he entered the name in his notepad.

"Okay, Malone," Harris fixed the guard with an intense look, "let's have the whole thing. We've got seven people who visited with Hunsinger last Tuesday. We have two people with keys. Anybody else have access to Hunsinger? Anybody at all?"

Malone hesitated.

"This is a homicide investigation, Malone. I don't need to tell you what could happen if you don't level with us."

"Uh . . . Mr. Hunsinger tips pretty good."

"Not anymore."

"Yeah, that's right. Well, there was one more key out. But that was a while ago. I don't know if Mr. Hunsinger ever took it back or not."

"Come on, come on."

"Nobody needs to know that it was me who told you?"

"Nobody needs to know."

"It was Mrs. Galloway."

Ewing's eyebrows lifted as he noted the final name.

Harris warned Malone and his supervisor emphatically about commenting on the case, especially to the news media, while the investigation continued. He left the two appropriately impressed.

Harris and Ewing returned to Hunsinger's apartment to wrap things up.

"Ned," said Ewing in the elevator, "did you really recognize Malone from a bust in the past?"

Harris chuckled. "Not really. But I find it helpful from time to time to psych myself up for an interrogation by pretending to know the guy and pretending that I hate him. Keeps him on his toes too. Didn't you notice?"

2

"GOD, I HATE MONDAYS. AND IF there's anything I hate more than Mondays, it's Monday mornings." Lieutenant Harris rubbed his eyes elaborately.

It did not help Harris's diurnal distress that he had begun a fresh homicide investigation last night that had kept him up rather late. Nor did it help that his partner in the case could be depended upon to be in good spirits even on a Monday morning.

"You're in good company, Lieutenant," said Sergeant Ewing cheerfully. "Willie Moellmann doesn't like Monday mornings either. But success does wonders for a guy's spirits."

"Huh?"

"Quickest autopsy I ever witnessed."

"Hunsinger?"

"Yup."

Most homicide detectives attended the autopsies of cases they were working. It being the despised Monday morning, Harris had relied upon the dependable Ewing to attend this morning's. Ewing had not disappointed him.

"Of course," Ewing added, "it didn't hurt at all that Doc pretty well knew what he was looking for."

"Was it the strychnine?"

"Yup. All the symptoms check out—just like we found

Hunsinger last night." Ewing ran down the notes he had taken during the autopsy. "'Terrified expression, fixed grin, and cyanosis.'" He looked up. "That's the purplish discoloration of Hunsinger's skin; he couldn't get oxygen. Strychnine's really a horrible death. Want the details?"

"Spare me." Harris's Monday syndrome had dissipated. He was now fully alert. Moellmann's progress had galvanized him. "Was it the DMSO?"

Ewing nodded. "Weird delivery system, but damned effective. Doc had a book on it." He again turned to his notes. He had copied the book's description of the manner in which dimethylsulfoxide works. "'It is most often administered by simply dabbing it on the skin; and, alone or as a carrier for other drugs, which DMSO often potentiates, it penetrates the skin to enter the bloodstream and be borne to all parts of the body.'"

Harris gave an impressed whistle. "And the strychnine was added to that?"

"Uh-huh. Doc says that with most people, even dabbing DMSO on leaves a red mark on the skin. But if you rub it in, it's most likely to cause a rash."

"Like the ones on Hunsinger's hands and head."

"Right. He poured the stuff on his hands, like you would shampoo, and massaged the stuff into his hair and scalp. Doc says the red marks on Hunsinger's chest and neck were caused by somewhat the same thing. Strychnine causes a tightness in the chest and a stiffness in the neck. Hunsinger probably grabbed at his chest and neck when the poison hit his respiratory system . . . but then you didn't want the details of what Hunsinger went through."

"Only if they're relevant . . . damn relevant."

"Relax, Ned. That's the end of relevancy."

"Where'd he get the DMSO? Anybody know?"

"Yeah. One of the other guys at the examiner's office was familiar with it. Seems you can get it all over town. Most health-food stores."

"I thought it was—"

"It is. But they can sell it as a solvent. Isn't that a peculiar turn of fortune? I'll bet the scientist who put DMSO together never thought it would be used to dissolve strychnine. Anyway, it carried the warning right on the label." Ewing again quoted from his notes, " 'Sold for use as a solvent only. Caution. This product not federally approved for medication.' And how about this: 'Warning: May be unsafe. Not approved for human use.' "

Both were silent a moment, contemplating the irony of it all.

"Okay," said Harris, "that's how Hunsinger got the DMSO. It'll be a good idea to check into how popular this stuff is with football players generally. But it leaves the bigger question: Where did he come up with the strychnine, and why?"

"We got an answer for the second question anyway. Our guys picked up some rodent bait last night in Hunsinger's apartment. It was saturated with strychnine."

"Rat bait! Wasn't that its primary use before they took it off the market?"

"Yeah, it was effective as hell with rats. Apparently, Hunsinger didn't favor a stick of dynamite when there was an atom bomb handy. I mean, why use a simple rat trap when you've got the Cadillac of poisons around?" He shook his head. "But it still doesn't explain where he got it."

"Yeah, well, okay. But I've got one more question before we start going off in all directions." Harris drained the last of his coffee. "We got a very inventive killer who's going to use DMSO as a delivery system for strychnine. Why doesn't the perpetrator drain the shampoo bottle and pour in the mixture of DMSO with the poison?"

"The perp banks on Hunsinger's compulsive nature. The Hun is going to reach for the second bottle from the left because that's where the shampoo is. Always."

"Okay, so the perp knows that Hunsinger's a compulsive. But it wouldn't be out of the ordinary for even a compulsive to glance at a label as he's using something."

"Except that Hunsinger had bad eyesight. He wore contacts."

"Right. So the perp knows that Hunsinger is a compulsive and also that he has poor vision."

"I get the impression that those two items were not exactly secrets to anyone who knew Hunsinger at all well."

"Okay." Harris appeared to have arrived at his final question. "Hunsinger, relying on his habit of always keeping things in their appointed place, automatically picks up the second container from the left. It feels just like his shampoo bottle. After all, the shampoo bottle is the same shape and size as the container of DMSO. He doesn't read the label because he can't make it out without his contact lenses. But the shampoo was a distinctive pink color and the DMSO is colorless. Why doesn't he notice there's no color?"

"Why doesn't he notice there's no color?" Ewing repeated thoughtfully. "Why doesn't he notice there's no color? Unless . . . unless . . ."

"Our first stop," Harris announced, "Hunsinger's eye doctor."

"But first, we'd better give a call to Inspector Koznicki."

"Walt? Why?"

"I think he'll want to know that his old buddy Father Koesler is back in the homicide business."

It took less than half an hour to drive to West Dearborn, where Thomas Glowacki's office was located.

Yes, Dr. Glowacki, the late Hank Hunsinger's ophthalmologist, was in. Did they have an appointment? Well, the doctor was very busy. Oh, the homicide department! Well, in that case, would they wait just a few minutes in the doctor's private office?

Dr. Glowacki, tall, thin, with a full head of brownish

hair flecked with gray, entered the office briskly. Harris noted the doctor wore bifocals. It gets to everyone, he mused.

"This is regarding Mr. Hunsinger?" The doctor looked appropriately concerned. "A pity. I read about it in this morning's paper. A great pity."

"We know you're busy, Doctor," said Ewing, "so we'll try not to take up much of your time. We've got a few questions about Mr. Hunsinger's sight—he was your patient, wasn't he?"

"Oh, yes, for a great number of years. The receptionist—my wife—could tell you exactly how long." Glowacki manifested great satisfaction that his wife was also his receptionist. It was anyone's guess as to the source of his satisfaction: that husband and wife could function as a team; that wife was competent enough to keep his records; that he was saving a ton of money on her salary.

"That's all right." Ewing eschewed the history. "We're more concerned with the condition of Mr. Hunsinger's sight as it was just before he died."

"Yes, yes. A most interesting case. A most rare case. Of course, he had astigmatism for many years—for most of his life. But it was correctable with lenses."

"We were more concerned with his color perception."

"Yes, I was just getting to that. Colorblind."

The two officers could not suppress triumphant smiles. Suspicion confirmed.

"I am not referring to a color deficiency," Glowacki continued. "I mean Mr. Hunsinger was colorblind, literally color*blind*. Do you know how rare that is?"

Both shook their heads. They urged him to elaborate. This could prove most relevant.

"In general," the doctor explained, "99.5 percent of women and 92 percent of men have normal vision with regard to color. Which means they can distinguish between all the colors of the spectrum. Now, among those relatively few people who have problems with color perception, there are three groups. I can tell you about them without becoming overly technical."

The officers nodded. Ewing prepared to scribble notes.

"The largest number of people who have a color deficiency are called anomalous trichromats." Glowacki glanced at Ewing's pad and spelled the term. "They can see the same major color characteristics as people with completely normal vision. But they tend to have problems with tones that are close together in the color spectrum, like orange and pink."

"How about white and pink?" Harris asked, thinking of the bottles of shampoo and DMSO.

"To the anomalous trichromat they would appear as exactly the same color."

Again the officers smiled. That alone would have been sufficient to explain Hunsinger's fatal error. But the doctor had indicated that the deceased's color perception was much worse than that.

"The second group, called dichromats"—again Glowacki spelled—"have what's called a red-green deficiency. That means they confuse colors like the red fruit and green leaves of the cherry tree. Their vision is unable to separate colors that occur at the same position on either side of the color spectrum—those with the same wavelengths. But, like the trichromats, these people are still able to see colors and distinguish among most of them."

Glowacki paused. There were no questions or comments from the officers.

"You see," he continued, "most people think that if a person such as those I've just described has any trouble at all identifying any colors, that the person is colorblind. Technically, that's not true. Such people are color-deficient.

"The true colorblind person is called a monochromat." He did not bother to spell. "The monochromat is unable to match one color with any other color. Everything, to the genuinely colorblind person, is either white, black, or gray."

"Until now," Harris commented, "I thought Hunsinger had done his apartment in Art Deco. Everything is white, black, or gray."

Glowacki nodded vigorously. "I've never seen Mr. Hunsinger's apartment, but I'm not surprised. Without assistance a colorblind person could not help making serious blunders in decorating an apartment. Even a color-deficient person probably would err. For a person like Mr. Hunsinger, it would make great good sense for his decorator to use black, white, and gray. That, after all, is exactly the way he saw life."

"This question just occurred to me," said Ewing. "Wouldn't his colorblindness be a serious problem for him playing football . . . you did know he played football?"

"Of course. No, it didn't hinder him. Remember, he saw things in the same way a normally sighted person sees a black and white television picture. There were times when his colorblindness was a help to him."

The officers registered incredulity.

"For instance, when two competing teams wear the same colors; say, blue and white. It happens. It can be confusing for the person with normal color vision. But as far as Mr. Hunsinger was concerned, his team was wearing dark pants and white shirts. While the other team wore white pants and dark shirts. That's the way all team colors appeared to him."

"One more—maybe the final—question," said Harris. "To your knowledge, did many other people know Hunsinger was colorblind?"

Glowacki thought for a moment. "I rather doubt it. No one learned it from me. I have never discussed it with anyone other than Mr. Hunsinger. Now it no longer makes any difference to him. But I got the clear impression that while he lived he wanted it kept a secret. He was, after all, a member of an infinitesimal minority. Less than one percent of males are colorblind. I don't know if it was because he was a private person or he was ashamed of his condition or he was just exceptionally vain."

"If you had to guess?" Ewing prodded. It was important that they learn all they could about the victim.

"Well," Glowacki pulled at his lower lip, "I'm no psychologist. But if I had to guess—and this is just a guess—I would say he was too vain to have admitted to being colorblind."

"Reasons?"

"I remember when contact lenses first became popular, Mr. Hunsinger was among the very earliest to use them. I sensed he had always been embarrassed to appear in public wearing glasses. He used to come in quite regularly because the frames were bent out of shape. They'd been in his pocket getting bent when he should have been wearing them. Then, as I say, at his earliest opportunity, he got contacts, so people wouldn't know that his vision needed correcting. Even though the contacts he first wore were rigid lenses."

"Is there a problem with rigid lenses?" asked Harris.

"They have a tendency to pop out rather easily. You can imagine how troublesome that would be in a violent game like football! So as soon as the Toric soft lenses came out he started wearing them."

"The difference?"

"Well, for one thing, soft lenses need more elaborate care than the rigids. I'm sure that after a game, Mr. Hunsinger's eyes would be sensitive and red. He'd surely remove the lenses and clean them."

"As a matter of fact," Ewing commented, "they were 'cooking' when Hunsinger died."

Glowacki again shook his head, reminded that the man they were discussing had been murdered only yesterday. "Yes, he'd do that. First thing after getting home. Mr. Hunsinger was a bit of a compulsive."

"So we've been given to believe."

"And also proud," the doctor continued. "Proud of his physique. Proud of his appearance. Proud of his accomplishments. Too proud, I'm sure, to ever let it be known that he belonged to an exclusive minority of people who are colorblind. He considered that a blemish, a defect. But one that was, as far as others were concerned, invisible. And I'm sure he did everything in his power to make sure it stayed that way."

The officers thanked the doctor for his time and information. They advised him that his late patient's colorblindness was becoming a significant factor in their investigation and warned him not to reveal the fact to anyone, at least while the investigation continued.

They got in their car. Harris inserted the key in the ignition, but did not turn it. Instead, he drummed his fingers against the steering wheel. "I've got a feeling that we've got the essence of the thing. How about you?"

"Yeah," Ewing agreed, "the perpetrator didn't bother to pour a mixture of DMSO and strychnine into the shampoo bottle because he—"

"Or she—"

"Or she—knew it didn't matter. Hunsinger, seemingly an ironclad victim of habit, would reach for the second container from the left, assuming that everything was in its proper place—as everything in his life was. The bottle was the same shape and size as the shampoo container. He couldn't read the label because his contacts were in the 'cooker,' where they always were when he showered after a game. And he couldn't tell the liquid in the bottle was white instead of pink because he was colorblind."

"We are looking for someone with a motive for killing Hunsinger," said Harris, "someone who had the opportunity to kill him and who knew his compulsive routines: knew of his showering at home after a game, knew his eyesight was bad—and knew that he was colorblind."

"Of all that, it seems the best-kept secret was his colorblindness."

"Well, let's get crackin'."

"Right. On to good old Father Koesler."

In 1954 Robert Koesler was ordained a priest to serve in the Archdiocese of Detroit. He was ordained in Blessed Sacrament Cathedral on June 4. The next day, Sunday, June 5, he offered his first solemn Mass at 10:00 A.M. in his home parish, Holy Redeemer. In the congregation at that Mass were Grace Hunsinger and her seven-year-old son, Hank.

Conrad Hunsinger, Grace's husband and Hank's father, was not there. Conrad was not present because he was not a Catholic, and, further, he never attended any church service. Grace was there because a first Mass of a returning ordained young man was an extremely important parochial event for deeply religious Catholics. And Mrs. Hunsinger was a deeply religious Catholic. Hank was there because his mother made him attend.

In three months, Conrad Hunsinger would be dead. Very sudden. A heart attack. Very sad. Robert Koesler would not know any of this. In August 1954, he would be working in his first parochial assignment on Detroit's east side. He and Conrad Hunsinger had never met.

To a degree, Grace Hunsinger had watched Bobby Koesler grow up. She had attended at least one Mass almost every day of her adult life. Frequently she would kneel back in the shadows of the enormous Romanesque Holy Redeemer church and watch little Bob Koesler, altar boy, in cassock and surplice, serve Mass. She knew, from the churchy gossip of other daily Mass attendants, when he went away to the seminary. She noted, on his return during vacations, that he still played the part of a faithful altar boy well into his twenties. From time to time, she wished the church bug had bitten her son. It was not to be.

Koesler knew Grace Hunsinger, although not by name. He knew her as a quiet gentle lady who seemed always to be in church. There were several like that, mostly women, mostly middle-aged to elderly, who seemed to be in church most of the time, especially during Masses and novenas. He had no way of knowing that one day, many years later, the unseen son of this nice lady whose name Koesler did not know would, for a short time, play an extremely important role in his life.

That day, June 4, 1954, was the culmination of all that Robert Koesler had dreamed of since he was of an age to remember dreams. As far back as he could recall, he had always wanted to be a priest.

Shortly after he had gone to the seminary in the ninth grade to test his vocation, *Going My Way*, one of the greatest recruitment films of all time, was released. Inspired by that movie, lots of little Catholic boys concluded that it might be neat to grow up to become Bing Crosby's Father Chuck O'Malley, turn a bunch of juvenile delinquents into a celestial choir, rub elbows with Rise Stevens, stand backstage during a Met performance of *Carmen*, become savior of parishes on the brink of financial disaster, and reunite an old Irish pastor with his aged Irish mother when they both should have been dead.

Great as *Going My Way* was, Bob Koesler hadn't needed it for motivation. Long before "...just dial 'O' for O'Malley," Koesler was convinced the priesthood was the life for him. He viewed the twelve years of preparation—four high school, four college, four theologate—as just so many obstacles to be overcome, so many hurdles to be leaped. And he took them pretty much as hurdles, clumsily kicking over many on the way.

Koesler's professors as well as his contemporaries would agree that his seminary career was "interesting." By no means a serious student until perhaps the final few years of the seminary, Koesler could more frequently be found on the athletic field or the stage.

But at the end of twelve years his determination to be a priest was more firm than ever. The seminary officials found no good reason to deny him; some even found good reasons to recommend him. So, on June 4, 1954, came his ordination, followed by his first Mass, with, unbeknownst to him, Grace and Hank Hunsinger in attendance.

The years of his priesthood were, like his seminary career, "interesting." After three parochial assignments, he was appointed editor of the *Detroit Catholic*, a weekly newspaper owned by the Archdiocese of Detroit. For that post, his lack of qualification was remarkable. Somehow he mucked through, learning much along the way. Eventually he became what he was now: pastor of St. Anselm's, a suburban Dearborn Heights parish.

By far, the most "interesting" turn of events took place in 1979, when Koesler stumbled onto a clue in the murder of a Detroit nun. Thence he was drawn into the investigation of what turned into a series of murders of priests and nuns. From this grew a close friendship with Inspector Walter Koznicki, head of the homicide division of the Detroit Police Department.

Since that first homicide investigation involving Koesler, he had, through a sort of recurrent kismet, been drawn into other similar investigations. At times, he became involved because the murdered victims were members of the Catholic clergy, other times because victims were found in Catholic churches, still other times because the dramatis personae in the investigation were members of his parish. Now it seemed he was about to become involved in yet another homicide investigation because the victim happened to be a member of a Bible study group that included Koesler.

When Inspector Koznicki had phoned earlier this morning and requested Koesler's participation in at least the early stages of the investigation into the death of Hank Hunsinger, the priest had been stunned. At breakfast he had read in the *Free Press* about Hunsinger's death and was shocked. As in the death of most murder victims there was a special element of surprise in Hunsinger's demise. It was so unexpected. This was a strong young man, a man whose body was not prepared for death. And readers did not have to wait to reach the sports pages to learn of the murder of the tight end; it was splashed on page 1 with companion stories throughout Section A.

Koesler had not been able to talk at length with Koznicki. After accepting the inspector's invitation to render whatever assistance was possible in the investigation, Koesler had to marshal his rectory forces to cover for him, locate a priest to fill in at daily Mass, and reschedule several appointments.

All had been done. Now he awaited the promised arrival of Lieutenant Harris and Sergeant Ewing, both of whom he knew from previous investigations.

Although he had met Hunsinger several times in the Bible study group and had seen him play football any number of times either in person or on television, Koesler remained unaware of their connection through Holy Redeemer parish. He had known Grace Hunsinger by sight. But he had not known her name. He had never met the young Hunsinger. Even though the seven-year-old had been dragged to Koesler's first solemn Mass, Koesler of course had no way of recognizing the young lad's presence. And Hunsinger himself had long ago dismissed the memory as that of one more meaningless ceremony.

Koesler did not know it, but he was in for a big surprise.

"This is probably going to sound like one of those ultimate philosophical questions," said Father Koesler, "but, why am I here?"

"It wasn't our idea." Lieutenant Harris was the less diplomatic of the two officers.

In a flash, Koesler pictured the scene. Koznicki suggesting the priest be included in at least the beginning of the investigation. Harris objecting, undoubtedly strenuously. Koznicki closing the discussion considerately but firmly.

"Actually, Father," Ewing explained, "you, all by yourself, are our control group."

"Huh?"

Harris was driving. They had picked Koesler up at his rectory and were now en route to the Silverdome.

"You see," Ewing continued, "between the time a new security system was installed in Hunsinger's apartment building and the time that Hunsinger was killed, seven people were recorded as his visitors. All seven came the same evening. You were one of them. All seven had the opportunity to case . . . er . . . study the security system and discover an easy way to beat it. If one of them did that, he's our man."

"Then I'm a suspect?" Koesler hoped his question was facetious.

Ewing laughed. Koesler's hope was affirmed. He breathed more easily.

"No, you're not a suspect. Like I told you in the beginning, you are our one-person control group.

"You see, it didn't take us long to discover the connection between you seven. Now comes the interrogation. We have no sure way of knowing whether this or that person is answering all our questions truthfully. You are the only one we can rely upon to tell the truth. It just may work out that we can measure the truthfulness of the others by your answers and recollections.

"There are, by the way, three other people who had or may have had keys to the apartment: Hunsinger's mother, his mis—uh, girlfriend, and, possibly, Mrs. Galloway. But then, you wouldn't know any of them, would you?"

Koesler shook his head.

"Okay, so we'll concentrate on the members of the discussion group. Let's start with Hunsinger while we've got a little time. Why would a guy like him join a Bible discussion group anyway?"

Koesler hesitated. "I haven't given it that much thought. For one thing, for athletes to join some sort of Christian organization is very prevalent... like the Fellowship of Christian Athletes, for instance. You know, there's more than one religious discussion group just within the Cougars.

"Now that I think of it, though, it *was* an odd group. On the surface, they seemed to have nothing in common but football. Some actually played the game; then there was the trainer, of course, and the two in management.

"But it seemed to me that something was going on just beneath the surface. For one thing, there was a good deal of conflict. The arguments that occurred between the Hun and Bobby and Kit, I always felt, were more than mere differences of opinion.

"Then, in the group at large, I got the impression that most of them were there because they just had to know what the others were doing, what the others were thinking. A couple of the players attending represented the highest paid athletes on the team. The welfare of the players, how they were spending their time away from the field, seemed a special concern of the trainer. And of course the players wanted to get every clue they could as to what plans management had.

"As for Hunsinger specifically," he shook his head, "I just don't know. It might have been his way of saying, in effect, You guys think you know me, but you don't. You don't know where I'm coming from. You think I'm incapable of anything spiritual, but I've read my Bible too... and just because I don't turn the other cheek doesn't mean I don't know what you're getting at." He shook his head again. "But then, I don't usually spend a lot of time trying to analyze people's motivations; I tend to just take them at face value.... Maybe Hunsinger thought he *needed* some higher-up help..."

"All in all, Father," Ewing had been jotting notes, "you're not describing a very altruistic bunch."

"After a few get-togethers, I didn't think I was attending very altruistic meetings either. But it was a fascinating study in human behavior nonetheless. I learned some things. And not just about human behavior. About Scripture too. Each of these men had his own peculiar interpretation of Scripture. Through those interpretations, I think I learned something about each of them and also got some fresh insights into Scripture."

Ewing had half turned toward the rear seat. He now swung his left arm over the front seat and faced Koesler. "I'm going to tell you some things now, Father, that we hope no one outside the investigating team will learn. Things that are vital to our investigation and are not to be revealed to anyone else."

Koesler nodded and smiled. "I'm good at keeping secrets."

So far, the news media knew only that Hunsinger had been poisoned. Ewing now explained in detail the manner in which the dead man had been killed.

At the end of the account, Koesler sighed. It had been an ugly if quick way to go. The older he grew, the more dismayed he became that anyone would take it upon himself that another should not live. That conviction stretched from abortion to war to capital punishment.

"You've been involved in enough of these investigations to know that we're looking for someone who had a sufficient motive to kill, had the opportunity, and actually did the deed," Ewing continued. "But, in this case, there are a few other things we're looking for along the way. We think that in order to use the method he did to commit murder, the killer had to know certain things about Hunsinger. So, let's see what you knew about him and, maybe, what you think the others knew."

Koesler nodded.

"To begin with, were you aware of anything peculiar about Hunsinger's behavior?"

"Peculiar?"

"One might even call it neurotic."

"Neurotic . . ."

"Compulsive," Ewing finally clarified. He was beginning to wonder about the advisability of including the priest in this investigation.

"Compulsive! Oh, my, yes. I don't think anyone could have been around Hank very long without noticing the repetition of one routine after another: the precise placing of his Bible, pen, pad; he even got upset if anyone disturbed anything in the apartment—and if anyone did he had better put it back in its exact position. But then," Koesler expanded, "I've always thought that if a Catholic was going to become neurotic, compulsive behavior was a natural vehicle to choose, even subconsciously." Koesler smiled as he launched into one of his favorite routines.

"After all, we provide our people with so many numbers: one God, two natures, three persons, four cardinal virtues, five processions, seven sacraments, nine Beatitudes, nine First Fridays, Ten Our Fathers and ten Hail Marys, twelve promises to St. Margaret Mary, fourteen Stations of the Cross. Probably one of the most popular images for a Catholic is a rosary. And there you've got the Catholic carefully counting out ten Hail Marys for each decade, five decades in the small popular rosary, fifteen decades in the full rosary. And it's the rosary that's entwined in the Catholic's hands when he or she is laid to the final rest.

"Mind you, I don't claim that all Catholics become compulsive. Only that I'll bet the majority of Catholics who become neurotic at least go through a phase of compulsive behavior."

Silently, Harris hoped Koesler would be able to hold down the quantity of his responses.

"Okay," said Ewing, "how about the others in the

group? Do you think they were aware of his compulsiveness?"

"Oh, yes. Remember I told you about how he insisted on everything's being in its proper place? He almost forced his guests to join him in his compulsiveness."

Better, thought Harris.

"Now, here's a second consideration, Father. Were you aware that Hunsinger had any problems with his vision?"

"His vision? Well, I assume he had some problem; I mean, he wore contact lenses. At least I noticed one of those lens-disinfectant containers—what do they call them, cookers?—in the apartment."

"Would the others in that group know about the lenses?"

"Again, I assume so. Surely his teammates would see him putting the contacts in, taking them out . . . wouldn't they? Surely his employers . . . the trainer . . . would know . . . wouldn't they?"

"We're not so sure they all knew. We do know that Hunsinger was very reserved when it came to anything that might be construed as a personal defect or deficiency. But that's an interesting observation about the lens cleaner. Do you recall where you saw it?"

"Yes. When I visited the bathroom, it was on a dresser in the bedroom."

"Then the others could have seen it?"

"Uh-huh. Anybody who looked into the bedroom—and we all did—would be likely to see it. That is, if you could get your eyes away from all those mirrors.

"Another thing, about the strychnine. Hank bragged about having it in the apartment. Said it was the atom bomb of rat poisons. Everyone in the discussion group would have known it was there."

"Okay. One final thing, Father: Were you aware of anything else that might have been wrong with Hunsinger's vision?"

"You mean besides the fact that he wore glasses—or

contacts? No . . . I didn't even know the reason he needed corrective lenses. Was there something else?"

"He was colorblind, Father, totally colorblind. We just visited with his eye doctor. All Hunsinger could see was white, black, and gray."

"Amazing!" A new light came into Koesler's eyes. "Say, that would explain why Hank's apartment was decorated the way it was, wouldn't it? I never really wondered about it, just thought it was sort of . . . masculine. Maybe because that's the way I ordinarily dress: in black and white. But that certainly explains the decor of his apartment."

"Now, think carefully, Father: Did any of the others ever give any indication they might have known about Hunsinger's colorblindness?"

Koesler gave the question careful consideration. "No. There was a bit of what I considered to be just banter . . . the kind of thing you might expect from athletes. But no, nothing at all that had to do with color. There were some remarks about Bobby Cobb's color—he was the only black in the group—but it seemed to be given and taken in good humor. I am rather sensitive to that sort of thing. But it didn't trouble me. No, as far as I can recall, no one made any reference at all to colorblindness."

"Well, there it is," Harris noted.

The other two peered at the distance. The outline of the Silverdome was barely visible.

Ewing looked at Harris. "Well, where do we begin?"

Harris smiled. "My personal philosophy is, start at the top."

"The top it is."

In the remaining time, Ewing, consulting his notes, explained to Koesler all that Dr. Glowacki had told them about color deficiency and colorblindness.

One of the fringe benefits of these police investigations, thought Koesler, was that he always learned something.

* * *

At forty-four, Jay Galloway easily was the youngest owner of a professional football franchise. And he appeared even younger. Of moderate height and build, he had an oval, wrinkle-free face and a full head of dark brown hair untouched by gray, parted in the middle, and shaped in a mod cut covering the top tip of the ears and just touching the back of his shirt collar.

Galloway was a native of Minneapolis. His father had been a successful salesman, his mother a homemaker. He had a younger brother and sister.

Environment has its effect on the developing personality. But it is an unpredictable effect. Jay Galloway was a case in point.

Born James Randolph Galloway, he developed in a solid, typical WASP family. Security and stability were there. The family attended a nearby stylish Lutheran church nearly every Sunday. Galloway's father, besides being a successful ad salesman for the *Minneapolis Star*, was active in the Boy Scouts of America. Mrs. Galloway kept an extremely neat home; loved, humored, and obeyed her husband; was active in the ladies' society of Mt. Olivet Lutheran Church, and tried her very best to instill in her children the virtues of piety, reverence, honesty, truthfulness, diligence, and industriousness. In this, she was sustained by her husband.

Jay Galloway grew up in a state whose reputation for cold snowy winters was fabled. He grew up in a city that was famous as a municipality that had been carefully planned; had a well-monitored government cleaner than that of almost any other large urban area; was headquarters for many large corporations and businesses whose management demanded and got an attractive city in which their executives would be eager to live; was liberal in politics and conservative in almost everything else. The eleven lakes within the city were open to the public. No one privately owned property contiguous to any of the beautiful lakes. Taxes were high, but education took the top dollar.

While the downtowns of other cities decayed and gurgled in death throes, downtown Minneapolis with its mall and skyways remained vibrant long after Mary Tyler Moore was done throwing her cap up in the air outside Dayton's. General Mills, 3M, Cargill, International Multifoods, and similar corporations were generous in community donations, providing an ideal atmosphere for raising families. No branch of city government had an excess of authority without having another segment of government there to provide checks and balances. One graduate of the University of Minnesota Law School who specialized in criminal law moved to another state after passing the bar, because he did not think there was enough crime in the Twin Cities to provide a lucrative legal career.

The Guthrie was among the very best and most famous of regional theaters. Chanhassen was among the most successful dinner theaters in the nation. Yet both theaters regularly staged classical, tried-and-true productions.

And that was pretty much the way Minneapolitans grew up—in relative safety, in good health, well educated, with a penchant for planning ahead carefully, proud of their city, programmed for white-collar jobs, and convinced the Ford assembly plant just outside St. Paul was an anomaly.

Like their theaters, Minneapolitans did not take many risks. They followed their ancestors in vocations, or carefully trained for established professions. They lived well and patiently waited their turn for membership in escalatingly prestigious country clubs.

That is how the Galloway family lived. That is how their three children developed. That is how young Jay Galloway grew. For a short time. Then he began to forge a lifestyle that was nearly the antithesis of his impressive environment.

Environment has its effect on the developing personality. But it is an unpredictable effect. So it was with Jay Galloway.

After graduation from the University of Minnesota, he was employed by the *Minneapolis Tribune* as an advertising salesman. Following in his father's footsteps, but not along the identical path. His father was an ad salesman for the *Star*. But it was an understatement to call them sister publications. They were more like twins. Readers of both papers would have been hard pressed to discern a difference in their editorial policies. They were housed in the same building. They were both properties of the Cowles Publishing Company. And when one looked high enough into the management hierarchy of both papers, the personnel was identical.

So, young Jay began in the approved Minneapolitan fashion.

All his life, he'd heard his father run on about the sales game. Jay had studied sales and business management in college. He was, it was universally recognized, a natural. Some salespeople counted up to seven noes before they accepted a negative answer. Jay Galloway never gave a client an opportunity to turn him down. His standard method was to make an excellent sales presentation, usually by phone, then interrupt himself before reaching the point where the client would have to accept or decline. "Don't make up your mind now," Galloway would say, "Think about it. I'll get back to you."

Galloway had some sixth sales sense. Unerringly, he would perceive the moment the sale was made. And he would move in for the sales kill. Of course, his technique was not effective in every case. But his success ratio was extremely high. He made good money and his prospects were excellent.

He courted and married Marjorie Palmer. In this union, he attained the carousel's brass ring. Marjorie had been the University of Minnesota's dream girl, the campus beauty par excellence. Jay and Marj had attended the university at the same time, she a year behind him. He had made his play for her then and found only that she did not recognize his existence. Her tastes ran to whatever football player happened to be Big Man on Campus.

After graduation, Galloway finally caught her attention when he attained some considerable standing as a young man of means in the community. From that moment on, it was the full-court press. Dining at Charlie's Cafe Exceptionale, the Blue Horse, Lord Fletcher's, the Rosewood Room; dancing at the Orion Room and Chouette's; evenings at the Guthrie or Chanhassen. Afterward, sometimes his place, sometimes hers.

It was a society wedding. St. Mark's Episcopal Church. Honeymoon in Hawaii. They settled into *the* Minneapolis suburb of Edina. They decided not to have children. It promised to be a good life. Together they would tread the path to success and fulfillment as had so many other successful Twin Cities couples. They were Beautiful People.

But he grew restless. He found depressing the prospect of following forever in his father's footsteps, even though Jay was certain to soar beyond his father's achievements.

He began to find staff meetings a crashing bore. He fidgeted through what had been routine three-martini lunches. He became distracted during sales presentations. His acquisition of new accounts slowed, then stopped dead in the water. He began losing dependable old accounts. His employers were very concerned. They sent him off to a private, company-owned retreat on the north shore of Lake Superior. They hoped that in seclusion and peace he would find himself.

He did.

But the self he found was new. It did not fit into the Minneapolitan mold prefabricated for him by his parents and peers. He would be his own man. No longer would he work for others. He would become an entrepreneur—the guy who gives the other guys ulcers.

But more than anything else, he would become Somebody. No longer would people identify him as Jay Galloway, ad salesman. He would become Jay Galloway, celebrity. No soiree would be complete without him. He would have his picture in the newspapers regularly, as well as on the TV screen, as part of the news and, perhaps, the entertainment scene. He would leave behind this relative anonymity that was now his lot. He had to become Somebody.

That was what he concluded during the first half of his retreat. Just how he would become Somebody was the subject of the final portion of his retreat.

At length, he decided to follow the maxim, Go with what you know. He knew newspapers. He would start his own. Nothing to attempt to compete with the *Star* or *Tribune*. He hadn't the clout to take on even a small portion of the Cowles empire. He would begin a kind of shopping guide for the thriving Minneapolis downtown.

And so he did.

He invested everything he owned, mortgaging up to his hairline, to start his publication. He found there was more to this business than he had realized. In the beginning he found it necessary personally to stand at the corner of the Mall and pass out complimentary copies of his tabloid to indifferent Minneapolitans. He was close to panic.

That was when he sensed Marjorie was beginning to drift. It began with disenchantment with Jay. In her eyes, he had blown it all. Their comfortable life had degenerated into counting coins. Dinner out had degenerated into eating at the Jolly Troll occasionally. Marjorie completely lacked her husband's vision of a rosy future. She began to see other men.

Galloway learned of his wife's dalliances. He was neither terribly hurt nor surprised. But the fact that he felt neither emotion was surprising. Something subtle and subconscious had happened. He had harbored a latent feeling of contempt for her. The feeling had begun the moment she consented to marry him. It had grown steadily since then. He still was not cognizant of the contempt, only that he felt neither strong anger nor surprise.

It was a phenomenon that would occur within him time and again throughout his life. He would court the very best—executives, staff, athletes, women—and the moment they consented to associate with him, either as employee or mistress, he would lose all respect for them. But never consciously.

If ever he had gone into psychotherapy honestly, he might have discovered that he was simply projecting his self-loathing onto others. Unconsciously, he had no respect for himself. Thus, subconsciously, he could not respect anyone who proffered services or love.

In any case, his downtown paper began to thrive. It was a tribute to his tenacity and talent at salesmanship. While remaining complimentary to readers, the ad sales skyrocketed. As with most ad salespersons, he was slipshod about picking up the pieces, attending to detail. Thus it was fortunate for him when he could begin hiring a staff.

He was able to take on a full-time editor, who was given a rather generous budget for attracting freelance writers. He then hired two more salespeople. His greatest coup—a singular tribute to Galloway's salesmanship—was in luring his old friend, Dave Whitman, from International Multifoods to become business manager of the paper.

Whitman was such a prize that Galloway almost—but not quite—retained his respect for his friend. The others he hired he quickly but quietly began to despise. They became aware that there was something peculiar about their relationship with their employer. He noticed there was something peculiar about his relationship with his employees. But no one could identify just what was going on.

From the paper, Galloway moved into the pizza business—a sleeper enterprise in the capitalistic society. He took with him Dave Whitman. Together they managed to garner solid, six-figure incomes. Thence they moved into the subculture of professional football. As he did with his Minneapolis paper, Galloway sold his interest in the pizza business. Now all his financial eggs were in the Cougars basket. He worried a good deal about that. The income from attendance, television, and other sources was extremely gratifying. But the expenses, particularly in players' salaries, were enormous. And growing annually. Unlike other owners, Galloway had no resource to satisfy expenses other than the income created by the Cougars. He had cause to worry.

One of his major worries involved Hank Hunsinger. The Hun posed a serious dilemma for Galloway. On the one hand, Hunsinger drew a crowd, not only on the playing field when he carried the ball, but in the stands. A hefty percentage of the Silverdome crowd came to see the Hun. But, on the other hand, his salary demands grew more preposterous by the year. There was a time coming, if indeed it had not already arrived, when the two would counterbalance each other and the Hun's salary and fringe benefits would offset the crowd he drew.

It was just possible Hunsinger stood in the way of Galloway's master plan: to be Somebody. Galloway could not let that happen. He could brook no impediment to his goal. He had to find a solution to the problem of the Hun.

"I understand you have to investigate this matter." Galloway, fingers trembling slightly, lit a Camel. "But I'm a very busy man. And you don't have an appointment."

"We haven't time to make appointments during a homicide investigation," Sergeant Ewing explained affably. "We've just got to go where the investigation leads."

"But I don't know anything about it," Galloway protested. "Besides, I'm trying to put this whole thing back together. I still can't believe we've lost Hunsinger!"

Koesler thought Galloway made it sound as if he had lost a prized tool.

"Look, Mr. Galloway," said Lieutenant Harris, "we can ask you a few questions, get a little information from you here and now. Or we can all go downtown to police headquarters, where you can make a statement."

"Y-you can do that?" In moments of great stress, Galloway suffered a slight stammer.

Harris nodded.

"Okay." Galloway blanched at the very thought of being taken to police headquarters where the dregs of society were led through the corridors. He virtually collapsed into his black executive chair. With a vague wave, he motioned the others to seat themselves. He glanced at Koesler. "What's he doing here?"

"The department," Ewing explained, "has decided to use Father Koesler as a consultant in this investigation."

"Why?"

"That's all you need to know," said Harris.

Galloway appraised the two officers. From all he'd seen on television and in the movies, they were playing the tough-cop/nice-cop routine. He decided he would be able to handle Ewing with no problem. But he'd better be cautious about Harris. He was not entirely correct.

Galloway sank deeply into his chair. He dragged on his cigarette. It was several seconds before he exhaled through his nostrils. He sank his thumb into his cheek. The cigarette was clenched between his index and middle fingers. A thin curl of smoke followed the contour of his head, then disappeared above him. His eyes darted from one officer to the other, waiting for the questions.

"Mr. Galloway," Ewing began, "we want to pinpoint the last time Mr. Hunsinger was in his apartment before he returned to it after the game."

"H-how should I know?"

"Well, when did he have to join the rest of the team before the game?"

"Oh, that'd be yesterday morning at eight at the Pontiac Inn for the pregame meal and taping."

"Then he might have left his place at—uh, how long does it take to get out to the inn from Jefferson and the Boulevard? About 45 minutes, doesn't it? So, about seven or seven-fifteen?"

"I suppose. Why don't you find out from the doorman?"

"We did ask the doorman. But in investigations like this, we crosscheck. We may well ask you questions that we have asked others. There's no telling where an investigation will lead."

"Oh."

"Just a minute, Mr. Galloway," said Harris, "I thought it was the custom for teams to stay at a hotel the night before a game, even if they were playing at home. How come your team doesn't get together until game day itself?"

Galloway glanced nervously at Harris. He was the one to be wary of. "We decided long ago it would be better for the players to be at home until just before the game whenever possible. Helps relax them. So, when we play at home, we assemble on the day of the game."

Harris, Ewing, and Koesler each had the same thought: staying at home saved an overnight hotel bill. To Harris's thought was added: you stingy bastard.

Ewing resumed the questioning. "Mr. Galloway, were you aware that Hunsinger had any physical problems or flaws?"

"Physical problems?"

"Any impairment?"

"Well, he had a chronic problem with his shoulder. And his knees were in horrible shape. But anybody who's played as long as the Hun would have to have a lot wrong with him."

"Anything, any impairment not connected with football?"

Galloway took another long drag and jammed the cigarette butt into a large ashtray. As with most smokers, he failed to completely extinguish the cigarette; it continued to smolder as he lit another. "His eyes? You mean his eyes?"

"That's right."

"Yeah; he wore glasses. Contacts. He was nearsighted or something."

"Anything else?"

"Not that I know of. Actually, he was in pretty good shape for the length of time he'd been in the game."

"I mean anything else about his eyes?"

Galloway frowned. "Something, I think it was astigmatism. You'd better check with Dave Whitman, or with Jack Brown, my trainer. They know more about the physical condition of the players than I do."

"What do you know about Hunsinger's death?"

"Just what I've read in today's papers. I've been on the phone all morning. But I haven't been able to find anyone who knows more about it. Or, at least anybody who'll talk. He was poisoned. That's all I know."

"It was strychnine."

"Strychnine!"

"We found a container in the apartment. Did you know it was there?"

"No. N-no. I don't think so. Why would I?" For some time he had been swiveling his chair from side to side. It was obvious he was nervous and wanted this interrogation over as quickly as possible.

"Mr. Galloway, do you know of anyone who would want to kill Hunsinger?"

For the first time, Galloway showed a brief smile. "Just about everybody he ever played against."

Ewing returned the smile. "We're trying to narrow this investigation, Mr. Galloway. We're concentrating on those who might have had access to his apartment and might have both a motive and the means. Specifically, right now, six of the men who met at his apartment in the discussion group."

"The discussion group!" Galloway seemed genuinely shocked. "That was a Bible discussion group, for God's sake. Besides, with the exception of the good father here, we were all with the same team. Why would any of us want to hurt the Hun, let alone kill him?"

"Think, Mr. Galloway."

Galloway butted another cigarette, left it smoldering in the tray, and began drumming his fingers on the desk-top. "Hoffer, I suppose. He played behind the Hun. He may have resented the Hun, but"—he shook his head—"not enough to kill him. No," he shook his head again, "the idea is just preposterous."

Softly, without moving in his chair Harris asked, "What about your wife, Mr. Galloway?"

"What!" Abruptly Galloway lurched forward as if he were about to stand. "Marjorie! What has she got to do with this?"

"We have information that she was a very close friend of Hunsinger at one time." Harris retained his calm manner.

"B-but that was ages ago. A year or more. There isn't anything between them any more."

"Then you knew about the affair?" A hint of a smile played at Harris's lips.

Galloway's shoulders caved slightly. He had been trapped. Even though he had known Harris was the dangerous one.

They were on the brink of a confessional precipice. Ewing, for one, did not wish to cross it at this time. "Were you aware of Hunsinger's attitude toward routines... habits, Mr. Galloway?"

Galloway remained erect in his chair. He would not chance relaxing again during this conversation. "Routines! Hell, yes. Everybody knew the guy was compulsive. Hell, he was a compulsive-obsessive!"

"You say that was general knowledge?"

"Everybody in the league knew it. Everybody who read the sports pages knew it. The guy wouldn't play if a shoestring got crossed." Galloway looked from one officer to the other, then glanced at his watch. "Is that about all? I really have a lot to do."

"Just a few more questions, Mr. Galloway," said Ewing.

"Can you account for your whereabouts yesterday between 7:00 A.M. and 6:00 P.M.?" Harris asked.

"M-me! My whereabouts!" Galloway flushed. His lips trembled. He clearly was angry. "What do you mean, my whereabouts! Are you accusing me of this thing?" He reached for the phone. "I think I'd better get my attorney!"

"Before you do that"—Ewing raised a hand; Galloway did not lift the receiver—"you should know that you are not being accused of anything at this time. We are merely conducting a preliminary investigation. We are going to be asking this question of quite a few people."

Galloway removed his hand from the phone.

"Now," Ewing continued, "can you tell us what you did yesterday between 7:00 A.M. and 6:00 P.M.? Try to be as thorough as possible."

"Okay. I got up about six-thirty, had some coffee, read the papers. Got down to the Pontiac Inn about ten. Joined the gang for some brunch. Went directly from there to the stadium. After the game, I went out to dinner with some friends from GM. That would take me up to about ten last night."

"So you were in the company of others from six-thirty in the morning until ten last night?" Harris asked.

"Not exactly. I was alone until I got to the inn."

Harris raised his eyebrows. "So no one can corroborate your story until after ten yesterday morning?"

"I've had about enough of this, Lieutenant." Galloway stood and leaned forward, his whitened knuckles pressing against the desktop. "Are you saying that I'm a suspect in this murder?"

"No one has said that," Harris stated.

"It doesn't make any sense," Galloway continued. "Why would I do a thing like that? I had no reason at all."

"How about, just for the sake of pursuing the idea, jealousy or revenge for what he did to your wife?" Harris suggested.

A sardonic smile cracked one side of Galloway's mouth. He would rather not have addressed the subject at all. If Harris had not tricked him into admitting knowledge of the affair, he would have responded in some vague manner. As it was, he had to answer openly. And he was prepared to do so.

"Your source, whoever it was, about the affair my wife had with the Hun failed to fill you in on the status of our marriage. My wife and I are separated. We have been for over a month. Hunsinger was not the cause . . . although he may have been the final straw. You can ask any of the gossip columnists. They'll tell you my wife really gets around. It's going to be a messy divorce. The media can hardly wait. They'll tell you."

The ensuing moment of silence was awkward if not embarrassing.

Galloway continued. "Aside from the fact that, frankly, I don't give a damn about my wife, I really would be a fool to do anything harmful to the Hun. He was a meal ticket. The local hero. God, his fans go back to high school around here. A lot of the fans come out just to see him. You can check for yourselves. On home dates, when it's known beforehand that he's hurt and not going to play, there have been more no-shows than at other games.

"And now, gentlemen, the Hun will be permanently absent from our games. I've got to address that problem. And it'd better be a pretty damn smart move I make, whatever it is. That's what I'm busy with this morning. So if there are no further questions—"

"Not just now, Mr. Galloway," said Ewing. "There may be more later. Thank you for your help."

The two policemen and the priest rose and left the office in silence.

"Want some lunch now?" Ewing asked.

Harris checked his watch. "Let's hit on the other executives while we're up here."

"Okay," said Ewing. "On to Dave Whitman."

They began walking down the corridor, eerily quiet in the gigantic stadium.

"Whatcha think, Father?" Ewing asked.

"Well," said Koesler, "for what it's worth I think he lied about the strychnine."

"What?"

"As I told you, Hank clearly mentioned that he had a supply of strychnine in the apartment. And not only was Mr. Galloway present, but I remember his making some comment about it."

"No shit!" Ewing murmured.

"I should never doubt Walt Koznicki," said Harris. "Every once in a while he is capable of an absolutely inspired idea."

"Bring it in. Bring it home. We had to do it. They depended on us."

Although he had an exemplary father, young Dave Whitman's role model of choice was his paternal grandfather, a railroader of the old school.

Whitman's father, Robert, was a surgeon. He also was for many terms a Minnesota state senator. A rare combination. Understandably, he was held in high esteem in the community. Also understandably, he was seldom home. On those few occasions when he was both home and not otherwise occupied, he spent as much time as possible with his son and two daughters.

The daughters were very close to their mother. Dr. Whitman thought that appropriate. But he was particularly pleased that young Dave attached himself to his grandfather. As he grew up, the doctor had related well to his father, Bernard. Especially since he was forced to be away much of the time, Dr. Whitman could think of few others he could wish his own son to copy more than the man the doctor had patterned himself after. In fact, when in a nostalgic mood, the doctor frequently envied his son's relationship with the old man.

Before David was in his teens, Bernard Whitman was nearing his eighties. Although of English rather than Scandinavian extraction, Bernard was a stereotype of what one might expect a native Minnesotan to be. In his late years, Bernard looked as if he'd been chiseled out of rock. Years of facing a frigid unrelenting winter wind had cut deep ridges in his face. Once he had been a huge man. Now his big-boned body was pencil-thin, skin taut over the bones. His hands remained large and gnarled.

Many an evening, Dave would sit at his grandfather's knee near the fireplace and listen eagerly to the oft told tales.

"Things were different when I was a lad, David. I was a country boy up near Duluth. There was no Reserve Mining. Just the Lake." (Grandpa never gave Superior its name, but always referred to it as if it were uppercased.) "And some homesteaders, some Indians, and the land to care for so it would care for us. And I was eager and ambitious. From the first time I ever saw a train I knew that was going to be my life.

"I started as a hostler, a laborer. I'd clean the shop and the pits, prepare the engines, knock the fire out, clean the ashes. That's the bottom, David."

Dave had guessed, before being told, that that was so.

"Then I became a fireman in the engine. That was hard work."

Dave's eyes would drop from his grandfather's face to

his workworn hands; he could understand just how hard that work had been.

"Then I passed an examination to be the engineer, gained my seniority, and got to be able to pick my runs. When business got bad, I'd go back to being a fireman. In the 1929 depression, I lost about twenty years' seniority for two or three days."

Grandpa was with the Minneapolis, Northfield & Southern Railroad for fifty-one years. Regularly, he would sum it up for his grandson: "Indeed, David, it was a thrill. We'd travel under all kinds of conditions—storms, faulty engines. But there was the thrill of getting the fireman to get up speed. We had to get 'er over the hill. There were no excuses. We had to come through."

Of all his grandfather's many reminiscences, David was most impressed by two quasi-creeds by which Grandpa lived. One, in proof of maturity, was, "There were no excuses; we had to come through."

When at last grandfather retired from the railroad, "I was still eager for something ahead of me to inspire me."

He found it in the Minneapolis Society for the Blind. "I always pitied the handicap of the blind. I got sympathetic watching the blind travel. Well, sir, one day the Society for the Blind had an open house, and I attended.

"I always wondered how a blind man could operate a power saw. It seemed like suicide to me. So I sneaked away from the open-house crowd and walked over to talk with some men who were working with wood. One of the supervisors asked me if I would like to volunteer. Right then I knew that this was where I wanted to be.

"First I had to learn how to use power tools before I could learn how to teach the blind in their use.

"But I was left alone to teach them. Which was good. I never liked to have a boss over my shoulder. All my life I had to depend on myself to bring myself in."

That was the second maxim by which grandpa lived. Young David Whitman determined to live his life in the same way. He would make no excuses. And, to the extent possible, he would have no boss over his shoulder. Certainly he would never depend upon a boss for motivation. He would depend upon himself to bring himself in.

Tempering these challenging goals was a subtle but almost everpresent sense of humor. When filling out application forms for the University of Minnesota, Dave had answered the question "Church preference?" with "Gothic." Fortunately for the fledgling collegian, the admissions dean also had a sense of humor.

After an outstanding tour through academe, he was recruited by and joined the public relations section of International Multifoods. As IM expected, he was very good. He quickly built excellent relations with the community—and with the media, to whom he was a genuine help. They learned to trust him.

However, there was a boss over his shoulder. Whitman certainly did not depend on anyone else for motivation in his work. But bosses, even approving bosses, would not go away.

Thus, when his childhood friend, Jay Galloway, pressed Whitman to join an independent venture in publishing, his inclination was to abandon the giant corporation and its multiple bosses and get in on the ground floor of something new and exciting. It took him a considerable time to convince his wife, Kate, of the wisdom, even of the necessity of the new gamble. But he succeeded, as he knew he would.

It was not long before disenchantment set in. It was not that Whitman did not believe Galloway could succeed. Indeed, it was probable he would. But no sooner did Whitman begin working for Galloway than an air of contempt began to be detectable.

Whitman could have ignored that. But Galloway had an irredeemable habit of cutting corners, playing fast and loose with rules, relying only on hope to get away with his unending fiscal peccadilloes. Sometimes Whitman wished Galloway would just commit one serious crime rather than all those minor offenses, the total penalty for which would be approximately the same as for a felony.

Whitman had been nearing the end of his endurance when Galloway came up with the idea of buying into and eventually owning the Cougars. The prospects were too good. Whitman, after a fierce internal battle, reinvested in Galloway.

They moved to a new city, a new state, a new enterprise. But nothing else had changed. Galloway was still mucking about in areas unsuited to his talents. Once again, Whitman was nearing the end of his tether when a fresh thought occurred.

He would nudge Galloway out of the picture. He would maneuver Galloway into an intolerable position with the Cougars. And then, out. Finally, Whitman would be where he was destined to end: in the driver's seat. No boss over his shoulder. Depending on himself to bring himself in.

It would require some bold strokes. But Whitman had one such stroke in mind. It would take a lot of planning. He knew well the problem Galloway had with Hank Hunsinger. Whitman, indeed, was the management representative who had to negotiate the contracts containing those outrageous demands with the Hun. If it had been up to him alone, Whitman would have taken a much more hard-nosed attitude toward Hunsinger, including letting him go, to see if he could pursue his career with some other team.

But Galloway insisted on keeping the Hun, whatever the cost. Galloway seemed to Whitman to be unrealistic about the Hun's value to the team. And that, Whitman decided, was Galloway's Achilles' heel. Whitman began to devise a complicated scheme. It would require very careful planning. But then, planning was his forte.

All that was required was that he get up a head of steam, get 'er over the hill, and bring 'er in.

* * *

Distractions were second nature to Father Koesler. And he was suffering from a persistent one now. The twin rows of pipes on Dave Whitman's desk had nearly mesmerized the priest. He had never seen so many pipes outside a tobacconist's. Clearly, Whitman was a serious smoker.

Between attempting to count the pipes, Koesler had been listening to the interrogation. They had covered the length of time Whitman had been associated with Galloway, the tragedy of Hunsinger's death, and Whitman's awareness of the player's obsessive compulsiveness.

"Were you aware of any physical impairment, outside of injuries, that is?" Ewing asked.

"Yes, of course." Whitman consulted Hunsinger's file. Earlier, when the officers and Koesler had entered his office, Whitman's secretary had brought it in. "He had a sight problem: astigmatism with a touch of nearsightedness. See for yourself."

Whitman offered a sheet of paper to Ewing, who glanced at it, then gave it to Harris. It was a record of Hunsinger's health status. The report mentioned the vision problem, but made no mention of any color deficiency. Apparently, he had been able to keep his colorblindness out of his official record.

"He wore contacts," Whitman continued.

"There was nothing else wrong with his eyes?" Ewing asked.

"Not to my knowledge."

"Are you aware of how Hunsinger died?" Harris asked.

"He was poisoned, wasn't he? At least, according to the media."

"It was strychnine," said Harris.

Whitman raised his eyebrows. He sucked hard on his pipe, but it had gone out. He tapped the dottle out of the bowl and inserted a pipe cleaner in the stem. He returned the pipe to its place on the rack, removed the next pipe, and began the elaborate procedure of filling, tamping, and lighting it.

"Were you aware that Hunsinger kept a supply of strychnine in his apartment?" Harris continued.

"Uh-huh."

"How's that? Did you see it?"

"No. He told us about it. At one of our meetings, he mentioned how he'd had a problem with rodents in the apartment. He said he'd gotten the problem under control with, as he put it, 'good old-fashioned strychnine.'"

Koesler nodded at this. Whitman's description was exactly how the information had come out.

"Do you know how he got it?"

Whitman shook his head. "Didn't ask. But it surprised me. Strychnine's a controlled substance, isn't it?"

Ewing nodded. "Speaking of surprises, Mr. Whitman, you looked surprised when Lieutenant Harris mentioned that strychnine was the poison that killed Hunsinger. Why was that, if you knew that strychnine was in the apartment?"

Whitman scratched the side of his head with the stem of his pipe. "I guess I was surprised that whoever killed him had used a poison that was already in the apartment. I guess that would have to mean the killer would have to have known that it was there in advance."

"Like you did," said Harris.

Whitman smiled self-consciously and blushed simultaneously. "Silly of me . . . trapped by my own logic."

"Mr. Whitman," said Ewing, "part of your responsibility here is to sign up the players, negotiate their contracts, isn't it?"

"Yes."

"Would you say Mr. Hunsinger had a good contract? I mean, measured by comparable contracts for comparable players?"

"I'd say it was an excellent contract. But fair. If the Hun hadn't liked it, he could have played it out, become a free agent, and maybe gone to another club."

"But isn't this his market?" Ewing pressed on. "I mean, because of his local background, he'd be more valuable here in Michigan than anywhere else."

"True, as far as it goes. But the Hun was a premier performer—a pheenom, as they say in this business. He would have gotten good money no matter where he went."

"But not more than he'd get here. Which would give you a bargaining tool. I mean, after your final offer, say, you could point out that he would not get as much anywhere else, right? Sort of take away the whipsaw possibility."

Whitman exhaled a thick cloud of smoke. He smiled. "That's why they call it negotiating. During negotiations, it would be just me and the Hun getting together in our own little huddle."

"Just you and Hunsinger? Didn't he have an agent?"

"Nope."

"Isn't that kind of odd? Everybody's got an agent."

"Almost everybody. A long time ago, the Hun had an agent, when he signed his first couple of contracts with us. Then—no. The Hun was no dummy. After the first couple of go-rounds, I think he figured he could do as well as any agent, and also, he didn't want to give 10 percent to anybody."

"And you, you didn't have an attorney or anyone with you?"

"It's my responsibility. I bring it in."

"And you're capable, all by yourself?"

"I am capable of doing whatever I'm responsible for."

"Sort of a lone wolf," Harris commented.

"Not exactly. Just a philosophy of mine. I take responsibility for completing what I set out to do. And I make no excuses."

Harris and Ewing wondered, if ever so briefly, whether that encompassing philosophy might extend to murder. Koesler, harking back to a day when workers were more conscientious, thought it a laudable philosophy.

"What does Hunsinger's death mean to your team?" Harris asked.

Whitman shrugged. "Undoubtedly, it will hurt attendance. You'd have to ask the coach about the implications for the team's playing strength."

"It also blots out an extremely expensive contract, doesn't it?"

"That's just shortsighted, Lieutenant. It may be true—no, it's definitely true, that whoever we bring up to the Cougars will not get a contract close to what the Hun had. There isn't a tight end in football who ever equaled the Hun's contract. But we're going to have to pay someone to fill out the team. And we're certain to have a falloff in attendance. Happened every time the Hun missed games in the past.

"So, from a financial standpoint, it's like cutting off one end of a carpet and sewing it on the other. Whatever money we save on the Hun's contract we'll lose at the gate." Whitman extended both hands, palms upward, in a gesture of futility. "Now, is that everything, gentlemen? I've got a very busy day ahead of me. Mondays are bad anyway. And, what with the Hun . . ." He didn't bother completing the statement.

"Just one more thing," Ewing responded. "Can you account for your whereabouts through the day yesterday?"

Whitman took several deep puffs from his pipe, rekindling tobacco that had almost gone out. He seemed to be collecting his memory. The officers noted that, unlike Galloway, Whitman showed no reluctance to account for his time.

"We got up about seven, jogged our five miles, had some breakfast, read the papers, got ready, and went to the stadium about noon."

"Excuse me," Ewing interrupted, "but who is 'we'?"

"My wife and I."

"The two of you were together throughout the whole morning?"

"Why, yes." Whitman seemed surprised at the question.

"I see. Okay, continue, please."

"Well, we watched the game from our box. After the game, we went out to dinner with some of our friends. Then we went home, watched a little TV, the eleven o'clock news, and then retired."

"Then you were with your wife or others all day?" Ewing asked.

"Far as I can remember."

"Just a moment, Mr. Whitman," said Harris. "If I recall correctly, you said you arrived at the stadium at noon. But the game didn't start till two. What about those two hours?"

Whitman looked disconcerted—at having forgotten the two hours, or because they had spotted the gap?

"I was up in my office catching up on some business."

"Anyone with you?"

"Why, no. I was alone."

"Alone? Where was your wife during all that time?"

"I can see you haven't been to many Cougar games, Lieutenant. Or, at least, you haven't come early to the games. There's a regular ritual many fans enjoy before a game. It's called tailgating. It can become a genuine banquet. That's where my wife was, Lieutenant, with some friends of ours at a tailgating party."

"So there are two hours for which you have no corroboration."

"I suppose so. Why should I need any?"

"During that time, you could have left the stadium." Harris pressed the point.

"I could have. I didn't. Why would I?"

"Between the time Hunsinger left for the stadium and the time he returned, somebody went to his apartment and set the trap that would kill him."

For the first time in this interview, Whitman placed his pipe in the ample ashtray and sat forward. "Are you accusing me of killing Hunsinger? Are you serious?"

"No one is accusing anyone of anything—yet," said Ewing. "But the investigation will proceed. We may have more questions for you later, Mr. Whitman. In the meantime, it would not hurt if you could think of anyone who could establish that you did not, indeed, leave this office between noon and two yesterday."

"And for your part, gentlemen," Whitman was standing, "it might help your flimsy suspicion if you could come up with a single solitary reason why I would even think of cutting off an attraction like Hank Hunsinger."

In better restaurants it was called ground round or chopped steak. To Father Koesler, it was hamburger. And he had built a considerable reputation as the gourmand of the local hamburger circuit. As an expert—acknowledged or self-appointed—he disdained as hopelessly inferior the beef served in all fast-food chains, with the possible exception of Wendy's.

Nonetheless, he was eating in a fast-food restaurant and it was not Wendy's. It had been selected by Lieutenant Harris. Sergeant Ewing had concurred. Father Koesler's opinion had not been solicited.

They were at the coffee stage of the meal. The one bright spot in this lunch as far as Koesler was concerned was that they served brewed decaf.

Luncheon conversation had been studied. The officers could not talk shop without leaving the priest awkwardly out of it. Koesler sensed that policemen might not be interested in parish matters or theology. So they advanced through lunch pushing one word after another.

"You come here often?" Koesler essayed.

"First time for me."

"Me too."

"I thought . . . since you found it . . . and it was so close to the stadium . . ."

Harris smiled. "We don't come to the stadium that often either."

"Too expensive," Ewing said. "And, besides, you have to invest too much time getting out of that parking lot. How about you, Father?"

"Only once in a long while. Actually, once since I joined the Bible discussion group. I thought I ought to patronize the business of the other members of the God Squad. But since attending in person, I realized that TV just doesn't cover the game."

Ewing sat back and for the first time appraised Koesler carefully. Redistribute the weight a little and take off maybe thirty years and he would at least look like a pro football player.

"How about you, Father? Did you ever play the game?"

"Me? Yeah. But I went through high school and college in the seminary and we played touch. Which sounds a lot more innocent than it was." He grinned. "No conditioning, no pads, the blocking identical to tackle football—and there were some pretty big guys playing.

"Teams like the Cougars have thirty seconds to huddle and get the next play under way. Our plays originated in maybe a three-minute huddle. And we didn't call the plays in shorthand. It was more, 'You block so-and-so. You block so-and-so. You go out for a deep pass. You go out for a short pass. You go out in the flat and buttonhook—that means turn around—and you get out and cut behind the wheelbarrow.'

"So there's a limit to how much I am able to identify with the Cougars.

"Before I got involved in this discussion group, the closest contact I had with a pro football player was a gentleman I'll never forget. The name wouldn't mean anything to you. But he played in the years just after the professional league was formed in 1922. I met him in his last days. He had terminal lung cancer. We became quite good friends. When he died, I had his funeral Mass and because I'd come to know him so well, I gave a eulogy that, I guess, was kind of affecting.

"Anyway, after the Mass, I went back to the rectory to get ready to go to the cemetery. The doorbell rang. It was a huge, elderly gentleman, who, it turned out, had been a teammate of the deceased. I don't know whether he was embarrassed or just didn't have the words to express himself, but he stammered something like, 'I just wanted to tell you . . . I mean . . . I just wanted you to know . . . uh . . . that . . . I thought . . . well . . . you played a good game!' "

The two officers smiled.

"I got to thinking about my friend this morning while I was listening to Mr. Galloway and Mr. Whitman explain what the loss of Hank Hunsinger would mean to the Cougars. How attendance would drop as it always did when he had to be out of a game.

"I remembered that my friend had told me of a similar experience. He had been a good player, but not nearly as famous as players like Red Grange and Bronco Nagurski. In fact, attendance in those early years was very poor until Grange became a professional. Anyway, my friend told me that when word got out that one of the superstars would not be able to play, attendance always suffered. But when, inevitably, a superstar retired, it had no effect at all on attendance.

"It was as if the fans felt cheated when a superstar—a pheenom I believe they call them now—would not perform. The star played last Sunday and he'll probably play next Sunday. But this Sunday, when I pay my hard-earned money, he's not going to play. So I'm not going to pay until he plays again.

"Whereas, when the player retired, the fans didn't feel cheated when he no longer played. In fact, if it went anywhere, attendance used to go up because the fans wanted to see who would be taking the star's place.

"So I thought it rather odd that both the owner and the general manager would assume that the Hun's permanent loss to the team would necessarily hurt the gate. Seems to me attendance is just as likely to improve."

There was a moment of silence. Toward the conclusion of Koesler's monologue, Harris had paused with his coffee cup halfway raised. It was still in that position. "Out of the mouths of babes," Harris murmured.

"Galloway and Whitman know, of course, who they've got back of Hunsinger. And they know how good he is. Who is it?" Ewing asked.

"Kit Hoffer," said Koesler, "and I think he's quite good. But he hasn't had much of a chance to play . . . what with the Hun's being the superstar."

"I think we'd better get back to the stadium and check out the new kid in town," said Harris. "Then we'll know a little bit more about just how motivated management was in keeping Hunsinger alive and well."

Monday mornings in the Cougars' locker room and training facility were devoted mostly to the walking wounded. The wounded who could not walk were usually in the hospital.

By the time Harris, Ewing, and Koesler entered the locker room in search of Kit Hoffer, much of Monday's customary routine had taken place.

The players had begun to straggle in about nine. Some were dressed in the identical clothing they had worn when they left the stadium the evening before. They hadn't been home. They had partied long and late. Most of these were in the arms of a bleary-eyed but good-humored hangover. Others, the more mature or serious athletes, were rested and ready to go.

A high percentage of those who had seen considerable game time yesterday now needed at least patching. Trainer

Jack Brown had been steadily taping extremities, chests, and groins. At eleven-thirty, the team doctor arrived, checked the halt and the lame, and examined the more seriously maimed.

In general, the Cougars were far more subdued than usual. Most of the conversation, naturally, revolved around Hank Hunsinger. It was truly shocking for one athlete to contemplate the death of a fellow athlete, much less his murder.

After the examinations were completed, the trainer and the doctor delivered their reports to the coach, so he could begin to consider the personnel around whom he would build this week's game plan.

It was at this point that the detectives and the priest entered the locker room. A few questions to players, some in varying stages of dishabille, others wrapped like mummies, disclosed that Hoffer, Cobb, the coach, and several assistants were on the field in the stadium. And yes, that was out of the ordinary for a Monday. But the coach wanted Cobb and Hoffer to have the maximum time in working together.

The three walked up the gentle incline toward the field with its artificial surface. Koesler considered the view from the field awesome, a sports cathedral. Not far from them, a group of men were clustered. Four wore team jackets. Koesler recognized only Coach Bradford. The three others, it would turn out, were assistant coaches on the offensive team. In nondescript sweat clothes were Bobby Cobb and Kit Hoffer. Koesler vaguely hoped the officers wouldn't immediately halt the workout. He wanted to watch for a short while at least.

So did the officers.

At about the 10-yard line, Cobb and Hoffer stood approximately six or seven yards apart, roughly where they would be had the rest of the team been in playing position.

Cobb, holding a football in his right hand, turned toward Hoffer. "Okay, let's try a dragout. Right. On two."

Cobb hunched as if crouching behind an imaginary center. Hoffer assumed a three-point stance.

Cobb called out, "Hut! Hut!" and slapped the ball against his left hand as if it had been thrust there by the center. He retreated rapidly, four, five steps.

Hoffer began a pattern, swinging slightly to his right, and continuing downfield. Abruptly, he broke for the sideline, looking over his right shoulder.

The ball was thrown behind Hoffer. He tried to twist his body in the opposite direction; his legs became tangled and he fell, rolling over and over.

Cobb cursed. One of the assistant coaches returned the ball. The others shouted either correctional advice or encouragement. Coach Bradford stood silent and motionless, arms locked across his chest, face expressionless.

Hoffer, obviously feeling as graceful as a puppy whose legs are its worst enemy, returned to the imaginary line of scrimmage.

The two players conferred with one of the assistant coaches, then set up for another play. This time, Hoffer lined up to Cobb's left.

"Okay, Hoff! Gimme a dragout and go! Left! On one!"

Cobb crouched. Hoffer balanced on his toes and the knuckles of his right hand.

"Hut!" Cobb slammed the ball and backpedaled.

Hoffer slanted slightly to his left, heading downfield. He abruptly broke toward the left sideline, then, just as abruptly, headed downfield at full speed.

Koesler thrilled to the exuberance of it: Hoffer, like an animal, seemed to run for the joy of running.

Cobb sent the ball in a high, deep arch. Hoffer slid to a halt, keeping his balance with one hand on the turf. He returned several yards and caught the pass just before it touched the turf. Clutching the ball to his chest, he fell and rolled over several times. Then he lay on his back, holding the ball up as high as he could, like a trophy.

"Bobby!" an assistant coach yelled. "Tell me what the hell good it is to outrun the safety and have to come back for the ball!"

Coach Bradford might have been carved from stone.

"Okay, Hoff! Let's try a little curl! Right! On one! Hut!" Cobb retreated.

Hoffer ran straight downfield ten to thirteen yards, then stopped and curled back toward scrimmage. The ball was delivered just as he turned. He barely saw it. He dropped it.

The assistant coaches shouted.

What seemed to be a frown appeared on Bradford's face.

At twenty-five, Kit Hoffer was young by anyone's standards. Yet he was a little old to be a rookie. The cause of his retarded career might have been buried somewhere in his background.

Hoffer had just missed the 1950s, the decade many say was America's last age of innocence. Born in 1960, he would live through the age of power explosions: student power, radical power, black power, drug power, fem-lib power, consumer power, rock power, rocket power.

Much of that had taken place beyond his awareness. He was only a teenager during Watergate. And Vietnam was over before he would have been forced to go.

Actually, despite growing up during a time of turmoil, Kit Hoffer had had a comparatively tranquil youth.

An only child, he had worshiped his father, Harold. And the affection was returned. Kit wanted to grow up just like his dad. Fortunately for that wish, he took after his father in that they were both mesomorphs with an abundance of bone, muscle, and connective tissue. Harold was, and Kit would grow to be, a muscular athlete with a large skeletal frame. And, as was so often the case, the son would far surpass his father in both size and athletic ability.

Harold Hoffer had grown up in New York City. He had attended Catholic schools, and had been an outstanding athlete from grade school through college. But while his scholastic career had been exceptional, he was not quite up to the standard of a professional in any sport. He went into sales for American Airlines. He was highly successful, using many of the contacts he had made during his life as a sports hero. He was transferred to Dallas-Fort Worth, the once and future headquarters of American.

Harold had married while living in New York. Kit was born there. When they moved to Texas, Kit was too young to know that everything about him would have been perfect if he had been Baptist. That anomaly diminished significantly as Kit grew and grew and grew.

He attended public school. But his parents made certain that he also attended catechism instructions faithfully. By so doing, he learned the Commandments, the Sacraments, and the Creed, over and over. His parish was not in the catechetical avant-garde.

For a while, young Hoffer toyed with the notion of becoming a priest. But he discovered two effective barriers to that vocation. He liked girls far too much to go through life without a wife. And his grades never reached a level that would encourage an academic career demanding scholastic achievement.

By no means was he stupid. He could have become a serious and successful student. But his desire to follow in his father's tracks forestalled that.

His parents would have been pleased enough had he wanted to be a priest. But his father would have been convinced that his son had missed a vocational vehicle. So father and son played endless catch, shot numberless baskets, hit countless baseballs. At the proper time, Kit began to invest regular hours in pumping weights and working out on exercise machines.

It worked. In senior high school, he was all-state in football, baseball, and basketball. Most major colleges tried to recruit him. The best package was offered by, in effect, his hometown university, Southern Methodist.

He had it all. All but luck.

College baseball and basketball have their value. But neither attracts the publicity nor garners the income for the school that football does. Considering Kit's build and natural talent, Harold and his son put all their chips on intercollegiate football. Kit became fullback for SMU. The best fullback in the conference. Perhaps the best in the nation.

But almost every time SMU would play one of its traditional rivals—a Notre Dame or a Texas A & M—on national television, for one reason or another Kit Hoffer would be sidelined. An injury, the flu, once, unbelievably, housemaid's knee. Thus, he gradually earned a reputation for unreliability. The word went round that Kit Hoffer could not be counted on for the big ones.

It was unfair. Kit Hoffer played, and played well, against Notre Dame, Texas A & M, Texas, Oklahoma, but generally not when national TV covered the event. Unlucky.

He should have been chosen in the first round of pro football's draft. He went in the eighteenth, to Chicago. Just as training camp opened, his mother died. He was late for camp. Unlucky. By the time he got there, he had fallen hopelessly behind in learning Chicago's system. Two veteran fullbacks were well ahead of him. The coach decided to go with the two veterans. Unlucky.

His father got Kit a job in sales with American Airlines. His was a very big name among sports fans in the Metroplex area. Many travel agents and business people wanted to be seen in the company of the big, if former, college football star at the Fairmont, or the Pyramid or the Carriage House. Kit did well for American Airlines. But his heart wasn't in it. His heart was in football.

The next season, as a free agent, he was invited to Tampa Bay's training camp. On the first day of contact drills he injured a knee. Because he was unable to participate in any further drills or practice, he never did catch up—and failed to survive the final cut. Unlucky.

He returned to Dallas, where he continued to please influential people who reserved a lot of space in air travel. American Airlines was pleased with his work. But he and his father shared a common disappointment. They knew it was all a matter of bad luck. However, there seemed to be nothing either could do about it. Kit stayed in shape, working out regularly at the Y.

The following season he contacted no one. And no team contacted him. But he continued to maintain his excellent physical condition. He played softball, basketball, and touch football with amateur groups, while keeping in mind that he could not afford to forget to hold back. Otherwise, he would be likely to injure someone.

He married. He and his childhood sweetheart had agreed to wait till his career in pro football was well established before marrying. That they went ahead with the marriage was a tacit admission that he had given up hope.

Then the phone call came from Coach Bradford. The coach wanted to reinforce the position of tight end. He was certain Kit could master the new position. Yes, even if he made the team he would be playing behind Hank Hunsinger. But nobody lasts forever. And he would finally attain his dream of playing professionally.

Kit, his wife, Grace, and his father agonized over the decision. They even went to their parish priest and had a Sunday Mass offered for guidance. They decided to take the chance. Actually, Harold and Kit had known from the start what the decision would be. The agonizing had been for Grace's benefit.

For once, he sailed through training camp uninjured

and unencumbered. He more than mastered the position of tight end. But there was that brick wall: Hank Hunsinger. A no-cut contract, and orders that he play every moment he was capable of playing. Unlucky.

Kit had practically no opportunity to even work out with the first string. In practice, he was on the squad of reserves that ran the plays of the coming week's opponent for the benefit of the Cougars' first-string defensive team. Kit had little more than a nodding acquaintance with Bobby Cobb, the perennial starting quarterback.

And so it would go, he was convinced. The recipient of one bit of rotten luck after another.

Unless . . . unless he could make his own luck.

Bobby Cobb and Kit Hoffer had reverted to the simplest pass patterns. Little more than playing catch. But as they grew increasingly successful, Hoffer grew increasingly confident. The shouted encouragement of the assistant coaches became more sincere. Coach Bradford watched the progress intently but impassively.

Hoffer jogged back to what passed for the line of scrimmage.

"Okay, Hoff, let's just try that curl again. Right! On two! Hut! Hut!"

Hoffer left the scrimmage line driving and at full speed. As he reached a point just behind where the middle linebacker would play, he planted his right foot and curled back toward scrimmage. At the moment he turned, the ball was there, in a tight spiral, thrown hard and aimed at his chest.

By now, Hoffer was becoming accustomed to the quarterback. Kit anticipated the ball, the spot, the velocity, the tightness of the spiral. He opened his large hands and "looked the ball in," letting the spiral drive itself into his hands. No sooner had he made the catch than he spun away and was driving downfield, the ball securely tucked in the crook of his left arm.

Perfect.

Koesler looked over at Coach Bradford. He didn't smile. But he did something with his lips. Perhaps it was the suppression of a smile. The assistant coaches were going wild. They sensed the new combination was beginning to jell.

Hoffer trotted back, his fine blond hair bouncing as he jogged. He wore a wide, self-satisfied grin.

"Okay, Hoff! Let's go for the big enchilada. Let's try for the flag with a one-step fake inside. And, Hoff, when you make your break, turn on the afterburners. I'm gonna lay this sucker dead over your right shoulder. Right! On one! Hut!"

Hoffer drove from the line, running low, moving toward some invisible target. After some fifteen or twenty yards straight downfield, he planted his right foot, took one feinting step to his left, immediately planted the left foot, and broke for that corner of the end zone where the small red flag was planted. As he broke, Cobb lofted a high, deep pass downfield.

Hoffer glanced back as Cobb released the ball. Instinctively, the tight end knew where the pass would come down. He extended himself, lengthening and quickening his stride. As he neared the goal line, he knew the pass was too long. He would never be able to get both hands on it. He would be lucky to get one hand on it. He stretched every fiber of his being as far as possible. The tips of the fingers of his right hand made contact with the descending ball. He wiggled it toward his palm. Stumbling, he crossed the goal, the ball firmly, triumphantly held in his right hand. None of those watching had ever witnessed a better effort or a better catch.

The assistants went wild. Bradford kicked the turf and shook his head.

Harris, Ewing, and Koesler approached Bradford.

"Nice catch," Harris understated.

"I don't believe I've seen better." Bradford shook a

full head of unruly salt-and-pepper hair. His accent was an Oklahoma-Texas mix. His permanently tanned face was creased by too much sun and wind.

"Looks like Hoffer could be an adequate substitute for Hunsinger," Harris offered.

"Adequate?" Bradford raised an eyebrow. But for a few extra pounds around the middle, Bradford could have been the image of the classic cowboy. "Adequate?" he repeated. "Better than adequate, I'd say. He's bigger, heavier, faster, and younger. The Hun had a few moves it'll take the kid a couple of years to learn. But he'll learn 'em. 'Sides, most of the Hun's moves lately have been for self-preservation. He was gettin' a bit long in the tooth."

"So why didn't you play Hoffer?"

Bradford's eyes, for one brief moment, lifted to the owner's empty box. "Orders from upstairs."

"Management tells you who to play?" Harris, having judged the coach to be as tough internally as he appeared on the surface, was surprised.

Bradford's sigh spoke volumes regarding long, heated arguments over who had final control over the game itself. "They sign the checks," he commented simply.

"But why? If Hoffer could be better than Hunsinger was?"

"They're convinced the crowd comes to see Hunsinger. Nothin' I could say'd change their minds." He looked sharply at Harris. "Now, don't get me wrong. Hunsinger was plenty good and he was popular, and a great many people did come to see him play. But you can educate fans. They'll turn to sumpin' better if you give 'em a chance."

"Hmph." Harris stored this information with the rest he was gathering. "We'll need to talk to Hoffer and then to Cobb."

Bradford nodded. "I figured you wanted to talk to somebody when I seen you come up the ramp. You got your work to do. I'll cooperate much as I can."

Cobb and Hoffer were standing together surrounded by smiling assistant coaches.

"I think," said Cobb, "I got it figured out now: I throw the goddam ball far as I can and Hoff runs under it and catches it. Man," he cuffed Hoffer playfully on the shoulder, "we got some fine times comin' up. We shall overcome!"

Everyone laughed.

"Hoff!" Bradford called, "these gentlemen wanna talk to you."

Hoffer dropped the prized football to the turf and trotted over. Bradford performed introductions, then left.

Ewing led Hoffer through the questions that were becoming all too familiar to Koesler. Yes, Hoffer was well aware of Hunsinger's compulsions. Even though Hoffer was a rookie with the Cougars, it had taken no time at all to learn to keep clear of Hunsinger's obsessions. And there were lots of them. Hoffer guessed that not only his own team, but everyone in the league talked about Hunsinger's endless routines.

Yes, he was aware that Hunsinger had a sight problem; he wore corrective lenses, didn't he. Nearsightedness, maybe. Hoffer seemed not to be aware of any further vision problem Hunsinger might have had. Just needed glasses.

It was when they reached the subject of Hunsinger's having strychnine in his apartment that Hoffer's information caused the officers to perk up.

"Shoot, yes . . . I knew he had that poison in his apartment. I was with him when he got it."

"Oh? How and where did he get it?"

"Well, it was when we were in Houston for an exhibition game. Well, it wasn't, you know, during the game; it was, like the night before the game. And the Hun took me and Murray—that's our kicker—out to supper."

"Just a minute," Harris interrupted, "why would he do

that? Doesn't the team usually eat together before an out-of-town game?"

"Basically, yes. But different teams, you know, do it different ways. We always eat together the day of the game. But when it's, like, not game day and we're on the road, well, you know, we get expenses."

Funny, thought Koesler, how even fairly well educated college grads took on the contemporary speech patterns so prevalent in pro sports.

"We want to get this straight from the beginning," said Harris. "Why would Hunsinger take you and . . . uh . . . Murray to dinner? Did he take you often? Were you especially close to him?"

Hoffer snorted. "I don't rightly think you could call us close. Basically, I think he wanted to, like, dominate the people on this team. And he'd, you know, start with the rookies. The night we were in Houston, I think he maybe wanted to introduce me and Murray to, like, the world of booze.

"We went to La Reserve, which they tell me is like the best restaurant in Houston. The Hun had the money. No doubt about that. Well, from the time we sat down and all through the meal, the Hun kept ordering whiskey neat—no ice, no water; just, you know, whiskey. He put 'em down one after the other. And poor Murray matched him drink for drink."

"And you?"

"I been there. I knew what that booze would, you know, do. After a couple, I just turned 'em down. The Hun could hold booze by the quart. So he was okay the next day for the game. Poor Murray was sick as a dog. But the Hun pulled him through for the game. Got him kind of sobered up. Threatened him if he should so much as, you know, york on the field . . . made him very dependent, you know . . . just like he wanted." Hoffer shook his head. "That's the way the Hun was."

"The strychnine?" Harris pressed.

"Oh, yeah, I was just, like, comin' to that. Toward the end of the meal, when Murray was about to slip under the table, along comes this dude—I've seen enough of them in Dallas: plenty of hat and plenty of cattle. Well, this guy sits down at the empty chair at our table. He didn't have any, you know, trouble finding us. The Hun and me were bigger by several times'n anybody else in the place. Then the guy recognized the Hun.

"You know how it is, Lieutenant, with some people: they just want to be seen with football players. Basically, they want to go back to work and say, like, 'I had a few drinks with the Hun Saturday night.' That's the way it was with this dude."

"And how did this go over with Hunsinger?"

"It coulda gone either way. The Hun coulda knocked the dude on his ass. But, by then, you know, Hun was feelin' no pain. So he takes the dude in like a long-lost buddy. Even buys him a drink. God, Lieutenant, you'da thought the dude had died and gone to heaven.

"Next thing I know, the Hun is tellin' this guy about his swank apartment in Detroit. The dude is, like, lappin' it all up. But, Hun says, the only problem with this apartment is it's got rats. 'Can you imagine that?' says Hun. 'Payin' all that money and havin' to put up with rats!'

"'Funny thing,' says this dude. He happens to be, like, I think he said, something like a county agent for the state Department of Agriculture. He handles this poison that is just made for rodents: strychnine. Gets it from someplace in New York. Comes as some sorta chemical compound. They turn it into liquid form, pour it on bait, use it for, like, ground squirrels. Promised he would send the Hun some.

"Basically, Lieutenant, that's how he got it: from some dude in Texas who could handle it legally."

The interrogation was drawing to a close. No, Hoffer could not say for sure who else knew the strychnine was in the apartment. But he was pretty sure the others in the discussion group knew. As he recalled, Hunsinger had mentioned it once when they met at his apartment.

"One final thing," said Ewing, "can you account for your time yesterday? Don't leave any large unverifiable gaps, if you can help it."

Did they imagine it, or did Hoffer seem to blanch? "Well, basically, I'm gonna have to start with a gap. See, I, like, got up about six-thirty. I tried not to wake my wife, and I don't think I did. Then, after I got ready, I stopped off at church for a while, to, like, pray for good luck in the game."

"You went to St. Anselm's?" Ewing asked. He glanced at Koesler, who seemed surprised.

Hoffer nodded

"What time was that?"

"It was about seven."

"But, Kit," said Koesler, "we don't have early Mass until eight o'clock."

"I know, Father, but the janitor opens the church just before seven. And I stopped in just to pray for good luck."

"Did anyone see you there?"

"Afraid not. Wasn't anybody around that early. The janitor just opens up and leaves."

"He goes on his rounds checking all the other buildings," Koesler corroborated.

"So then what happened?" asked Ewing.

"Well, after I got done praying, I left for the Pontiac Inn. But I misjudged the timing. I got there about eight-thirty, quarter to nine. I got the hell bawled out of me and, like, I woulda got it worse except Bobby Cobb was late too. He didn't arrive until a little after nine. And he woulda got it worse than he did 'cept he's one of the team's pheenoms."

"How about the rest of your day?"

"Well, there was the meal and taping and trip to the stadium and the game with the rest of the team and all. Then, you know, after the game I went with my wife to dinner with some friends. Then, like, the wife and I went home."

"But there's no one to attest for your time until eight-thirty or eight-forty-five. Which means you got to the hotel up to forty-five minutes after the rest of the team, after Hunsinger."

"Excepting for Bobby Cobb."

"Except Cobb."

"That's about it, Lieutenant."

"One more thing," Harris added. "Hunsinger's death, it sort of opens the way for you, doesn't it?"

Hoffer lowered his head. "Lieutenant, it's a cryin' shame that the Hun is, you know, dead. And I'm sorry it happened. But I guess you'd have to say that I, like, got lucky for a change."

They advised Hoffer there would probably be more questions, then left to locate Cobb. If nothing else on the surface made Hunsinger's death of interest to Cobb, there was that hour's tardiness that might prove interesting.

As they walked down the tunnel toward the Cougars' locker room, Koesler said, "That's odd, Kit stopping in church the morning of the game."

"What's odd about it, Father?" Ewing asked.

"Just that Kit and his wife were at the four-thirty afternoon Mass on Saturday. That satisfied his obligation to attend church on Sunday. Catholics, generally can be depended on to attend Mass once on the weekend. And that generally is about how often they are involved in formal prayer of petition. I would expect Kit to pray for victory and survival when he attended Mass on Saturday. I wouldn't expect him to repeat the process the next day, just because it was Sunday."

"Are you sure he was there Saturday afternoon?" Harris asked.

Koesler chuckled. "I'd have to be blind to miss that hulk in church."

That Koznicki and his hunches, Harris thought approvingly; having Koesler along is cutting neat corners on this investigation.

On June 11, 1963, Governor George Wallace stood in the doorway of the University of Alabama, attempting to bar two black students from registering. Governor Wallace proved himself no prophet by promising, "Segregation Forever! Integration Never!"

Years later, the Reverend Jesse Jackson, urging blacks to make optimal use of educational opportunities, and in allusion to Mr. Wallace's symbolic blockade, observed, "Nobody is standing in the schoolhouse door now."

Quite independently of the Reverend Mr. Jackson's observation, Robert Leland Cobb spontaneously reached the same conclusion.

Born in 1956 in Kalamazoo, Michigan, Cobb grew up in that city. His father taught English in Kalamazoo High. His mother was a homemaker. He was an only child.

From the beginning of his conscious life, he was essentially an introvert. As early as possible, his parents introduced him to the joys of reading. He took to literature quite naturally and readily. His love of reading, together with a contemplative bent, prompted him to measure his world with precocious maturity.

It did not take him long to experience and learn what it meant to be black in an essentially white town. For a small city, Kalamazoo was heavy with institutions of higher learning: Nazareth College, Kalamazoo College, Western Michigan University. There were an unusual number of hospitals and schools of nursing. It was almost literally worth one's life to find a mere general practitioner; most medical doctors were specialists. The UpJohn Company was so objectively large and significant it was practically the only game in town.

When little Bobby Cobb first understood the significance of being black-skinned, he was uncertain what to do about it. This deferral of judgment set a pattern in his life. Seldom would he act precipitately.

Although neither of his parents was particularly large, Bobby gave every promise of becoming a giant of a man. His father could trace this promising physical development to his paternal grandfather, a onetime slave whose feats of strength were storied.

In keeping with his father's respected position in the community, Bobby's family lived in the comfortable northwest section of Kalamazoo. They were about the only blacks living in that area.

Bobby observed that as time passed and he grew to be so much larger and stronger than his friends and schoolmates, he became more accepted. Even those with racist tendencies treated him with a certain civility, even deference. It did not much matter to Bobby that their attitude might spring from fear. In any case, Bobby's polite articulateness won him acceptance in the homes of his white friends.

Jackie Robinson's years as major league baseball's first black player were gone long before Bobby's time. But, unlike so many of his contemporaries who knew nothing of what had preceded them, Bobby learned everything he could about Robinson, and also about Paul Robeson, the black athlete who had earned letters and a law degree at Rutgers and had gone on to electrify the world as singer, actor, and activist.

Cobb was good at sports, very good. And he would get better. If he applied himself assiduously, he could become a professional athlete, probably in the football arena. At that point, he could do as many of his brothers had: carve out an athletic career and have nothing to turn to when age put him on the shelf. But no, that would not be for Bobby; he lived, and would live, in a white man's world. And no amount of blackspeak or adopting of African names would change that fact.

His athletic ability easily would win him a scholarship

to most any university of his choice. Under normal circumstances, that would be Western Michigan. He studied that option. Only one athlete from WMU had made it big: Charlie Maxwell, nicknamed Ol' Paw Paw after the western Michigan town that was Maxwell's point of origin. Maxwell had played baseball for a number of years for the Detroit Tigers. His career was marked by penchants for hitting home runs on Sundays and hustling back to the dugout after strikeouts. No, not WMU. Scouts would have to dig to find him there. And nothing must be left to chance.

He settled on Michigan State University. It had a big-time football program. But not so big that one could not be serious about one's academic life. And Bobby did intend to be serious. He would be an attorney. And he would be one in the white man's enclave. The white man's world would be his field of combat. He would be articulate, well-educated, cultured, poised, cool, and armed with a well-publicized sports portfolio.

He was already handsome in a white context, with caucasoid features and chocolate-colored skin—evocative of a king-sized Harry Belafonte.

And that caused a problem which demanded the careful planning that was becoming his general modus operandi.

During Bobby's teens and young adult years, in both college towns of Kalamazoo and East Lansing, consciousness-raising became very popular. Racist as well as sexist attitudes were roundly condemned, especially by high school and university students. But not infrequently an opposite swing of the pendulum would occur. Not only were racial disparities downplayed, but there was a mindset group of white females whose objective it was to merge with black men.

This, Bobby promised himself, would not happen to him. The quantity and at times superior quality of young white women students who plainly made themselves available to him were tempting, most tempting. But giving in to that temptation was not a part of his plan. The stratum of white society he would be a part of was not altogether prepared to accept miscegenation. So, neither was he.

Things went pretty much as planned. There were few surprises in Bobby Cobb's life. And when an occurrence extraneous to his plan threatened to upset his modus vivendi, he always managed to bring things to order expeditiously.

He was an All-Everything in high school football. Most of the major colleges had heard about him, even though he came from little Kalamazoo. Feelers came in from as far away as Florida and California. He chose Michigan State, as he had planned long before MSU recruited him. He continued to develop both mind and body. He was cordial to, but stayed clear of, white coeds. He first dated, then courted, a gorgeous girl whose complexion was soft chocolate like his. They made a fine-looking couple. He knew the white world he would enter would accept the two of them unreservedly.

From his sophomore through his senior year he quarterbacked a football team whose success depended, in large part, on his excellence. He graduated cum laude and was drafted by the Cougars in the first round. He married his college fiancée. He was counseled to take no more than one semester a year in his postgrad march toward a legal degree. That way neither the demands of law school nor those of professional football would be too taxing.

Now he was in his seventh season with the Cougars and only a few short months away from taking the bar examination. His marriage was a success. He had two rather perfect children, a boy and a girl.

His program was right on schedule. There was but one fly in the ointment. Hunsinger.

It was part of Bobby Cobb's plan that he be Numero Uno with the Cougars—the star attraction. It would not do to court the most illustrious law firm in Detroit unless one were indisputably the most prestigious candidate in applying for entry into the partnership. And that prestige must be across the board, in studies as well as professional accomplishment.

As it turned out, he was Numero Dos. Hunsinger always managed to get a tad more publicity. He was good copy, mainly because he was flamboyant. He could afford to be; he was not seeking the buttondown life of a corporation lawyer. He wasn't searching for anything but pleasure, security, and fame, in that order.

Worst of all, Hunsinger didn't deserve the publicity he received. He was beginning to go over the hill. He wouldn't even be getting in all that playing time were it not for those jackasses in management who assumed the capacity crowds were coming primarily to see Hunsinger in action.

Another part of Cobb's plan was that the team he represented be of championship caliber. Nothing but the best for the area's top law firm.

In Cobb's eyes, for some reason, Hunsinger seemed to try his best to ruin the careers of his teammates—introducing the younger members to booze, breaking curfews, entertaining playmates, and flirting with drugs, including cocaine, and stopping just short of heroin.

For six full seasons Cobb had tried to neutralize Hunsinger. For six seasons Cobb had made little headway. In fact, it appeared to Bobby Cobb that Hunsinger's popularity and his influence upon the Cougars were stronger than ever.

Hunsinger stood directly in the path of Bobby Cobb's carefully laid plans.

Something would have to be done.

"Where did everybody go?" Ewing asked of the assistant trainer, the only person in the locker room.

"Oh, they're probably in the projection room."

"Bobby Cobb in there?"

"Uh-huh."

"Get him for us, will you?"

"Sure."

The assistant trainer did not need to ask who the two plainclothes detectives were, nor who the priest was, nor why they were at the Silverdome. Word had gotten around.

Moments later, Cobb entered the locker room. He wore cutoff jeans and a T-shirt. Koesler marveled, as he had many times this day while viewing partially clad pro football players, at the muscle tone. It was as if a Renaissance sculptor had chiseled out an entire team. None of them seemed to have a neck. Massive shoulders sloped gracefully into a head. It made him wonder about the cartoon Father McNiff had described wherein the lady explained to her companion that the football players were wearing falsies. Up close and in person it was obvious that, except for protection, the players needed no padding.

Ewing greeted Cobb. "Sorry to have to disturb you."

"No sweat. You just saved me from suffering through yesterday's game again. Watching us fumble it away. They were just getting to Hunsinger's fight. Come to think of it, that's the last film of the Hun in action."

Koesler was unable to tell whether there was a touch of relief, remorse, or just thoughtfulness in Cobb's tone.

"How can I help you?" Cobb asked.

"Just a few questions. We're trying to get to know a bit more about Hunsinger and some of the people around him. What kind of man was he?" Ewing asked.

Cobb smiled. "That's a big order."

"I mean, did he have any eccentricities?"

"Eccentricities? What pops to mind immediately were those weird routines—compulsions, I guess you'd call them. Used to drive me nuts watching them."

"Many of them?"

"Oh, yeah, let me count the ways. Shoelaces had to lie flat against his shoes. Going on or off the field he would run by the right side of the goalpost only. First step up the stairs had to be with the left foot. Before going into a game the first time he'd have somebody slap his shoulder pads exactly three times. The long white sleeve of the sweatshirt we wear under our jerseys always had to be visible. He always sat in the last row of the plane—claimed it was safer . . . shall I go on!"

Ewing smiled. "You watched him pretty closely."

"Couldn't help it. Fascinating. Besides, it wasn't boring. Every so often he'd come up with something new to add to the list."

"How about showers?"

"Showers? You mean the way he showered? Never noticed. I'm usually last in the shower and last out of the stadium."

"Not the quality, the quantity."

"Quantity? Oh, you must mean the double showers." Cobb grinned. "The Hun led an . . . uh . . . an active social life. He wanted to . . . uh . . . smell nice for the ladies. So, particularly after a game and the crowd in here and the TV lights, he figured he needed more help than he got here in the locker room."

"Was this common knowledge? I mean, it sounds kind of personal."

"Yeah, well, you see, a team gets closer, maybe, than any other group. We get to depend on each other. So we get to know a bit more about each other than you might expect. Besides, there are those who prefer to keep some personal secrets and those who like to brag. The Hun was a talker."

"Were you aware," Harris took over, "that Hunsinger had a vision problem?"

Both officers studied Cobb's reaction to the question. They detected nothing out of the ordinary.

"Shit, yes—sorry, Father—I mean, I used to spend enough time on my hands and knees down on the turf looking for his damn contacts. That was before he got the soft lenses. The hard lenses used to pop out a lot."

"Again, common knowledge?"

"The team almost took up a collection so he would get the soft lenses. We all spent time lookin' for his lenses."

"Were you aware Hunsinger kept a strong poison at his apartment?"

"You mean the strychnine. Sure. Like I said, the Hun was a talker. He blurted it out when we had a meeting of the discussion group at his place."

The sound of many male voices talking loudly and simultaneously interrupted the interrogation. The team had finished viewing the films of yesterday's game. Now they filed through the locker room.

"Show's over," Cobb observed. "Are we just about done?"

"Just about. What happens now with the team?"

"The coaches'll run us for a while . . . just to loosen up after yesterday's battering."

"One last question then," said Harris. "Can you account for your time yesterday?"

"Let's see..." Cobb nibbled on a knuckle. "I got up about seven, kind of overslept and then started running behind."

"You were late getting to the Pontiac Inn," Harris stated.

Cobb looked at him sharply. "Yeah, that's right."

"How late?"

"Forty-five minutes, maybe an hour."

"Isn't that kind of late for rising at seven? The brunch meeting didn't begin till eight."

"I had a flat on the way to the stadium."

Harris looked skeptical. "Did you call anyone? Triple-A?"

Cobb shook his head. "Happened at an empty stretch of I-75."

"Anybody stop to help you?"

Again he shook his head. "Ever see I-75 early on a Sunday morning?"

"Was your family awake before you left for the stadium?"

"No. They usually sleep in till about ten."

"So no one would be able to attest to your whereabouts until you arrived at the inn at eight-forty-five or nine?"

"What are you getting at?" Almost from the beginning of this interrogation, Cobb had understood its purpose. Now that the intent had become so obvious, he thought it best to get the cards on the table.

"Nothing, Bobby." Ewing was conciliatory. "But Hank Hunsinger is dead and we have to find a murderer. And to do that, we've got to ask questions. As, for example, what does Hunsinger's death mean to you?"

Cobb glanced pointedly at Harris and hesitated, as if refusing to answer any more questions. But finally he spoke. "Nothing. Hun's death means nothing to me. By a series of coincidences we happened to be on the same team. That was the end of it. No, I'll take that back: You saw it for yourselves up there," he gestured toward the field. "I'll be throwing to a better player. And if you want to know whether I knew Hoffer was that good, the answer is no. I've had practically no time with him since he joined the club this season.

"Now, is there anything more?"

"Not now, Bobby. We may want to talk to you again," said Ewing in parting.

Cobb lightly jogged out of the locker room and headed up the ramp to join his teammates in their running exercises.

"That's a lot of time unaccounted for at the beginning of his day yesterday, isn't it?" Koesler asked.

"Yup," said Ewing. "Since Hunsinger arrived at the inn on time, he would have had to leave his apartment by about seven. If Cobb went there, he could have gotten there anytime between, say, seven and eight, and still have had plenty of time to get out to the inn by nine. It would take only seconds to switch containers and pour the strychnine into the DMSO." Ewing paused and reflected.

"But have you noticed?" Ewing continued. "So far, everyone we've talked to has an unaccounted-for gap in yesterday's schedule. And in each case, the missing time is sufficient for the person to have gone to Hunsinger's apartment and made the switch."

Harris shrugged. "Sometimes you can't raise a suspect. And sometimes there's too many."

"Who's next?" asked Ewing.

"We'd better grab that kicker before he gets away. But first, I want to call headquarters."

While Harris was gone, Koesler studied the locker room. Just a series of open wire cages, each containing a set of shoulder pads on a shelf topped by a helmet. Wide open. No privacy. He could imagine Cobb studying Hunsinger indulging in one obsessive compulsion after another. It would be hard to hide anything in this setting. Not that Hunsinger had tried to hide anything, from all they'd been told. Perhaps he should have tried to be more secretive.

Harris returned. "There are prints all over the apartment. But then a lot of people had been there lately. However, only Hunsinger's prints on both shampoo and DMSO containers. And another thing. Hunsinger's latest girlfriend, that Jan Taylor who found his body. Jackson checked her out. She's got a roommate who testifies that they were together all day Sunday until Taylor left to join Hunsinger. The timing checks out. She's clean."

"It figures," Ewing commented, then turned to Koesler and smiled. "Father, you're not holding up your end."

"What's that?"

"Praying for success."

They offered him a contract guaranteeing a salary of $35,000 and containing a health-care package and little else. He thought he'd died and gone to heaven. Of course, it meant that he might never return to Dunderry, at least not to work there. That was the best part.

Dunderry was an estate of approximately a hundred acres. It had been taken from its native Irish owners in 1573 and settled by a transplanted English landlord. Though the property had been passed down through generations of the Birmingham family, the present Georgian mansion had not been built until the late nineteenth century.

At about the time of the official establishment of the Republic of Ireland in 1949, the then Lord Birmingham lost interest in Dunderry. He became an absentee landlord. The Murray family became his tenants.

The Murrays came from Gurteen, less than ten miles south of Ballymote. Dunderry stood at the outskirts of Ballymote. Both Gurteen and Ballymote were in County Sligo.

Three of the seven Murray brothers pooled all their resources and entered into a mortgage on Dunderry, much to the relief of Lord Birmingham. The Murray brothers moved their considerable families into Dunderry. Space was not a problem; the mansion was huge.

The Murray plan was to make of Dunderry a sheep farm. The secondary plan was to make of the mansion a bed-and-breakfast establishment. The combined plans put food on the table. And that was about all it did. That the sheep were sheared, the once magnificent gardens maintained at least to a minimal degree, and the occasional overnight guests satisfied was a tribute to the industriousness of the Murray families and all their many children.

Into the large family, in 1965, was born Niall, fourth son and seventh child of Liam and Meg Murray.

Niall learned the rudiments of farm life not long after he learned to walk. He was given responsibility for a list of chores as soon as he was physically able to carry them out. The list of chores grew right along with Niall. As a side effect of all this work, Niall was building a strong body. He would not become a huge adult, but he would be hard packed, with sinewy power.

At the age of only four, he began his formal education at Ballymote National School. Discipline was rigid, obedience and performance expected. Although it had been years since physical punishment had been banned in schools, that did not preclude a cuff on the ear from time to time. Teachers guilty of sporadic hitting had little fear that the punishment would be reported. Pupils quickly learned that the blow suffered in school, if reported at home, most likely would be repeated there.

At age fourteen, Niall attended St. Nathy's College in Ballaghadreen. St. Nathy's was the equivalent of high school in the States. A Catholic boys' school with a priest as dean and a faculty comprising clerics and laity. If anything, the discipline and demands were far more intense than at Ballymote National.

There were times during Niall's four years at St. Nathy's that he was invited to friends' homes. At some of these visits, he learned that Dunderry was a mansion in name only. The experience was akin to that of one who grows up in poverty, not desperate poverty, but poor nonetheless. As long as everyone in his milieu lives in roughly the same circumstances, the boy is unaware that he lives in what others would term poverty.

Niall, in his visits to some Ballaghadreen homes, discovered that not everyone lived with sheep; that outer clothing does not have to carry an animal odor; that toilets, even though indoor, need not appear to be the outdoor variety; that multiple consanguine families need not live together; that every able-bodied person in a home need not work at every conceivable moment.

He was by no means the only one in the Murray clan to learn these facts. But as he assimilated them, some unpredictable inner conviction was formed. He would escape. He would flee the inheritance of Dunderry. There was a better life out there, and he would have it.

But how?

One possible avenue was the natural progression, taken by many of his predecessor classmates, from St. Nathy's to Maynooth. St. Nathy's, as a Catholic school, was a feeder to the seminary. Many's the lad who had been force-fed a liberal arts curriculum featuring Latin; been an altar server over many years; been exposed to the example of so many clerical professors; then matriculated at Maynooth to pursue studies that might lead to the priesthood. For many Catholic students in Ireland, the progression was as natural as going from third to fourth grade.

But that was not for Niall. He'd had a belly full of discipline, starting with his earliest memories at Dunderry, then St. Nathy's. Spending his adult life curtsying to some bishop hardly described an escape for Niall.

Besides, he wanted to get as far from Dunderry as possible. He felt that if he remained in Ireland, Dunderry would get him in much the same way a vortex sucks under a drowning person. His future lay in the States. He was sure of it. There, in the land of the free, his horizons would be limited only by his talents and his ambition.

Of course, it was possible to get to the States through Maynooth. For many years, a goodly number of Irish priests had been imported to the States, technically excardinated by their Irish bishops and incardinated by American bishops. The trend was particularly strong throughout Florida. In Florida the imports were called by the local clergy, FBIs. Foreign-Born Irish. The term was used pejoratively.

Again, Niall had no intention of trading obedience owed an Irish bishop for that owed an American Irish bishop.

He was aware of the Irish Clergy Connection because he made himself aware of every possible shred of news about what went on in America. He read all the American literature and journals he could find. And when he chanced upon any potential avenue of entry to the States, he zeroed in on it.

Thus it was that Niall learned that there had been a blend of sorts between distinctive United States and European sports. Football—American, not Irish—rivaled baseball as America's favorite sport. Niall took special note of and interest in the phenomenon of soccer-type kickers, many of European origin, becoming specialists in attempting field goals and extra points for American football teams.

Why not? He'd played a lot of Irish football. He was a strong young man. And, in remote preparation for such an event, he'd gotten a mail-ordered American football and kicking tee. On one of the seldom used fields of Dunderry, he'd set up regulation-sized goalposts. As often as possible, he would cajole or bribe one or another of his brothers or sisters to shag the ball. For him, practice made not only permanent, but near perfect. Repeatedly, he would split the uprights from distances approved by American standards.

Then, as if fate had ordained it, he read that the Pontiac Cougars, before each training season, staged a sort of open house for amateur athletes to try out for their team.

The open tryout was the brainchild of owner Jay Galloway. His intention was twofold: to whip up more local interest in the Cougars; and, on the off chance that some genius talent might be uncovered, to sign that talent to a minimum contract.

Niall could not know Galloway's intent. Nor would he have cared had he known. The opportunity seemed perfect—God-sent, in fact.

Despite warnings and dark prophecies from family and friends, he spent nearly every pence he'd saved and purchased a plane ticket to Michigan. He promised his fiancée, Moira, whom he'd been courting these two years since graduating from St. Nathy's, that he'd send for her as soon as he'd made good with the Cougars. She alone believed in him.

It happened. The Cougars coaches, who usually daydreamed through these ragtag tryouts, scarcely could believe their eyes. This Niall Murray—not a potbellied, overstuffed, noncoordinated dreamer—was a trim, powerful, natural athlete.

At first, the coaches were content to watch him put kick after kick through the crossbars from the 10-yard line, about the distance of a PAT. Then they began moving him farther and farther from the goalposts, adding difficult angles to the increasing distance. Rarely did he miss.

Few of the coaches could recall, in their experience, anyone like him.

The assistant coaches fetched head coach Bradford, who generally retreated to his office during these tedious tryouts. He, of course, agreed wholeheartedly with the others. Altogether, they treated Murray like a piece of rare Waterford. They got him a good room in a good motel and made sure he had sufficient money for expenses.

The coaches immediately found general manager Dave Whitman, who informed owner Jay Galloway that a rough-cut diamond was all but signed. Then, before anyone could say "agent," Niall Murray was under contract to the Cougars.

It did not matter to Niall that he would be the lowest paid Cougar, nor that he would be among the lowest salaried players in the league—$35,000 to Niall was as good as a million. It got him off Dunderry and out of Ireland. Forthwith he sent for Moira Malloy.

Hank Hunsinger arranged for their wedding at Holy Redeemer after the Hun's mother pulled a few strings with the good Redemptorist Fathers. Hunsinger also arranged Niall's bachelor party, at which the Hun introduced him to marijuana.

Niall could not quite fathom why he had been singled out for special attention by Hunsinger. The other Cougars treated him like an alien at best and a toy at worst. Some mocked his brogue, others taped him to the goalpost. But as time passed and his consistently excellent performance exhibited itself, his teammates had to acknowledge that the Mick would be winning games and helping them make more money. Now Niall was unreservedly accepted into their company.

From the very outset Hunsinger had accepted him. Actually, more adopted than accepted. And, correspondingly, Murray had become dependent on Hunsinger. After a while this dependency became apparent even to Niall. However, since, from his first days with the Cougars, he had accepted an enormous amount of help from Hunsinger, Murray could find no way of terminating his dependency.

And as long as this dependency continued, Murray felt himself drifting further and further from his goals. He wanted to be superior at his job as a place kicker for the Cougars, make an escalating amount of money, and secure a future for himself, his wife, and the family they would have. Meanwhile, the Hun continued repeatedly to try to lead him into chemical dependency and infidelity.

He decided his relationship with Hunsinger was one of aversion-attraction. Niall was truly grateful for all the Hun had done in the beginning, even though the ill-intentioned basis was becoming apparent. Niall acknowledged to himself that somehow he must free himself from the harmful hold Hunsinger had on him.

There was no doubt in Niall's mind that he would have to do something. The only question was how far he would have to go.

Around and around the track circuiting the playing field the team jogged. Koesler watched, fascinated. These finely conditioned athletes ran so effortlessly. They were running ostensibly to loosen up from the aftereffects of yesterday's game. Some needed more than others.

Lieutenant Harris informed one of the coaches that Niall Murray was wanted for interrogation. As Murray neared the group, the coach waved him out of the drill.

"It's grateful I am to you for that." Murray toweled his head as he stood with Harris, Ewing, and Koesler.

Introductions were made and explanations given, specifically for Koesler's presence. The introductions and explanations were becoming less and less necessary. Word of the interrogations, their purpose and scope, was circulating throughout the team.

Yes, Murray was well aware of Hunsinger's compulsive behavior; wasn't everyone? Niall also knew of the Hun's astigmatism and nearsightedness. Team members by and large were aware that Hunsinger kept some sort of device in the training room for cleaning, or "cooking," his contact lenses after practice. Only after practice? Then did Murray know what Hunsinger's postgame routine was? Of course. He took a cursory shower here and then went back to his apartment where he took care of his lenses, showered again, and prepared for the Big Evening. Everyone knew that.

"Were you aware of anything else being wrong with Hunsinger's vision?" Ewing asked. "I mean, besides the astigmatism and nearsightedness?"

"Oh, then, you must mean that the poor man was colorblind."

Murray's unequivocal delivery of this unexpected answer stunned the officers and Koesler.

Harris recovered first. "How did you happen to know that Hunsinger was colorblind?"

"It came out of a night when we were, as they say, hoistin' a few. For once, I used the brains I was born with and let the Hun get well ahead of me with the creature, and the poor man was after running off at the mouth about the bad tricks fate had played on him. Among them was the fact that he was colorblind. But once it was out and the Hun realized what he'd said, he swore me to secrecy . . . I don't suppose it matters anymore now, does it?"

"As a matter of fact," said Ewing, "it does. Very much. Have you told anyone else?"

"Oh, I did not; certainly not! It was a secret! I told no one. I just thought . . . now that he's dead—"

"No, no. It is terribly important that you continue to keep this to yourself." Harris was unsure how most effectively to extend the embargo on the knowledge of Hunsinger's colorblindness. He decided to tread lightly; Murray seemed likely to react better to trust than to threats. "We can't reveal the reason for this secrecy just yet. But it is most important to our investigation that you go right on keeping it a secret."

Murray nodded, as if he had turned a key in his brain. The Hun's secret defect would remain unrevealed by him.

"One final thing," said Ewing, "can you tell us what you did yesterday?"

"Ummm . . . I can. I think. Let's see; we got up about half-five; went to six o'clock Mass. It's over by seven . . . no sermon, ya know. Too early. Left home about quarter past seven. Got to the inn just at eight. Had the pregame meal. Got taped up. Attended the special team's meeting. Then it was out to the stadium. Got suited up. Then there was the warmups and the game."

"And after the game?" Ewing had not bargained on such detail.

Murray blushed slightly. "Well, then, I shoulda gone straight home. But I didn't . . ."

"Oh?"

"Some of the lads convinced me we all needed some—what did they call it?—comin' down from a high. So they took me to this party in Grosse Pointe. And I'm afraid I had a mite too much to drink." He decided to omit the girl and the cocaine. After all, they had not passed the stage of being temptations, and he hadn't actually used either one. "But then, before I did anything more foolish,

Bobby Cobb came by and took me home where the wife got in her licks as well."

Ewing looked up. He'd been taking notes. "That pretty well covers the whole day, doesn't it?"

"That's what you asked for, wasn't it?" Murray seemed embarrassed, as if he had revealed more than was required. "You wanted to know what it was I did yesterday, did you not?"

"Yes, that's right," said Ewing. "That's what we wanted to know."

"Will that be all then?" Murray had worked up a sweat while running and wanted to take a shower before catching a chill.

Ewing dismissed him with an admonition to remain available for further questioning.

Murray trotted down the incline toward the locker room. Hindsight told him, especially now that the Hun was dead, that all his suspicions about his relationship with Hunsinger had been accurate. Even that bit of advice the Hun had given before the field goal in yesterday's game. Murray had been bothered on and off since then, wondering whether it might be a sin to think of doing it with your wife without actually doing it. He thought he'd ask some priest. He was pretty sure what the priests back home would say. But the priests over here appeared to be more liberal. Maybe he'd get a chance to ask that Father Koesler. He seemed to be the sort of priest you could trust.

"How about that!" said Ewing. "The only one so far who admits he knew Hunsinger was colorblind . . . and he's got an alibi for all day."

"Do you take his word for it?" Koesler asked.

Ewing smiled. "Oh, no. Not any of them. We're just gathering statements. Then we'll check each one's story. Somewhere in this crowd is the murderer. And the murderer will lie. He—or she—has to. But we'll break it down and get whoever it is."

"We'd better get to the trainer before he closes shop for the day," said Harris.

"Right you are."

The three men walked toward the locker room. There was an eerie stillness in the huge, empty stadium. Koesler was relieved to leave it.

It wasn't fair. It just wasn't fair. That was all the boy could think.

His father agreed, but that was not his only thought.

The doctor had just been in the boy's room and delivered the prognosis. The boy had a heart murmur so pronounced and so potentially threatening that there could be no thought of strenuous exercise in his future.

That was what was not fair. Young Jack Brown had been destined for a life of sports stardom. Everyone agreed on that. His father had pushed him along that trail from preschool days. When Jack reached the fourth grade, he was already bigger and stronger than his classmates. By bending a few rules, he played on the seventh- and eighth-grade extramural athletic teams from the time he was a sixth grader. By the time he was in the eighth grade, a Dallas high school coach thought enough of Jack's ability that the coach moved the Brown family into his school district so that Jack could play there.

Then, during summer vacation between sophomore and junior years, he was stricken with polio. In 1944 many who contracted polio died. So young Jack Brown was extremely fortunate to be alive. That was the thought uppermost in his father's mind.

Yes, it was not fair that such a budding athletic career should be ruined by a chance exposure to that dread disease. At the same time, they were lucky to have Jack still with them.

In due time, Jack was released from the hospital and returned to his school. Not long after the scholastic year began, football practice commenced. Jack could do no more than stand on the sidelines and watch his former teammates go through the drills. It hurt. But by then, he had pretty well adjusted to a life without the heady joy and challenge of athletic competition. He had no idea what he would do with that life.

The coach had a difficult time concentrating on practices with his best player reduced to a spectator. One day he asked Jack if he would accept the position of team manager. After talking the offer over with his parents, Jack took on the job. At least it would keep him close to the sports he loved.

There had never before been a team manager for this south Dallas school. So the job became defined as Jack performed it. He took care of the equipment, brought drinks onto the field, applied iodine and calamine lotion, and made some bandages. There was a scarcity of tape because of the war.

It was the beginning of a new career. Jack was awarded a partial scholarship at the University of Houston to act as assistant trainee in the university's sports program. In 1951 he graduated with a degree in physical science.

Finding a job as a professional trainer was a larger problem than Jack had anticipated. He might not have caught on anywhere had it not been for a few Texas coaches and trainers—friends of Jack's—and their interest in and intercession for him. But through them and their sports contacts, Jack uncovered several promising leads. Nothing outstanding, mind; after all, he was just a fresh college grad with no professional experience.

Interviews with some Canadian football teams proved largely unproductive. Some offers were made, but the money was always less than he needed for sustenance as well as to satisfy debts he had incurred while attending college.

Finally, he was hired as an assistant trainer for the New York Rangers hockey club. It was a sport with which he was largely unfamiliar, but hockey players needed conditioning and incurred injuries just as did football players. Hockey players, since they were on skates, did not hit, clutch, and hold each other as violently as did footballers, but there were the boards around the rink into which the skaters were regularly slammed. And in those days, players did not wear the helmets and masks popular today. Pucks traveling around a hundred miles per hour wreaked their own special damage on exposed heads and teeth.

It was while Jack was with the Rangers that he met and grew to admire Gordie Howe, the durable and memorable winger of the Detroit Red Wings.

It was also while in New York that Jack met several of the better boxing trainers, known more popularly as corner men. New York then was the world capital of prizefighting. Some of the trainers were generous enough to teach Jack how they taped their fighters' hands; how to get the protection where it was needed without cutting off circulation or restricting movement; how to slip the strips between the fingers. From that time, Jack's football players would have their hands taped after the fashion of prizefighters.

After serving his apprenticeship with the Rangers, Jack was hired by Ball State University through the good auspices of then assistant coach Buck Bradford, who had followed Jack's career from his high school days. Bradford, who had great confidence in Jack's ability, integrity, and understanding of athletes, took him along as Bradford became head coach at Texas A & M, then Oklahoma, and now the Cougars.

Jack Brown watched his profession evolve over the years he practiced it. In his early days, it was carrying water and fixing bandages over cuts. Then it moved on to ice packs, towels, hot packs, and massages. Trainers were expected to acquire something of a pharmacist's expertise in pills and linament.

Then came the National Athletic Trainers Association and its board of certification. At one time, the title, Certified Athletic Trainer, was, in an exercise of cronyism, passed on to a very few veteran male athletic trainers. Now, the initials AT,C after one's name were highly sought after and awarded only after long and demanding scholarly study and practice.

Those associated with Jack Brown professionally knew that he admirably fulfilled the responsibilities of an up-to-date athletic trainer, whose functions were to prevent athletic trauma and treat any conditions that might adversely affect the health or performance of an athlete. Such functions included management—first aid, evaluation, treatment, and rehabilitation—of athletic trauma or other medical problems that affected the athlete, as well as counseling the athlete in such health-related areas as nutrition, relaxation, and tension-control and personal health habits.

Trainers were expected to be able to manage and operate such therapeutic agencies and procedures as hydrocollator, hydrotherapy, dinthermy, ultrasound, cryotherapy, cryokinetics, contrast bath, paraffin bath, and infrared, manipulative, and ultraviolet therapy.

In short, Jack Brown exemplified the modern athletic trainer who has made the long journey from water-bucket brigade to just this side of a medical degree.

But of all the expertise he had acquired in his years as trainer, that of which he was most proud was, oddly, taping. No mean skill, it involved not only the routine taping of ankles—required even for practices—but the building of castlike pads, made of fiber glass, covered with a protective layer of foam rubber and held together with tape.

Like most trainers, Brown was dedicated to his players, to their conditioning and rehabilitation. He could never forget the disease that had robbed him of a playing career and from which, for him, there had been no rehabilitation. He found no greater joy than to nurse an athlete from a position on the shelf to a spot in the active lineup.

That was why he simply could not understand Hank Hunsinger. Brown had encountered bad-tempered people in his long career. He had known athletes who were the antithesis of the grateful lion from whose paw Androcles had pulled the thorn.

But Hunsinger—bent to destroy other athletes—was something else. Brown had never taken any courses in psychology, and had never regretted the lacuna until he met Hunsinger. The Hun was sick, Brown had at length concluded, but it was a sickness that was impervious to massage, a whirlpool bath, or the panacea of taping. And while Brown fretted over what to do about this condition, Hunsinger roamed about seeking teammates to devour.

Most recently, the victims were the two rookies, Hoffer and Murray. Hoffer, after a bad start, seemed to be handling Hunsinger adequately. But Murray seemed to be more easily led into Hunsinger's world of wretched conditioning, debauchery, and chemical dependency.

There was no turning away from it; something had to be done. But what? Since the bad influence Hunsinger was having on the team resulted in poor conditioning and, as a result, in injuries, it seemed to Brown it was up to him to rectify the situation.

That would mean, as far as he could figure, something would have to happen to Hunsinger. But after all these years of repairing and healing bodies, could Brown bring himself to a denial of everything he stood for?

Harris, Ewing, and Koesler stood outside the training cubicle wherein a player was consulting with Brown.

Koesler studied the closed door. A series of cartoons had been taped to it. Many had turned yellowish-brown with age. Two were at his eye level. Both were by an artist named Cochran and looked as if they had been clipped from *USA Today*. One showed a coach admonishing a huge player, saying, "You're a sadistic bully who has no compassion for his fellow man, Foswell. I like that in a linebacker."

The other depicted a coach saying to a trainer on the sidelines, "Jones has a broken leg. Go out and spray it."

He could abide someone who lived his life by cartoons. Koesler felt he himself frequently did.

Shortly after he had asked them to wait until he had finished, Brown dismissed the player and invited them into his office.

The initial interrogation of Brown proved predictable. He knew of Hunsinger's obsessions, his astigmatism, that he showered again at home after the games, and that he had a supply of strychnine in his apartment. Brown gave no indication that he knew of Hunsinger's colorblindness.

Neither Harris nor Ewing expected any more. The only real surprises so far had been Hoffer's explanation of how Hunsinger had acquired the strychnine, and Murray's admission that he knew the dead man had been colorblind.

One more question and they would move into the second phase of the interrogation: getting the subjects to talk about each other.

"One more thing," said Ewing, "would you tell us what you did yesterday? Be as complete and thorough as you can."

Brown reflected momentarily. "I got to the inn about six-thirty in the morning. I always get an early start, especially on game days. The guys started showing up about seven-thirty. We had something to eat. Then I started taping. The guys take turns eating and getting taped. Then about ten, I came here to the stadium to get ready to apply the special braces, get out the medication—things like that.

"The team started getting here about noon. We did the final taping. Then there was the game. After that a few guys needed some first aid. I checked out some injuries that would need the doc's attention. Then there was the cleaning up.

"I left here about eight, eight-thirty and went right home and had some dinner."

"I see," said Ewing. "Was there anyone at the inn when you got there at . . . uh . . . six-thirty?"

"My assistant got there just a few minutes after I did."

"How about when you left here last night at about eight or eight-thirty?"

"Again, my assistant."

"How about that period in midmorning?" Harris asked. "What was it—you said you left the inn to come here about ten and the players didn't get here till about noon. Anybody with you then?"

"No, I came alone."

"Nobody here when you got here? Anybody here at all between ten and noon?"

"No."

"Anybody see you come in?"

"Maybe. But I don't remember seeing anybody."

"So you were alone here for a couple of hours, but there isn't anybody can attest to that?"

"I guess so. I had to get things ready here for the game . . . like I told you. Is there anything wrong with that?"

"Not yet. Did you notice any of the players show up late at the inn yesterday morning?"

"Sure. There's almost always a few."

"Hoffer and Cobb among the late arrivals?" Ewing resumed his questioning.

Brown nodded. "Near as I can remember, Hoffer said something about going to church, and Bobby had a flat. Didn't matter. Coach chewed 'em out."

"How did Cobb and Hunsinger get on?"

"Okay, I guess. There's always a kind of special relationship builds up between a quarterback and his receivers. The longer they stay on the same team, a kind of—whatchamacallit—ESP builds up.

"See, like during a play, a pass play, let's say the blocking breaks down and the receiver has already run his pattern. They could be separated twenty, thirty yards, but about then a good quarterback may want the receiver to come back for the ball. The receiver, if he's on the same wavelength, sort of senses this and comes back for the ball. It's amazing. I've seen it work quite a few times. It worked between Bobby and the Hun. But Bobby is a good quarterback and the Hun is—was—a good receiver.

"'Course, there wasn't a helluva lot of love lost between them. That happens. But they were able to communicate on the field."

"So," Ewing tried to sum up, "you'd say they were able to anticipate each other."

"Kinda."

"How about Hunsinger and Hoffer?"

"Well, Hoff played behind the Hun, so that didn't make for all that friendly a relationship. In the beginning of this season, seemed like the Hun tried to take Hoff under his wing, but it seemed Hoff wasn't havin' any of it. 'Course, Hoff played behind guys in the past—high school, college. Even tried out with a couple of pro teams before this year. So he knows what it is to have to wait your turn."

"How about the owner, Jay Galloway . . . and the general manager. How'd they get along with Hunsinger?"

Brown shrugged. "They don't get taped."

In spite of himself, Ewing smiled. "I know you're not as close to them as you are to the players, but it's a team; you must have some opinion on their relationship with Hunsinger."

"Depends on what time of the season you're talkin' about. Around contract time, Mr. Whitman didn't think too kindly of the Hun. He drove a hard bargain, a real hard bargain."

"And Galloway?"

Brown put the adhesive tape he'd been toying with on the shelf. "Pretty well known Mr. Galloway wanted the Hun on the field at all possible times. Thought a goodly percentage of the fans came out to see the Hun. Mr. Galloway's probably takin' this pretty hard."

"You agree with him? About all those people coming out to see the Hun?"

Brown shook his head. "Guess I've seen too many come and go. Franchises somehow survive the players."

"And how did you and Hunsinger get on?"

Brown paused, then shook his head. "The Hun was no malingerer. He took his licks—gave some too—and came back for more. He knew there were lots of strong, fast kids out there achin' for his job. He was a good player, far as that went.

"But the thing you gotta remember about the Hun is that he was the only person he cared about. If you were in his way, he'd try his damndest to run you over. 'Bout the only guys who got on with him were the ones he impressed. Some were impressed with his money. Some were impressed with his reputation. He was almost a legend. He holds—or held—nearly all the league records for a tight end. And he played the position longer'n anyone else ever. He was an established hero to some of these kids when they were growin' up.

"But you were either impressed with him or you didn't care much for him. He wasn't easy to like . . . too much for himself and almost nothin' for the team. That's the way the Hun was."

"And you?"

"I taped him, patched up his bruises. Outside of that, as far as he was concerned, kept pretty much to myself. Only way to get through life."

"Okay," said Harris, rising from the chair, "I think that'll be all for now. We'll probably have more questions. So stay available."

Brown nodded.

The three men left the locker room and began the steep incline toward the parking lot outside the stadium. The vast lot, nearly empty, was dotted by only a few cars.

One could see the significant potholes, cracks in the asphalt, and areas of just bare ground. Koesler mused that it must be some sort of moral crime to charge—and extravagantly—to park there.

They entered the city-owned car. "Do you mind, Father," Ewing asked, "going with us on one more call?"

"No, of course not." Koesler was surprised. He had been asked to participate in this interrogation segment of the investigation only because of his particular association with the God Squad discussion group. And the questioning of those members was now completed.

"Actually, we've got two more calls—Mrs. Galloway and Hunsinger's mother—to make before we go back to headquarters and get together with the others investigating this case. Delivering you to your parish is right on the way to Mrs. Hunsinger's."

"If you don't mind my asking, why Mrs. Galloway and Mrs. Hunsinger?"

"They had keys—and thus access—to Hunsinger's apartment. We have to check them out."

Koesler could understand why Hunsinger's mother might have a key to his apartment, but did Mrs. Galloway still have a key?

"All we know is what we hear on the gossip circuit. She and Hunsinger had an affair awhile back. He gave her a key. We have no idea whether she returned it or might have had a copy made. We've got to check it out . . . touch all bases, you know."

Interesting, thought Koesler.

Sergeant Ewing would have no way of knowing how far from actuality he was when referring to Koesler and a gossip circuit in the same sentence. The priest neither collected nor spread rumor. And thought himself the better for it.

She could remember drowning. Even though she was only six at the time, the memory had never left her. Not that she constantly thought about the event. But it certainly had changed and formed her life.

It had happened when she, an only child, accompanied her father aboard his sailboat on Lake Calhoun in Minneapolis. The wind was up and the lake's surface disturbed. Marjorie Palmer and her father were alone on board. He had strapped her in a lifejacket... too tightly, she decided. She loosened it.

Her father had just begun a tack when an unexpected wave slapped the boat. Marjorie lost her balance. As she tumbled out, her head struck the side of the boat. She struggled only momentarily before going limp. Her body slipped out of the loosened lifejacket. And down she went.

It took her father several minutes to locate her in the roiled water. When he did, he grabbed her and shot to the surface. Afterward, he was unable to recall how he had managed to get her and himself back aboard. He hadn't thought to lower the rope ladder before diving off the boat. He had thought only of rescuing his daughter or dying in the attempt. Without the ladder, it was pretty improbable that he would be able to get back in the boat, much less get his daughter's limp body back in. Everyone attributed his feat simply to the phenomenon that in extreme emergencies, people are capable of almost superhuman strength.

Once back in the boat, he had administered artificial respiration until Marjie began to breathe again. But she was still unconscious. Fortunately, the occupants of a nearby powerboat witnessed what had happened. They sped Mr. Palmer and his unconscious daughter to shore, where an ambulance sped her to Hennepin County General Hospital.

It was in the emergency room that the bump on her head, just over the right ear, was discovered. The doctor performed a lumbar puncture, hoping to find the spinal fluid to be clear. It was streaked with red.

The medical staff did what it could. They fitted her

with catheters and IVs. Nurses came in periodically to turn the small patient to prevent bedsores. They administered physical therapy, moving her small arms and legs so the joints would not stiffen. But no one could predict whether she would ever feed herself or move her own body again.

Hours became days. Days melted into weeks. Marjie remained unconscious. Her classmates, her playmates—indeed, because of media coverage, most Twin Citians—prayed for her. One or the other of her parents was with her constantly.

One day, some three and a half weeks after the accident, Marjie's eyes fluttered, then opened. Her father, seated at her bedside, had been staring at his daughter's closed eyes for so long that at first he did not believe his own. Then, of course, emotion overcame him.

The Twin Cities celebrated. A lot of prayer and concern had been invested in that little girl. And it had paid off. The Sunday following her recovery, sermons were preached on the theme of Jesus curing the sick, especially children. Little Marjorie Palmer was a celebrity.

Her recollection of her coma was published in area newspapers and discussed in radio and television newscasts. It was not that much. She remembered striking her head as she fell. She remembered slipping under water. She remembered trying to breathe and swallowing water. She remembered being terribly frightened.

Then, there had been a brilliant light. As her eyes grew accustomed to the light, she was certain she had seen Jesus. He was waiting for her, smiling, arms outstretched. Gone was her fear. She felt very comfortable. Then, it was as if she had drifted into a deep, peaceful sleep, remembering nothing more until she awoke and saw her father crying tears of joy.

That had been almost ten years before Elisabeth Kübler-Ross made afterlife experiences popular. Little Marjorie's experience made her even more of a celebrity.

From that time on, Marjorie Palmer held the firm belief that God had a very special purpose for her. That was why He had returned her to this world. She would have died after but six years on earth if God, perhaps as a result of all those prayers, had not restored her to life. Her parents, firmly believing this to be so, impressed the message on their daughter so repeatedly and forcibly that she had little alternative but to believe.

It was not simple growing up knowing she was divinely destined for some unknown but obviously earthshaking purpose. On top of all this, Marjorie was a bright girl, who learned easily and won top grades. She was also a beautiful brunette with a spectacular complexion. Little wonder she became the most popular coed at the University of Minnesota.

Looking back now, at her life from the time of her "drowning," through her college days, she could find no reason why she had let Jay Galloway into that life. In the jigsaw puzzle of her existence, he was the piece that didn't fit. When she forced him in regardless, he destroyed everything.

Though they had attended the university at roughly the same time, she didn't recall him there. She had traveled with a crowd several levels above Jay Galloway's expectations at that time.

Then had come the massive frontal assault he called courting. She had to admit that, at least through the courting stage, he was fun. Even the sex was good. Better than anything she had experienced until then. Better, in fact, than anything since, including Jay Galloway.

It started on their honeymoon. In the Hotel Liliuokalani, he began to treat her like a whore. She almost expected him to pay her after they copulated. She could not understand it . . . nor would he discuss it.

As life with Jay Galloway continued, Marjorie slid subconsciously into her role as, not his wife, but a high-priced mistress.

How far she had fallen! From a privileged soul who had had an encounter not merely with death but also with God. She'd been programmed to believe that hers was a divine mission. God had saved her for something significant.

To be the debased consort of Jay Galloway?

It was when he sank everything they owned into that miserable tabloid, when they had been reduced to eating stretched-out leftovers and borrowing money—from her parents, his parents, everyone—she was pushed around the bend. She seemed to descend, in her husband's eyes and her own, from being a high-priced mistress to a two-bit whore. She abandoned the last shreds of self-respect and acquired a well-deserved reputation for sleeping around.

As their financial condition improved with the success of the paper, followed by another success in the pizza business, culminating in this present adventure with the Cougars, she simply became more selective about her sleeping partners, whether of one night or of some duration. It seemed her only way of striking back at the man who had dragged her from the heights to the eighth circle of hell. Her condition might be best described by the ancient adage *Corruptio optimi pessima*, ("When the best is corrupted, it becomes the worst"). And she owed it all to her husband.

She had planned Hank Hunsinger as the coup de grâce to her relationship with Jay. She had long thought that her husband and the Hun deserved each other. They used each other shamelessly. Galloway urging Hunsinger to play even when badly injured, reminding him that one doesn't make the club from the tub, and that a good part of the crowd had come to see him. And that any loss of playing time would certainly be reflected in the cash value of his next contract.

Hunsinger, for his part, gleefully wrung every last cent he could get out of Galloway's wallet each time a new contract was negotiated. It was no longer that the Hun needed the money; he just enjoyed the torture he could inflict on the penurious Galloway.

Marjorie's strategy, then, was not only to have an affair with Hunsinger, but also to make sure her husband knew of it. Knew that the two people he despised, one for marrying him, the other for working for him, were mocking him through the gossip columns. Knew that the money, expensive gifts, and investments she would insist Hunsinger lavish on her all had their source in Galloway's carefully doled-out fortune. In effect, she would force her husband to support her twice over.

Her plan worked, at least to the extent that the affair did mark the end to any conjugal relationship. Until recently, the Galloways had continued to live together and be seen together, but there was no longer any intimacy between them. A divorce was in their immediate future.

However, Marjorie had very badly gauged how much an affair with Hunsinger would drain from her already depleted emotional reservoir. Even life with Galloway had not prepared her for the degree of humiliation Hunsinger was capable of inflicting.

Long after she felt that she had achieved the revenge she had plotted against her husband, Hunsinger would not permit their affair to end. He demanded that she beg for the shame he heaped upon her. When he was finished with her—and only then—he casually dismissed her.

She could not forget and would not forgive.

Marjorie attended the Cougar games faithfully. It was one of the few agreements she and Galloway had reached. Besides, she derived deep satisfaction from the physical punishment Hunsinger had to absorb in those games.

But it wasn't enough. It never could be sufficient reparation for the brutality he had wreaked against her. There had to be something more. As time passed, the memory of her ill-fated fling with Hunsinger, instead of fading, became more intense and piercing. With increasing frequency, she found herself indulging in elaborate plans of revenge.

As her ace of trump, there was always that duplicate key to his apartment.

Lieutenant Harris needed more time and many more words to explain to Marjorie Galloway what Father Koesler was doing in her home. She was the only one of this morning's interviewees who had not known him through the God Squad, or through any other circumstance, for that matter.

During the explanation, Koesler experienced one of those awkward sensations that was by no means unique in his life. He felt like an appliance being described by a salesman. After a demonstration, should the housewife decide against him, he would be put out on the porch and discarded. He stood, hat in hands, while he was being spoken of in the third person, offering it up for the suffering souls in purgatory.

At length, Koesler was accepted into the Galloway home, as accepted he must be. Marjorie Galloway led them to the living room, airy and spacious, but, Koesler thought, not particularly well decorated. He felt that something was wrong with the decor, but he couldn't identify what. He smiled inwardly; what did he know about decor? There were times when he was inordinately grateful he ordinarily wore basic black and white. If he were a businessman, it would be all browns, blues, grays, or greens. He would never try a contrasting color combination; the chances that the colors would complement one another were no better than fifty-fifty.

The priest listened attentively as Lieutenant Harris and Sergeant Ewing covered the now familiar territory of their preceding interrogations.

Yes, she certainly knew Hunsinger was compulsive and that he regularly showered at home after a game. The question was answered with a slight shudder. As if the memory of Hunsinger's postgame shower was somehow disturbing. She claimed not to know there was any strychnine kept in the apartment. That would jibe with the fact that they had broken up approximately a year before; Kit Hoffer had stated that Hunsinger had gotten the strychnine during the preseason games, which would have been about three months ago. Her professed lack of knowledge hinged, of course, on her not having returned to the apartment since her affair with Hunsinger ended.

Yes, she knew about the contact lenses and the nearsighted astigmatism. But painstaking questioning by the officers failed to elicit any evidence that she knew anything further was amiss with his vision.

Koesler tended to believe people. Probably it had something to do with his training. Many years before, in the seminary, he had been taught that a priest hearing confessions is obliged to presume that the penitent is telling the truth, whether speaking for or against him- or herself. He had followed that principle throughout his many years of hearing confessions. And the presumption spilled over into his general attitude toward people.

But Mrs. Galloway's seeming ignorance of Hunsinger's color dysfunction stretched Koesler's credulity almost to the breaking point. How well could a person disguise a problem like colorblindness? Sufficiently for a spouse or a paramour to be ignorant of it? Maybe. But the priest had his doubts. And, he thought, if he doubted, what must be the state of mind of the detectives, who, after having been lied to regularly over the years, are programmed to distrust at first blush rather than to believe?

Koesler also noted that Mrs. Galloway was fielding these questions rather smoothly, as if she knew what was coming next. The only thing so far that had seemed to surprise her had been his presence.

And, indeed, she had been forewarned. Jay Galloway had phoned her immediately after his interrogation. He wanted no discrepancies in their responses to the detectives' questions. Since he had been informed that Koesler's presence stemmed from his having been a member of the God Squad, and since Marj was not a member, it did not enter Galloway's head that Koesler would be present at Marj's interrogation. So he had not mentioned the priest. Thus her surprise.

"One thing more, ma'am," said Ewing, "could you tell us what you did yesterday? Try to be as thorough as possible."

Marjorie Galloway sighed. "I must have awakened at about nine. Had breakfast, read the papers . . . a rather leisurely morning, all in all. Went to the game. After the game, went to dinner with some friends. Then returned here. Watched some TV. Went to bed.

"Now you're going to ask me if anyone can corroborate all this, right?"

Good-naturedly, Ewing nodded.

"Right!" She smiled. "You see, I've watched 'Hill Street Blues' too."

Ewing smiled in return.

"Well," Marjorie proceeded, "the answer is yes and no. I sat in my husband's box for the game. So lots of reliable people can account for me there. I had dinner with the van den Muysenbergs—he's the Dutch consul. That was immediately after the game until nearly nine. And, from what I read in the papers about the Hun's death, that should pretty well take care of my afternoon and evening alibis.

"However, I'm at a loss for a morning alibi."

Ewing looked up from his notepad; Harris raised both eyebrows.

"I live alone now. Have for the past month. Actually, for all practical purposes, for the past year. There is," she nodded in Father Koesler's direction, "something to be said for celibacy. I have assembled an unenviable track record of living with people. Now I'm trying life alone, and enjoying it. At least I have more peace alone than I've ever experienced with anyone else.

"Gentlemen," she looked from Harris to Ewing, neglecting Koesler, "I admit what you already know: that Hank Hunsinger and I were . . . an item . . . for a long while a year or so ago. It was a sordid affair well chronicled in the gossip columns. But you can't think for a minute I killed him! Why would I?"

Ewing shrugged. "Revenge?"

Marjorie smiled sardonically. "'Hell hath no fury . . .'? Trite! And it's been more than a year! If I'd ever thought of it at all, why would I wait till now?"

"An idea whose time had come?" Ewing suggested. "Look, ma'am, nobody is accusing you of anything."

"Then why are you asking me all these questions . . . as if I were a suspect?"

"We're asking questions of lots of people, ma'am," Ewing responded. "Just trying to get the general information we need to home in on the perpetrator."

"Well, look at it this way: You said the poison used was strychnine and that it was found in the Hun's apartment. I can tell you it wasn't there when I was . . . seeing him. And you probably know that. So, how would I know there was strychnine available in the apartment?"

"You had a key—"

"I had a key! I had a key! Of course I had a key! But when we broke up I gave it back to him . . . I threw it at him!"

If that was a lie, or if she had the key duplicated before she returned it, thought Ewing, that would be a very interesting lie.

"Of course," said Harris, "we'd have no way of knowing whether you returned the key, would we?"

"I assume you're having the apartment searched. You should find an extra key among his belongings."

Unless, thought Koesler, he's given it to another woman. . . .

"We may find more than one key. But that would not necessarily indicate one of them was from you."

"I returned it!" She said it defiantly.

"Maybe you did. But what if you had the key duplicated before you returned it?"

"I didn't kill him."

"No one has said you did. This is just the first round of our investigation."

Unexpectedly, she relaxed and appeared quite confident. "I think the rule of law is that I am presumed innocent. The burden of proof—of *proof*—is on you."

Harris nodded acknowledgment of her correct assessment of the situation.

"Thank you for your time, Mrs. Galloway." Ewing rose and, as if it were a signal, so did Harris and Koesler. "As Lieutenant Harris indicated, we will very probably be needing more information from you."

"Anytime." Her response held no indication of sincerity.

She showed them to the door. As they departed, she called out, "Oh, by the way, Father. I guess I'll be seeing you tomorrow night."

"What?" Koesler was nonplused. "I don't understand."

"The so-called God Squad is meeting here tomorrow evening."

"Here?" said Ewing. "I thought—"

"That I was separated from Jay? You're right. But I still hostess for him on occasion, and this is one of those occasions . . . part of the rather complex deal we're working out." She smiled at Father Koesler. "Although this will be the first time I've served the God Squad."

The door closed, leaving the three men standing awkwardly on the porch.

"Did you know there was to be a meeting here tomorrow night?" Harris asked Koesler.

"Yes."

"Interesting."

"We'll have you home in no time," said Sergeant Ewing, as their car rapidly moved south on Telegraph Road.

"Will you be off duty then?"

Ewing chuckled. "No way. We've got lots more to do before we call it quits today."

"Where to next, if I may ask?"

"For starters, we're going to talk to Mrs. Hunsinger."

"I didn't know he was married."

"He wasn't. Well, he was. Then, divorced. Long time ago. Remained single ever since. No, I meant his mother."

"Oh, that's right; you mentioned her. But isn't that a bit farfetched? His own mother?"

"She did have a key, remember?"

"Oh."

"Have to touch all the bases."

Koesler fell silent. He tried to picture Hunsinger's mother, not knowing what she looked like. Not aware that he had known her in the distant past.

Whoever she might be, his heart went out to her. Especially since she must be quite elderly now, it would be particularly painful to lose her son. Koesler was sadly familiar with the situation. He had assisted many an elderly parishioner on the occasion of the death of a mature son or daughter. In old age particularly, one tends to accept the inevitabilities of nature, the natural progression of life and death. But one hopes for the continued love and solicitude of one's children. One expects to be buried by one's children. Usually, in Koesler's experience, there is a particular poignancy when the expectations of nature are upset.

Exacerbating this, these officers would soon be asking her some of the same questions they had asked earlier of those who might be considered suspects in Hunsinger's murder. The detectives were only doing their job from which there was no escape. But Koesler grieved that Hunsinger's mother would have to be subjected to this sort of questioning.

He could not decide whether a police interrogation such as this was better or worse than the questioning by the reporter who feels compelled to thrust a microphone into a grieving parent's face to ask, "How did you feel when you saw the truck run over your child?"

All he could hope was that Harris and Ewing would be gentle when they met with Mrs. Hunsinger. He had every reason to expect they would.

The car came to a stop. It was not the sort of stop made for a traffic light. An air of expectancy pervaded the car.

They were in front of St. Anselm's rectory.

"Oh," Koesler said, "we're here. Thank you very much."

"Not at all," Ewing responded. "Thank *you*. You've been a help, Father. If anything else comes to mind, give us a call."

They pulled away, leaving the priest suspended midway between the rectory and the church. After a moment's consideration, Koesler headed for the church. An investigation into a deliberate murder might be the daily fare of homicide detectives, but it was a rare and deeply disturbing episode for a suburban parish priest. He felt he needed time to reflect on all he had heard this day. And after many years of searching he had never found a better place for silent, prayerful reflection than a quiet church when there were no services going on. There was something about the building's memory of being packed with worshipers, the faint odor of incense that clung to the pews and furnishings, the present emptiness that urged Koesler to sit back and look at God and let God look at him.

She had planned on becoming a nun. It seemed logical. She was raised in a large, pious German Catholic family. And she was rather plain. At least that's how she thought of herself. Mostly because others treated her as if she were. She was the middle child of seven children. None of her siblings appeared to hold out any hope that someone someday would offer Grace Koenig a proposal of marriage. So Grace did not consider marriage as her vocational vehicle in life.

In that state it was only natural that Grace Koenig would prepare herself for life in a convent.

She grew very close to the Sisters, Servants of the Immaculate Heart of Mary, more simply known as the IHMs, who taught in her parish school, Holy Redeemer. And they grew very close to her.

She was not a gifted pupil, but she applied herself without stint. She earned consistently good grades. That gave everyone hope that she would be successful in the IHMs, for the nuns in that religious order were all teachers.

Grades alone did not a teaching sister make. Grace knew that. Both priests and sisters taught Grace that a religious vocation had to be worked at. She, along with all other parochial students of the time, learned that the real heroes of life were the young boys who went away to the seminary to become priests. Next in line for heroism were the little girls who went to the convent to become nuns. Nuns, of course, were second class to priests, but then, as nearly everyone of that time knew, girls were second class to boys.

Then there were the Great Unwashed who got married. Marriage, as anyone who studied the catechism knew, was for "the procreation and education of children." Sex was around to propagate the human race and to relieve concupiscence. And that, pretty much, was that.

If Grace Koenig was not to be found at home, more than likely she was in the convent, helping the nuns clean or cook, or repair their religious garb. Some of her more spiteful classmates took to calling her Sister Grace. Some who were familiar with the Latin litany in honor of the Blessed Mother aimed at Grace such high-class barbs as "mater purissima" ("mother most pure"), "mater castissima" ("mother most chaste"), or "virgo fidelis" ("faithful virgin"). None of this much troubled Grace. To paraphrase Irving Berlin—which Grace would never do—she had the Mass in the morning and prayers in the evening. And with the Mass in the morning and the prayers in the evening, she was all right.

In due course, Grace graduated from high school. The brand new St. Mary's Convent, the IHM motherhouse in Monroe, Michigan, awaited the assumed entry of Grace Koenig into religious life. Mother General was surprised when Grace did not arrive.

After graduation, Grace's parents took her aside for a serious talk. There was no problem with her going to the convent. There was no way they could forbid her to go, though she was an obedient girl. The commitment to religious life for most of her scholastic years had been a given. But didn't she think she owed the family something? Her father had supported her all of her life. Even paid for her parochial school education when he might have sent her to a public school. In return, she had made no financial contribution to date. And she surely would make none after she took the Sisters' vow of poverty.

Would she, then, consider entering the work force for a year or two, maybe three, so she could make some fiscal contribution before entering the convent? After all, she was a very young woman, still in her late teens. She would have plenty of years as a nun. Most of them died in their eighties and nineties. You could read it for yourself in the obituaries.

She consented, reluctantly. And that is when a small segment of history was altered.

She got a job in Hudson's in downtown Detroit. Since she would be a saleslady, she thought she owed it to her customers and employers to fix herself up a bit. With what her parents allowed her to keep of her first paychecks, she got a permanent, some new, if inexpensive, clothing, and some cosmetics.

Then, a funny thing happened: Grace Koenig became pretty.

Her thin, Germanic face hadn't benefited by wearing her straight blond hair in a boyish bob. The permanent was a strong aid, as were lipstick, rouge, and eyeshadow. Her very attractive figure, hitherto concealed in modest, baggy dresses, was now evident.

Her immediate superior complimented her. That was a first. She noticed other salespeople and an occasional floorwalker taking a second look at her. That was a first. Then came that memorable moment when a customer very politely asked her for a date. That, very definitely, was a first.

She absorbed a lot of kidding at home about her dating. She blushed when her siblings poured it on. But she was determined to continue dating Conrad Hunsinger as long as he was willing. He always treated her like a lady and never tried to get fresh. About the only problem of which she was conscious was that Conrad was not a Catholic. If push came to shove, he would admit to being Lutheran. But he never went to church.

They became engaged. They were married, at Holy Redeemer, at a side altar in the basement of the church. It was a small wedding with a modest reception and a traditional honeymoon at Niagara Falls.

Perhaps not altogether traditional. Conrad learned that he would never see Grace unclothed, unless she was ill and he had to nurse her. She learned that he wanted no children and would always use a prophylactic. At least once, an accidentally perforated condom failed, resulting in little Hank Hunsinger.

Although Conrad never darkened a church door, Grace continued to attend daily and Sunday Mass. She went to confession each Saturday. Among other sins, she regularly confessed birth control. Regularly she was severely chided, but absolved. Then she would go to communion every day until the inevitable night when Conrad would fit himself with a prophylactic and, in the darkness, work her nightgown up in his practiced manner and quickly reach a grunting climax. Then she would not go to communion again until she could go to confession again and be absolved.

After many years of this frustrating vacillation from a state of sanctifying grace to mortal sin and back, she chanced upon a young Redemptorist priest, fresh from the seminary, armed with the latest in Catholic theology.

Her confession was routine. It had been a week since her last confession. She had lost patience with a neighbor and with her husband several times. She had forgotten and tasted food she was preparing on a fast day. And she had committed birth control once.

The new priest asked if she intended or wanted to practice birth control. No, it was her husband's idea. Then, Father said, all she had to do to escape all guilt was, first, never instigate intercourse when she knew it would end in illicit birth control and, second, try not to get any enjoyment out of the evil act. Then the entire burden of guilt would be borne by her husband.

It was, for that era, enlightened advice.

She had never been given advice easier to follow. In her entire married life, and before, for that matter, she had never initiated anything that could be described as foreplay. And she had never derived any pleasure from sex. She was not even certain she was supposed to get any pleasure from it. She had paid careful attention as a series of unmarried priests and nuns had taught her about marriage. Their instructions were always couched in vague, cautious, and circumspect terms. For most of these dedicated men and women, intercourse was an act they had read about in theological textbooks, but had never experienced. The general theme of their instructions was that men wanted sex and women were supposed to give it. Since the purpose of sex was the "procreation and education of children," and since women could not bear children much more often than every nine months, men usually wanted sex more often than was absolutely necessary.

In any case, as long as there was none of the hanky-panky of artificial birth control going on, should either spouse request or demand intercourse, the other spouse "owed" it, because coitus was also referred to as the "debitum," the debt. In practice, since men were the animals who always wanted sex, the burden of satisfying the debt fell to women. Grace never associated the rendering of a debt with pleasure.

Thus, the knowledge that she could pay the debt accompanied by birth control without sin was a heaven-sent revelation. And it was possible because a young priest had learned the principle of the indirect voluntary, a recent application of traditional Catholic theology. In effect, Grace was materially, not formally, cooperating with her husband in a sinful deed. But because her cooperation was not voluntary, but actually even against her will, she was without sin. It troubled her that this theological conclusion shifted the entire blame to Conrad. But her husband seemed to be bearing up under the burden rather well.

It never occurred to Grace that Conrad's decision provided her with a canonical reason for a Church annulment of her marriage. There were few enough reasons why the Church would consider a marriage null and void from its inception. Denying a partner the right to that complete action which could produce children was one such reason. Technically, it was termed "contra bonum prolis"—"against the good of children." It never occurred to Grace to challenge the validity of her marriage because she never got over being grateful that Conrad thought she was pretty and had wanted to marry her.

Then there was little Henry, the ever-present reminder that the better designed forms of birth control do not always work. Even the presence of Henry would not have weakened her nullity case, had she chosen to pursue it. It was Conrad's decision to deny Grace all but birth-controlled intercourse that constituted the canonical impediment to a valid Catholic marriage. The accident had no bearing on it.

Conrad accepted Hank much as a gambler accepts a loss at the gaming table. Grace greeted Henry as a miracle baby, which, given the odds against his happening, he nearly was. She loved the child with a chaste, carefully controlled love.

Now she became more painfully aware of Conrad's complete absence from church as she dragged a reluctant son to Mass every Sunday and occasionally on weekdays. When Conrad died, leaving behind a seven-year-old son, Grace was desolate.

If anyone needed the strong influence and guidance of a father, Henry certainly did. He had his father's large physique and gave every indication he would grow to be an even larger man.

The nuns were a godsend. She knew not what she might have had to do if they had not offered her work in the convent. God knows they paid little. But it was enough. And God knows they tried their best to help with young Henry. But no one could control him. She could not stop him from hanging around with a bad crowd. She worried about him constantly. But worry changed nothing.

Although she did not understand athletics very much, she was proud of Hank's—everyone called him Hank—accomplishments. And he was always good to her. This, she had to admit, was almost his sole redeeming virtue. Particularly when, after signing a professional football contract, one of the first things Henry—she could not stop calling him Henry—did was to offer to buy a new house for her.

But she insisted that she wanted to live out her days in this house that held so many of her memories. And right across the street from her beloved Holy Redeemer. So Henry paid the mortgage and saw to it that the exterior and interior of the home were kept in tiptop shape. He provided her with more money than she needed or used. She gave much of it to the Redemptorist foreign missions.

She read about Henry's on- and off-the-field exploits, of course. It disturbed her deeply that he had acquired the reputation of being an unfair and dirty player, as well as that of a rake, a libertine, a womanizer, a playboy. On his infrequent visits, she admonished him. She left notes for him when she went to his apartment to make sure everything was clean.

That, largely, was a waste of time. She did it only because, like many mothers, in her eyes her son would never grow up. Each time she visited his apartment, everything was in perfect order and spotlessly clean. Nevertheless, she would run a dustcloth over tables and shelves.

In her own way, she was as compulsive as he.

Both Grace and Hank had concluded, independently of each other, that he had "caught" his compulsiveness from her. In point of fact, though not in the way they thought, he had. During his adolescence, the conflict between what his mother expected of him and the sort of life he actually led produced an overwhelming conflict within him. Unconsciously marshaling his emotional defense mechanisms, he channeled all that conflict into an obsessive-compulsive neurosis. A relatively mild defense as neuroses go. Obsession fitted in so beautifully with all the numerical truths he was learning in his catechism, it was a natural, if subliminal choice.

As time passed, Grace wondered, with greater and greater frequency, what could be done about Henry. He remained her only son, but he was obviously hurting others. She felt somehow responsible. Something had to be done. But what?

It was a question she had never been able to answer.

* * *

Both Lieutenant Harris and Sergeant Ewing were lifelong Detroiters. If they had been Catholic, they would have known that the intersection of Vernor Highway and Junction Avenue was a famous corner in the eyes of west-side Catholics. It was at that intersection that the hub of the enormous physical plant of Holy Redeemer parish was located. If Ewing and Harris had been a bit older, they undoubtedly could have recalled a time when Redeemer High School had constituted a major athletic power in Detroit.

But that was history. Now the once financially comfortable parish struggled to stay afloat in a neighborhood where there was no longer at least one Irish-owned bar per block. Long before, when affluent Catholics had begun moving out to the suburbs, the then Cardinal Edward Mooney had mused that he wished some of the larger parochial structures had been built on wheels so they could follow the families that built them to the suburbs. Redeemer would have been chief among these movable edifices.

Harris and Ewing were standing directly across from the mammoth church with its flight of stone stairs climbing to the mosaic church exterior. Impressive. They turned to face 1731 Junction, Hank Hunsinger's ancestral two-story home and present residence of his mother and her companion. It was well kept up and preserved. But then, so were most of the homes on the block. A careful eye would note that 1731 had had a tad more money poured into its maintenance.

They mounted the stairs and rang the doorbell. Neither looked forward to this interview. Interrogating a mother after her son's death, especially when the death is caused by murder, was not fun.

They waited patiently several minutes before the door was opened a crack. They could see the links of the chain lock that prevented the door from being opened fully. Behind the chain was a small, wrinkled, suspicious visage.

"Mrs. Hunsinger?" Harris tried.

"Mrs. Quinn," clarified the face.

The two detectives identified themselves, showing their badges and identification cards. Finally convinced, Mrs. Quinn let the detectives in and showed them into the living room, where Mrs. Hunsinger, handkerchief held to her face, sat in a padded rocking chair.

Only a few of the room's furnishings appeared to date back to the time the Hunsingers had first moved in. Most of the furniture—end tables, hutches—was contemporary and fairly new. All in all, the room was tastefully outfitted and decorated.

The officers identified themselves to Mrs. Hunsinger. It was obvious she had been crying. But now she seemed composed. The two men and Mrs. Quinn seated themselves.

"We're sorry about your son's death, Mrs. Hunsinger," said Ewing. "But we need some information to help us solve his murder. So we have to ask you some questions."

"I did it," Grace Hunsinger said quietly.

"What?"

"I'm responsible for Henry's death."

"I don't understand—"

"It all began when he was a little boy and hanging around with that bunch of hooligans. Of course, if his father had lived, it might have been different. There just was so little I could do . . ."

"But you said—"

"As the boy is, so is the man. If I had been able to control him more, he might not have turned out as he did. So many people seemed to hate him. It could have been different if I had been able to do things just a bit differently. Still, he was a good boy. He certainly took good care of his mother . . ."

After being initially startled, Harris and Ewing relaxed.

It was a typical case of a parent blaming herself for all the circumstances that contributed to the downfall, death, or murder of her son. Even though most of these circumstances were beyond her control and, indeed, may well have been clearly his responsibility. But the two men did not interrupt as the grieving woman continued to find reasons, in her background, in her late husband's background, for all the evils of her boy's life. Finally, inevitably, she ran out of excuses for her son.

"Poor, dear Henry," she concluded. "So young. To think that I must bury my son . . ." She covered her eyes with her handkerchief and wept silently. After a short while, she seemed to gather some inner strength. Her shoulders no longer quivered. She dried her eyes and looked at the officers. "But you have your work to do, don't you? I believe you said that you had some questions you wanted to ask me."

Ewing opened his notepad. He'd been studying Mrs. Hunsinger. He guessed she had been a handsome woman. Even now, she had a striking presence. And, he estimated, she must be in her seventies. "Mrs. Hunsinger," he began, "could you tell us something about your son's compulsiveness?"

"Compulsiveness? I don't know what you mean. He was neat. I taught him that. One of the few good things I was responsible for. A place for everything and everything in its place. Do you find anything wrong with that, young man?"

Ewing, startled by her response, looked at Harris, who, in a sort of silent message, first returned Ewing's gaze, then directed it significantly around the room. What Ewing saw answered his question. There was a place for everything and everything was in its place. The pictures were hung perfectly, the carpet had been freshly vacuumed, and not a speck of dust could be seen.

Of course. Why should she think her son's behavior

out of the ordinary when it was but a reflection of her own compulsiveness?

"No, nothing wrong, ma'am. It's just that not everyone is as neat and clean as your son was. The way he kept everything in perfect order and the way he would always do everything the same way all the time . . . well, it made him a bit . . . uh . . . different."

"A virtue, I'd say."

"Yes, ma'am. Could we talk a bit about your son's eyesight . . . his vision?"

"My fault once again."

"Ma'am?"

"So rare. Far less than one percent are colorblind. And yet, medical science is always coming up with cures for ills we grew up with. Who'd ever think someone would come up with a cure for polio? There may even be some cure for colorblindness, some operation, some medication. We were never rich enough to afford anything like that. But Henry assured me over and over that it was all right. That it didn't interfere with his football. He was a good boy."

"Yes, ma'am. Did you know that your son kept a supply of a poison known as strychnine in his apartment?"

"That was only recently. I warned him about that. I left him a note. He didn't need anything as powerful as poison. His rodent problem could have been handled the good old-fashioned way—with traps. But no; he had to do it his way. Just like his father. I told him in my note that it was dangerous."

"Speaking of your note, ma'am, just how often did you visit your son's apartment."

"Irregularly. Perhaps once every other week. There wasn't much to do, though. Henry kept everything in pretty good order. Used to let the refrigerator get kind of empty. I'd bring him milk. He'd never get it on his own. Then he wouldn't eat a nourishing breakfast with cereal. I'd call first, though."

"Ma'am?"

"Never knew when he'd have . . . company over. Ran into a hussy there once. Wasn't wearing a stitch. And not a bit ashamed or embarrassed about it. I certainly was. Didn't want that to happen again. So, I'd always call first."

"But you had a key? Your son gave you a key?"

"Of course. How else would I get in when he wasn't there?"

Ewing looked at Harris. Once again communicating wordlessly, Harris indicated they should wrap up this interview.

"One final question, ma'am. Can you tell us what you did yesterday?"

Mrs. Hunsinger exhibited a small, self-conscious smile. "It's one of the things that goes when you get older. Usually I can remember things that happened ages ago clear as a bell. But the closer we get to the present moment, the harder it is . . . Mary Frances . . . Mary Frances!"

Mrs. Quinn had dozed off. Her head drooped down near her bosom. The officers had quite forgotten she was there. When Mrs. Hunsinger called her name, it startled everyone, including Mrs. Quinn.

"Oh! Oh . . . yes . . . what is it?"

"These gentlemen want to know what we did yesterday."

"Yesterday. Yes . . ." Mrs. Quinn was slowly coming out of her nap. "Well, let's see. We got up about eight as usual and got over to church for nine o'clock Mass. We never eat before we go to communion. Everybody else does now. That doesn't show the proper reverence for our Eucharistic Lord. So we don't have breakfast until after Mass."

Harris began to think that it would take Mrs. Quinn all of today to recount yesterday.

"Then, after the nine o'clock Mass, we stayed for the ten o'clock. We always hear two Masses at least. One in thanksgiving for the other. Then we came home. It was harder than usual getting back across Junction. Do you remember, Grace? The traffic was really unusually heavy yesterday."

Mrs. Hunsinger nodded agreement.

"Then we had breakfast. Just cereal and coffee. We eat lightly, you know. It's better for you when you get older."

"Ma'am," Ewing interrupted, "just touch on the high spots. I mean, we don't need to know everything."

"Oh, I thought you wanted to know what we did yesterday."

"Yes, ma'am." Ewing grew resigned; there was nothing he could do about her meandering in any case.

"Then we read the papers. The *Free Press* didn't get here until late. Now that was strange because the *Free Press* is the morning paper and the *News* is the afternoon paper. But yesterday the *News* got here before the *Free Press*."

Harris sighed audibly. Mrs. Quinn remained undeterred.

"Then there was the pregame show. We never watch television on Sunday unless Henry's team is playing. And with that man who talks all the time, we wouldn't watch it at all if it were not for Henry. Then the game started and we watched. Who won the game, Grace?"

"I think the other team."

"Whatever. Then we turned off television and listened to records. It was the Beethoven symphonies, wasn't it, Grace?"

"Yes . . . no; it was Brahms."

"Yes, that's right. It was Brahms. And before the Fourth Symphony we had dinner. We made frozen dinner so we didn't have to cook. Otherwise, we wouldn't have been able to watch the game. You had the roast beef dinner and I had chicken . . . isn't that right?"

Mrs. Hunsinger nodded.

"Then, after dinner, we listened to the radio. We always listen to the classical music station, WQRS . . . although we can't stand the modern composers. It's just noise. Not like Beethoven, Brahms, and Chopin. Then, after that—"

"Excuse me, ma'am," Ewing interrupted, "but that would bring you up to about eight o'clock yesterday evening, wouldn't it?"

"Yes, I guess so."

"Well, it just so happens that's all the time we need accounting for."

"Oh."

"So we'll be leaving now."

The two officers rose and started hastily for the door. They were stopped in their tracks by Mrs. Hunsinger's anguished tone.

"Where's my son?"

"Beg pardon, ma'am?"

"Where's my boy?"

"Mr. Hunsinger? I would guess the medical examiner is finished with h— uh . . . I suspect the body has been delivered to the mortician. You do have one, don't you?"

"Yes. The Hackett Funeral Home across the street on Vernor."

"Well, then, that's probably where the b— where your son is now."

Ewing opened the door and Harris preceded him out.

"Will you be coming to the funeral?" Mrs. Hunsinger asked.

"The funeral?"

"Yes. I suppose it will be on Wednesday. There's no reason to postpone it. Everyone who might attend is already here in the Detroit area. Will you be coming?"

"We'll certainly try, ma'am. Depends on what our schedule will be then. And, thank you, ma'am, for your time. And"—his look bore pity—"our condolences, ma'am."

"Yes, thank you."

"Come in," said Mrs. Quinn to Mrs. Hunsinger. "You'll catch a chill."

3

FATHER KOESLER ARRIVED AT THE Pontchartrain Wine Cellars at 11:30 A.M., fifteen minutes early.

The habit of being early for appointments had begun, as nearly as he could recall, with his mother insisting that he not keep others waiting. By now, the habit was so ingrained that it was virtually impossible for him to be late. At times, embarrassed at his reputation of being the only person on time for meetings, parties, whatever, he would plan elaborately to arrive exactly on time. But on those occasions, something unforeseen, such as a rapid traffic flow, would occur and he would find himself ringing the doorbell just a few minutes early.

It took a few moments for his eyes to adjust to the Cellars' quiet lighting. When he could see, he found himself gazing into the smiling face of Joseph Beyer, proprietor and, by choice, maître d' of the Wine Cellars.

"I've been wondering about you, Father," Beyer greeted Koesler. "You've been away entirely too long. Been keeping out of mischief?"

Koesler smiled. Beyer was the only one of Detroit's famous restauranteurs Koesler not only knew personally but on a first-name basis. They had met by accident socially and had liked each other from the outset. It helped that each of them liked most people they met.

"Trying my best, Joe," said Koesler. "I'd tell you more, but you're not my regular confessor."

"So what brings you downtown, Father?"

"I'm supposed to meet Inspector Koznicki for lunch. But I'm early."

"So what else is new?"

Until now, Koesler had not known that his reputation had reached to Joe Beyer.

"In this case, my time of arrival was on purpose. Lunchtime here is the survival of the earliest." He glanced around the nearly empty room, which would soon be filled to overflowing. "So, got a table?"

"For you, yes. But we don't serve Polish people."

The knack of a dry sense of humor is the ability to keep a straight face while saying something utterly ridiculous. Joe Beyer had the knack.

"I'm glad that you, not I, will be the one to tell that to Walter Koznicki."

Beyer chuckled as he led Koesler to a corner table where things would be somewhat quieter.

"Molly here today?" Koesler's reference was to Mrs. Beyer.

"Uh-huh. Working on the books. She's the smart one." Beyer supervised the seating of Koesler. "Get you something from the bar?"

"I think I'll wait for the inspector."

"Okay. The waiter'll be along in a minute."

Koesler did not have long to wait. It was 11:40—he had just checked his watch—when he saw the inspector enter. Koesler really could not have missed Koznicki's arrival. The inspector was a very large man. Though roughly Koesler's height, Koznicki had a much heftier build. Actually, it was more his aura that gave him the appearance of being larger than life.

Koesler noted that there was no hesitation on Beyer's

part in leading Koznicki to the table. "Change your policy?" the priest asked as Koznicki was seated.

"Yes," Beyer chuckled. "I checked with Molly. The policy is intended for only very small Polish people. And not even then if they are accompanied by large Polish people." Placing two menus on the table, Beyer returned to the door as the luncheon crowd began to assemble.

"What was that all about?" asked Koznicki.

"Oh, just another example of Joe's fey sense of humor." He smiled, recalling the time he had arrived at the Wine Cellars expecting to meet *Free Press* columnist Jim Fitzgerald, only to be told by Beyer, "We don't serve Irish here."

"Good of you to join me on such short notice, Inspector."

"Not at all. It was good of you to set aside your schedule yesterday and assist in our investigation. I have spoken with Lieutenant Harris and Sergeant Ewing. They tell me you were of significant help."

"Thanks. I don't know how much help I was, but whatever, I paid for it last night. Just couldn't get to sleep for thinking about it. All that I heard yesterday just kept buzzing around in my head. And the one interrogation I didn't sit in on—Mrs. Hunsinger. It was the second shoe that hasn't dropped. How did that go? Can you say?"

"Certainly, Father. But perhaps we ought to consult the menu before the waiter comes."

"Of course."

Neither man needed to study the menu in any great detail. They had lunched in the Wine Cellars many times.

After scanning the menu, Koznicki recounted the interview with Mrs. Hunsinger and, briefly, with Mrs. Quinn. He told of how startled the detectives had been at Mrs. Hunsinger's "confession" until it became clear that she was blaming herself in a wholesale manner for every evil done to or committed by her son, including his colorblindness. And how Mrs. Quinn, in great detail, had recounted their Sunday activities.

Koesler smiled. He could imagine the detectives fidgeting during the overly detailed narration.

The waiter appeared. Koesler ordered a Chablis, Koznicki a rosé. Koznicki would have the Dover sole. Koesler requested the club sandwich, silently promising that he would cut back at dinner.

"Odd, is it not, Father, the vast array of penitents there are in the world. We find some people confessing to real crimes. Others seem to be professional penitents, confessing to everything imaginable. Then there are those, usually parents or someone in authority, who seem to absorb the guilt of their children or subordinates."

"Yes." Koesler nibbled on a bread stick. "As a matter of fact, I was reading something about that in the paper recently. I was trying to recall it as you were speaking. It wasn't exactly the same thing you were talking about, as I recall, but it was similar. Oh, yes, now I remember: It was about victims—like rape victims or battered wives or accident victims or even people who are terminally ill.

"The thing all these people had in common is that what had happened to them was beyond their control. The article said that there is a tendency among such people to take the blame, to assume some responsibility for what had happened to them.

"There were a couple of reasons for this, according to the article. One reason for blaming oneself is that it can give meaning to something that seems incomprehensible. As if it were better to accept blame than to have to admit that life has no meaning or is unfair.

"And the other reason is that when a victim takes on the responsibility for what happened to him or her, the victim may thus be able to retain some feeling of control. One of the examples was a rape victim chiding herself: 'It was at least partly my fault . . . I should have known he was up to no good.'

"Maybe that's what Mrs. Hunsinger had in mind, at least subconsciously. She was assuming responsibility for things her son had done to others, things that happened to him, even his death. Better that than admit that some nameless fate was responsible for what happened to him, that her prayers had been fruitless, and that there was nothing she could do to help him.

"Which is not to say I agree with that. On the contrary, I feel very strongly that, while we may be less than completely responsible for everything we do as we grow up, at some time in our young adult or adult life, we must take full responsibility for our choices as well as for the consequences of those choices." Koesler sipped his wine. "They are not the fault of our parents or our siblings."

"I could not agree with you more, Father. I believe it is one of the deep sicknesses of our society today. So many people, not a few of them accused of crime, want to shirk all personal responsibility and pass it on to their parents, teachers, the times we live in—anything—everything but their own decisions and choices. And, as you suggest, Father, too often parents are too inclined to step in and take on the unjustified guilt. But the reasons you discovered in that article are interesting. I had not heard them."

"Yes. In effect, Mrs. Hunsinger cannot comprehend or deal with her son's death, nor with what he probably did to prompt someone to murder him. So she internalizes the whole thing and says that it's her fault. However terrible that may be, it's preferable to dealing with reality—admitting she had no control over the circumstances that led to her son's untimely death."

The waiter brought their lunch. Neither would have more wine.

Koesler extracted the toothpick that seemed intended to hold his club sandwich together. "I assume Mrs. Hunsinger's was the only confession you got yesterday."

"Oh, quite absolutely." Koznicki pierced a wedge of

lemon with his fork and squeezed it over the fish. "But you would know; you were present during the interrogation of the others."

"Yes. They were all sort of defensive . . . not that I blame them. And they all had excuses—what do you call them?—alibis. Were the detectives able to check those out yet?"

"Oh, yes. Their whereabouts have all been substantiated. And yet, all but two have gaping holes in their Sunday schedules that could have allowed them the opportunity to have committed the murder."

"Oh?"

"Yes. This much we know: Mr. Hunsinger was on time for the team meeting at the Pontiac Inn at 8:00 A.M. According to the building guard, he left his apartment around seven. He happened to stop in the lobby and check something with the guard before leaving.

"The important thing is to establish a time span during which the killer definitely had the opportunity to enter the apartment, mix strychnine into the DMSO, and switch the bottles of DMSO and shampoo.

"And that time frame extends from at least seven in the morning to approximately six in the evening, when he returned to his apartment after the game.

"Now, consider the team's owner"—Koznicki extracted a notepad from his jacket pocket, flipped it open, and read from it—"one Jay Galloway."

"I think I remember." Koesler interrupted as much to allow Koznicki to eat as for any other reason. "He said he was living alone and he didn't arrive at the inn until about—what was it—about ten that morning?"

"That is correct."

"Which means that he could have gone over to the apartment, perhaps waited for Hunsinger to leave, gone up, and done it, and still had plenty of time to get to the inn. Too much time, in fact. Galloway could have gone to the apartment any time up to about nine o'clock. But he claims to have no motive. He claimed to have lost a lot by Hunsinger's death."

"But it was you yourself who supplied a very plausible motive in his not being able to satisfy the fans if Hunsinger did not play for the Cougars—unless . . . unless it became impossible to give them Hunsinger not because management had callously traded him but because he was dead."

"Do you think that's a realistic motive?" Koesler asked somewhat self-consciously.

"Excellent. Then there is the general manager." Koznicki flipped a page in his notepad. "David Whitman."

"His time gap was, let's see, from noon till the game started at 2:00 P.M. Figuring about an hour's drive either way between the stadium and the apartment, that would be a pretty tight fit, wouldn't it?"

"Yes, but possible. Possible. However, we have yet to establish a motive for Mr. Whitman. What he might have gained from Hunsinger's death is not clear. Nor is there evidence of any animosity toward Hunsinger on Mr. Whitman's part. Certainly not any evident hatred that could motivate a murder."

"Let's see, then; there's my parishioner, the one who got me involved in this thing from the beginning by inviting me to attend the Bible discussion group."

"Yes, Kit Hoffer. He has unverifiable time from about six-thirty until he arrived late at the inn, about eight-forty-five. Which means that he could have driven to the apartment by seven-thirty, left fifteen minutes later—ample time to mix the poison and switch bottles—then driven out to the inn, arriving there, as he in fact did, at eight-forty-five. His motive, of course, would be clear. According to the testimony we have gathered, as long as Hunsinger was on the team and apparently able to walk, he would, specifically at Mr. Galloway's orders, play—and thus Mr. Hoffer would not. And if Mr. Hoffer did not play, his salary—his entire future—would suffer."

"Yes. Then there was this bit about going to the church

the morning of the game to pray. I know he was at Mass the evening before. I suppose it is possible he'd go back for a visit Sunday morning, but normally I would have assumed he did all his praying Saturday at Mass."

"Would it not be an ironic twist of fate, Father—if Mr. Hoffer should prove to be the guilty party—that your testimony would be at least partly the cause of his being found out. And he is the very one who brought you into this case."

"I don't want to think about that possibility. Of all the people I met with yesterday, Kit Hoffer is the one I most want to be innocent."

"I know how you must feel, Father. Understandable . . . one of your parishioners and all. But we must apprehend the perpetrator, whoever it is." Koznicki finished the final morsel of Dover sole, touched napkin to lips, and turned another page in his pad. "Then there is the quarterback, Robert Cobb."

"Yes, he was late, too, wasn't he? Even later than Kit Hoffer."

"That is correct. Fifteen minutes later than Mr. Hoffer. So, a very similar opportunity to do in Mr. Hunsinger. And fixing a flat tire with no witness to corroborate is a pretty flimsy alibi. However, once more we were at a loss to establish a motive. It would seem that though there was no lack of ill feeling between the two, they did work well together on the playing field. That must have made Mr. Cobb's job more easy and successful."

"Probably the same holds true for Jack Brown, the trainer, doesn't it? I mean, I didn't think there was any reason in the world why he would want to kill Hunsinger."

"That is true as far as the interview you attended yesterday. But in further questioning of some of the other players—interviews carried out by other detectives on this case—a little more light was shed on this matter."

"Oh?" Koesler finished the sandwich and began to nibble on another bread stick.

"It seems that Hunsinger lived on the mere edge of the conditioning one would expect of a professional athlete. A fact that would force Mr. Brown to have to work harder to keep Hunsinger in playing condition. But what is even more germane is that Hunsinger went out of his way to lead others on the team into temptation. It far surpassed the breaking of curfew. It led to chemical abuse, even cocaine."

"I wonder why he would do that?"

"Several hypotheses have been advanced. The most popular theory seems to be that Hunsinger wanted, perhaps needed, to dominate, to control others. This seems so because he regularly tried to trap the younger, newer members of the team. If he could trap a newcomer, then he had control from that time on."

"So the trainer would have to watch these young athletes be drawn into the bad influence of Hunsinger and have their careers—their lives—possibly ruined. But would that be sufficient motive for murder?"

Koznicki shrugged. "Perhaps. Athletic trainers devote their professional lives to keeping athletes healthy, or, at least in good operating condition. The conduct of Mr. Hunsinger would have been in direct conflict with the trainer's goals. He, perhaps next to a medical doctor, could most fully understand what these drugs could do to men . . . men he had pledged himself to keep healthy."

Koesler's bread stick was gone. The waiter cleared the table. Koznicki ordered tea. Koesler asked for decaffeinated coffee.

Koesler felt very gustatorially satisfied. He wondered if he should have any dinner at all. "I realize that I'm talking to a professional and all I know about this sort of thing is what I read and see on TV, but if I had to make a guess, it would be Mrs. Galloway."

"You are being far too modest, Father. You have been a significant help in not a few of our cases in the past.

Nor would I deny you on your guess, your intuition, as it were."

"That's really all it is: intuition. She doesn't have any alibi until kickoff, when she showed up in the owner's box. So, there's ample time. No one knows whether she ever returned the key to Hunsinger's apartment. And even if she did, she could easily have had a duplicate made. And revenge is an awfully powerful motive."

"All that you say is true, Father. But there is the matter of the elapsed time. Approximately a year passed between the time that Hunsinger broke off his affair with her and his death. That is a rather extended period to sustain feelings of revenge."

"But not unheard-of. A strong emotional feeling—particularly an obsession—can last a lifetime. I've seen that happen. Perhaps it was an emotion whose time for execution came."

"Perhaps, Father. But I think the odds lengthen with time. Then, again, there is the strychnine. If she had been gone from his apartment for a year, how would she know about the poison, which he had had in his possession no more than a matter of a few months at most?"

Koesler shook his head. "I don't know, except that if she had a key to his apartment, she could have gone in at any time and—what do they say in the movies?—cased the joint. She certainly knew when he would not be there. All she had to do was read the paper. There were practices, games—best of all, out-of-town trips for away games.

"As a matter of fact, now that I think of it, that could just explain why she might have done it now instead of a year ago. Suppose she is nursing this long-term hatred. She goes up to the apartment sometime when she knows he won't be there and finds the strychnine. The discovery triggers desire for revenge. She hatches this plot and does the deed. She mixes the strychnine in with the DMSO and leaves it on the shelf in the spot reserved for shampoo.

She knows all about Hunsinger's storied obsessions. She knows he will automatically reach for the shampoo in its usual spot. She knows he will not be wearing his lenses in the shower. He will not be able to read the label and the bottles are the same shape.

"And now we reach the final question." Koesler slapped his brow with the palm of his hand. "Why doesn't she bother to disguise the color difference? Even if Hunsinger could not read the label, he could certainly notice the different coloration. I still wonder, Did Mrs. Galloway know that Hunsinger was colorblind?"

"That we do not know."

"Is it possible to hide so basic a defect from a lover? Never having been, or had, a lover, I am not in the best possible position to say."

Koznicki chuckled. "It is a good question, Father. We know that his colorblindness was a condition Hunsinger felt most reserved about. He even managed to keep it out of the team's physical-health record. Apparently, he was also able to keep knowledge of his condition from his teammates . . . no easy feat, considering how very closely they live for much of the year. If he was able to keep the defect from his teammates, could he also have kept it from a paramour . . . ?" Koznicki left the question hanging.

"Which, I suppose, brings us to the one Cougar player who freely admitted that he knew about Hunsinger's problem: Niall Murray."

"Ah, yes, Mr. Murray. Fresh from Ireland and he finds himself in the midst of a *murder* investigation. The one who knows everything and does nothing."

"What do you mean, Inspector?"

"Mr. Murray is well aware—as are almost all his athletic colleagues—of Hunsinger's compulsions. He knows Hunsinger needs corrective lenses for astigmatism. He has heard of Hunsinger's . . . uh . . . active social life, which dictates a second shower at home after games. He knows about the poison in the apartment. He has at least a slightly reasonable motive in that he is one of the new young players Hunsinger has tried to corrupt . . . although, even with that in mind, he seems to have considered Hunsinger a good source of advice and counsel, not a subject for murder.

"And finally, he and Mrs. Hunsinger are the only ones to admit knowledge of Hunsinger's colorblindness."

"Yet," Koesler picked up Koznicki's review, "Murray and Mrs. Hunsinger are the only ones who have an alibi with no holes for the entire time in question on Sunday. Now I see what you mean by he knew everything but did nothing. Something like that old saw about the medical profession: an internist knows everything but does nothing; a surgeon knows nothing but does everything; a pathologist knows everything and does everything, but it's too late."

"Yes," Koznicki smiled, "something like that."

"Isn't it odd that out of eight possible suspects, the six who have the strongest motives for doing harm to Hunsinger"—Koesler could not bring himself to use the term murder, even though the use of strychnine could have no other purpose—"also have the most opportunity. While the two with the least motive each have airtight alibis."

Koznicki shook his head. "If this were fiction, and I were writing it, I would alter the plot so that the police would have an easy job of it. But this is life. And life, I believe is not painted in bold black and white strokes, but rather in shades of gray.

"Somewhere, among these people, is one who had the motive, the opportunity, the necessary knowledge, including—whether he or she will admit it—awareness of Hunsinger's colorblindness. The one who did the deed. We will find that person."

Koznicki pronounced the final sentence so decisively that, with really nothing more to go on but this statement, Koesler was convinced.

The waiter brought their beverages. Tea for Koznicki, decaf for Koesler.

"What do they do today?" Koesler asked.

Koznicki's eyebrows arched in a metaphorical question mark.

"I mean the Cougars," Koesler clarified. "What's their schedule for Tuesday?"

"Oh. Well, as far as the players are concerned, this is, for all intents and purposes, their day off. For the coaches, quite another matter. They will be closeted throughout the day, reviewing film of next week's opponent, which is"—Koznicki consulted his notes of the day's schedule that he had received from Lieutenant Harris—"New York. Then, gradually, through the day, they are to devise a game plan for next Sunday's contest. While the coaches will be busy with their game plan, we will be occupied with ours. We have teams of detectives who will be continuing the investigation and interrogating the suspects."

"*Teams* of detectives!" Koesler sipped the steaming decaf. "Isn't that rather . . . prodigious?"

Koznicki waved an impatient finger. "It is not fair; I know that, Father. We have only so many homicide investigators. And we must spread them too thinly on all the cases we must investigate. But every so often a case such as the murder of Mr. Hunsinger comes along, and public pressure—from the news media, the mayor's office, the community finally—simply demands as speedy a solution as possible.

"This is not good. On the one hand, we must take detectives from cases they are developing, to spend more of their valuable time on this case. On the other hand, this demand for a solution can, if we are not very careful, cause mistakes, which, under ordinary, less pressured circumstances, we would not make.

"Every day—and frequently more than once a day—reporters are all over the fifth floor, and demands are made for newspaper and television interviews. The reporters have their job to do and are under pressure from their editors. They want, if not a solution, a constantly developing story, when oftentimes there are no developments.

"As I say, Father, it is not fair. But that is the state of a notorious case such as this."

"You're right. It isn't fair. And you're also right: it is life."

"By the way, Father," Koznicki signaled for the check, "I understand that the Bible discussion group is scheduled to meet this evening. What do you call yourselves? The God Squad . . . is that correct?"

"Yes. I guess so. Under the circumstances, I assumed it would be canceled or at least postponed. But according to Mrs. Galloway yesterday, the meeting is on. And I was really flabbergasted when she said it would be at her house . . . I mean, her husband's house . . . I mean their house. I guess I mean her house. I mean," Koesler floundered, "what with their relationship, I didn't think the meeting could possibly take place there. In any event, I thought it better not to attend."

"Oh, no, Father," Koznicki appeared intent. "It is very important that you attend. Already you have contributed much to this case. Perhaps not in a quantitative sense, but surely in a qualitative degree. One never knows what may be revealed at a gathering such as the one tonight.

"And it is safe to assume that there will never be an assembly of the God Squad to equal the one to take place tonight. One of your members is dead and, with the exception of yourself and young Murray, all the other members are suspect to one degree or another. There will be a special dynamic tonight that in all probability will never be repeated. We will need eyes and ears to that dynamic and, to paraphrase a popular religious metaphor, we will have no eyes nor ears but yours. We are dependent on you, Father, to glean what could be most important information. No one but yourself can do this for us."

"Inspector, I am reminded of an experience some young friends of mine had years ago when they were conducting a prayerful demonstration against the Vietnam War. They were young Jesuit priests who were praying on the steps of the Pentagon. There were only five of them and they didn't even draw a crowd. People—top brass, other officers, enlisted men, civilians—just kept passing by with no more than furtive glances in their direction.

"Finally, after a few hours, they decided to call it off and go home. Besides being ineffectual, they were getting cold. Just before they were about to disband, an older Jesuit priest, one of their superiors, came up to them and specifically ordered them, under their vow of obedience, to disband. Their only thought, at that point, was that they had been the victims of administrative overkill.

"That," Koesler concluded with affectionate emphasis, "is how I feel. All you really had to say was, 'I wish you'd go,' and I would have gone."

Koznicki smiled appreciatively. "You know, Father, I knew that before I started. I knew if I asked you to go, you would. But if that were all I had said, you would not have been motivated, really motivated, to observe and listen tonight as carefully and astutely as you will now."

"Inspector, you know me too well."

The waiter presented the check, which Koznicki quickly grabbed, over Koesler's protestation. "Inspector! This was my party. I'm the one who invited you to lunch. Please, let me have the check!"

"Some other time, Father." Koznicki smiled at his friend, glanced at the check's total, covered it with a credit card, and handed both to the waiter. "It is my pleasure. Please allow me to take care of it."

It was useless to argue. Koesler shrugged resignedly. The waiter retreated happily. He figured he was likely to get a more realistic tip from a layman than from a priest.

In Koznicki's case, Koesler knew the inspector was motivated by simple friendship. But the incident caused him to wonder in general. Was it that the laity considered priests to be so poorly paid that they could not afford to pay their own way, let alone someone else's? Was it that the laity wanted to pay their priest's freight in return or anticipation of some spiritual favor . . . a sort of pious buying of votes?

It was true that a priest's salary, with the exception of those diocesan priests who earned a side income, was technically well below a living wage. However, it increased significantly in value when one considered perks and gratuities that scarcely ever quit. Free room and board, free medical and dental expenses, and on and on.

Almost every time he considered the subject, Koesler would entertain positive thoughts about the aborted worker-priest movement of France. Particularly since he had delegated so many pastoral responsibilities that hitherto had been considered the private preserve of him whose hands had been consecrated, he wondered if he should go out and at least try to get a job.

He spent very little time on that thought. For what secular work was he qualified? Who would hire a priest? What would be the reaction of his ecclesiastical superiors? His peers? Knowing the answers to those questions, he did not generally waste time on considerations that were doomed to a dead end.

Although he didn't much want to attend the God Squad meeting tonight, he would. For one, he would not disappoint his friend, Inspector Koznicki. Additionally, it might be instructive.

But first, this evening, he would drop in on the wake of Hank ("The Hun") Hunsinger.

"Good evening, Father. Who is it you're here to see?"

"Mr. Hunsinger."

The funeral director looked disappointed. Hackett Funeral Home was not designed to act as the penultimate resting place for the Hun. It was an ancient, boxlike structure that simply wasn't large enough to accommodate the numbers who had come to mourn or merely view the deceased athlete.

Hank Hunsinger's was not the only body presently preserved in Hackett's. José Gonzales' remains also were on display in a very small slumber room. The funeral director had hoped Koesler had come for the Gonzales group. It was past the appointed time for José's farewell rosary. Once the rosary had been recited, most of the Gonzales people would depart, leaving more room for the ever-fluctuating crowd for Hunsinger.

So it was with less than his usual peculiar mixture of accommodation, reverence, sympathy, and affability that he escorted Koesler through the crowd and into the parlor containing the Hun's remains. From that point on, Koesler was on his own. As well he might be; he had gone through similar scenes countless times.

Standing just inside the door, the priest attentively surveyed the room. Its panels slid aside, the room was several times its original size. Still the hallways were full of people waiting for the opportunity to file past the bier and have a last glimpse of the Hun. The line of people doing just that was moving almost imperceptibly. None of this was of any practical concern to Koesler. Marked by his roman collar, he could squeeze by anyone, go anywhere in the room he wished. People would step aside and even apologize for being in his way.

As he looked around, he saw few familiar faces. Except for the multitude, it was his standard experience at a funeral home. A few, a very few, spoke to each other in whispered tones. There was the muffled shuffle of feet advancing toward or retreating from the casket. Most of the people sat statuelike on the small folding chairs staring straight ahead as if they too had died.

Here and there, Koesler recognized isolated members of what was becoming a familiar cast of characters: the God Squad. They were to meet at the Galloway house after these services. Mrs. Galloway was nowhere to be seen. She must, Koesler assumed, be preparing for the arrival of the men. Or maybe she had just decided not to attend the rosary for Hunsinger.

The scene of relative inactivity had a soporific effect. Koesler's mind wandered back to a similar scene many years earlier in this very home. His father had died after a long illness and his wake was held here at Hackett's. Koesler had arrived to find a group of his friends gathered in the hallway. They were taking up a collection among themselves for stipends for Masses for his father. It had taken him several minutes to convince them that they were bringing coals to Newcastle. All of his many priest friends were offering Masses for the happy repose of his father's soul; one thing no one needed to be concerned with was prayers for any priest's relative.

Koesler was also reminded of the eve of his father's funeral. That night, he and his mother were the last on hand at the funeral home. They stood alone beside the bier. He urged her to leave with him. She spoke, but not to him. To his father. That surprised him; he had never known his parents to be overtly affectionate with each other. "Good night, my darling," she had said. "I'll see you tomorrow morning for the last time before we meet in heaven." He nearly broke down.

The following year, his mother followed his father.

"What do you think of the house, Bob? Is this SRO or isn't it?"

Koesler's reverie was shattered. It was Father Peter Forbes, pastor of Holy Redeemer. They knew each other casually but with the familiarity almost completely reserved to priests.

"Yeah," Koesler responded, "you've got a good crowd tonight. I was just remembering the wakes for my parents. They were held right here and with just about as many people as are here tonight."

"But a different crowd, Bob." Forbes had not been

stationed at Redeemer when Koesler's parents had died, but the Redemptorist spoke from experience. "Most of these folks are here out of curiosity. The death got lots of publicity. And after all, Hank Hunsinger was a celebrity, especially in this town. These folks want to tell their friends they attended the Hun's funeral. Some of them just want to see a celebrity—even a dead one. Besides, there's a live one over there." Forbes nodded in the direction of Bobby Cobb.

Cobb and his wife were among the very few blacks in the crowd. Besides being a celebrity in his own right, Cobb and his wife were so outrageously attractive that they were the object of many a surreptitious glance.

"There are some genuine mourners here, of course," Forbes continued, "but I'm sure most of them are curiosity seekers. Even though I wasn't here for your parents' funerals, I'm sure you had a big turnout of people who were genuinely sympathetic and supportive."

Koesler nodded affirmation. It was always thus with parents or close relatives of a priest. Besides the relatives and friends of the family, there were many parishioners and former parishioners, as well as priestly classmates and friends, to swell the total. And always they formed a group of sincere and sympathetic mourners.

"Was there a problem with the funeral?" Koesler inquired.

"Problem?"

"I mean with Christian burial. I got to know Hunsinger only over the past couple of months or so. But I got the impression he hadn't seen the inside of a Catholic church—or any church, for that matter—in a great number of years."

"It's true; that could have been a problem," Forbes reflected. "There is one overwhelming reason we really went to bat for this one: Mrs. Hunsinger. She has been so faithful and exemplary a Catholic all her life, we just couldn't let her down. Hell, even the Chancery guys got the point after I explained it to them."

"But they did give you a hard time?"

Forbes gave a low, almost soundless whistle. "Oh, my, yes. They were concerned with scandal. I must say I don't much blame them. Hunsinger has always gotten a lot of publicity. Just about everybody knew what his private life was like. And it was also common knowledge that he couldn't have cared less about church. If the guys downtown had known Mrs. Hunsinger, maybe they wouldn't have been so stubborn."

"Maybe. But I doubt it."

"Anyway, I must admit a few hot words were exchanged before they finally gave in and let us have the funeral. Mrs. Hunsinger has been so good and faithful for so long, I just couldn't let her down. I think I might have been tempted to just outright disobey the Chancery if they hadn't given in. Thank God I wasn't forced into that position."

"How's she taking it?"

Forbes and Koesler had not yet moved from the doorway. So Koesler had still not met Mrs. Hunsinger.

"Pretty hard." Forbes shook his head. "Not unexpected. Parents just don't envision burying their children. When it happens, especially suddenly and tragically like this, it's a double shock. But she's holding up pretty good through it all. I've been trying to keep her busy . . . as busy as possible, anyway. Earlier today, we went over the Scripture readings for the Mass tomorrow. I don't know why I should have been surprised at her knowledge of the Bible; she's been reading it all her life the way other people read novels. After the funeral, I think I'm going to try to get her involved again in the parish. She's been a kind of recluse over the past several years. Be good for her to get outside herself. Be good for the parish, in fact."

"I've never met her."

"Really! Now that surprises me . . . your growing up in the parish and all. Come on over and I'll introduce you."

Koesler, by far the taller of the two priests, took on the blocking role as he led the way toward the casket.

As soon as he saw her seated in the front row, pencil-thin yet exuding an inner strength, Koesler recognized her. He had never known her name. But he remembered that familiar face from all those years he had served at daily Mass and all those years he'd come from the seminary on vacations. So she was Mrs. Hunsinger. It was the queen of clichés, but it was all that came to mind: small world. He was yet to discover just how small.

Father Forbes, arriving on the scene in Koesler's wake, was just about to begin introductions when Koesler abruptly sat down next to her. "You're Mrs. Hunsinger, aren't you?"

She smiled, pleased that he recognized her. These were the first words he'd ever spoken to her. "Yes. And you're Father Koesler."

Introductions being unexpectedly unnecessary, Forbes moved off to greet and console, if consolation were called for, some of the aunts and uncles of the deceased, Mrs. Hunsinger's sisters and brothers.

"I used to see you in church all the time," said Koesler. "You used to sit in the back of the transept on the Epistle side."

"Yes." She nodded, still wearing an attractive if shy smile. "I always knew you would be a good priest. You were a very good altar boy. Always so reverent and attentive. Even through your final years in the seminary."

Only now did it occur to Koesler just how long a period they had been wordlessly watching each other. Almost twenty years from the time he first began serving at Mass in the primary grades, through high school, college, and the four years of theology.

The thought crossed his mind that this would not likely have happened if they had been Protestants. The Separated Brethren, as they were now called, with their custom of congregating, mingling, offering "the hand of fellowship," never would have let nearly two decades pass without even a greeting. Only in the Catholic Church . . .

But this was not why he had come to the funeral home.

"I'm so sorry about the death of your son," said Koesler, coming to the point. "I hadn't known him very long—"

"We were at your first Mass."

"Pardon?"

"Henry and I attended your first solemn Mass right here in Holy Redeemer; in June of '54, wasn't it?"

"Yes, but—"

"If only I could have somehow gotten him to follow in your footsteps, this wouldn't have happened. It's all my fault, you know."

Koesler recalled Inspector Koznicki's saying that during her interrogation Mrs. Hunsinger had lapsed into the self-blame that so often afflicts parents when a child doesn't live up to their expectations. Mrs. Hunsinger's confession of guilt brought to mind a very similar statement made by the father of the young man who had shot President Reagan and three others. At the ensuing trial, the father said, "I am the cause of my son's tragedy."

"You musn't say that, Mrs. Hunsinger. I'm sure you did all you could."

Koesler had no firsthand knowledge that she had done all she could. He simply could not believe that a woman who practically lived in church would not do all she could to make certain her son would grow up well. "Besides," he said, grasping at straws, "Hank . . . er . . . Henry was not by any means without some very good qualities. Why, I wouldn't even have met him if he hadn't been a member of a Bible discussion group. Anyone who devotes an evening a week to a deeper understanding of the Bible can't be all bad."

"Do you think so?" She seemed to be testing the straw he extended, to see if it were strong enough to hold to.

"Yes, of course. And we have no idea what his private

prayer life might have been. But, once again, that Bible study very probably had a very positive effect on his prayer life." It was pure speculation on Koesler's part, but it was by no means the first time he'd indulged in such conjecture. Mortal life was ended for Hunsinger. If the priest's faith were valid, Hunsinger had lately appeared before God in judgment and was now living in eternity. It remained for the living to find some means, any means, to console the living.

"Perhaps," Mrs. Hunsinger mused, "if his father had lived . . . you know, he died just a few months after your first Mass. And Henry was so young, so impressionable at the time."

"Absolutely." Koesler plucked at the straw Mrs. Hunsinger, grateful to find another excuse for her son's flagrantly dissolute life, was extending to him. "It's very difficult for one parent to fulfill a child's need for both parents. Sometimes, impossible. No matter how hard the single parent tries.

"But in the final analysis, Mrs. Hunsinger, at some point in life a young person grows up. And, short of the most gross mistreatment throughout youth and adolescence, as an adult he must take full responsibility for his actions, for his life. And he also must take full responsibility for the consequences of those actions. At that point it's needless, pointless, and maybe even self-destructive for parents to continue to absorb the blame for their children's actions. You do understand that, don't you, Mrs. Hunsinger?"

She nodded, but she was gazing straight ahead at the open coffin. Koesler could not determine whether she was weighing or discarding his words. At any rate, he was worried about her obviously distressed state and concerned that he apparently had been unable to ease her out of it. He wondered if it were possible that she might harbor thoughts of suicide. With her strong adherence to Catholicism, it was unlikely that she might attempt that;

on the other hand, in her depressed state she might not be entirely in her right mind. In which case, no one could foretell what might happen.

"Do you have anyone with you?" Koesler asked after a brief silence.

"Anyone with me?"

"Yes; someone staying with you?"

"Oh, well, of course there's Mrs. Quinn."

"Mrs. Quinn?"

"Yes, right here." Mrs. Hunsinger indicated the elderly woman seated next to her on the side opposite to that where Koesler was seated.

Koesler had been unaware of Mrs. Quinn's presence. Contributing to this circumstance was Mrs. Quinn's state. Her head was softly bobbing in the general direction of her bosom. She was in the midst of a small nap.

"Mary Frances! Mary Frances!" Mrs. Hunsinger nudged her gently.

"If the number's B-8, then I've got a bingo," Mrs. Quinn murmured. Obviously a vestige of her dream.

In spite of himself and in spite of where he was, Koesler could not suppress a smile. Long ago, the traditional four marks of the One True Church had been increased by one, to read: One, Holy, Catholic, Apostolic, and Bingo. Surely, Mrs. Quinn's faith was strong.

"Mary Frances." Mrs. Hunsinger was getting her attention. "This is Father Koesler. You remember I told you all about Father Koesler."

"Oh . . . oh, yes. Father Koesler." Mrs. Quinn extended her hand.

"Pleased to meet you, Mrs. Quinn." Koesler took the proffered hand, thinking that it might better be put to use rubbing the sleep from her eyes.

"So," Mrs. Quinn blinked in a conscious effort to fully awaken, "this is Father Koesler. Grace has told me what a fine boy you were, so faithful to your altar appointments. And so reverent."

These ladies were perhaps twenty or thirty years older than he. And though he was in his midfifties, Koesler couldn't help but feel that he was a boy again, being affirmatively evaluated by the good ladies of the parish. He half expected one of them to affix a gold star to his forehead.

"I am the same, Mrs. Quinn, only now grown a bit older." He smiled. "The two of you live together, do you?"

"Oh, yes, Father," Mrs. Quinn responded. "We have for years now. Two old widows taking care of each other as best we can. We seem to match pluses and minuses. Sort of like . . . whatchamacallit . . . a yin and a yang. But we get along as well as two old ladies can these days. It's a mercy we found each other."

"Yes," Koesler affirmed, "it is a mercy you're together now. I'm especially pleased that you don't have to be alone at this time, Mrs. Hunsinger. I'm sure Mrs. Quinn will be a big help to you."

"Well, I certainly hope to be, Father."

"Ladies and gentlemen," Father Forbes announced, "we're going to say the rosary now . . ."

Whereas there had been only the soft shuffling of feet approaching the bier, now it sounded like a subdued stampede as many tried to reach the exit before being trapped by the prayer.

"If you are seated," Father Forbes continued, "you may remain seated. If you are standing, considering the crowd here tonight, you probably ought to remain standing." Catching sight of the many who were making good their escape, he added, "But if you wish to kneel, you may." He turned toward the coffin and knelt. "In the name of the Father, and of the Son, and of the Holy Spirit. Amen. I believe in God, the Father Almighty . . ."

Koesler decided to offer this rosary for the deceased, who certainly needed all the spiritual help he could get, as well as for the success of the impending gathering of the God Squad. A meeting that, in all candor, he dreaded.

* * *

"I think we ought to observe a moment's silence in memory of Hank Hunsinger." Jay Galloway, host for the evening and thus leader of tonight's discussion, bowed his head.

So did everyone else at the large round dining table, with the exception of Father Koesler. He was not averse to offering another prayer for Hunsinger's soul, but he considered himself, for this evening, Inspector Koznicki's eyes and ears. As much as possible he wanted to observe faithfully what would happen here tonight in case what transpired would help the police solve Hunsinger's murder.

Seated at the table clockwise from himself were Bobby Cobb, Jack Brown, Jay Galloway, Niall Murray, Kit Hoffer, and Dave Whitman. Marj Galloway, having set hot and cold hors d'oeuvres on the table, was seated in the adjoining living room, whence the sound of the television set, volume turned very low, could still be heard.

He and Mrs. Galloway were, thought Koesler, color-coordinated this evening. Each was attired in black and white. The priest, as usual, wore his clericals. Mrs. Galloway wore a simple long-sleeved black dress with frilly white lace at the collar and cuffs. Why, Koesler wondered, was she wearing black? Was it in deference to the deceased Hunsinger? Or for no specific reason? No matter; even the modest dress did not detract from her elegance.

Koesler was haunted by the same feeling he had had on his previous visit to this house. Something was wrong, but he could not identify what. He looked carefully about the dining room. Nothing out of place that he could see. It must have been the other room, the living area. But what?

He would have to remember to look more closely when he was leaving.

He wondered what the others were doing with their moment of silence. Praying? That could be a reasonable assumption with a group assembled for Bible study. On the other hand, it was more than likely that someone in this room—or the next—had killed Hank Hunsinger. What would be going on in that person's mind during a moment of silence in memory of Hunsinger? A prayer that he or she would not be found out? Scary thought.

Galloway cleared his throat. It might have been the dependable cough of a heavy smoker. In this case it was a signal that the moment of silence had expired.

There was a shifting in chairs and the rustle of Biblical pages being turned.

"Last week," said Galloway, "we considered the raising of Lazarus from the dead, and we agreed we'd continue on from there this week. So, that's John, chapter 11, verses 45 to 53. You want to read that, Dave?"

Whitman adjusted his half-lens reading glasses to read the passage:

"Then many of the Jews which came to Mary, and had seen the things which Jesus did, believed on him. But some of them went their ways to the Pharisees, and told them what things Jesus had done. Then gathered the chief priests and the Pharisees a council, and said, What do we? for this man doeth many miracles. If we let him thus alone, all men will believe on him: and the Romans shall come and take away both our place and nation. And one of them, named Caiaphas, being the high priest that same year, said unto them, Ye know nothing at all, Nor consider that it is expedient for us, that one man should die for the people, and that the whole nation perish not. And this spake he not of himself: but being high priest that year, he prophesied that Jesus should die for that nation; And not for that nation only but that also he should gather together in one the children of God that were scattered abroad. Then from that day forth they took counsel together for to put him to death.

The reading was followed by an extended, almost embarrassed, silence.

Father Koesler, as was his habit, had read the assigned text shortly after the previous meeting. Of course, he had read it in the Catholic Confraternity edition. He had nothing philosophically or theologically against the King James Version. He agreed, in fact, that there were few English translations that equaled the grandeur of the King James. But he found the archaic style confusing. And he always found it difficult enough understanding some parts of the Bible without complicating the process. In any case, he had read the text and was prepared for its prophetic impact.

The others in the God Squad, as was their habit, had not read the assigned text beforehand. Understandably, they were now deeply struck by the obvious connection between the Gospel verses, which spoke of plotting a deliberate murder, and what had actually taken place within their small group in just the past week.

At length, Jay Galloway, as leader, tried to get the verbal ball rolling. "Anyone?"

Another silence.

"Well, quite obviously, it hits home, doesn't it?" said Koesler.

"If you're referring to the death of the Hun, I wouldn't think so," said Whitman. "After all, the Gospel text is talking about Jesus Christ. And I don't see what Jesus Christ has to do with Hank Hunsinger."

Kit Hoffer snorted, thought better of it, and stifled a laugh.

Koesler felt a flush of anger rising at the back of his neck. "That was a cheap shot, Dave. In the first place, no matter what you care to think of him, there was a connection between Jesus and Hank Hunsinger, just as there is a connection between Jesus and all of us.

"And secondly, I was referring, of course, to the Pharisees agreeing that one man had to die and then beginning to plot the assassination. Just two days ago, someone murdered one of our number as the culmination of a devilishly intricate plot. So, there is, I think for a double reason, a connection."

What angered Koesler was the dismissal of Hunsinger as being of no consequence to Jesus Christ, the Savior of all people. At times like this, Koesler was immeasurably grateful that after death he would be judged by an all-loving God and not by any small-minded human.

"I happen to agree with the Father," said Murray. "I think it more than a coincidence that the very text we read tonight has to do with plots to commit murder when here not two hours ago there we were in the presence of the last remains of our companion. I say it's more than a coincidence; it's the very providence of God, as well."

"Do you think we could get back to the verses of the Bible we agreed to discuss," said Galloway, more as a command than a question. "After all, this is a Bible discussion group. We didn't come together to talk about Hank Hunsinger. If we wanted to get maudlin, we could have gone to a bar, lifted a few, and reminisced about the Hun."

"Mr. Galloway's right," said Brown. "I always thought it was odd that anybody would plot to kill a man like Jesus Christ. I mean, He never did a mean, nasty thing to a soul. And you know, it never made any sense at all to me that anyone would want to kill Him. I mean, the way this Gospel text reads, why, man, that's Murder One."

"I can see why you'd think that, Brownie," said Koesler. "Particularly if you think of all the people He cured and preached to and helped. All the common people with whom He spent almost His entire lifetime. But there were the others. In His case, they were the religious leaders who happened to be the Establishment of His society. He accused them of putting heavy burdens on the backs of other people while they lived high off the hog. He challenged the Pharisees constantly. And this is the way they reacted."

"But I still don't see why they had to kill Him," Brown protested.

"You've got to remember, Brownie," said Whitman, "that there was as much politics going on as there was religion. Back then, Israel was part of the Roman Empire. The Romans were sort of benevolent in dealing with their provinces. As long as a province paid the Roman tax and made no waves, the Romans left them pretty much alone.

"Oh, there was always a Roman governor on the scene—that's the role Pontius Pilate played in this drama. And there were Roman soldiers there to keep order. But the important thing for an insignificant little province like Israel to remember was not to make waves."

"And Jesus made waves?" Brown seemed incredulous. "I don't understand."

"The people were beginning to follow Him in droves." Koesler picked up the explanation. "Maybe it could be called a popular uprising. As much as the Pharisees opposed Jesus and warned the people that He was a dangerous leader at best and a charlatan at worst, still the people followed Him in growing numbers.

"Of course, most of the people, including His Apostles, refused to take His word that He was not interested in establishing an earthly kingdom. His followers preferred to believe that He would lead them to freedom from the Romans. I suppose the Pharisees believed the same thing. Now, remember, the Pharisees were living a very comfortable life. Of course it would have been nice to be free of Rome. But in the meantime, things were cool for them. They did not want their comfortable lifestyle to be upset. Certainly not by a revolution. They were very nervous about Jesus and His ragtag followers.

"Then, when Jesus raised Lazarus from the dead, His popularity was never greater. The Pharisees perceived that what they considered Jesus' political strength was now enough so that He could indeed, were he so inclined, get a revolution off the ground.

"So, we read in today's text"—Koesler consulted his Bible, which happened to be the New American Bible—"that after some of their spies report to them, the result was that the chief priests and the Pharisees called a meeting of the Sanhedrin. 'What are we to do,' they said, 'with this man performing all sorts of signs? If we let him go on like this, the whole world will believe in him. Then the Romans will come in and sweep away our sanctuary and our nation.'

"So, that's what the Pharisees were afraid of: that the Romans would learn of this troublemaker and come and lean on the Jews and then the Pharisees' sweet life would be swept away. Then, they said, 'it is better for you to have one man die than to have the whole nation destroyed.' That's why they began to plot Jesus' death. That was their motive. They wanted to save their own skins. They wanted to preserve their good life."

"Yeah, motive," Cobb murmured, "everybody's got to have a motive."

"What was that?" Galloway glowered at the quarterback.

"A motive . . . a reason. People do things for reasons. The Pharisees wanted Jesus out of the way so they could continue on with their sweet life. Somebody wanted the Hun out of the way. But why?"

"I thought we'd agreed we weren't going to get into that," said Galloway.

"There's no escapin' it, if you ask me," said Murray. "It's on everybody's mind, there's no escapin' it. He was at our meeting last week; he was on the field with us not more than two short days ago. And now he's gone. And 'twasn't as though he'd got some terrible sickness and passed away quietlike in a nice clean hospital bed. He was murdered, he was. Somebody plotted it, just like them Pharisees in the Gospel. And what's more, the police think that one of us might be the culprit!"

He'd said it! He'd said what was on everyone's mind.

Several long moments of silence followed as those around the table reevaluated each other. They'd worked together. They'd played together. Relied on one another. Was it possible one of them could be a murderer? Was it likely that one of them had killed Hank Hunsinger?

"That's it, Mick," said Cobb, "one of us might be the killer. By this time we pretty well know what all of us were doing on Sunday. Hoff and I were late for brunch. Mr. Galloway didn't get there till ten. Mr. Whitman was alone from noon till game time. Brownie here was alone from ten till noon. Only the Mick has a corroborated alibi. We all knew the Hun kept strychnine in his apartment. We all knew the Hun's peculiar habits. He was all set up like Jesus was. The Pharisees were scared He was going to rile up the Romans and they would come down on the Jews. That was the Pharisees' motive. Question is: Which one of us had a motive to off the Hun?"

After a moment's reflection, first one, then another, then all the others were looking at Kit Hoffer.

"Hey! Wait a minute!" Hoffer protested. "What is this? You guys nuts or somethin'?"

"You played behind him," Whitman stated. "As long as he was on the field and was physically able to play, you were going to ride the bench. Who had a stronger motive than you?"

"Hey! Like, Hunsinger was getting into a granddad's age. He couldn'ta lasted much longer. Like, all I had to do was wait him out. I didn't have to kill him, for God's sake."

"Still, he was on the field and you were riding the bench," Whitman insisted. "And guys who manage to play longer than anyone can expect just seem to go on and on. Look at Gordie Howe and George Blanda. Look at Pete Rose. How many kids got tired of waiting for guys like that to hang 'em up? Who knows what was going on in your mind? You could have thought of guys like Howe and Blanda and Rose and wondered whether you could wait the Hun out. You were already a little late on the scene as a rookie. If Hunsinger could've hung on for another few seasons, you might not have had much of a career left. How's that for a motive?"

Hoffer's face was flushed. Anger? Embarrassment? Guilt? Koesler wondered.

"Look, I didn't have to wait for Hunsinger to hang 'em up! I'm good! Damn good! Ask Bobby. There's only one reason I wasn't playing. And, begging your pardon, sir, it was you." Hoffer pointed at Galloway. "Everybody knew it was your orders to the coach to play the Hun all the time that kept him on the field. Coach Bradford would have used me. I know he would've. But he had orders from you. I had no reason to kill the Hun. *He* wasn't keeping me off the field; *you* were."

From Koesler's position at the table, he could see into the living room where Marj Galloway was seated. She appeared to be paying careful attention. But to what? The television's volume had been turned so low, it would have been nearly impossible for her to hear it. That, along with the increasingly loud exchanges in the dining area, made it likely she was listening in as accusations progressed.

"Wait a minute," said Galloway. "If we've got to talk about the murder and not what we agreed to discuss, I want to make myself perfectly clear. Okay, I ordered Coach Bradford to play Hunsinger. He was the franchise. He's the one who made it big at Western, U of M, then the Cougars. A good part of the crowd came out to see the Hun. And by God they were going to see him as long as he could get on his two feet and walk."

"There's no doubt about it at all," said Murray. "You'd certainly not have any reason to want the Hun dead."

"Of course not," Galloway agreed. "Why would I want him dead? He was the team's meal ticket. He was worth a lot to me, not only alive, but healthy."

"Unless . . . unless," Whitman mused, "having Hunsinger dead was the only way you could satisfy the crowd."

"Wha-at!"

"I'll be the first to agree that when we had to report that Hunsinger was a doubtful starter or that he was injured and couldn't play at all, the gate went down. But that's because they expected him to be able to play, and being no-shows or not coming out to buy a ticket was the result of their thwarted expectations.

"But what if Hunsinger were out of the picture entirely: retired, or even better, dead? Then the fans would just have to adjust to the fact that watching the Hun on Sundays was simply no longer in their future. But football certainly was going to continue to be part of their lives. The question, then, was, Did we have another attraction for them? I submit we did.

"First, there's Bobby Cobb, who never got the ink he deserved while the Hun grabbed all the publicity he could. And second, there's young Hoffer here. I told you all about him, showed you the scouting sheets. On paper, anyway, he would have made a perfect substitute for the Hun. So, if Hunsinger were to die, the fans would know with an irrevocable sense of finality that he was gone. And you would be able to replace him almost immediately with a younger athlete who showed every promise of being a more than adequate substitute."

Koesler felt somewhat vindicated that his supposition on Galloway's motive was ratified by not only a second opinion, but an extremely well-informed one.

"Your whole premise is crazy, Dave." Galloway was very definitely angry. "Even if what you say were true, why would anybody risk murdering somebody just to replace a proven star with a might-be star? It's crazy."

"Maybe, maybe not. I mean, it's common knowledge that your money is completely wrapped up in the Cougars. And Hunsinger was costing us an arm and a leg. Without Hunsinger on the roster, our payroll takes a pleasant nose-dive. We already have a modest contract with Hoffer and maybe we can bring up a rookie to fill the vacancy. And there you have it"—Whitman spread his hands in a gesture of finality—"an instant path to greater solvency."

A strange smile played at the corners of Galloway's lips. "If anybody wanted to believe your rather incredible scenario, Dave, it would provide as much motive for you as it would for me."

"Wha—? You've got to be kidding! You own the team, not I!"

"For the moment, yes. But it can't be much of a surprise to you that I've been watching your moves very closely. I've been watching you eat up those stock options. And, most of all, I know you. You're the guy who finishes what he starts. If you'd stayed with Multifoods, you'd probably own the company by now. And I know damn well that you've never liked working for me. Not from the very beginning. You want the Cougars. You want me out. Of course, I'm going to fight you all the way. And I think I can win. But my confidence in my ability has nothing to do with your plans for a takeover."

"That's nonsense! It's ridiculous!" Whitman almost rose out of his chair.

Koesler thought the accusation was probably neither nonsense nor ridiculous. It made sense to him. In addition, it supplied the missing motive for Whitman. A motive the police had not been able to uncover. He made a strong mental note to inform the inspector of this development.

"The only thing you've got right," Whitman maintained, "is that I've always regretted coming to work for you. You're a convincing bastard, Jay, but you should have stayed a salesman. Starting with the pizza business and capping the climax with this football team, you're in over your head. You should have stayed in sales and I should have stayed in public relations. You shouldn't screw around in people's lives."

There was a deathly silence. It seemed fortunate that Galloway and Whitman were separated by the full diameter of the round table.

Koesler glanced into the dining room. No doubt about it, Marj Galloway was paying dedicated attention to what was going on in here.

Finally, Jack Brown broke the silence. "Since you brought this whole thing up, Bobby, about the Hun's murder," he turned to face Cobb, who was seated at his right, "it just pains the hell out of me that everybody has left you out of this conversation."

"What d'you mean, Brownie?" Cobb rejoined. "What's biting at your ass?"

"Well, it's like what Mr. Whitman was sayin' just a few minutes ago. He was talkin' about how Bobby Cobb never got the publicity he shoulda got while the Hun was out doin' a good job of takin' care of Number One."

"With apologies or gratitude, whichever is appropriate, to Mr. Whitman, I get my share of headlines and I'm on the tube regularly. I get paid on time. Why should I give a damn whether the Hun gets three more lines than I do?"

"You can tell that to people who don't know you, Bobby, but I know you good. You gotta be on top. You think ahead. You lay good plans. Just like you set things up good in a game, keep the offense moving, and plan the next series of downs. I mean, you got your life all set up. And there's nothin' wrong with that. But you gotta be Number One. You sure as hell would know if the Hun got three more lines than you did. And, by damn, you would care. But with the Hun gone, you wouldn't have to worry any more; whatever anybody else on the team did, you would very definitely be Number One. And that's what you want."

"Sure I want it. But is that any believable reason to kill a guy?"

Koesler had his doubts about that too. It didn't seem to him to be a sufficient reason to commit murder. But, again, it could supply a motive, no matter how unsubstantial, where there had been none before. While Bobby Cobb had had the opportunity to kill Hunsinger, the police had been unable to come up with any motive for him to do so. Now there was one. Koesler would also report this exchange.

"But while we're on the subject," Cobb continued, "how about you, Brownie." Brown's objection was stifled when Cobb continued. "And why would a trainer, whose only job is to keep players healthy, kill one of those players? Well, what if the player in question took it upon himself to lead as many teammates as possible into temptation? What if he tried especially to drag newcomers and rookies down into the drug scene so they would be dependent on him for supply and support?

"What if the trainer, who knows his players almost as well as they know themselves, knows that all this is coming down? Wouldn't the trainer think it was vitally important to protect his players from this one-man plague? Doesn't this bring us right back to tonight's Bible reading: 'It is expedient for one man to die.'?"

"Bobby, Bobby . . ." Brown shook his head. "You should know me better than that. No matter what was going on, I couldn't kill somebody . . . one of the players. It's just against everything I believe."

"All we've got is your word on that, Brownie."

"Bob, that's all you got from everybody at this table. The Father is not in on this. The Mick is the only other one here with an all-day alibi. Everybody else at this table had the opportunity to do it to the Hun. And we have, maybe foolishly, devised made-up motives for each other. All of us can deny the accusations that have been made against us. But that's all you got: some accusations and some denials. There isn't a speck of proof in any of it."

The word "foolishly" struck a responsive chord in Koesler's mind. Instead of an innocent Bible discussion this evening, the members of this group had said things to each other, made embarrassing accusations, many in some anger and long-suppressed hostility.

It had long been a conviction of Koesler's that words

spoken in the heat of emotion, especially in anger, can become as permanent as words carved in stone. And because of such words, friendships had been permanently destroyed. Looking around the group now, with the exception of Murray and himself, they were all glaring at one another. Relationships between these men would, he thought, never again be the same. That was, somehow, saddening. He was quite certain he was attending the final meeting of this God Squad.

"Brownie," said Whitman, "we are forgetting one of the so-called suspects who isn't sitting at this table and who also had the opportunity to kill Hank Hunsinger."

"What?"

"I was wondering when you would get around to me, gentlemen."

Marj Galloway stood, leaning against the doorjamb, in the arch separating the living room from the dining area. In one hand she held a straight-back chair. She proceeded to the table and seated herself between her husband and Jack Brown.

She looked straight at her accuser, Dave Whitman. Neither blinked.

"Seems to me you're doing a lot of accusing, Dave," said Galloway, bitterly. "First Hoffer, then me, now my wife. Is it just possible that, to borrow from Shakespeare, you are protesting too much?"

Whitman did not take his eyes from Marj. "If anything, I may be getting warmer."

"Think so?"

Koesler had to admit Marj Galloway was cool. She gazed steadily at Whitman. If anything, she seemed to be suppressing a smile.

"You," said Whitman, "had the best opportunity of any of us. The way I heard it, you had unaccounted-for time right up to the opening kickoff. You—let's be honest—knew Hunsinger and his personal habits better than any of us. And, now that we're concentrating on motives, you had perhaps the best reason of all."

"Oh?"

"'Hell hath no fury like a woman scorned.' Revenge is as old as Cain and Abel."

"Really, Dave, you'd have a much more viable reason for saying that if the Hun had been found dead a year ago. I've had a lot of time to forget, if not forgive. And time heals lots of wounds."

"Time," Whitman pursued, "also provides the opportunity to plan. We don't have to pussyfoot around your affair with Hunsinger—"

Galloway made as if to interrupt, but Whitman cut him off by talking over Galloway's objection.

"Everybody knew about it, Jay. Hell, all you had to do was read the gossip columns. Neither of them tried to keep it a secret. And the assumption, never denied by you or anyone, Marj, was that it was Hunsinger who dumped you. You couldn't have helped being bitter. You had to have had access to his apartment while the two of you were still together. You could have kept the key or easily had a duplicate made.

"What if you hear—or, for that matter, discover for yourself—that the Hun had gotten a supply of a lethal poison? And you've had almost an entire year, not, as you say, to cool down, but to have your humiliation and anger fester. Seems to me you had the very best knowledge, opportunity, and motive of anyone."

There was a prolonged silence as the seven men stared at Marj.

"A nice guess, Dave," she said. "But that's all it is: a guess. I've been listening to you all very carefully, and that's all you've been doing all evening: guessing. The only ones who've escaped the guessing game have been Niall and the Father here. And that's only because neither of them had the opportunity or a motive. As for the rest of us, each of us knew the Hun well enough to know his peculiar habits. Each of us theoretically had the opportunity. And, I suppose as a kind of tribute to how really rotten the Hun was, each of us seems to have had a reason to dislike him, at the least, and, at most, hate him enough perhaps to kill him.

"But what we lack here, gentlemen, is what I think they call in the crime trade the smoking gun.

"You can talk all night long, Dave, about how much I hated the Hun and how good an opportunity I had to kill him, and all I have to do is sit here and deny it. And that is all any of us has to do: simply deny it. No one, including the police, can put any one of us at the scene. All they can say is that one of us could have been there. So, what you've done tonight is to complete an exercise in futility. And I would suggest that since everybody who could have been accused of the crime has been, maybe this party ought to break up."

Koesler considered that the evening had been somewhat more than an exercise in futility. Some real animosity had built up around all these accusations. He wondered how or if some of these people could ever work together again.

But evidently, Marj Galloway's invitation to call it a night had been taken seriously. The men had closed their Bibles and were preparing to leave. Unlike the conclusion of previous meetings of the God Squad, there was no light repartee tonight. Only awkward, stony silence.

Koesler, like the others, prepared to leave. As he walked through the living room, he recalled that something about that room had disturbed him both when he had visited here for the first time yesterday with the police and again tonight. What was it? He looked around the room.

The color scheme . . . it was the color scheme. The walls of the living area were papered in a sort of pale apricot, but the upholstered furniture was done in a purplish red. Even to Koesler's uncultivated and untutored eye, the hues seemed to clash. He found it curious that both Jay and Marj had such poor taste and that no one had ever rectified things. It seemed strange, but, in the light of the murder they had just been discussing, of comparatively little moment.

In a very few minutes, all of the men, with the exception of Jay Galloway, had left. Instead of being the last out the front door, he closed it and doubled back to the kitchen where Marj stood at the sink disposing of the uneaten hors d'oeuvres.

Silently, Galloway approached his wife. As he moved directly behind her, she stiffened as she became aware of his presence.

He put his arms around her waist, his hands resting against her flat abdomen. She stood stock-still.

"You were magnificent tonight, honey." His voice was almost a whisper. "Any other woman would have folded at Dave's accusation. But you stood right up to him. I was proud of you."

"What's this all about, Jay? Why didn't you leave with the others?"

"I told you, I'm proud of you. When you take over a situation like that and are in command of the whole thing . . . damn, but I find that a turn-on." His hands slid up her body until they found her breasts. He cupped them and squeezed. It was one of his many habits that disgusted her.

He never had been able to understand why anything he did would disgust her. He had tried everything he did to her on other women before doing them to her. Of course, the other women either were prostitutes or were looking for a favor from him and were willing to overlook a lot to get it.

She tried to pull his hands away, but couldn't. She turned quickly. The element of surprise worked; she was free of him. Something in her face made him take a step backward.

"Hey! What is it with you? We're still married, you

know. We might be living apart, but we're still husband and wife. And we're not apart right now. We're together in our house. You're still legally my wife and I want you." He stepped forward and again grabbed at her breasts. "They may not be large, but they're perfect. I remember every contour of them—"

This time she was successful in slapping away his hands with unexpected force.

"That's all you're ever going to have of me: a memory!"

"W-what do you mean?" Not having his way was one of the stresses that always affected his articulation.

"You never listen, do you? Dave said it all tonight when he told you that the thing he regretted most was ever going to work for you."

"Th-that's crazy! He's had a good life. Made a lot of money."

"And along the way lost much of his self-respect, just like everyone else who gets involved with you. It isn't so much that everything you touch turns to dross; it's more that you don't really like yourself, and you can't believe that anyone who would work for you—or marry you, for that matter—can be any good. How could they be worthwhile and still agree to work for you, or marry you?"

"Wh-when did you get a psychology degree?" All this talk was dampening his arousal.

"I don't need a degree. I had to go through the school of hard knocks to learn about you. It dawned on me after the Hunsinger affair. All the way down that trip through hell I could never figure out what I was doing with that maniac. But after we broke up, the whole thing became clear. I guess I needed somebody as rotten as Hunsinger to shake the cobwebs out of my brain.

"It started right after we got married. Before, our sex was great. But you were still trying to win me then. You couldn't be sure I was 'worthless enough' to actually marry you. So you treated me with respect. But once you married me—or, rather, once I married you, that proved to your satisfaction that I was without value; otherwise why else would I consent to be your wife?

"From then on, you treated me like—no, worse than—a prostitute. I was a thing. A thing you could take to bed and use at your whim. Or a pretty thing you could take out on important occasions and show off. But always you used me. Until I began to see myself the way you saw me: worthless. So I became available to almost anyone who wanted to use me in much the same way as you did.

"But Hunsinger brought me to my senses. You, at your worst—and that was something to behold—were never as low as the Hun.

"Now I've got a life to put together. And that life definitely does not include you. I know you're going to find this difficult to understand, but we're through, finished, over, closed, and shut.

"Now, you may leave. And close the door after you!"

Galloway backed away from her. "If you change your mind, you know where to find me."

"If I change my mind, I hope somebody has me committed."

Galloway left the house. He wanted her now more than he had in years. He would not realize that his desire was the direct result of her rejecting him. Now that he no longer possessed her, he respected her once more. But, as he had proved time and again, he was a very good salesman who would not take no for an answer. Like everything else in life, this would require some planning.

As soon as Father Koesler returned to St. Anselm's rectory, he phoned Inspector Koznicki at home.

Koesler recounted the evening's events as carefully as he could recall them. What had begun as a rather routine Bible discussion—albeit with an electric atmosphere—had quickly deteriorated into a maelstrom of anger, hostility, and recrimination.

As best as Koesler could recall, Dave Whitman had

accused Hoffer, Galloway, and Galloway's wife. Jay Galloway, in turn, had accused Whitman. Jack Brown had accused Bobby Cobb, who had returned the favor.

He was careful to relate the new motives for Whitman supplied by Galloway, and for Cobb as supplied by Brown.

"Very good, Father . . . excellent." Koznicki congratulated the priest on his reportage and added, "Our detectives have been busy today and are formulating some very definite opinions. I shall make sure they learn of your contribution first thing in the morning. We are hopeful of wrapping up this case tomorrow."

"That soon!"

"It has been two full days since the murder, Father. And, as you well know, the longer a case continues, the less likely we are to reach a solution."

"You're right, Inspector, of course. I was speaking as the amateur I am. Just because I haven't the slightest idea who did it is no reason to assume that the experts are not close to solving the case."

He could hear Koznicki's soft chuckle.

"Will you be attending the funeral tomorrow, Inspector?"

"Yes, indeed. It is at—" Koznicki tried to locate the obituary in the afternoon paper.

"At 9:00 A.M.," Koesler supplied, "at Holy Redeemer."

"Of course. Will I be seeing you there, Father?"

"Yes. I plan on concelebrating. I got to know Hank fairly well during the discussion meetings. And I must confess I've gotten to know him even better during the investigation of his murder."

"Yes. I think you might say, Father, that he can use all the prayers he can get."

"I quite agree. Well, I'll . . . see you in church," Koesler concluded lightly.

Before retiring, the priest poured himself a glass of sherry. He sipped it slowly as he let the events of the past couple of days drift through his mind.

It was fortunate for the wheels of justice, he concluded, that society did not have to wait for him to solve a crime. But he was glad that the police seemed close to a solution. For his part, Koesler was forced to agree with Marj Galloway. There was no smoking gun . . . at least none that he could detect. Just lots of opportunities and lots of motives.

The smoking gun everyone seemed to be looking for apparently was the knowledge of Hunsinger's colorblindness. So far, the only ones who had admitted such knowledge were Niall Murray and Hunsinger's mother. Neither seemed to have a motive for the crime and both had daylong alibis.

Somebody else had to be holding the smoking gun, but Koesler could think of no way to figure out who.

Well, then, he concluded as he downed the last of the sherry, here's to the police.

4

HACKETT'S FUNERAL HOME WAS, especially for this early in the day, unusually packed.

Seated next to each other in front of the wall near the still open casket were Niall Murray and Kit Hoffer. Each wore a black suit, with white shirt and black tie. They were two of the six pallbearers.

They were waiting while Father Peter Forbes completed the wake prayers. When he had finished, the ceremony would move to the church. Murray and Hoffer conversed sporadically in whispers.

"I don't fancy tryin' to lug that casket up all them steps of the church," said Murray.

"Me neither," Hoffer replied. "That coffin plus the Hun must weigh a ton."

"You're a poet as well."

Both successfully smothered snickers.

"Beats practice," Murray commented after a period of silence.

"Beats practice?"

"Just sitting here."

"We'll pay for it later this morning. You can bet on that altogether."

"You know, I was kind of surprised the coach let us off to come to the funeral. After all, this is Wednesday.

Should be a full day of work. Especially with New York coming up. I mean, like, we are really going to be behind."

"Put your trust in Coach Bradford, will ya now, man? Even as we speak, he is probably sittin' in this very funeral parlor plannin' on how he is goin' to sweat our asses off this afternoon. Besides, we are here for one reason and one reason alone. It would look very bad indeed in the papers and on TV if we hadn't shown up for the Hun's funeral."

"Like, so much for respect for the dead."

Once again, they successfully stifled a laugh.

Father Forbes finished the prayers and left immediately for the church to prepare for the funeral Mass, known since Vatican II as the Mass of Resurrection.

Mrs. Hunsinger's brothers and sisters and Mrs. Quinn gathered about her and assisted her into the waiting limousine for the extremely short trip to the church.

Father Forbes found himself pressed for time. He had to hurry back to the church, vest for Mass, and be ready to greet the cortege as it reached the church doors. Ordinarily, it was not his custom to visit the funeral home just before the funeral. He'd done so this morning as a special courtesy to Mrs. Hunsinger.

He was surprised when he entered the huge sacristy to find Father Koesler waiting and completely vested for Mass. It was just a couple of minutes before nine and the funeral bell was tolling. "Bob! What are you doing here?"

"I'm going to concelebrate the Mass with you." It was Koesler's turn to be surprised. He had taken it for granted that Forbes would assume he would come to concelebrate. Before the Second Vatican Council, for priests to concelebrate a Mass was most rare. It would be difficult to think of any occasion besides a priest's ordination Mass when there was a concelebration. But after Vatican II, concelebration became extremely widespread. Nearly every time more than one priest was present for a Mass, it became a concelebrated Mass.

"But you can't," said Forbes.

"I can't?" Koesler's mind went through a quick computer check looking for a reason why he could not concelebrate. He found none.

"While granting permission for Church burial for Hunsinger, the Chancery specifically forbade that there be a concelebration."

"What! They can't do that!"

Forbes smiled. "They can do just about anything they want."

"But they gave permission for Church burial. And that's that. They can't tack on any other conditions."

"It was a quid pro quo. I had to plead with them for permission to bury. They were most reluctant. I hunted all over the place to find someone, anyone, who would testify that Hunsinger had gone to Mass in recent memory. Or that he had even tipped his hat while passing a church. Nobody. I'm afraid that Hunsinger just gave up on the Church. So now, of course, the Church, in the form of the Chancery, has the opportunity to give up on Hunsinger. So, initially, they denied him Church burial.

"I guess when they finally gave in, they felt they had to get something in return. So they imposed the condition that it not be concelebrated. I don't even know whether they thought there was a chance that another priest would show up. I know it didn't cross my mind until I saw you vested and ready to go."

"Okay, okay. I don't want you to get in trouble." Koesler began to divest.

"But there's nothing in the Chancery's regulation says you can't assist at the Mass." Forbes quickly began to put on the vestments that had been set out for him on the vestment case. "Would you take care of the first two readings?"

"Sure." Koesler left his cassock on and slipped a white linen surplice over his shoulders.

Forbes indicated the selected readings in the lectionary.

The procession started down the aisle toward the front doors of the church where the cortege was awaiting the clergy's greeting. Forbes and Koesler were preceded by four small altar boys, two carrying lighted candles, one carrying a processional crucifix, and the fourth carrying an aspersorium—popularly referred to by the priests as a bucket—in which rested the aspergillum and the holy water.

Forbes sprinkled the casket with the holy water, then, assisted by the attending morticians, spread an ornate white cloth over the casket, meanwhile praying, from the Ritual, that as Henry Hunsinger had been buried with Christ in baptism, he might now be clothed in the white robe of the Resurrection.

The procession returned to the altar area. The mourners, participants, or just curious were handed liturgical leaflets enabling them if they were so inclined to follow the service and join in the prayers and hymns. Very few would do so. Thus, having invited the community to sing the entrance song, the organist sang in solo voice, "God loved the world so much, he gave his only Son, that all who believe in him might not perish, but might have eternal life."

The Mass began with Father Forbes leading the brief introductory rites.

Koesler sat on a straight-back chair in front of which was a kneeler. Briefly, he consulted the lectionary to refamiliarize himself with the Biblical texts he would read.

After Father Forbes read the collect prayer, it was time for the first two Scripture readings. Koesler mounted the pulpit.

"The first reading is taken from the Old Testament, Second Book of Maccabees, from the seventh chapter:

"It also happened that seven brothers with their mother were arrested and tortured with whips and scourges by the king, to force them to eat pork in violation of God's law. Most admirable and worthy of everlasting remembrance was the mother, who saw her seven sons perish in a single day, yet bore it courageously because of her hope in the Lord. Filled with a noble spirit that stirred her womanly heart with manly courage, she exhorted each of them in the language of their forefathers with these words: 'I do not know how you came into existence in my womb; it was not I who gave you the breath of life, nor was it I who set in order the elements of which each of you is composed. Therefore, since it is the creator of the universe who shapes each man's beginning, as he brings about the origin of everything, he, in his mercy, will give you back both breath and life, because you now disregard yourselves for the sake of his law.'

"This is the word of the Lord."

A few scattered voices responded, "Thanks be to God."

The organist essayed "The Lord Is My Light and My Salvation" as a psalm response, but, again, it became virtually a solo.

Koesler began the second reading. "This is a reading from St. Paul's letter to the Romans, the sixth chapter:

"Are you not aware that we who were baptised into Christ Jesus were baptised into his death? Through baptism into his death we were buried with him, so that, just as Christ was raised from the dead by the glory of the Father, we, too, might live a new life. If we have been united with him through likeness to his death, so shall we be through a like resurrection. This we know; our old self was crucified with him so that the sinful body might be destroyed and we might be slaves to sin no longer. A man who is dead has been freed from sin. If we have died with Christ we believe that we are also to live with him. We

know that Christ, once raised from the dead, will never die again; death has no more power over him.

"This is the word of the Lord."

Again, a few voices: "Thanks be to God."

Koesler left the pulpit.

Forbes entered it to read the Gospel. "A reading from the Holy Gospel According to Mark:

"His mother and his brothers arrived, and as they stood outside they sent word to him to come out. The crowd seated around him told him, 'Your mother and your brothers and sisters are outside asking for you.' He said in reply, 'Who are my mother and brothers?' and gazing around at those seated in the circle he continued, 'These are my mother and brothers. Whoever does the will of God is brother and sister and mother to me.'

"This is the Gospel of the Lord."

A few scattered voices: "Praise to you, Lord Jesus Christ."

It was time for the homily.

Father Forbes began in time-honored fashion. He offered the condolences of everyone he could think of to everyone he could think of.

Koesler, one of those in whose name sympathy had been offered, scanned the group being singled out for condolences.

"Mrs. Grace Hunsinger," began Forbes. She sat ramrod straight, looking neither right nor left; her face was covered by a black veil. You can't hardly find that kind of mourning any more, thought Koesler.

"Mrs. Hunsinger's many brothers and sisters, uncles and aunts of the deceased," Father Forbes intoned. They looked like hardy stock, judged Koesler. They're probably still wondering why such a sturdy, healthy young relative lies dead.

Forbes continued his enumeration. "Mrs. Quinn, long-time companion and friend of Mrs. Hunsinger..." At mention of her name, Mrs. Quinn's head bobbed upright. She had nearly fallen asleep. Koesler hoped, rather absently, that she would not have one of her habitual dreams and wake up shouting "bingo" in the middle of the Mass.

Koesler would not fall asleep. He scarcely ever did during the homilies of others. But neither did he pay attention. He scarcely ever did that either. He would mentally compose his own homily. He almost always did, amid many digressions and distractions.

Yes, homilies had changed since Vatican II, even for a funeral or, more currently, the Mass of Resurrection. Before the Council, eulogies containing personal praise of the deceased were discouraged. One was expected to preach on such eschatological themes as death, judgment, heaven, hell, purgatory; the possibility of the Church Militant (those yet alive) helping the Church Suffering (those in purgatory) by prayer. Now, whenever the priest knew the deceased, a eulogy, mixed with a bit of eschatology, was the order of the day.

There was a distinction too, at least in Koesler's mind, between pre- and post-Vatican II preaching. The preaching common during his early priestly years he would have called sermons. These had had little if anything to do with the Scripture readings of the Mass. If it was decided that now was the time to inveigh against the evils of steady dating or French kissing, then that was what the sermon was about.

After the Council, more and more priests were led to link their preaching to the subject of the Scripture readings of the Mass. It was a style Koesler liked. When there were two readings (or, more commonly, on Sundays or special occasions such as funerals or weddings, three), the initial trick was to find some connection between the readings and develop that as the homiletic theme.

Thus, as Father Forbes began his homily, Father Koesler mentally began his.

The three readings of this Mass put Koesler in mind of a valiant mother, faced with the sudden death of her sons, who comforts herself, first with St. Paul's sublime insistence on the fact of Christ's Resurrection and ours through Him. And her second consolation comes from the evenhandedness of God's mercy. Anyone who wishes to do the will of the Father is mother, brother, or sister to Christ.

Of course, putting Henry Hunsinger in the company of those who wanted to do God's will was stretching things a bit. But that was the very point of the Christian understanding of death and judgment: that God does not judge by human standards. Koesler would never forget the simple words he had seen stenciled on the wall of Detroit's Carmelite convent: "When you die you will be judged by Love."

This was the theme he would have developed had he been delivering the homily this morning. It was the theme of the homily he now preached to himself. He did not even wonder what Father Forbes had preached.

After the homily the Mass of Resurrection proceeded without incident. Occasionally, Koesler looked about the crowded church. He had seldom seen so many extremely large men in church at the same time. The Cougars were in attendance to a man. He was reminded of the comment made by President John Kennedy when awarding a medal to one of the astronauts at a White House ceremony. He said, in effect, that one could tell the difference between the astronauts and the politicians assembled for the ceremony; the astronauts were the tan and healthy ones.

Similarly, one could distinguish the football players from the ordinary humans; the players were the ones with no necks, just huge shoulders sloping upward into large heads.

Father Forbes reached that part of the Mass called the

consecration. According to Catholic faith, when the priest repeated the words of Jesus at the Last Supper, the bread and wine again were changed into the reality of Christ come again as food for the soul. As Forbes pronounced the words of consecration, so did Koesler in a whisper. Thus, Koesler managed to foil the capricious decision of the Chancery forbidding concelebration at this Mass. It was such an absurd, childish dictum that he felt rather good about violating it.

From his vantage in the sanctuary, somewhat elevated above the floor of the body of the church, Father Koesler could easily see the people in the pews. As Mass proceeded toward communion, he tried to pick out the suspects.

You couldn't miss Kit Hoffer and Bobby Cobb. Not only were they large; they were both pallbearers and thus in the front row. Hoffer was kneeling; Cobb was seated. Another distinguishing point: non-Catholics seldom knelt in church. Kneeling, for most of them, was foreign to their worship experience. So, while Catholics knelt, non-Catholics sat.

Jack Brown was in the second row, just behind the pallbearers. He seemed ill at ease. Koesler wondered why. Did he find the Catholic ceremony awkward, or was something else troubling him?

The Galloways were seated in about the fourth or fifth row, Koesler could not quite tell which. Jay Galloway seemed . . . what? Self-satisfied?

Marj Galloway was not satisfied. That was obvious and so was her reason for being upset. Koesler was certain that if she could have carried it off without attracting too much notice, she would not be here. And if she could have helped it, she would not be sitting next to a man she no longer loved. Had Koesler been present at the epilogue to last night's meeting, he would have understood just how much in fact she despised her husband.

Koesler could not locate Dave Whitman, though

undoubtedly he was somewhere in the congregation. Koesler wondered if it would be possible for Whitman and Galloway to continue to work together after the words they had exchanged last night.

The congregation stood for the Lord's Prayer. Non-Catholics generally have no objections to standing. Then most everyone knelt again as communion time arrived.

Koesler assisted Forbes in distributing communion. Thus he was nearby when Grace Hunsinger received communion from Father Forbes. And thus Koesler was startled when, having received communion, she began to sob and almost collapsed. Instinctively, he moved as if to assist her. But her relatives were quick to come to her aid and support her.

The weeping of this brokenhearted mother finally supplied the somber, bleak character this funeral, until now, had lacked. Hardly anyone in this church lamented Hunsinger's death. They were surprised, yes, but hardly heartbroken. So, till now, it had been a rather bland occasion at which a number of people were expected to be in attendance and to which many others were drawn by curiosity.

Now, hearing the heart-rending sobs of Grace Hunsinger, everyone was deeply affected. Who could remain unmoved in the presence of a grieving mother?

Koesler could sense, almost tangibly feel, a new awareness of death and grief in the congregation. Somewhere in this church, he was now certain, was the murderer of Hank Hunsinger. Could he or she not be affected by this mother's desolate tears? Would this not alter the status quo? Would the murderer's defenses not be lowered? Might the guilty person not actually be moved to confess?

Although he had not intended to do so, Koesler at that moment resolved to return to the Hunsinger home after accompanying the casket to the cemetery.

Indeed, the priest concluded, it was long past time when he must stop thinking of Henry Hunsinger's death as a murder investigation in which, by pure accident, he himself was involved. Leave the solution of crime to the experts. One of his duties as a priest, a duty he entirely welcomed, was to at least try to console those who mourn.

The return drive from Holy Sepulchre Cemetery to Holy Redeemer was a long one. Father Koesler had lots of time to think. Deliberately, he forced out of his mind thoughts of the ongoing murder investigation and concentrated on the business at hand: death and dying.

It was in one of the Epistles—Koesler thought it might be Paul's letter to the Hebrews—but in any case, the Bible stated it clearly: "It is appointed for each man once to die. And after death the judgment."

After death the judgment.

After death, what?

The question thoughtful humans had been asking through the ages. There could be no doubt that each of us who live will die. Then what? Nothing? Anything? Reincarnation? As a lower form of life? As another human? Or, as the Bible clearly teaches, judgment? Then, heaven? Hell? Purgatory?

No living person, pondered Koesler, can prove the answer to any of those questions. It's a matter of choosing something in which to believe.

The Christian is offered the Resurrection in which to believe. The Christian is supposed to put all his or her chips on Christ. If Christ did not rise from the dead, then, in St. Paul's opinion, we are the most to be pitied because our faith is in vain. But, the Apostle goes on to write, the most important reality of all is that Christ did rise from the dead. And if He, human as well as divine, is alive, overcame death, then everyone lives after death. A most consoling faith.

What sort of belief would a person such as Hank Hunsinger have about a life after death? From the little Koesler had been able to learn, he doubted that Hunsinger had given much if any thought to the question. Even though he had somehow found his way into a Bible study group, there was little indication that he thought about death and its consequences at all. It probably was the combination of not being religious along with being young and, though periodically injured, healthy. The Hun would have had no occasion to ponder death and a hereafter.

No matter. Now he knows all the answers.

Although Koesler did not often find himself on the southwest side of Detroit these days, it was easy and reassuring to recognize and remember the old neighborhood. As he drove down Junction Avenue, he passed the stately St. Hedwig's Church, a Polish parish. Amazing how well the neighborhood had been preserved! So many Detroit neighborhoods had been allowed to deteriorate and decay.

Finally he reached the celebrated intersection of Vernor and Junction and the familiar sprawling brick buildings that were part of the vast plant that was Holy Redeemer. He found a parking space just across the street from the Hunsinger home.

The doorbell was answered by a woman who identified herself as Rose Walker, one of Mrs. Hunsinger's sisters. Koesler could see the resemblance. "It's so good of you to come back, Father. We have a buffet set up in the kitchen. Would you like something to eat?"

"Maybe a little later. Right now I'd like to talk with Mrs. Hunsinger for a few minutes, if that's all right."

"Of course. I'll take you to her, Father. She'll be pleased to see you."

Mrs. Walker led the way into the living room. Koesler located Mrs. Hunsinger immediately. She was seated near the large front window. Near her sat a man in a straight-back chair. Neither was speaking. Again, from the family resemblance, Koesler guessed it might be her brother.

Mrs. Walker made introductions. Suspicions confirmed; the man was one of Mrs. Hunsinger's brothers. He excused himself to let the priest be alone with Grace.

Koesler was very glad he had decided to return to the home after the ceremonies. There was almost no one here besides Grace Hunsinger's immediate family. For most, the special occasion of a funeral had given way to an ordinary Wednesday, and work was waiting. For others, the show was over.

Mrs. Hunsinger appeared to be very calm, but also very remote, as if contemplating some tranquil mystery. She had held up well at the mausoleum too. Just that one moment at communion when she had been overcome by emotion.

He could understand that. For many Catholics, himself included, communion was a time of the most intense prayer and communication with God. It was not at all uncommon for one, in a stressful demanding moment such as the funeral of a loved one, to find the intense emotional impact of communion overwhelming.

"Mrs. Hunsinger?"

"Oh? Oh, Father Koesler." She had been unaware of his presence. A brief smile of recognition and welcome crossed her face.

"I thought we could talk a little bit."

She nodded, but without animation.

"How are you feeling?" Koesler felt like taking her hand in his as a consoling gesture. But, as was his wont, he remained reserved.

"All right now, I suppose."

She was dry-eyed. If he had not witnessed her breakdown in church, he would have found it difficult to believe it had happened.

"You know, Mrs. Hunsinger, according to our faith, it's all over now."

"What's that?"

"Henry. It's three days since he died. He is well into eternal life."

"That's what troubles me."

"You shouldn't be troubled. The way you and I were

raised and the way we were taught our catechism, death and judgment were presented in a more frightening way than they are today."

Even though a good number of years separated the two, Koesler could be fairly certain that both he and Grace Hunsinger had been taught identical Catholic doctrine. So little of that doctrine had been changed before the Second Vatican Council.

"Our early impression of God," Koesler continued, "was heavy with vengeance. We could lead decent lives in the state of sanctifying grace and then maybe slip and eat one pork chop on a Friday and if we died before getting to confession God would zap us into hell. And, while that oversimplifies things a bit, it is pretty much the way we were taught.

"Now, I think, we tend to view the morality of a life as a whole rather than consider its individual episodes. Not that an act of theft is good. But that the act of theft flows from a lifestyle where an individual act of thievery might be more a mistake than typical of the way that person would ordinarily operate."

"But Henry's lifestyle was not all that good—"

"Perhaps not . . . at least not as far as we can judge. But Henry has been judged by God . . . by an all-loving and forgiving and understanding God. We mustn't lose faith that Henry has found that God can find ways unknown to humans to forgive. We leave Henry to our Father in heaven with great confidence and hope. It's all we can do."

They were quiet. Koesler was content to allow his words to sink in. He sought only to give Mrs. Hunsinger confidence to help her over her terrible loss. It would do Henry's mother no earthly good to remain tortured by her son's sudden death following upon—to be kind—a not exemplary life. He hoped he had given her some reason for optimism.

"You walked right along there." Mrs. Hunsinger was staring out the front window.

"Pardon?"

"On the day of your first Mass. The procession came out of the rectory and went down the street and up the steps into the church. I was standing right there." She pointed, Koesler had no idea where. Somewhere along the route the procession had taken. He remembered the day clearly.

"It was a warm, sunny day. I was standing there holding little Henry's hand. Then we went into the church for your first solemn Mass. It was beautiful and you sang so well.

"Then after the Mass, we came outside again and waited while the procession returned to the rectory. When you passed by, all recollected and pious, I remember I squeezed little Henry's hand and told him he should grow up and be just like you.

"But," she sighed deeply, "it was not to be."

Koesler looked at her for a long time. She continued to gaze through the window at the facade of Holy Redeemer Church, lost in her memories. He took one of her hands in both of his and pressed gently. She did not react. She continued to sit and gaze.

Finally, he rose and stepped away. He was startled to find that he had almost backed into Mrs. Quinn. He was additionally surprised to find Mrs. Quinn fully awake.

"How is she, Father?"

"I think she's all right. I wish I could have been better able to comfort her, though."

"Time, Father. It'll take time. It always does. Both of us have lost our husbands. And we know only time can heal a wound like that. It's probably worse with the loss of a child, even if the child is a grown man. That I wouldn't know; I've not lost any of my children, praise God."

All the while Mrs. Quinn talked she was leading Koesler toward the kitchen. As he passed through the various rooms in the old house, he was impressed with how neat and tastefully decorated they were and how well kept up. He commented on this.

"Well, thank you, Father. It's kind of you to notice. Grace and I do our best and we try to make up for each other. And Henry provided handsomely. He wanted us to move. He was willing to buy us a house or build one wherever we wanted. But Grace wanted to stay close to her Holy Redeemer. And I can't say I disagree with that.

"That would be a point in his favor, wouldn't it, Father . . . I mean, as he stands before our Savior in judgment . . . that he was kind to his mother?"

"I'm sure it would be," Koesler assured. Somehow, he'd found himself doing a lot of consoling, particularly in view of the fact that this funeral had not been his responsibility.

Mrs. Quinn led him into the kitchen, where a buffet consisting mainly of sandwich ingredients had been laid out.

In the kitchen was a considerable crowd; almost everyone who had returned here from the cemetery. Koesler guessed, after a cursory study, that most of the people were relatives of Mrs. Hunsinger.

Awkward. He definitely was odd man out. Oh, the group was respectful enough, but he was not family. What had been a rather lively conversation before he entered was now somewhat subdued.

As speedily as he could, Koesler worked his way through the crowd, made himself a modest ham and cheese sandwich, and worked his way out of the kitchen to an empty corner of the dining room. There, alone, he wolfed down the sandwich.

One thing was certain, he had to get out of there.

Suddenly it occurred to him that this was his day off. Or at least what was left of it. He found Mrs. Quinn and asked if he might use the phone. She showed him to a small desk in an alcove beneath the staircase. Fortunately, no one else was in the area. He dialed a number from memory.

"St. Clement's," a matronly voice answered.

"I'd like to speak to Father McNiff, if he's available."

"Just a moment, sir."

After several long moments: "Father McNiff."

"Anybody ever tell you that you physically resemble Carroll O'Connor?"

"A few." McNiff's voice revealed he knew the caller.

"Anybody ever tell you that your philosophy of life resembles Archie Bunker's?"

"Not to my face they don't." McNiff chuckled.

"Patrick, old fellow, why did I know that you'd be hard at work at the rectory on your day off?"

"The work of the Lord must be done in season and out of season. We who have put our hands to the plow must not turn back."

"How very Biblical of you."

"And you, Robert, are you calling from some sleazy bar while your hirelings keep St. Anselm's together?"

"No, I'm calling from a private home," he admitted with some embarrassment. Until having made the indictment against McNiff, Koesler hadn't realized that he had, in effect, been working on *his* day off. "And what I'm calling about," he hurried on, "is to ask you to join me for dinner."

"Sure. When and where?"

"How about Carl's Chop House about six?"

"Done."

"Don't work too hard."

"Don't play too hard."

Koesler arrived at Carl's at twenty minutes to six. Early again! Well, he would go to prepare a place for McNiff.

He asked the hostess if he could be seated in the Executive Room, and told her he was expecting McNiff. She asked if Father McNiff would also be wearing a clerical uniform. If McNiff were not in clericals, Koesler replied, the next Pope would not be a Catholic.

The Executive Room was cozier but not substantially different from the other two large dining rooms. But the Executive Room featured Kay Marie, the redhaired queen of waitresses, who had been at Carl's since the Year I, and whose aunt was a nun, which always gave Kay Marie and Father Koesler something to talk about.

The busboy brought the extremely generous relish tray, breadbasket, cottage cheese, and creamed herring. Koesler began to wonder if he'd been too hasty in designating Carl's as their rendezvous. Ordinarily he dined here only as a special celebration or after a significant weight loss. Carl's portions were bigger than life. It was a classic place for a pigout. He promised himself that he'd get some exercise tomorrow. Where, he did not know. Maybe he'd go for a walk.

"Evening, Father. Alone tonight?" Kay Marie brought him out of his dietetic reverie.

"No; expecting a colleague. How's your aunt?"

"She's thinking of retiring."

"Oh? How old is she?"

"Eighty-four."

"It's a thought."

"What'll it be tonight?"

"How about a martini, up?"

"Different. You're usually a manhattan. Bourbon manhattan."

"Great memory, Kay. I'm going to leave the manhattans to my companion this evening."

He had filled his salad plate with the first of the preprandial delicacies and was gnawing on a bread stick when McNiff arrived.

"Good!" said Koesler. "Now the next Pope can be a Catholic."

"What?" McNiff seated himself. "This isn't going to

be another of those nights where you pick on the Pope, is it?"

"Absolutely not. Going to leave the Holy Pope of God—your phrase—out of it entirely."

"Good!"

Kay Marie returned. McNiff would have a manhattan. All was well.

"Remember your first drink, Pat?"

"At your hand. Of course. There's been many a sip since then."

"You're lucky you laid off those first ten years. By now your liver would be embalmed."

"See the remarkable prescience of Holy Mother Church."

They understood each other's hyperbole.

Kay Marie took their orders. McNiff would have Dover sole. Koesler would have the ground round. Kay Marie sighed. She could have brought Koesler's entrée without asking.

"Wasn't that something," said McNiff, "about Hank Hunsinger! Who woulda thought when we saw him play last Sunday that he'd be dead that night?"

"A real surprise."

"Say, I hadn't thought about this before, but what does that do to that Bible discussion group—what did you call it?"

"The God Squad. I don't know, Pat. We met last night. But I'd bet that group, qua group, never meets again. So I don't think I'll get the chance to introduce you to the bunch."

"That's all right." It wasn't, but McNiff wouldn't admit it. "I've got plenty to do."

"Matter of fact, I went to the funeral this morning."

"Hunsinger's?"

"Uh-huh."

"How was it?"

"Not particularly sad until his mother broke up."

"That'll do it."

"It was from her house that I phoned you."

"So, working on your day off! Physician, heal thyself."

"I'll drink to that."

Kay Marie brought the salads. Both McNiff and Koesler would have another drink.

"Say, remember Robideau?"

"Sure." Koesler was grateful for the turn in their conversation. He was trying to forget the funeral, the investigation, the whole Hunsinger affair.

"He was notorious for not paying attention to whom he was burying or marrying. He got help with the weddings because he could carry their marriage license along with him. But he had real trouble with funerals.

"Well, one day he had this funeral and not only did he not know whom he was burying, he forgot whether it was a man or a woman. He had a devil of a time preaching. He used phrases like 'the loved one,' 'our dear, departed friend,' 'the deceased.' Finally, he decided to get off the fence; after all, he had a fifty-fifty chance of being right. So he said, 'We must remember to keep him in our prayers.' At that, he became aware that one of the pallbearers was shaking his head no."

"Good old Robideau." Koesler laughed. "He preceded me by several years at St. David's. They said they were always afraid he would start a fire in the confessional because of the speed with which he kept opening and closing the confessional screens. Someone once accused him of absolving with both hands and both feet."

They ate steadily. Their drinks would do them little harm. And the entrées had not yet arrived.

"There was a hypochondriac in the parish," Koesler continued, "who was also really ill—"

"Sort of like the paranoid guy whom everybody actually does hate," McNiff interjected.

"Right. Well, it was the feast of St. Blaise and this lady called Robideau and actually asked him to come to her house, since she was bedridden, and bless her throat. Robideau of course was not about to do any such thing. He told her to prop the phone between her ear and the pillow, pretend her arms were blessed candles, and cross them underneath her chin, and he would give her the blessing over the phone."

McNiff snickered. "Reminds me of an incident they tell about that happened in Grand Rapids. This lady's husband died. They had bought a couple of lots in a public cemetery and she couldn't get anyone to come and bless the grave. It wasn't that she couldn't get anyone to get off his ass and go bless the grave; the guys who were willing to go would check with the Chancery and discover that the Chancery wasn't giving permission to bless graves then.

"But she finally finds this one guy—must have been a clone of Robideau's—and pleads with him. So he asks her which way is the cemetery. North, she says. So the guy swings his chair around so it's facing north and he traces a large sign of the cross in the air.

"The good news is he didn't charge her a stipend."

They both chuckled.

The busboy cleared away the dishes and trays and Kay Marie served the entrées. A huge *amandine* fish. The largest hamburger steak in captivity, smothered in mushroom gravy. And mounds of French fries.

Oh, yes, thought Koesler; a very long walk tomorrow.

As the two got down to serious eating, Koesler reflected on the stories they had exchanged and undoubtedly would continue to recount.

As long as he could remember, at least among his peers in the sacerdotal fraternity, priests were wont to recall and recount stories of the past. Some more than others. The recent phenomenon of Catholic nostalgia had led to such books as the popular *The Last Catholic in America* and the spinoff play, *Do Black Patent Leather Shoes Really Reflect Up*? In all probability, had there been no Vatican

II, there would not be this wave of Catholic nostalgia because everything would still be pretty much the same. Very little would have changed. Most Catholics would not know or would not be informed that many of the things they had done seriously a quarter of a century earlier were now considered funny.

But stories of "the good old days" had been and would remain favorites among priests, with or without Vatican II.

"You know," said McNiff as he loaded tartar sauce on the fish, "I got a document yesterday in the mail from the Tribunal. They wanted the document to be put in the parish's secret archives. Put me in mind of when I was at St. Mary Magdalen in Melvindale—"

"With old Jake Parker." Koesler was relatively certain that McNiff would not be coming up with any old Jake Parker stories that hadn't been told before. But, what the heck, they were good stories.

"Right." McNiff warmed to the memory of old Jake Parker. "So, anyway, I got a document then, too, from the Tribunal, to be placed in the secret archives. So I went to Jake, told him the problem, and asked where the secret archives were. And he said, 'Father, they're so secret, even I don't know where they are.'"

They laughed. Good for the digestion.

"Didn't you miss Melvindale your first time out?" Koesler recalled.

"Yup. Drove right through the little suburb. Finally asked a cop where Melvindale was, and he said, 'Father, you just left it.'

"But that's the way Jake looked at it too. Once I got another missive from the Tribunal. This time they wanted me to do a notary job on a marriage case."

"You don't get those as much now as you used to... at least I don't."

"That's right. But back then, I was getting them almost every week. And I'd have to go out and call on somebody—who was usually pretty hostile—and ask a lot of personal questions. Well, anyway, I'd had it, so I went in to see Jake and I told him, 'I've had it with these notary jobs. What would they do to me downtown if I don't do it? If I just refuse to do it, what could they do to me downtown?'

"And Jake says. 'Father, they couldn't do anything to you; you're already here.'"

They laughed again. As anticipated, Koesler had heard the story previously. But when consummate raconteurs such as Myron Cohen or Flip Wilson begin to tell their stories, one looked forward to hearing one of their familiar anecdotes.

"Actually"—McNiff had polished off the fish and was working on the few remaining fries—"I think old Jake was ashamed about being in Melvindale, though I don't know why; it's a nice enough little town. But for some reason, he just didn't think anything good happened in Melvindale.

"Now that I think of it, it might just have been something in old Jake's personality.

"I remember for years I used to get at him to ask for another assistant. We had almost three thousand families and there were just the two of us. But he wouldn't do it because he was afraid of being turned down. Finally, one fall, he broke down and asked the Chancery for another priest. Well, his worst fears were realized: he didn't get one. They turned him down. And those were the years when every September and June they shifted hundreds of priests to different parishes and all the new appointments were published in the *Detroit Catholic*."

"I remember it well. I was the editor. I used to publish those new assignments. We'd start on page 1 with pastoral appointments, then stick all the assistant assignments on page 2. It always took at least the entire page. Sometimes they ran over onto page 3.

"I remember once our reporter wrote a mock account,

which opened, 'Seven tons of priests were transferred . . .'"

"Exactly. Well, the day the new assignments were published—none of them being to St. Mary Magdalen, Melvindale—old Jake sat at the dining-room table all day long with the *Detroit Catholic* in front of him, opened to the assignment page. And every time somebody would pass by, old Jake would call him over and point to the page and say, 'Look at that! Just look at that! You couldn't put your finger on one of those assignments and say, 'Now there was a smart move.'"

Koesler hadn't heard that one before. "It's rationalization like that that can lead to mental health."

Having finished the ground round, Koesler was sloshing the fries in mushroom gravy. Oh, yes, it would have to be some walk tomorrow. "Reminds me of when I was at Patronage of St. Joseph parish. It was just me and the pastor, Father Pompilio. Then a monsignor from the Chancery was going to take up residence at Patronage. He was offered a single room, just like the one I had. But a Chancery monsignor wasn't about to take that lying down—literally. So Pomps was obliged to surrender his very nice three-room pastoral suite to the monsignor. Later, he explained to me how, in the end, he had outsmarted the monsignor: The single room was closer to the ceiling fan in the hallway than the suite was."

The busboy asked if they were finished. Silly question, thought Koesler; he knew he was supposed to ask, but still it seemed obvious that all that was left were the empty plates.

He cleared them away and Kay Marie ascertained that McNiff would have coffee and Koesler decaf and that neither would have dessert. Koesler considered the thought of dessert obscene.

McNiff patted his tummy appreciatively. "We haven't got a corner on the sort of logic that, as you say, leads to mental health. Before we had our own school in Melvindale, a bunch of nuns used to come in several times a week to teach catechism in the church. And that, of course, was fine with me. I've always said the art of being a truly fine catechist is finding somebody else to teach catechism."

Koesler nodded approval.

"But old Jake Parker insisted that we go over at least once and talk to the little kids who were going to make their first communion. So this one time I went over, reluctantly, and waited while this nun, their teacher, introduced me. She said, 'Children, Father is going to talk to you now. And I want you to pay good attention to what he's going to say. After all, he spent twelve years getting ready to teach you.' I wondered why she brought that up and where she intended to go with it. Then she added, 'Of course, I spent twenty-three years in preparation . . .' I felt like the village idiot. But I guess she managed to preserve her mental health."

Kay Marie brought the beverages. McNiff asked for the bill.

"Well," said Koesler, "I doubt you'd find many nuns that uptight today. Maybe it's as simple as back then some said there were three sexes: men, women, and nuns. But today they know they're women. They dress like women instead of like ancient statues. They're permitted, even encouraged, to be mature, much more in charge of their own lives than ever before in history.

"But back then, you're right: they could be a bit stiff-necked. One of the toughest groups I was ever associated with were the nuns at Patronage. Even for those days, those gals were on the strict side. I spent most of my time trying to talk our parochial kids into sticking it out and staying in school.

"Being with that group is probably what made the two funny ones stand out as much as they did."

"You had two funny Salacians? That may be a record."

McNiff began to compute the tip.

"Yup, two; count 'em, two. One Tuesday, after Our Lady of Perpetual Help devotions, the two of them came back into the sacristy. They were the sacristans, which post became the only outlet they could find for their humor. One of them, a Sister Dulcilia—hard to forget a name like that—asked me if, when I blessed religious articles after the devotions, did the blessing include crosses. I said sure it did. So Dulcilia, pointing to her companion, said, 'That's fine; next week I hold Sister here on my lap.'

"Another time, I arrived in the sacristy to prepare for Perpetual Help devotions. As usual, the Sisters had laid out the appropriate vestments on the vestment case. I was already wearing my cassock and collar. So I put on the surplice and found that the Sisters had pinned to it one of those ribbons from a funeral floral arrangement with the word 'Friends' on it.

"I just left it that way and wore it for the devotions. All the nuns were sitting in the front pews. I wish you could have seen the faces of the two jokers when they saw I was wearing the funeral ribbon. They told me they got in a lot of trouble over that one . . . 'a scandal to the good people of the parish' and all that.

"Now you'd think that might have cured them. But some time later, when they were certain I was scheduled for the early weekday Mass, they laid out the vestments the night before. They had a purple stole, a green maniple, and a black chasuble."

"Don't tell me," McNiff interrupted, "you didn't have the first Mass!"

"With their luck, it couldn't have happened any other way. Father Pompilio wanted to go on an early morning fishing trip and traded Masses with me. Fortunately, he didn't report them. But he was convinced they were certifiably insane."

"Remember," McNiff spoke through his laughter, "the time when everybody thought I was insane?"

"The time—? Hmmm . . . there were so many. But since

you're talking about Melvindale, it's probably the one where you came back for the parish fall festival."

It would not occur to Koesler to head McNiff off at the pass merely because the anecdote was ancient and oft repeated. Good stories remained good even when retold.

"That's the one. It was, O Lord, three or four months after I was transferred from Melvindale and I had nothing more to do with the parish. But old Jake Parker wasn't feeling all that good and he asked me to come back and stand in for him at the fall festival. That's where I was insane: in agreeing to do it.

"Well, it was just your ordinary parish festival with simple little games and prizes and a few rides. All except for the big card game in the rear of the tent. The ushers got kind of carried away and were hosting a full-scale gambling concern—poker, blackjack, that stuff. And that's when the good old Melvindale police got into the act: closed us down, made some charges. Meanwhile, old Jake Parker is up in bed nursing a cold while I am trying to handle the cops."

Purple stole, green maniple, and black chasuble. Why was this thought continuing to distract him? Koesler tried to pay attention to McNiff's story.

"And that wasn't even the worst part. Who does the *Free Press* reporter call for a statement—Jake Parker, the pastor and the one responsible for it all? No, he calls me. And what do I say? I say, 'Why don't you tell your editor that you couldn't find Father McNiff?' And what does the *Free Press* reporter write in next morning's paper? He writes, 'A certain Father McNiff, when contacted about the police raid, stated, "Why don't you tell your editor you couldn't find Father McNiff?"'

"It was at that point that all my peers and classmates were willing to pronounce me certifiably insane."

"And rightly so."

They split the bill plus tip evenly. Kay Marie bade them

good evening and asked them to pray for her aunt the nun. When McNiff, after asking, was informed that the nun was eighty-four and pondering retirement, he asked Kay Marie to have her aunt pray for them.

During his drive home, Father Koesler tried to listen to WQRS, the classical music station. But it was offering chamber music, which Koesler easily could live without. He switched off the radio and smiled as he recalled the stories, some old, some new, that McNiff had told. And he smiled as he recalled the stories, all old, that he had told.

But his preoccupation with the vestments of mixed colors still puzzled him. The problem was not intrinsic to the story. Koesler had told that story many times; never had he been troubled or puzzled by it.

From time to time he wondered if he were coming down with Alzheimer's syndrome, or whether it was just the natural disintegration of the brain cells that accompanies aging. But then, in good time, it would all come together and make sense.

So he was confident that at some unpredictable time the elusive link between the color-confused vestments and whatever they reminded him of would be made clear. Probably it would happen while he was showering. For some strange reason, the routine of showering always cleared his mind for some of his better thinking.

5

FATHER KOESLER WAS SHOWERING. It was a quarter to eight on a bright Thursday morning. Mass was at eight-thirty. As usual, the priest's mind wandered in an undirected path.

Something, some inner feeling, some intuition told him the police were going to catch the killer of Henry Hunsinger today. This was, after all, the fifth day of the investigation. And Inspector Koznicki had told him more than once that the longer a case remains unsolved, the less likely it is that they will arrive at a solution.

Then there was the assurance by Lieutenant Harris that they would, indeed, solve the case. The professional confidence of Harris and Sergeant Ewing, Koesler was convinced, simply could not be gainsaid.

At any rate, the police would not be the only ones busy today. Koesler faced the crush of business that had piled up, due in part to his early participation in the investigation as well as to his day off yesterday. For one thing, shortly after breakfast there would be two days of mail to attack. Oh, well, everything in its allotted time. It would, in any event, be a busy day.

After showering, shaving, and dressing, he had just a few minutes to look over the Scripture readings for today's Mass. After all his years of being a priest, reading and meditating on the Bible and preaching, it did not take him long to come up with a two- to five-minute commentary on the Scripture of the day.

This was another of the many changes resulting from Vatican II. In the first decade of his priesthood, Koesler would offer a sung Mass entirely in Latin and there was never a homily or commentary during the week. This custom of preaching daily, if briefly, was much more demanding of the priest. It also made a lot more sense.

Seven people were waiting in the church. The usual customers. Koesler knew them all well. By the time he vested and was ready for Mass, there might be one or two more present.

The Mass began as informally as a very formally structured ceremony could. In no time, he reached the Gospel reading. It was from St. Mark, the eighth chapter. Everyone stood as he read:

"*When they arrived at Bethsaida, some people brought him a blind man and begged him to touch him. Jesus took the blind man's hand and led him outside the village. Putting spittle on his eyes, he laid his hands on him and asked, 'Can you see anything?' The man opened his eyes and said, 'I can see people but they look like walking trees!' Then a second time Jesus laid hands on his eyes, and he saw perfectly; his sight was restored and he could see everything clearly. Jesus sent him home with the admonition. 'Do not even go into the village.'*"

The congregation sat and looked expectantly for today's message.

"That little story," said Koesler, "is my favorite miracle. It's so much more . . . well . . . human than the usual miracle. This is not a grand show of power like stilling the angry winds that are whipping up the waters of the Sea of Galilee or calling Lazarus back from the dead after three days in the tomb.

"This is a more tentative kind of cure, if you will, instead of miracle. Can't you just see Jesus rubbing a little spittle on the blind man's eyes and saying, 'How's that? Do any good?' And the guy says, 'I don't think you've got it yet. All I see is stick people walking around like trees. Have you got anything else up your sleeve?' And Jesus says, 'Okay, give me one more shot at it.' And He touches the blind man again. Then the blind man says, 'I can see everything very clearly now. I think you've got it! By George, you've got it!'

"It puts me in mind of my favorite scene in a fine silent movie on the life of Christ, called *King of Kings*. This scene follows one where the Christ is in a small village curing people right and left, just by an act of His will. Then, He leaves the village and goes out to the countryside. He is exhausted. He leaves the dusty country road and sits in the shade of a large tree.

"The Apostles form a ring around the tree, keeping the crowd, which has followed him from the village, at a distance. Then, a little girl sneaks underneath the arm of one of the Apostles, who reaches out to grab her before she might bother Jesus. But He waves the Apostle aside and greets the child with a smile. She shows Jesus her ragdoll, which is ripped.

"You can see the wheels turning in His mind. He has just finished working wondrous miracles. He seems to be weighing what He should do about the little girl's doll. Should He wave His hand over it and make it miraculously fixed? Finally, He extracts a straw from the doll's innards and with it, He carefully and slowly mends the doll and returns it to the little girl.

"Now it's just an apocryphal story thought up by some clever screenwriter. But I think it captures the spirit of Jesus. That little girl probably wouldn't even have understood a miraculous cure for her doll. But that a very important man would take the time to mend her doll would be an act of kindness she would never forget.

"I don't think I even need explicitly apply the lesson to our daily lives. But somewhere out there today we're likely to encounter someone who's got some trouble. Let's look for that someone and mend the trouble.

"And, as they used to say on the TV show 'Hill Street Blues,' let's be careful out there."

The remainder of the Mass passed uneventfully. Except that something was troubling him. But again, he was unable to put his finger on it. Something to do with this morning's Gospel . . . but what? In his mind's eye, he could almost see his brain cells exploding and disintegrating.

After Mass and a few prayers of thanksgiving, he returned to the rectory. St. Anselm's secretary, Mary O'Connor, had attended his morning Mass and had preceded him to the rectory.

As usual, she offered to fix him some breakfast. As usual, he declined her offer. As usual, he sliced a banana over a bowl of Granola. As far as Koesler was concerned, there was much to be said for routine.

Reflecting on routine reminded him of Hank Hunsinger, whose life had been so compulsively riddled with routine. Koesler tried to drive the thought away. He had resolved to get back to parochial duties and let the police do the job for which they were so well trained and capable.

And he would have succeeded in expelling the thought if it hadn't been for the puzzles that still nagged him. Last night's story about the nuns laying out various colored vestments for him, plus this morning's distraction that had some inscrutable connection with this morning's Gospel. Were they connected? Were they connected with Hunsinger's murder? If so, how?

Breakfast finished, he went to his office, where, predictably, Mary had stacked two days of mail. A couple of significant piles. Armed with his letter opener, he attacked the first pile. A good offense, he thought, is a good defense . . . or something.

The first letter was from a convent of contemplative Carmelite nuns.

"Reverend and Dear Father:

"There is nothing more sacred to our faith than the altar breads which, upon the words of consecration, pronounced by priests such as yourself, Reverend Father, become the living presence of Our Lord and Savior, Jesus Christ.

"Thus, careful attention must be paid to the preparation of these sacred wafers.

"Most purveyors of altar breads subject the process entirely to insensitive machines. From the mixing of the dough, to the baking, to the cutting.

"This is not true of the work of our convent. No, Reverend Father, none but the virginal hands of our Sisters touch the sacred altar breads..."

Koesler could not go on. He was laughing too hard. So, it takes virginal hands to replace vulgar machines. He could envision the assembly lines of Detroit's auto plants. First there were the blue-collar workers on the line, followed by robots, followed by the virginal hands of hitherto contemplative nuns.

Probably he would order some altar breads from the nuns. They deserved some patronage after having entertained him. Then he would file their letter with his other prized possession: the letter from the company selling altar wine, all of whose Teamster drivers were Catholics.

The next envelope bore the extremely familiar address, 1234 Washington Boulevard. It was a Chancery missive, containing the parochial help-wanted listing. This too was a fairly recent wrinkle.

In the good old days, notice of a changed assignment had come in much the same fashion as a draft notice. Except that instead of "Greetings," the assignment letter would invariably begin, "For the care of souls, I have it in mind to assign you to..." There would follow the name of the parish that would be the priest's residence for the next approximately five years.

Now that priests were becoming an endangered species, it had become a seller's market. The Chancery now regularly listed openings in parochial assignments for pastors or associate pastors accompanied by thumbnail descriptions of the type of ministry expected. One applied, or did not, depending on one's interest. Seldom was pressure brought to bear. It may have been a better system than the previous practice. Koesler thought it was.

Suddenly, for no explicable reason, but, indeed, the way it usually happened with Koesler, everything fell into place. It was as if a curtain had suddenly lifted, revealing the stage. Suddenly the connection between the multicolored vestments, the blind man beginning to see, and the Hunsinger murder was clear.

It was a thrilling moment and Koesler savored it.

He needed to make only one phone call. If he received an affirmative response, it would be at least possible that he had found the solution to a murder.

Driving out to Dr. Glowacki's office with Sergeant Ewing, Lieutenant Harris was trying to figure out why he so resented this trip.

The bottom line, he finally concluded, was that he disliked having amateurs mess in his profession. There were just far too many people who considered themselves competent, without benefit of any training or preparation, to do police work. His intolerance of that sort of intruder doubled when the amateur meddled in homicide cases.

Especially when the homicide got a lot of publicity, the homemade experts seemed to come out of the woodwork—psychologists, psychiatrists, soothsayers, fortunetellers, mystics.

Of course, Father Koesler did not fit any of the stereotyped categories. And, Harris had to admit, the priest had been of help in the past. But it was not, he thought, a good precedent to invite amateurs in on a case. He wished his old friend, Walt Koznicki, who was coming to Glowacki's office in a separate vehicle, would not do it. It was about the only bone Harris had to pick with Koznicki.

They had discussed it a few times but had never reached a mutually agreeable solution. Koznicki would protest that Koesler was the sole exception to the rule banning nonprofessionals from cases. And Koznicki would explain that there were times when Koesler's expertise in things Catholic was helpful in certain cases. Harris would argue that, religious expertise or not, the police were well able to solve homicides without outside help.

They never reached an agreement. So the argument occurred less and less frequently. But Harris continued to believe that Koznicki's better judgment was clouded when it came to Father Koesler.

Besides, Harris had just developed a theory concerning the Hunsinger case and had anticipated testing it today. That had been before receiving the call this morning from Koznicki, who had been called earlier by Koesler. Harris had objected. But Koznicki made it clear that while he wasn't outright ordering Harris to Glowacki's office, neither was it merely an invitation.

Harris turned off Ford Road into the parking lot adjacent to Dr. Glowacki's office building. Koesler was already there. They exchanged greetings with the priest, Ewing more warmly than Harris. In a brief time they were joined by Koznicki. The four entered the building and were immediately admitted into Glowacki's consultation office.

It was Koesler's show. "I'll explain my idea as thoroughly but as quickly as possible," he began. "At the beginning of this investigation, when I was allowed to sit in on a series of interviews with possible suspects in the case, it soon became obvious that six of the suspects had the opportunity—and a sufficient motive—to kill Hunsinger. But none of those six possessed the final bit of information known to everyone in this room—that Hunsinger was colorblind and thus could not have detected that the liquid he thought was shampoo was white, not pink. I think that bit of information has been referred to as 'the smoking gun.' Am I right so far?"

"Well," Ewing said, "it's not necessarily that none of those suspects 'possessed' the knowledge that Hunsinger was colorblind; the fact is that, at least so far, we haven't been able to prove that one or any of them knew—or to get one or any of them to admit it."

"So far," Harris emphasized.

"Of course," Koesler admitted, "that was sloppy of me. All right. None of those suspects would admit they knew of Hunsinger's condition.

"But what if . . . what if we're looking for the wrong ype of person?"

Harris did not care for Koesler's use of the first person plural. But he said nothing.

"What, exactly, are you driving at?" Koznicki asked.

"A couple of unrelated things got me started thinking of another way of approaching this case. This morning I was reading a passage from a Gospel. It was about Christ curing a blind man. Only it wasn't one of those instantaneous cures. This one happened in stages. At first the man could see, but indistinctly. He could see people but they looked to him as if they were walking trees. In other words, he was no longer totally blind, but his sight definitely was impaired.

"The other thing that happened was that I was telling a friend about an incident involving a couple of mischievous nuns who deliberately set out a color-mixed set of vestments because they were certain I would have the first Mass the next day. They wanted to play a joke on me. But they blundered. The pastor traded with me and took the early Mass.

"Now, if I had seen that mixed bag of vestments, I would have understood the joke. But the pastor didn't have a clue as to what was going on. When he told me about it, all straight-faced, he didn't know what to make of it. And he suggested, in jest, I think, that maybe they were not in complete possession of their sanity.

"Don't you see?" Koesler, who had thought this theory through to its conclusion, mistakenly assumed the others would understand completely even without a complete explanation. It was a bad habit of his. Earnestly he continued. "Instead of accusing the nuns of being crazy, the pastor, if he didn't understand the joke, should have assumed the nuns were colorblind. Or"—he glanced at the ophthalmologist—"I should more correctly say color-deficient."

Koesler paused a moment, in vain, for some sign of comprehension or support from the others.

"Would you care to amplify whatever point it is you are trying to make, Father?" Inspector Koznicki was attempting, more than anything else, to rescue Koesler from the embarrassing silence.

"Certainly, Inspector. My point is just this: the man midway through his cure is not totally blind, but partially blind. Just as the nuns, if they hadn't been clowning around, presumably might not be totally colorblind, but merely color-deficient. I checked this all out with Dr. Glowacki earlier, before I phoned you."

"So," Harris was growing impatient, "you have a couple of nuns who are either joking, crazy, or color-deficient. So what?"

"So," Koesler continued, "that got me thinking about the murder of Hank Hunsinger. Well, to be honest, though I've tried not to, I have thought of little else these past few days.

"And, to try to sum this up, I thought of the police trying to find a suspect who knew that Hunsinger was colorblind and would be unable to distinguish one color from the next. But what if . . . what if it were not a case of knowing about Hunsinger's colorblindness? What if the murderer were color deficient and not able to tell the difference between the clear color of the DMSO and the pink color of the shampoo?"

There was another silence.

"That's so, isn't it?" Ewing turned to Glowacki. "That such a person would not be able to tell the difference between the colors?"

"Oh, absolutely," the doctor responded. "That was another thing the Father and I discussed this morning. We call the impairment a red-green deficiency."

"It's cute, Padre," said Harris, "but I'm afraid you've come up with a hypothesis without a foundation. We know that Hunsinger was colorblind. Someone else who knew it would know that he or she didn't have to be concerned about the color of the liquid containing the poison. There's no reason to think that it could have been the other way 'round—that the perpetrator couldn't tell the difference between the bottles."

"Well, I beg to differ with you, Lieutenant. But I think it does make better sense my way." Although the priest spoke firmly, he genuinely dreaded this argument. He wished that all of them, especially Lieutenant Harris, whose mild animosity toward himself Koesler had perceived, had bought his theory.

"Let me suggest this, please," he continued. "Suppose the killer were normal-sighted. Just to avoid fooling with pronouns let me assume the killer was a man.

"He goes to Hunsinger's apartment. His objective is to get the strychnine into the DMSO. He wants the DMSO to carry the poison into Hunsinger's bloodstream, quickly killing him. In order to get Hunsinger to use the tainted DMSO, the killer decides to mask the DMSO as shampoo because he knows that the Hun routinely showers at his apartment after the game.

"Now I'll grant you that the quickest and easiest way of doing this, since the containers of the shampoo and the DMSO are identical—I remember that correctly, don't I?"

Koznicki nodded slowly, encouragingly.

"Since the containers are identical, the killer simply exchanges the two bottles, relying on Hunsinger's compulsive routines to cause him to use the DMSO because it's in the spot reserved for the shampoo. Hunsinger uses the poisonous DMSO because he can't tell any difference in the bottle shapes, he can't read the label because of poor eyesight, and he can't tell the difference in the colors because he's colorblind."

"That's about the way it stacks up," Harris noted.

"All right," said Koesler, "but the killer has no plans to revisit the scene of the crime after the murder. In fact, he knows he can't. Because, again routinely, Hunsinger is showering to prepare for a . . . uh . . . date.

"So the killer knows that he will necessarily leave behind a scene that looks like this: There will be an open bottle of DMSO on the spot reserved for shampoo. And the police will quickly discover what is in the bottle and the cause of death. In effect, the killer is leaving a clue telling the police that he knows about Hunsinger's colorblindness—a condition that Hunsinger has gone out of his way to conceal.

"On the other hand, in the theory I propose, the scenario is the same, except for the reason for not exchanging bottles. Now the killer is not leaving a clue for the police. Now the killer is leaving a clear bottle instead of one with a pink liquid, for the very simple and reasonable reason that the killer himself cannot tell the difference."

Another silence.

"Two things wrong with that, Padre," said Harris, finally.

"One, you're thinking—or trying to think—like an investigator. Whereas criminals, in real life, rarely think that ingeniously. That's why we catch so many of them. You'd be surprised how many homicides are committed in the manner they are simply because that was the simplest way of doing it. It is very possible—probable—the killer didn't even advert to the different colors . . . or, if he did, didn't care.

"And two, your case is built on the supposition that one of our suspects is . . . uh . . . color-deficient. When there's no indication that that is so."

"Well, again, Lieutenant," said Koesler, "with all due respect, there may be one or another of the suspects with just that disorder."

Harris looked at him with disbelief. It was so strong the detective did not have to verbalize his doubts.

"It happened when I visited the Galloway home. The first time, when Mrs. Galloway was questioned, I was vaguely aware that something was wrong, but I couldn't say what. Then, the other night when our Bible discussion group met there, I became a bit more aware of what it was that was troubling me. It was the color scheme.

"Now God knows I am the last person in the world who might make a living at interior design. But the living room of the Galloway home is somewhat outlandish. I don't know what the rest of the house is like, but in the living room, they have the walls done in a sort of pale apricot and the upholstered sectional couch and chair are a purplish red . . . I believe they call it magenta."

Both Ewing and Harris had to admit to themselves that they had noticed what they considered the atrocious color scheme. Actually, they had been aware of it long before Koesler, but had simply ascribed it to bad taste and dismissed it from their consideration.

"That," said Koesler, "is the final detail I checked with Dr. Glowacki."

"Oh, yes. And I assured the good Father that such colors as he described—an apricot and a magenta—would be a classic kind of blunder of a red-green personality. You see, green plays an important part in this—"

"Is there any way of testing for this?" Harris interrupted. "Is there any way to prove if a person is . . . uh . . . color-deficient?"

"Oh, my, yes," said Glowacki. "It's right here in this little pamphlet, the 'Ishihara Test for Colour Blindness.' "

"May I?" Harris extended his hand and the doctor gave him the pamphlet. Harris began to page through it.

"You see," Glowacki explained, "there are ten pages of numbers in that little book. The numbers are formed by outlines of small colored circles."

"What's the point?" Harris had completed his scanning of the pamphlet.

"The point," the doctor responded, "is that normal-sighted people see one thing in that booklet, while color-deficient people see quite another."

"Could you demonstrate?" Koznicki asked.

"Of course. Sergeant Ewing, would you care to take the test?"

"Sure."

"Very good." Glowacki opened the booklet to the first page. "Do you see a number there, Sergeant?"

"Yes. Twelve."

"That's correct. Actually, if someone were to miss the twelve, one would be tempted to search for a white cane." The doctor perceived his attempt at humor was not completely appreciated. His visitors were all business.

"All right," he turned a page, "and this one, Sergeant?"

"Eight."

"That's correct. Now we get into the red-green color deficiency. The color-deficient person sees a three here. And this?"

"A five."

"The deficient person sees a two." The doctor continued turning pages.

"Twenty-nine."

"The deficient person sees seventy."

"Seventy-four."

"The deficient sees twenty-one."

"Seven."

"The deficient sees nothing here but colored dots."

"Forty-five."

"Again, the deficient sees nothing."

"Two."

"The deficient sees nothing." He turned another page.

"There isn't any number there." Ewing was surprised; he thought he might have erred.

"No, Sergeant, that's no mistake." Glowacki sensed Ewing's misgiving. "The color-deficient person sees a two here."

"Sixteen."

"Again, the deficient person sees no number here."

"Amazing," Koznicki commented. "And you say a person with this color deficiency actually sees these numbers that differently from the normal-sighted?"

"Quite. Yes."

"Now, you see," said Koesler, "if my theory is correct, someone in the Galloway household has this color deficiency. Either Jay Galloway or his wife, Marjorie."

"A layman can administer that test, is that correct, Doctor?" Koznicki asked.

"Of course. All one needs to know is what to expect the deficient person to perceive in this test. Father told me you were likely to want to test two subjects separately. So I took the precaution of borrowing another copy of the Ishihara test. You're perfectly welcome to borrow both, if you wish."

"You have been most cooperative, Doctor," said Koznicki. "Ned, you and Ray take one and check out Mr. Galloway. Father Koesler and I will take the other booklet and visit Mrs. Galloway. Call us at the Galloway home as soon as you have completed the test." He turned to the ophthalmologist.

"Thank you once again, Doctor. You've been an enormous help. And remember, not a word of this to anyone. Not until the entire investigation is completed."

As the three officers and the priest left his office, Dr. Glowacki was tingling. He had never before participated in a murder investigation. It was thrilling. He would, of course, keep their secret. Even from his wife, who would quite naturally want to know what the strange quartet had wanted. Just as she had wanted to know why he was sending her to borrow Dr. Graven's copy of the Ishihara test. She would learn all in good time. When he and the police had completed their investigation. And when, together, they had apprehended the person who had murdered his late patient.

If Dr. Glowacki was any judge, that would be soon.

Marj Galloway answered the door. As Koznicki and Koesler entered the house, they could see a couple of domestics dusting in the dining area. The living room was unoccupied. Mrs. Galloway invited them in, reluctantly, Koznicki felt, and seemingly with an air of foreboding and inevitability.

Both Koznicki and Koesler separately concluded that even without benefit of makeup, dressed in an old housecoat, and with her hair disheveled, Marj Galloway was a strikingly attractive woman.

"I hope," Koznicki opened, "that you do not too much mind our intrusion."

Marj shrugged as if to comment, And if I did . . . ?

"We will not take up much of your time," Koznicki proceeded. "We are continuing our investigation into the murder of Mr. Hunsinger. And I wonder if you would be so kind as to help us."

"Inspector—you did say you are an inspector?—ah, well, Inspector, when is this nonsense going to end? I had an affair with Mr. Hunsinger about a year ago. Apart from the football field, or at a great distance at a few social events, I haven't had anything to do with the Hun since we broke up. To be perfectly frank with you, I don't give a good goddamn that he's dead. But I had nothing to do with his murder."

"Sometimes," Koznicki's voice was soft and persuasive, "it is through your voluntary cooperation that we are able to establish just that: that you are innocent. We are not charging you with any crime. We ask only that you help us by taking a simple, uncomplicated test."

"A test? What kind of a test?"

"A vision test." Koznicki produced the Ishihara booklet.

"A vision test," she repeated. "Oh, what the hell; let's get it over with."

Koznicki held the booklet so all three could see the pages as he turned them.

"Twelve," Marj read.

Everyone could discern that one, Koesler remembered.

"Eight."

Uh-oh.

"Five.

"Twenty-nine.

"Seventy-four."

There was no doubt about it: Marj Galloway was not color-deficient.

"Seven.

"Forty-five.

"Two. "

It had to be her husband, Jay. Koesler could almost see, in his mind's eye, probably even at this very moment, Jay fumbling through the test, unable to correctly discern any number but the first.

"There's no number on this page at all."

Koesler could envision Lieutenant Harris grudgingly admitting the validity of Koesler's theory. The priest was not a vindictive person; he would not rub it in when next he met Lieutenant Harris.

"Sixteen.

"Is that it? That was pleasant. Did I pass? Do we go on to the Rorschach test? Do you have any nice little ink blots for me to identify?"

"You did very well, Mrs. Galloway." There was no trace of acrimony or chagrin in Koznicki's voice. Seemingly, he was genuinely pleased that she had done well.

Koesler, eyes darting from side to side, a reaction foreign to him, was waiting for something. The phone rang. That was it.

After several rings, which Koesler felt to be a dozen, the phone was answered. A moment later a no-nonsense working woman appeared in the archway. "Is there an Inspector Koznicki here?"

"I'll take it." Koznicki unfolded from the chair and went into the dining area.

"Koznicki," he identified to the caller.

"Ned Harris here, Walt. How'd it go with Marj Galloway?"

"She has normal color vision."

"Same with her husband. We had a devil of a time convincing him it wasn't necessary to call his lawyer about thirty seconds after we entered his office. But he settled down when he saw what the test was about."

There was a pause.

"There is more?"

"Yeah. We told him his wife was taking the test too. That was one of the reasons why he agreed to take it without benefit of counsel. He asked why we were giving both of them color vision tests. That was after he'd passed it with flying colors . . . no pun intended.

"So we told him that color perception was relevant to our investigation and that we'd noticed the rather odd color scheme of his living room, and we were just checking. I'll give you his exact reply."

Koznicki could hear the pages of Harris's notepad being riffled.

"He said, 'Marj doesn't have any trouble with color; she just doesn't have any taste. It's about the only flaw in an otherwise Ms. Perfect. I never paid any attention to her horrible sense of decor because she is such a good piece of ass.'" There was just an instant's hesitation. "I don't suppose you'd want to pass that entire quotation on to the good Padre."

"No."

"Now, would it be okay if we get on with the *police* investigation of this case?"

"Yes." Koznicki let the sarcasm pass without comment and replaced the receiver on the phone. He reentered the living room.

"Was that—" Koesler began.

"Yes. That was Lieutenant Harris. His results were negative also."

Koesler's spirits sank.

"We will be leaving now, Mrs. Galloway." As he spoke, Koznicki looked about the room, seeing it in a different light. It was true, the furnishings were an uncomplementary mixture of colonial, contemporary, and just about every other style.

"I hope you're finished. I mean I hope this is the last time I will be subjected to a random interrogation regarding a dead person I don't give a damn about." It was evident that Mrs. Galloway was not amused.

"Mrs. Galloway," Koznicki spoke firmly, "this is an investigation into a crime . . . into murder. We go where the investigation leads us. But we will make every effort not to trouble you further, unless it becomes necessary."

Outside the house, Koznicki told Koesler of Harris's report, omitting what it was that Galloway most appreciated in his wife.

It was a silent ride back to St. Anselm's. Koznicki felt very sorry for his friend. As for Koesler, he could recall, wincingly, times past when he had felt extremely foolish.

The present moment might not represent the nadir of foolishness in his life. But it ranked.

They did not have far to go. Just an elevator ride to the basement of the Silverdome. Harris and Ewing showed their badges and entered the Cougars' dressing room, only to find that almost everyone, including the man they wanted to see, was on the field. So they walked up the ramp to the playing surface. The Cougars were fortunate this week that no other major activity was scheduled for the Silverdome. Otherwise, their artificial turf would have been removed or covered and they would have had to search for some other practice facility.

The scene that greeted the two officers was one of organized chaos.

In one corner, offensive and defensive linemen crashed into each other. In another, linebackers stutterstepped as they practiced intercepting passes. From the other end of the stadium could be heard a recurring and resounding thunk as a football was repeatedly propelled off the foot of the punter to soar into the upper reaches. Midfield the passing personnel of the offense were scrimmaging against the defensive backs.

Through it all, the voice of Coach Bradford, who was with the scrimmaging players, could be quite clearly heard. "I wanna see some urgency in those third and fives."

They were practicing third-down formations, each scrimmage simulating a third down with five yards to go for a first down.

Bobby Cobb slapped the ball in his hand and retreated while the offensive players ran their pass patterns and the defensive players retreated to cover their zones. Cobb's throw was long and deep, intended for a wide receiver who was going full speed. Then the receiver, "hearing the footsteps" of the defensive back who was closing in, at the last moment backed off, and the ball fell harmlessly to the turf.

"Ritter!" The returning receiver hung his head. "I don't care how much you get paid," Bradford blazed, "but you're not gonna get it free. Desire, Ritter! Desire, drive, dedication, execution! They go together, Ritter!"

Harris and Ewing walked along the sidelines until they reached the Cougars' bench where the trainer, Jack Brown, was standing.

"Mr. Brown," Harris began.

"Brownie," said the trainer; "everybody calls me Brownie."

"Okay, Brownie, could we talk to you for a few minutes?"

"Sure. Do you mind if we go into the locker room? I've got some things to do down there."

"Good idea."

They retraced their steps to the locker room. Place kicker Niall Murray, left ankle encased in an ice pack, reclined on a training table. The detectives, of course, knew Murray, but not the man standing next to him. They were introduced to John Owen, the team's public relations representative.

Owen, face seemingly set permanently in a concerned frown, addressed Brown. "So, what we got?"

"An ankle."

"How bad?"

"Bad bruise and swelling. I'm hopin' the ice'll bring it down. It's gonna be sore."

"How'd he get it?"

"Special team drill. A pileup. Somebody kicked him. An accident."

"How many times you been told to stay away from the point of contact!" For the first time in this exchange, Owen directly acknowledged the presence of the person whose injury they were discussing. "Just kick the ball and get off the field."

"Aw," said Murray, "it's no fun that way at all."

"So how can we list him?" Owen went back to Brown. "'Questionable'?"

"Not yet. The injury is too bad for questionable. Better put him down as doubtful."

"Godalmighty! In one week we lost the tight end who's practically the franchise, and now the kicker. How the hell do they expect me to promote this team?"

"The kicker's down, not out," said Brown. "Just don't list him as questionable yet."

Owen, grumbling, departed.

Brown carefully removed the ice pack from Murray's ankle. The swelling made the ankle appear grotesque. In addition, there was a dark pinkish hue that reflected some internal bleeding.

"Looks worse than it is," Brown commented. He touched the ankle gingerly. Wherever his fingers went, small white prints appeared, only to resolve again into the angry pink. "But it's way too early to tell how it's gonna respond."

Brown began wrapping adhesive tape in a figure-eight on Murray's foot—around the ankle, across the arch, under the instep, back again over the arch, and around the ankle. "Too tight?"

"It's okay," Murray replied.

"What happens next?" Ewing was genuinely interested.

"Well," said Brown, "lucky it isn't his kicking foot or we'd really be in trouble. Still, the left ankle gets a lot of pressure. He plants all his weight on it when he kicks. I may just have to build a protective device for it."

"You build one?"

"Lots of times. Out of fiberglass. Then cover it with foam rubber. Then adhesive tape. Can provide some protection for almost any body part, especially the arms and legs. Usually, one of the officials will check it before the game . . . make sure we don't build a weapon."

Ewing looked around the trainer's quarters. He was

surprised at the number of cardboard boxes containing adhesive tape of various dimensions. "How much do you use, Brownie?"

"Don't rightly know. Lots. We're budgeted for $20,000 worth of tape for the season." Brown continued to tape the ankle, then reapplied the ice pack. "But you fellas didn't come out here to talk about the Mick's ankle."

"We wanted to talk to you about Hunsinger," said Harris, in a far more friendly tone than he had used during Brown's initial interrogation.

"We already talked about him." Brown clearly was reluctant to undergo another questioning.

"This is not like the last time, Brownie," said Harris. "We thought it might be helpful if we got a little more background on Hunsinger. Sort of find out more about what kind of guy he was. For one thing, the bottom-line image we've gathered from comments made about him is not very favorable. We thought we'd like a peek at the other side of the coin, as it were."

"That's right"—Brown sounded more relaxed now that he was reassured that this would not be a repetition of the interrogation—"nobody's had much good to say about the Hun. Well, he wasn't a Boy Scout."

"So," Harris hoisted himself onto an adjacent training table and sat there adding to the informal atmosphere, "maybe there isn't a flip side of the coin."

"Well, I'll say this for the Hun: he sucked up more pain and played through it more than a lotta guys I know."

"Was he hurt much?"

"Football's that way. Read the team reports from the league office any given weekend. There's usually more than three hundred players listed with more than four hundred injuries."

"How could that be—a hundred more injuries than players?"

"Multiples. The Mick's got an ankle. But he coulda been worse. He coulda got a left ankle, left neck, right hand. The worst I ever saw was Dorsett listed with general all-body soreness.

"But don't get me wrong; the Hun wasn't lookin' for trouble. Some guys do. They don't take enough care with their equipment. Take the shoe, for instance. For football, especially on artificial turf, a shoe is, or should be, protective equipment. But if it's not designed right for support, or if it's worn out, you can pick up a nasty ankle injury or what they now call 'turf toe.'

"But the Hun always got the best shoes, the best equipment. He may not have been a knight in shining armor when it came to his own personal conditioning. But that was his own personal choice. He decided he'd rather have fun than stay in tiptop conditioning. He also decided it was foolish to take needless risks with less than perfect equipment.

"And, as you know, he played just about every game. Just about every offensive play. And I can testify he had to suck up more pain than the average guy to do it."

"But what's so odd about that, Brownie?" Harris pursued. "Don't the players have a saying, goes something like—"

"You can't make the club from the tub," Murray supplied.

"Yeah," Harris agreed. "Doesn't everybody play even when they're in pain?"

"You don't understand—or you forgot: the Hun had a guaranteed contract. Owners and management always have that fear when it comes to players with a guaranteed contract: that they'll sit it out when they could be playing. And some do. I've known my share of players who float once they've got a contract with guarantees built in.

"But that's the way it is. There's always gonna be a certain kind of player who'll put out what he thinks he should do just to remain comfortable. Then there's those who always give 110 percent no matter how much they're paid.

"Then, see, the guys with guaranteed contracts who won't put out are just bein' shortsighted. No contract, guaranteed or not, is forever. So when the floater's contract is up, that's all she wrote. He's out.

"That's what the Hun knew. And that's what separated him from almost everyone else. He knew no contract was forever. And he was one who gave his 110 percent and—mostly 'cause of the years he put in—he played with more pain than any other player I've ever known. But not because he gave a damn for the team. Just because he knew no contract was forever. And he intended to get every penny he could from the game.

"And that pretty much explains the Hun."

"Interesting," Harris said. "Very interesting. But how did he do it? How was he able to keep on playing week after week, season after season with all those injuries and all that pain? Was he some kind of superman?"

"No; the Hun was no superman. But he had a king-sized determination. And we'd help him as much as we could."

"How's that?"

"Pills. Painkillers." Brown noticed Harris's eyebrow arch. "Oh, nothing illegal; the team doctor prescribed 'em. I just doled 'em out. The Hun got 'em after just about every game. Almost all the time, they did the job."

"What did you give him?"

"Dilaudid." Brown reached back to unlock the medicine cabinet. He removed a bottle from one of the shelves, took off the bottle cap, and shook a pill into his hand. He showed the pill to Harris and Ewing. "Dilaudid."

"Little, isn't it?" said Harris. "Looks like a BB. That could do the job? On a man the size of Hunsinger?"

Brown nodded vigorously. "Yup. That's why it's so little. Because it's so powerful. Works like morphine. Got a real kick. It did the job, even for the Hun." Brown chuckled. "But you're right about one thing: it's so little the Hun wouldn't believe it could kill all the pain. He wasn't one for moderation. As, for example, that poison he kept in the apartment—strychnine. Most people'd be content to use traps or some commercial product. Not the Hun; he's gotta have the king of rat poisons."

"So what did you do?" Harris asked.

"Huh?"

"What did you do to convince him one little pill would be enough?"

"Oh, yeah, right. Well, he wasn't one to take no for an answer. So I used to give him two pills . . . no, not two Dilaudid. The Hun may have been big but he was no horse." Brown reached again into the medicine cabinet, searching for another container. "I used to give him two pills. But I kept reminding him that one was all he needed. The warning that one was enough, along with always breaking down and giving him a second pill, worked. As long as the Hun thought he was getting double strength, he was satisfied. But the second pill wasn't much more than a placebo."

Brown found the bottle for which he'd been searching. He removed the container, opened it, and shook another pill into his hand, where it rested alongside the Dilaudid. He showed both pills to the officers. "Papazole. It's an antithyroid medication, but unlike the Dilaudid, it's of very weak strength. You could take lots of Papazole in this strength without doing yourself any damage. For all practical purposes, the Papazole was a placebo."

Harris studied the two pills. "You mean you were able to pass them both off as Dilaudid?"

"Sure, the Hun couldn't tell the difference."

"Well," Harris said with some satisfaction, "they look to be the same size and shape, but they're different colors. I mean, the Dilaudid is yellow and the Papazole is white."

"Sure. But the Hun couldn't tell . . ." Brown's voice trailed off; a look of extreme dismay appeared on his face.

"Because the Hun was colorblind." Harris completed Brown's statement.

"Brownie!" Murray exclaimed. "You knew! I thought I was the only one who knew as well!"

"Yes, Brownie knew." Harris could feel the adrenalin pumping. The familiar euphoria that came with closing in for the kill. "Brownie knew. But Brownie didn't tell anybody. Why is that, Brownie?"

"I . . . I didn't think it was important."

"Didn't think it was important? A man has a condition that affects less than 1 percent of all human males, and you didn't think it was important? We asked you, first time around, to list all Hunsinger's impairments and idiosyncrasies. You mentioned his compulsions and astigmatism, but not his colorblindness. Because you didn't think it was important? You said he had astigmatism, which affects a goodly proportion of the populace. But you neglected to say he was colorblind, a condition so rare it is almost unique? Because you didn't think it was important!

"Let me tell you what happened last Sunday, Brownie. At ten you left the Pontiac Inn. Instead of coming here as you usually do, you hurried to Hunsinger's apartment. You already knew about the new security system in the lobby. You were able to study it on the previous Tuesday evening when you came to the meeting of the discussion club. You timed your entrance to the lobby, synchronizing it so you wouldn't be caught by the sweeping closed-circuit camera. You flipped open the lock with one of your plastic credit cards.

"You went up to Hunsinger's apartment, got the strychnine, switched the bottles of shampoo and DMSO, poured the strychnine into the DMSO. The liquid in the bottle where the pink shampoo usually rested now was white. But you knew it didn't make any difference to your plan. The bottles were the same shape and size, just like those two pills you just showed us. You knew it didn't matter that the liquid in each of the bottles was a different color, just like you knew it didn't matter that the two pills you always gave Hunsinger, which were supposed to be identical, were, in reality, different colors. The different-colored liquid and the different-colored pills would make no difference to Hunsinger because you knew that Hunsinger was colorblind!

"Then you got out of the building the same way you got in, by synchronizing your exit through the lobby with the moving camera. And you hurried back out here to get here just before the team arrived from the inn. And that's what you did last Sunday. You killed Henry Hunsinger!"

"It's not true. I didn't do it."

"You got an explanation that's different from mine? One you can corroborate with any witnesses? You can't account for two hours last Sunday morning. No one can testify as to your whereabouts for those two hours. We've been looking for someone with a motive for killing Hunsinger. You had one: he was corrupting physically and morally everyone on the team he could. We've been looking for someone who had the opportunity: I just explained how you did it.

"And finally, we've been looking for the 'smoking gun'—the one who, along with motive and opportunity, knew that color meant nothing to Hunsinger because the poor bastard was colorblind.

"I think we've got our man." As Ewing began handcuffing Brown, Harris removed a card from his wallet and began to read, "You have the right to remain silent . . ." Brown, face ashen, looked at the floor. "I think I'd better talk to a lawyer."

Father Koesler, even late that day, was still embarrassed by his colossal faux pas. Imagine involving the police in a fallacious guilt theory! He wondered if either Mr. or Mrs. Galloway might sue for something or other. He'd heard of litigation for false arrest. He wondered if there were some such process for false accusation. Of course, neither of them was actually accused of anything.

But his had been such an egregious error that he thought mere embarrassment insufficient penalty.

Koesler had not felt so mortified since his school days. Well, perhaps once since then. Oddly, it had been during another homicide investigation. The one in which everyone was looking for a local monsignor who had mysteriously disappeared. That time too he'd had a theory that had proven to be without foundation. Yes, his embarrassment on that occasion had easily equaled his present chagrin. And for roughly the same reason.

When would he settle down and address only the questions he was asked instead of wandering around in a field wherein he was destined to remain an amateur?

It was nearing six o'clock. Ordinarily at this hour he would start dinner and watch the evening news. This evening he decided on only half his ritual. He wouldn't watch the news. Most likely there would be something about the Hunsinger investigation. There had been every evening, if only to report that there had been no progress. And he didn't want to be reminded of that investigation and his blundering participation in it. So he put two generous-sized hamburgers on a low fire, then went to his office to begin preparation for next Sunday's homily.

He had already decided to base his homily on the second Scripture, a reading from St. Paul's letter to the Romans: "It is rare that anyone should lay down his life for a just man, though it is barely possible that for a good man someone may have the courage to die. It is precisely in this that God proves his love for us: that while we were still sinners, Christ died for us."

Koesler always seemed to favor these Scriptures that emphasized, explained, or demonstrated God's incredible love for his creatures. People in general, in Koesler's view, did not often enough reflect on that reality. They thus missed one of the overpowering sources of consolation in life as well as a magnificent motivation for love of others.

Yet it was strange that he was again focusing on death. It seemed, since the murder of Hunsinger, that he could not escape the subject. And here he was again thinking of Hunsinger. He wished, as he had many times in the past, that he had more mental discipline.

The phone rang. That would distract from the homily preparation. Things simply were not working out very well this day.

"St. Anselm's."

"Bob?"

"Yes." He always felt vaguely uncomfortable when addressed by his given name, unless it was by a relative, an extremely close friend, or another priest. Most priests today seemed to be addressed by just about everyone as good old Tommy, Louis, or Eddie. Koesler readily admitted to being traditional enough to find a place for a sense of respect for an office. Especially the office of a priest.

"This is Pat," the now familiar voice of McNiff identified.

"Oh, hi, Pat. What's up?"

"Did you hear it on the news?"

"Hear what? I didn't have the news on."

"The five-thirty news. They got him. They got the guy who killed Hunsinger."

Koesler was almost afraid to ask, "Who?"

"The trainer. What's his name? Jack Brown. Showed him being taken into police headquarters. Handcuffs and all."

"What time did they arrest him; did they say?"

"Uh..." McNiff tried to recollect. "I think they just said earlier today. But it seemed like it was kind of bright out. I don't recall seeing any shadows. I guess it must've been around noon, or midday, at least."

"Pat, do you remember which police officers brought him in?"

"They didn't give any names, but there was a cop on either side of him... had ahold of his arms."

"Do you remember, was one white and the other black?"

"Yeah, I think that was it... holy crow, what do you think I do, memorize the news? I just thought you'd be interested."

"Yeah, you're right, Pat. Thanks a lot for calling."

Well, that was that. Koesler felt that it was safe to speculate that Brown had known about Hunsinger's color-blindness and that somehow Lieutenant Harris and Sergeant Ewing had found some way of getting Brown to admit his knowledge.

The priest felt certain that once the official duties were finished later this evening, Inspector Koznicki would call with both news of the arrest and some of the less publicized details.

Koesler felt so profoundly sorry for Jack Brown. How far the man must have been pushed to take another's life! And the life of an athlete, at that. The very type person he had dedicated his life to heal and restore.

Koesler decided he would pray for Jack Brown. He felt he had already said enough prayers for Brown's victim.

As Koesler finished his prayer, he smelled smoke. He hurried into the kitchen where he found two very burned hamburgers.

His shoulders drooped. The perfect end, he thought, to a not altogether perfect day!

A small man paced up and down the street, all the while restricting his travel to a single block. Each time he reached one of the two corners, he would pause and seem to reflect. He was neatly but inexpensively dressed, and clean shaven. A snap-brim fedora covered his Ivy League trim gray hair. He was perhaps in his late fifties, early sixties.

A single building stood on the block where he walked. It was 1300 Beaubien, Detroit Police Headquarters.

Inside, on the fifth floor, in the homicide section, three

men sat in an otherwise unoccupied squad room. All three felt the peculiar elation that usually accompanies the successful completion of a difficult job.

"What I don't yet understand," Sergeant Ewing said, "is what led you to the trail of Jack Brown. He seemed to me to be an A-1 straightshooter."

"That was my impression too," Harris said. "In the beginning I thought he was the least suspect of all of them."

"Then what was it, Ned?" Inspector Koznicki asked.

"Actually, Walt, I took a page from your friend, Father Koesler."

"Oh? How so?"

"Father Koesler is by trade a 'father confessor.' I mean, there are lots of people who are called father confessors. Anybody, actually, who is in a special position to receive others' confidences or give out advice. But a priest is the original father confessor. He is there and Catholics come to him and pour out their most intimate secrets. Eventually, the priest gets to know his people probably better than anyone else could . . . that about the way it works, Walt?"

Koznicki, smiling, nodded.

"Well," Harris continued, "I got to thinking about that, when, all of a sudden, this light goes on. At least on a physical level—and probably on several other levels too—who is more father confessor to athletes than their trainer?

"I mean, a player may try to fool his coach, an assistant coach, or somebody in management. But the one who patches up the cuts and tapes up the sprains is the trainer. The trainer alone on the team is the one who puts his hands on the bruises and torn ligaments. If a player is going to succeed, especially in a violent game like football, he's just got to confide in his trainer. The trainer is the very last person in the world a player could hope to fool. If anybody on a team could be called a father confessor, it surely would be the trainer."

"Therefore," Koznicki concluded, "you felt that Jack Brown must certainly know everything about Hunsinger, including that he was colorblind."

"That's it, Walt. And if I was right, why didn't he tell us about it when we first questioned him? We gave him every opportunity. He told us freely and voluntarily everything else about Hunsinger. Why not the colorblindness, if he knew?"

"So," Ewing said, "you were on a fishing expedition when you were talking to Brown this morning."

"Exactly. For once, I got to play the nice cop. I didn't know where it was going to lead, though. I just hoped that if we got Brown loosened up enough to be off his guard, he just might slip up. But, damn, he couldn't have been better! I could hardly believe my eyes when Brown stood there holding those pills, identical in every way except they were different colors. And then Brown tells us Hunsinger couldn't tell the difference!"

"Excellent work, Ned," said Koznicki.

The man who had been pacing up and down in front of headquarters had not drawn any special attention. Under ordinary circumstances no one was assigned to survey the outside of the building.

Police officers and others who had business at headquarters usually traveled briskly into or out of the building. They paid little attention to one another unless one happened to know a colleague; then greetings were exchanged. But no one would pay any special attention to a stranger on the street. None did now. None paused long enough to be aware that the stranger was pacing seemingly without purpose.

But when the stranger entered headquarters and appeared hesitant about where he was going and what he was doing, several officers noted his unconventional behavior. One approached him. "Can I help you?"

"Uh!" The stranger seemed startled. "Oh. I don't know.

I'm looking for somebody. Do you know where they took Jack Brown?"

"Who's Jack Brown?"

"They arrested him earlier. Or at least that's what somebody told me."

"Arrested him. What case? What for?"

"The Hunsinger murder."

"Oh, yeah; the football player. You want the fifth floor. Take the elevator there."

The small man pushed the up button and waited patiently.

"Thank God that one's over with," Ewing said.

"Right!" Harris replied. "We got almost hopelessly backed up on all the other cases we were working on."

"That is the way it is," Koznicki said, "when a case like this is played up by the media. The pressure to close the case is enormous. This is by no means the first time we have had such pressure. Nor will it be the last."

"Well, onward and upward," said Ewing.

"Uh..." said the small man in the doorway, "pardon me, but is this homicide?"

"It is," Koznicki said. "May we help you?"

"I hope so. I've got a problem. My name is Harold Drake. I'm a security guard out at the Silverdome."

Nothing Mr. Drake was saying seemed connected with anything else he said. Clearly, he was confused and ill at ease.

"Sit down here, Mr. Drake, and tell us what the problem is," said Koznicki.

"Well, it's about Jack Brown. I heard you arrested him today...for the murder of Hank Hunsinger?" It was uttered in the form of a question as Drake sat at the table the others were using.

All three officers felt tension build within themselves.

"I don't know if I should even be here," Drake continued. "I didn't even hear about it myself. My wife told me about it. She heard it on the news."

"You want to be a little more specific, Mr. Drake?" Ewing asked.

"Well, she—my wife, that is—said she heard on the news that Mr. Brown was arrested for the murder of the Hun. She said the guy on the news said that the cops—excuse me, the police—said that Brown allegedly—that the word?—left the Pontiac Inn last Sunday at ten o'clock and, uh, allegedly set up the Hun's murder, then got to the stadium by noon when the team arrived."

There was a pause.

"Well?" Harris said it angrily. He had a foreboding.

"Well," Drake said, "that couldn'a happened."

"What do you mean it couldn't have happened!" Harris was angry and incredulous.

"He was at the stadium. He was at the Silverdome."

"How do you know that?"

"'Cause I saw him. I was the guard on duty. Only I wasn't at the gate, at my post. I was inside, in an office inside the tunnel where I could see who came in but they couldn't see me. An' I saw Jack Brown come in and go into the Cougars' locker room. It was about a quarter past ten. An' he stayed in the locker room. He was there when the team came in about noon. Everything was just like it always is."

"And why would you not be at your post?" Koznicki asked. "Why would you be in an inside office?"

"I ain't gonna lie to you. Just not bein' at the gate puts me up shit's creek without a paddle.

"I done it lotsa times. I keep a pint in that office. Hid. I can go in there and have a wee nip and still see the outside door. If somebody comes in who ain't supposed to, I can just step outta the office and challenge 'em. It was just about foolproof until now.

"But I just can't see Mr. Brown in all this trouble when I know he couldn'a done it. Mr. Brown's been good to me. He's about the only one bothered to learn my name. Always says hello to me. A real nice guy. He couldn'a done it. I saw him come in and I know he stayed. Only he couldn'a known I saw him."

"Why didn't you tell us all this when we questioned you the first time, a few days ago?"

"'Cause I didn't wanna lose my job. I wasn't gonna tell anybody, anytime, ever. But when Mr. Brown got arrested . . ." Drake's explanation seemed prematurely complete. "Well, that's it."

The three officers questioned Drake for a half hour more, but could not break down his story or find a flaw in it.

At length they were forced to accept the fact that, although Jack Brown possessed the information that had come to be known as the "smoking gun," he now had a solid alibi. There was no other feasible conclusion.

Ewing took Drake's statement, had him sign it, and warned him to stay available for any possible further questioning. Drake then was permitted to leave.

"Where is Brown now?" Koznicki asked.

"Upstairs in a holding cell." Harris was sullen.

"What is his status?"

Ewing answered. "We've got the prosecutor's recommendation for warrant, but we haven't got the warrant yet."

"So he is still in our jurisdiction. I believe we had better cut him loose," Koznicki said.

"I'll do it." Harris's motive was more inquisitiveness than expiation. He took the elevator to the ninth floor, was admitted to Brown's cell, and informed him of the alibi provided by Drake.

"Poor Harold," said Brown. "I guess they'll can him for that. No alternative. Never mind; I'll see he gets a job. Least I can do. I owe him a barrel."

"Do you realize how much trouble you were in up till about an hour ago?" Harris said. "A first-degree murder charge and a pack of circumstantial evidence. I don't have to kid you, you're off the hook now. But I think we could've gotten a conviction. So what I want to know is why you didn't tell us in the initial interrogation that you knew Hunsinger was colorblind?"

"Well, I knew I was a suspect, although I didn't know why. From that point on, I wasn't gonna provide any more info than I absolutely had to. Somethin' like talkin' to the IRS: keep your mouth shut and don't volunteer information. 'Sides," he looked searchingly at Harris, "if I had told you I knew about Hunsinger, what would you have done?"

Harris thought for a moment. "Probably have moved you up a notch on the list of suspects. But not much more than that. It was your lie of omission that got you in over your head."

"Excuse me, Lieutenant, it isn't that I'm not learning something from all you're saying, but is it okay for me to go now? I mean, am I free?"

"Yeah, you're free. You can pick up your things at the desk down the hall."

"I guess you're back at square one, aren'tcha?"

"Uh-huh." Harris was as down now as he had been up an hour before.

"Well, sorry for that. But I'm just as glad I'm out from under."

"Tell me about it."

6

FATHER KOESLER TAPPED THE BOTtom of the box; the last few flakes of Granola dropped into the bowl. He sliced a banana over the fine grain, poured in some milk, and, presto, breakfast.

He spread out the morning *Free Press* and scanned page 1, trying to determine which story to read first.

His immediate attention was caught by a picture at the upper center of the page. It was a photo from the paper's files showing Cougar trainer Jack Brown standing on the sidelines, arms folded across his chest. The caption read: "Jack Brown, Cougars' trainer, arrested for the murder of Hank ("the Hun") Hunsinger and later released, all on the same day. Story on page 3-A."

That took care of any doubt over which story to read first. Koesler flipped the paper open to the second front page and began reading.

He continued to spoon in bananas and cereal, but lost interest in the remainder of the paper, following, instead, his own flow of thought.

Initially, he felt happy for Brown. Then he felt sorry for the police, who would now, as the story stated, have to begin practically all over. No wonder the inspector hadn't phoned him.

Though he had promised himself that he would waste

no more of his time with the question of who murdered Hunsinger, he found it impossible not to rehash the matter.

After all, there had been times when he had been of some help to the police in the solution of a few homicides. But now that he began reflecting on those past cases, he recalled that the help he had been able to provide had usually concerned something to do with things Catholic or something that he had learned by virtue of being a priest—information more likely to be recognized as such by him as a priest than by the police as law-enforcement experts.

Was it possible it could work again? Koesler left the dining table and began to pace the living room. This was an unlikely pursuit. A venture less prone to success than hunting for the proverbial needle. But he wanted to help. And he had proved beyond a doubt that when it came to genuine police procedure, he was of less aid than the rankest amateur. So he continued to pass the suspects, one by one, through a religious filter.

There was of course the Bible discussion group. That was religious. He sifted through things he had heard various members of the God Squad say in relation to the passages they had examined. But what to look for? Violence? The most violent statements he could recall, usually endorsing some of the more ferocious sections of the Old Testament, had come from Hunsinger.

As he continued to recall statements that had been made by individuals, something else, related but not identical, began to surface. He couldn't identify it, nor could he afford the luxury of waiting for a magic moment when, unbidden, it would make itself clear. So he continued to focus on individuals and their commentaries on the Bible. Meanwhile, he threw open a neutral gear in his mind that permitted a good deal of stream of consciousness to run freely.

Something. Something. Something. Something about

the Scriptures themselves. Not about anyone's comment on Scripture. The Scripture itself. An image came to him of the blind man Christ cured in stages so that he saw, but in a confused way. No, that couldn't be it; he'd been down that path before.

But it was Scripture that was knocking at the back door of his consciousness. But what Scripture? Something he'd heard or read recently. Something he'd tried to develop into a homily. Something he had looked at, in a confused way, like the blind man recovering his sight. Something looked at the wrong way. That meant there must be a right way of looking at it.

Of course! That was it! Looking at it the wrong way versus looking at it the right way.

Slow down, now. Must be cautious. Just recovered from a major league blunder. Can't be wrong a second time. Not so close to the first time. Let's just check all the seams. See if there are any holes. Well, yes, a few possible holes. But, by and large, it seemed to make sense. The more he thought about it, the more sense it seemed to make.

Just a couple of phone calls to set things up. Then, put the theory to the test.

"Thank you ever so much for meeting me here, Inspector."

"Not at all, Father . . . although I must admit your call surprised me."

"I don't blame you. After embarrassing you with the Galloways, I don't suppose you ever expected to hear from me again . . . at least regarding any investigation."

"Father, if only you knew how frequently we are wrong in our theories. Even in an investigation that eventually proves successful, we often encounter many dead-end roads. You have nothing to be embarrassed about or to apologize for."

"Nevertheless, I feel a bit awkward. I just couldn't

subject Lieutenant Harris or Sergeant Ewing to another round of my own serial, Father May Not Know Best. That's why I'm especially grateful you agreed to meet me here. Sorry, too, about the traffic. We had to park so far down the street."

"Walking is good exercise. We should do more of it."

Koznicki tipped his hat as they passed in front of Holy Redeemer church. Koesler had almost forgotten the gesture. But Koznicki's tip of the hat put the priest in mind of his own father's teaching him the custom. It was a sign of reverence for the presence of the Blessed Sacrament in the church. Koesler resolved to renew the custom in his own life. He never ceased to be amazed at how much he had to learn from others.

Koesler rang the doorbell and waited patiently. One could not expect old people to run to answer the door.

The familiar face of Mary Frances Quinn appeared. She greeted Father Koesler reverently but appeared a bit tentative toward his extra-large companion until Koesler performed the introductions. Mary Frances ushered them into the unilluminated living room. Again introductions were made.

Koznicki, after being seated, carefully studied Grace Hunsinger. Why did she remind him of a small animal about to be cornered? Her eyes darted about as if seeking some avenue of escape. Her breathing was rapid and shallow.

"Mrs. Hunsinger," Koesler began, "we won't take much of your time. I just want to talk to you a little bit about your son. But first, I wonder if you would mind looking at the numbers in this book and telling us what you see. Just take your time and read the numbers, if you will, as I turn the pages."

Koesler opened the book to the first page.

Grace adjusted her bifocals. "Twelve."

Everyone could read that, thought Koesler, as he turned to the next page with its number eight.

"Three."

Koesler turned to five.

"Two," Grace read.

Koesler turned to twenty-nine.

"Seventy."

Koesler turned to seventy-four.

"Twenty-one."

Koesler turned to seven.

"I don't see any number there at all."

"I think we need go no further," said Koznicki.

Grace removed her glasses. "What was the meaning of that?"

Her hands were trembling slightly.

"That was a test of your color sight, Mrs. Hunsinger," Koesler said. "It indicated you have what's called a red-green deficiency."

"I . . . I don't understand." Her hand fluttered at her hair.

"I think it means you couldn't know that when you mixed the strychnine with the DMSO and switched that bottle with the shampoo that there was a difference in the colors. The DMSO is clear. The shampoo is pink."

A remarkable transformation affected Grace. Her entire body seemed involved in the deep sigh she uttered. Her hands relaxed in her lap. "You know," she said so softly as to be barely audible.

"You tried to tell us often enough, didn't you, Grace?"

She nodded, giving every indication of being relieved.

"Grace!" Mrs. Quinn exclaimed. "What does he mean?"

"According to Inspector Koznicki here," Koesler proceeded, "and in what you said to me, you held yourself responsible both for your son's sight disability and for his death. But after making the statements, you backed away from them slightly, stating your responsibility in remote terms: that if you had done this or that differently, your son would not have turned out as he did. The confession was there, but it was sort of up for grabs.

"We chose to look at the statements through our viewpoint. Taking on blame for a child is common with many parents. Taking a greater responsibility for their children's behavior than they ought or need to. If we had been looking at those statements through your eyes, we might have taken them more literally. But that was not likely.

"But if we had been seeing things from your point of view, we would have asked ourselves why you felt responsible for your son's colorblindness. Because you just happened to be his mother and, as such, gave him his disability? I don't think so. If you had normal vision, and there were any hereditary cause involved, it could just as easily have come from his father. Why should you think you were responsible unless there was something wrong with your vision and you thought you had passed that defect on to your son? I checked with Dr. Glowacki, an ophthalmologist, and he said there is no evidence that colorblindness, total colorblindness, is hereditary. But that would not have prevented you from thinking it was so.

"But if you have a color deficiency—and you do—why does it not show up in your home decor? I think the answer lies with Mrs. Quinn. The first time I met you, Mrs. Quinn, I believe you told me that you and Mrs. Hunsinger take care of each other as best you can. That the two of you seem to combine your skills and abilities. You get along, I think you used the phrase, like yin and yang?"

"That's true," Mrs. Quinn said.

"Mrs. Hunsinger took care of the house, didn't she, Mrs. Quinn, doing much of the cleaning and cooking? You took care of the door and, among your other responsibilities, you probably took charge of the decorating?"

"Well, yes. Grace sometimes would get the strangest color combinations. I thought it was . . . well, not the best of taste."

"We've already been through that one," Koesler said to Koznicki, alluding to the Galloways.

"Then," the priest again addressed Grace, "we come to your son's death. How many times and how many ways you tried to tell us of your responsibility, not directly and plainly with no room for doubt, but trying nonetheless. I have a suspicion you wanted us to guess it."

Grace barely moved her head in a sign of affirmation.

"First, you told us outright, then hedged enough so that we proceeded to draw the wrong conclusion. Then, to me, the next most evident statement was at your son's funeral Mass.

"The evening before the Mass, I was talking with Father Forbes. He told me you had gone over the Bible readings for the Mass and had made the selection of which ones would be used. Yet when I heard the readings, I listened to them with my ears, not yours. Or, to return to the metaphor of sight, I saw them through my eyes, not yours.

"That first reading was an odd selection. I've never heard a reading from the Book of Maccabees used at a funeral before. The Protestant and Jewish Bibles don't even contain that Book. And yet, when I heard it, I listened with my understanding and I thought of you as the brave mother withstanding the all but unbearable grief of watching her children die. But that is not the way you saw that reading, is it, Mrs. Hunsinger? You saw it in the literal, obvious sense: Here was a mother willing to witness the death of her sons rather than see them break the law. It was the statement of why you did it.

"Henry had broken just about every law he encountered, and not a few Commandments. And he showed every promise of continuing in this unbridled lifestyle until long after your death. When you died, there would probably be no one who cared enough for him to stop him from hurting others. It was up to you. And so you did it. You were the modern mother of the Book of Maccabees, willing even to allow the death of her son rather than see him go on breaking the law.

"But I think we all tended to dismiss out of hand the

possibility that you might be responsible for the death of your own son. And on top of this sort of natural tendency not to take you as a serious suspect was your alibi. You spent the entire day with Mrs. Quinn here . . . isn't that right, Mrs. Quinn?"

"Why, yes. We started off with Mass in the morning—"

"Yes, I remember," Koesler interrupted. "Now please don't take this amiss, Mrs. Quinn, but practically every time I've seen you, you were taking . . . uh . . . a little nap. You do take little naps, don't you, Mrs. Quinn?"

"Well, that happens when you get older. You need it."

"Last Sunday, for example, if I remember correctly what Inspector Koznicki told me about your interview with the police, it was a very leisurely day."

"Older people need to rest and recoup what little strength they have."

"Yes, and—please don't take offense—I know you need your rest. But Sunday you got home from Mass, read the paper, watched the game on television, listened to some records, then had dinner . . . correct?"

"Just what we do every Sunday, except for the game. Sometimes Henry's team doesn't play on Sunday. And sometimes it isn't televised because, I think, not enough fans would come out to see it."

"Yes, that's right. And probably during that long morning and afternoon you took some naps."

"Oh, yes, of course. I need them."

"And some of those little naps could go on for an hour or more?"

"Oh, I don't know about that."

"Mrs. Quinn, every time I've seen you napping, you've never awakened spontaneously. Someone has always wakened you. Don't you think you might be able to nap for an hour or more?"

"Well, yes, I suppose so."

"And if, indeed, you had taken a nap and had awakened

to find that Grace was not in her chair, where would you have assumed she might be?"

"Oh, probably out to the kitchen to prepare dinner, or something like that."

"So, with all this in mind, do you think you could testify that Mrs. Hunsinger was actually here with you all day Sunday?"

"Well, I suppose not really. I mean, I didn't keep my eyes on her all day like some kind of watchdog."

"So much then for the alibi. Mrs. Hunsinger, you could have gone out almost any time Sunday for an hour or so, confident that your friend would either be asleep or suppose that you were somewhere in the house."

Grace did not react. Relaxed, smiling slightly, she continued to gaze steadfastly at the priest.

"And finally," Koesler said, "one more time when I foolishly viewed an event through my eyes and not yours—during the funeral Mass, at communion time, you broke down in tears. I projected my own feelings and figured that it was this highly emotional moment of sacramental union with our Lord that caused your emotional reaction. Whereas it more likely was the fact that you hadn't had a chance to go to confession. And you were receiving communion in the state of mortal sin. That's what caused the outburst!"

There was silence for several moments.

"Little Bobby Koesler," Grace murmured at length, "how proud your mother must have been of you. You were always so faithful. And on your ordination day, how proud she must have been of you—a priest of God, forever!"

"Mrs. Hunsinger," Koznicki said, "before you reply to all the things Father Koesler has said, I am required to inform you of your rights." He then removed a well-worn card from his wallet and read the Miranda warning to her. When he had completed the warning, after a slight pause, Grace spoke.

"Oh . . . it's true." She smiled tiredly. "All except the part about confession. Father should have remembered that confessions are heard very frequently at Holy Redeemer, even during morning Masses. I had been to confession Monday morning. But, mortal sin? How could that be? The plan came to me during prayer. Our dear Lord told me Henry must be stopped. How could a command given to me by our Lord Himself be a sin, much less a mortal sin? Henry had hurt enough people and more. And he would go on—just as Father Koesler said. No one would stop him.

"I prayed before I opened my Bible that our Lord would show me the way. And I opened the Bible to that very passage in the Book of Maccabees. That brave woman witnessed her sons' torture and death. She encouraged them to die rather than sin! That was what had to be: Henry had to die and it had to be at my hand.

"Father was right about everything but my tears at the funeral. I thought I had shed all the tears I possessed. When our Lord told me I must kill my very own son, I wept until I was sure I had no more tears. But I was wrong. At the moment of sacramental union with our Lord, I found there still were more tears to come. That was the reason."

Inspector Koznicki shook his head slowly, sadly. "This is one of the times, one of the very rare times, when it is not good to be a police officer," he said, almost to himself. And then, more loudly, "Mrs. Hunsinger, I am going to have to take you downtown with me. But take your time and gather all you need for a stay away from home. Perhaps Mrs. Quinn would help you."

"So, Father, it all happened the way you envisioned it." Koznicki took a small sip from his glass of cream sherry.

"I guess it did," said Koesler, "but with the wrong cast of characters."

The priest and the inspector had met at a small restaurant near St. Anselm's late the same afternoon on which Grace Hunsinger had been arraigned on the charge of murdering her son, Henry. Neither felt like eating. In fact, neither felt like drinking. What each needed was the other's company.

Koesler had been shaken to his core both by the fact that a respected Catholic matron had killed her only child and by the happenstance that it was he who had come up with the clues that led to her arrest. Koznicki, despite his many years with the Detroit Police Department, had never been more reluctant to make an arrest than he had been today.

"Now, Father, you are always too modest about your accomplishments. It was a most clever bit of deduction."

"Well, thanks, Inspector. But I'm not all that proud of it. First, I embarrassed Lieutenant Harris and Sergeant Ewing as well as myself. And undoubtedly the Galloways too. And I can only feel terribly sad about Mrs. Hunsinger. You know, Inspector, she and I spent a lot of years together that I was totally unaware of. All those years she followed my career as an altar boy and seminarian and priest!" Koesler shook his head. "I didn't even know she was looking."

"None of us feels good about Mrs. Hunsinger, Father. But justice has been served and this case is closed. And I still believe that it was very clever of you to have come up with the hypothesis that the perpetrator had a problem with color vision. How was it you did that?"

"I still don't know. It's all jumbled in my mind. I think the seed was sown when I saw the horrible mix of colors in the Galloway living room. You see, Inspector, I started this whole thing in the wrong ballpark."

"But you soon moved it to the correct location."

"An accident, I think. As usual, whenever I'm able to be of any help to the police, it's a matter of coming up with something that's just not in the usual sphere of police work. This time, the most significant clues I uncovered were found in the Bible. Mostly, the incident where Christ cured a blind man, but only in stages. And, of course, that text from Maccabees. Strange, now that I think of it, the Biblical text that provided the clue that led to a solution was the same text through which God 'told' Mrs. Hunsinger to kill her son. And of course I goofed entirely on the reason the poor woman broke down during the funeral."

"An irrelevant detail, Father."

Koesler cupped his bourbon manhattan in his palms, assisting the ice to melt. "Did she . . . I mean Mrs. Hunsinger . . . did she confess . . . I mean officially, to the police?"

"Yes, she made a full statement shortly after arriving at headquarters. She said she left her home shortly after she and Mrs. Quinn returned from Mass. She said that was a particularly 'nappy'—was the word she used—time for Mrs. Quinn. Mrs. Quinn invariably got exceptionally tired after attending two Sunday masses.

"So, about eleven that morning, or shortly thereafter, Mrs. Hunsinger left home, drove to her son's apartment building, entered through the basement, and took the elevator to his apartment. There she mixed the strychnine and DMSO and switched that bottle with the shampoo bottle. And, as you deduced, she was unable to tell that there was a different coloration.

"She returned home to find that Mrs. Quinn had not awakened once during her absence. And of course Mrs. Quinn assumed that Mrs. Hunsinger had been at home with her all through the day. Sergeant Ewing recalled that when he and Lieutenant Harris asked her what she had done all that day, she had Mrs. Quinn give an account of their time. She didn't even have to lie."

Koesler sipped his drink, caught one of the rapidly melting ice cubes, and held it in his mouth to complete the melting process. "What will happen to her now?"

"That is up to the prosecutor's office. I assume she

will be charged with murder in the first degree. No one could doubt, now, that she killed her son and that it very certainly was premeditated."

"And do you think she will be convicted?"

Koznicki smiled briefly. "I never speculate about such matters. Our police work is done now, save testifying at her trial." He looked at his clerical friend with a faint touch of amusement. "But for you, I will make a conjecture. If I were a good defense attorney—and you can depend on it, she will have one—I would love to have a client who can say with utmost sincerity, a sincerity that no prosecutor can break down, that 'our Lord told me to do it.' I would guess that Mrs. Hunsinger will eventually spend some time, perhaps the rest of her life, perhaps not, in some institution where she will receive psychiatric help. And with the money her son had already provided for her, the therapy ought to be first class."

Koesler shrugged. "What a waste; what a tragic waste! Such a good woman!"

"A good woman, yes . . . but," Koznicki touched a finger to his forehead, "somewhat unbalanced."

"Probably if we knew her complete background, it all might make some sense. I can't believe a good woman like Grace Hunsinger could just step outside her whole lifestyle and suddenly become a murderess. Or even that she could lead an otherwise normal, even very pious, life and then have this one psychotic episode."

Koesler deposited his glass on the table. This would be one of the rare occasions when he would not finish a drink. "One final point of information, Inspector. How could Grace Hunsinger know that DMSO would penetrate to the bloodstream and carry the poison with it? She hasn't any medical or pharmaceutical background. At least not that I'm aware of."

"Quite true, Father. She learned in the simplest possible way. It came out in her statement earlier this afternoon. We know that Mrs. Hunsinger, the compulsive mother of a compulsive son, regularly cleaned his already clean apartment. She would be aware of everything in it. Things like the intimate feminine apparel neatly tucked away, always changing as new women entered her son's life. And the X-rated videocassettes. And the ample supply of strychnine. And that strange bottle of DMSO in the medicine cabinet. Always concerned, if fruitlessly, about her son's use of illegal substances, she asked him about the DMSO.

"He explained its function, even going so far as to demonstrate. He put a drop of iodine on his hand, then, when it dried, he covered it with a drop or two of DMSO. She watched as the iodine disappeared, carried beneath the skin by the DMSO. At the time, she did no more than remind her son of the warning found on the bottle itself that the product might be unsafe, that it was not approved for human use.

"It was not until she received her 'divine commission' that she formed the plan of using the strychnine in conjunction with the DMSO. It was, as Dr. Moellmann observed, a very simple plan, yet ingenious in its simplicity." Koznicki finished his drink. "And that leads to a question that still puzzles me. Grace Hunsinger was a very, perhaps overly, religious woman. How could she take her son's life when in all probability he would thus have died in mortal sin? In this, she would not only be killing him, but condemning him to hell as well . . . would she not? This, Father, is your field of expertise."

Koesler shook his head slowly. "It's a good question, Inspector. I'm not sure how to approach an answer." He paused a few moments. "Perhaps you'll remember a movie that came out about . . . oh . . . thirty years ago, called *Night of the Hunter*. Robert Mitchum played a preacher who was a psychopathic killer. He had the word 'love' tattooed on the back of one hand, and 'hate' on the other. I'll never forget the scene where he's alone driving a car and talking to God—praying would be a sick use of the word to describe his monologue. He admits—brags almost—to God that he is a killer. But he reminds God that there's a lot of killing in the 'Good Book.' Well, Inspector, there is. The essence of the Bible, at least for the Christian, occurs when Almighty God allows His Son to be brutally executed. In fact, the execution may be said to be the fulfillment of the Father's will.

"When you move back into the Old Testament, killings multiply. And, not infrequently, they are in response to God's will. It starts with Cain killing Abel. Moses kills an Egyptian. God takes the firstborn of each Egyptian family. God wipes out the entire Egyptian army in the Red Sea. Whole cities are destroyed at God's command. And—in perhaps the most touching instance—to test his faith, Abraham is ordered to sacrifice his only son. Then, there is that rather obscure woman in the Book of Maccabees who encourages her sons to die under torture rather than sin. Grace Hunsinger was familiar with all of them. She, indeed, selected the Maccabees woman's story as one of the readings at her son's funeral. So she was no stranger to the phenomenon of God's occasional use of, in effect, a divine death sentence.

"Once she felt compelled to carry out the divine death sentence that had been passed on her son, he gave her no alternative. If we could compare his state of sin to a state of insanity, we would say he had no lucid moments. And she knew it. As you just stated, Inspector, she knew about the intimate feminine apparel, she knew about the X-rated TV cassettes. She knew about her son's whole dissolute life. She had no choice but to go forward with her plan and, as far as her son's soul was concerned, hope for the best."

"But," Koznicki said, "was there nothing the poor woman could do? Could she not have urged him to go to confession as the end neared?"

"On the contrary, Inspector, she would not have added sacrilege to her son's long list of sins. She would have been aware from her many years of parochial training that confession without a determination to change one's life—she would have known it as a 'purpose of amendment'—is not only useless but a sacrilege. Of what purpose would it be for her son to go to confession of a Saturday afternoon when he had no intention of going to Mass of a Sunday morning, no intention of ceasing his womanizing, no intention to stop manipulating others, no intention of doing anything at all about changing his life for—what she would consider—the better."

Upon reflection, Koznicki had to agree. He had had at least as much parochial training as had Mrs. Hunsinger, if not more. "Of course," he said, "but a moment ago, Father, you said something about Mrs. Hunsinger's hoping for the best?"

Koesler smiled and spread his hands on the tabletop. "Who knows? After death, who knows the immense power of God's forgiveness? We believe that after death there is a judgment. And, aided by Scripture and tradition, we think we know the rules under which we will be judged. But we don't really know how much God can and will forgive, nor how much He will not. All prayers after death, no matter how holy or sinful the deceased's life, presume nothing. They only ask mercy.

"Mrs. Hunsinger and I spent quite a bit of time consoling each other. I reminded her of God's infinite mercy as well as the fact that, for whatever reason, her son had freely joined a Bible study group. While she reminded me that at least he was good to her. And I would agree that filial devotion is very definitely a virtue."

"To know all is to forgive all?"

"Maybe. Or maybe to know all is to understand all."

Drinks finished, they made ready to leave.

"For the living, life goes on," Koznicki said, then added, "Oh, by the way, Father, will you be able to come over for dinner on Sunday?"

"Thanks, Inspector, but I've got tickets to the Cougars

game on Sunday. And parking at the Silverdome makes that an all-day adventure."

"Well, then, have fun."

"With Father McNiff along, it's always fun."

7

"THERE'S THE TWO-MINUTE WARNING, Eddie. The referee is informing both coaches that there's just two minutes left in the game. I know it's a cliché, but we've got another cliffhanger on our hands. The contest has come down to the final two minutes."

"It sure has, Lou. And with the score New York 35, the Cougars 30, we'll be right back after these messages."

"Whattya think, this is a real squeaker, eh?" Father Koesler almost shouted into his companion's ear.

"I think the operative word is cliffhanger," said Father McNiff. "Besides, I can't think very clearly. I'm trying to keep my nose from bleeding."

Koesler grimaced. "Patrick, that's about all I can take of your references to how far above ground level we are. It started with your asking the usher if he issued parachutes and it has come down to nosebleeds. I'm takin' it all too much to heart."

"Well, next time invest some money. I mean, I'm paying for my ticket and I don't mind paying a little bit more to get a decent seat. After all, Robert, we only go 'round once. Why not live now and then with a little better seat for a football game?"

"Hey, any time you want to be ticketbroker, be my

guest. These were about the only seats available. The really good seats are inherited from one generation to the next. Or they are the final item in a divorce settlement."

"Speaking of divorces, what did I read in the paper about the owners of this team getting a divorce?"

Koesler nodded. "If you can believe the gossip columns, that seems to be true. Funny, I had gotten the impression that the Galloways might reconcile. At least I gathered that from Jay Galloway. Apparently, Mrs. G. was having nothing to do with it; if you want to believe the rumors, it's Splitsville."

"Yeah, the columnist in the *News* claims it's going to be a newsy and messy divorce."

"Let those who like to read that stuff read it. As for me, reading about a nasty divorce is about as much fun as watching an autopsy up close and in living color." Koesler had to nearly shout the last words, for the time-out was over, and the two teams were gathering forces to do battle again. The spectator noise rose again.

"Well, what do you think, Lou? The Cougars have the ball on their own 20, first and ten, two minutes to go, and down by five. A field goal isn't going to make it. They've got to go for a touchdown. Think they can do it?"

"Dunno. The next two minutes will tell the tale. The Cougars break their huddle. They line up in a spread formation. It figures Bobby Cobb is going to have every eligible receiver going out for a pass. New York has its nickel defense in—an extra defensive back. There's the snap. Cobb fades. It's a draw! It's a draw play! He sent the fullback right up the middle. He's got ten . . . twenty . . . twenty-five yards before they can stop him. It's a first down and the Cougars take a time-out. It'll be first and ten at the Cougars' 45-yard line. How about that, Eddie?"

"Right you are, Lou. The Cougars really fooled New York with that draw. And it was an audible. Bobby Cobb called that one at the line of scrimmage. He saw New

York falling back for the deep pass and he set 'em up. We'll be right back after these messages."

McNiff thought twice about picking up his conversation with Koesler with all the pandemonium in the stadium. But he decided to give it another try. "You know, I don't want to drive this ticket thing into the ground, but you do know the owner."

"Galloway?" Koesler shouted back. "Just barely, and now, not on the best of terms."

"Won't there be any more meetings of the God Squad?" McNiff still harbored hopes of being included.

Koesler laughed. "Boy, I don't think so. That's dead as a doornail. I don't know that they'll even be speaking to each other. Did you see in the paper where Dave Whitman is going back to Minneapolis and Multifoods? Says they made him an offer he couldn't refuse. And maybe that's so. But I think he would have gone anywhere to get away from Jay Galloway."

"Pretty soon it's going to be Galloway against the world."

"That's the way it started," Koesler rejoined.

"I even saw in the paper where there's some dissension on the team . . . some bad blood between Cobb and the trainer."

Koesler nodded. "They had some angry words at the last meeting. Some people are reluctant to believe it, but I think there are times when the spoken word is more permanent than words carved in stone."

The time-out was over. The Cougars were returning to the line of scrimmage. Koesler and McNiff along with all the other spectators rose to their feet to give the Cougars all the encouragement their almost hoarse voices could muster.

"Here they come again, Lou. Their work's cut out for them, with only 1:45 to go."

"And they're in the shotgun formation, Eddie. I wouldn't be surprised to see them stay in that formation for the rest of the game. This is close to desperation time. Cobb takes the ball and fades. He can't find anyone open. He's scrambling and being chased. He's waving his receivers into different patterns. Uh-oh, the left linebacker almost got him. He's using up precious seconds. Okay, he's got his man. Hoffer came back from a deep post pattern and he's got the ball and is tackled on the spot. It's a fifteen-yard gain. The clock is still running! Why don't the Cougars call a time-out? Okay, finally they do. But letting the clock run like that may just have been a fatal mistake!"

"I'm afraid you're right, Lou. The Cougars now have the ball on New York's 40-yard line. They've used up their last time-out and there are just twelve seconds left on the clock. In all probability, the next play will be the last one of this game. And you can bet New York's going to have everybody way back covering what has to be one of those old 'Hail Mary' passes.

"You know, Lou, this game has largely belonged to Hoffer and, of course, Cobb. The question on everybody's mind this week has been, How badly are the Cougars going to miss the Hun? And I think young Hoffer has answered that question this afternoon.

"Although all Cobb's passes to Hoffer have been of the short variety, this is what you expect from a tight end. Tight ends are not deep threats. But for what he is, Hoffer looks like he's gonna fill the Hun's shoes and more. Even if the Cougars lose this afternoon—and right now it sure looks like they will—this Cougar team has found itself a premier attraction. The crowd has taken Hoffer to their hearts. He's gonna have a really great career."

"Oh, I'm glad I'm not in the land of cotton . . ." Bobby Cobb sang his parody of the Confederate anthem, "Dixie." Again, it was one of his ways of keeping his team loose.

And at this moment, he needed to remain as self-possessed as any of his teammates.

There were only a few seconds left in the time-out. And then, the final play of this game. Cobb beckoned Hoffer to bend close. "Well, Hoff, old man, we been foolin' with this short game all afternoon. These dudes from the Big Apple know by this time that you can catch a short pass with the best of 'em. What they don't know is that you got the afterburners of a rocket. I think it's about time to show 'em what you got."

Hoffer grinned from ear to ear. "Like, man, I thought you'd never ask."

"I'm gonna call an eighty-nine out of the shotgun. That'll get all the backs and wide receivers deep into the end zone, hopefully with most all the defensive backs. You delay a couple seconds, then give me a post pattern. If this works, I'll hit you on about the 5-yard line. You gotta get it in from there. If it don't work, that's all she wrote."

"Okay, Lou, the Cougars are coming up to the line. This is it."

"Right. The noise is deafening. Cobb is waving his arms, asking for quiet so his team can hear the signals. He's getting some cooperation. There's the snap. It's only a three-man rush. The Cougars' defensive line seems well able to contain that rush. As anticipated, every receiver is cutting deep, but the retreating defensive backs are with them step for step.

"Wait a minute. I didn't even see this: Hoffer has broken downfield after a delay. There's a linebacker with him, but he'll never keep up. Holy Christmas, I've never seen a tight end with that kind of speed.

"Cobb fires the ball. It's a clothesliner. It may be too hot to handle. Hoffer goes up at the five. Holy—I didn't think anybody could get up that high! Hoffer's got it on his fingertips. He gathers it in. And he's hit. One, two, three defensive backs all over him. But he hasn't stopped.

Those legs are still pumping. He's carrying three defensive players all over him! Now he's hit by the fourth back and he's toppling. He falls. He's down. Wait . . . wait a minute! The referee has both hands raised. Hoffer broke the plane of the goal line! He scored! He scored! He scored! I don't believe it! Four men on him and he scored! And the Cougars win it! It's a miracle! It's over; it's all over! The game's over and the Cougars win it!"

It's like a miracle, thought Koesler, as all around him went berserk. As far as he was concerned, it seemed to bring everything full circle. It all started last Sunday and it was all over this Sunday. It thoroughly satisfied the priest's deep-felt need for symmetry in life.

God's in Her heaven; all's right with the world.

ABOUT THE AUTHOR

William X. Kienzle, author of six best-selling mysteries, was ordained into the priesthood in 1954 and spent twenty years as a parish priest. For twelve years he was editor-in-chief of the *Michigan Catholic*. After leaving the priesthood, he became editor of *MPLS* magazine in Minneapolis and later moved to Texas, where he was director of the Center for Contemplative Studies at the University of Dallas. Kienzle and his wife, Javan, live in Detroit, where he enjoys playing the piano as a diversion from his writing. His previous novels include THE ROSARY MURDERS; DEATH WEARS A RED HAT; MIND OVER MURDER; ASSAULT WITH INTENT; SHADOW OF DEATH; and KILL AND TELL.